CHILDLINE

LINDA THORPE

First published 2017

This edition published in paperback 2017

Copyright © Linda Thorpe, 2017

Linda Thorpe has asserted her right under Copyright, Designs and Patents Act 1988
to be identified as the author of this work.

ISBN-13: 978-1-9743-8574-4

ISBN-10: 1974385744

ASIN: B0711717KG

Cover photo by Canva

"There are truths which are not for all men, nor for all times"

Voltaire 1764

1

'Perfect,' the man said to himself under his breath. He'd been beginning to think that nobody would be out on such a cold day and that he would have to change his plan and he so hated improvisation.

Ahead of him an elderly man, chilled and with eyes reddened by the acute cold, walked gingerly along the icy pavement together with an equally aged and frail yellow Labrador dog at his side. Nobody else was in sight, the norm for this time of day as the cold began to bite and the daylight ebbed away. He slowly manoeuvred the car coming to a halt slightly ahead of the old man and lowered the passenger-side window as if to ask for directions. He had already switched off the car's state of the art satellite navigation system just in case the old man became suspicious, but this proved to be unnecessary. As was the way with the British the old man was eager to offer help to a stranger as best he could.

'Lost are you lad?' he politely enquired.

The man smiled as he was only about thirty years younger than the wizened elderly gentleman who now peered through the car window. He had long since ceased to regard himself as a lad.

The man raised the Glock 17 pistol he had concealed on his lap and pulled the trigger shooting the old man squarely between the eyes. Thanks to the suppressor it made little more noise than the cracking of a twig underfoot. First shock registered in the old man's watery blue eyes then they clouded over in death as he slumped to the frosty grass verge.

The man stepped out of the car and unceremoniously pushed the old man with the toe of his boot until he rolled down into the ditch that ran alongside the road. Popping the lid on the car boot he now turned to the dog which sat on the cold verge awaiting his master's return, oblivious to his demise.

The dog wagged its tail as he approached. With his left hand holding the collar, he withdrew a scalpel from his right pocket and swiftly and expertly severed the dog's spinal cord about half way down its back. The dog whimpered and registered surprise but not overt pain as its hind quarter slumped uselessly to the floor. Pathetically it tried to drag itself away using its front legs alone. The whimpering increased as the hopelessness became clear but before it had managed to get even a few feet the man picked it up and swung it into the open boot in one movement before slamming the lid.

The whole exercise had taken a little under two minutes. The man looked around for any actual or potential witnesses but there were none as he had expected. He climbed back into his car and without thought or conscience continued on his way as if completely unaffected by what had taken place.

2

Friday 24th January 2014 – 17:00 – Oxford, England

Rosie Ware smiled to herself. She was happy, very happy. She had it all, brains, beauty, a rich loving family and now the hottest guy in her year at Oxford University. Things just couldn't get better she thought. Rosie was a student in her second term studying Biological Sciences at Magdalen College at one of the most prestigious universities in England, if not the world. After getting her degree she hoped to specialise in marine biology which was her passion. Rosie had just finished talking on the phone to Ben her new boyfriend and was packing her small rucksack ready for a quick exit and weekend visit home to attend her mother's 60th birthday party. It was too soon in her relationship to take Ben home to meet her folks, maybe next time, she'd have to wait and see.

If only she knew then that there wasn't going to be a next time.

She tied back her thick long blonde hair pushing it up under her beanie hat, adding two scarves and a pair of hefty mittens. She needed to wrap up warm given the fact that the temperature had plummeted to a chilly minus two degrees Celsius today and as evening approached it was getting even colder. She carried her bag down the hallway, throwing it casually over one shoulder in her usual haste to get moving and headed towards the rear door where she kept her bicycle in the small courtyard behind her student accommodation, ready for the short cycle ride to the railway station. It was at times like this that she cursed the ban on student cars in the city as she'd be able to afford a nice little runabout. She was oblivious to the fact that she wasn't going to get to her mother's party or even the station come to that.

3

Friday 24th January 2014 – Newcastle, Northern England

At the same time in the northern city of Newcastle, blissfully unaware of events down in Oxford, Sara Ware was excited. In less than four hours she would see her beautiful daughter. It had only been a few weeks since Rosie had returned to Oxford following the Christmas break but her visit just couldn't come soon enough. Sara always thought of them as more like sisters rather than mother and daughter as they just got on so well. It was surprising in a way as they couldn't have been more different. Sara was a plain, shy woman, barely more than five feet two inches tall with short mousey brown hair. No matter what she wore or what she had done with her appearance she never got beyond the frumpy or dowdy reflection that she always saw staring back at her in the bedroom mirror but she had a capacity for love that sometimes overwhelmed her. She directed that love at Tom her husband of forty years and her only daughter Rosie.

Both she and Tom had come from humble beginnings. She remembered the Saturday in December 1994 that had changed their lives. Tom had come running into the off-license where she worked in an evening with the news that they had won the newly formed UK National Lottery – not only that but they had subsequently found out that they were the only winners that week and so they didn't have to share the seventeen point eight million pound jackpot with anyone else.

As a teenager, on a family holiday, she had visited a clairvoyant on Blackpool's North Pier who had told her she would have three miracles in her life. She thought her first miracle had been meeting and marrying Tom, the love of her life, the second was the lottery win and her third was in August 1995 when Rosie had arrived.

Up to that point, she had given up the hope of having children. She had been forty-one years of age and had been through every available procedure in the hope of conceiving a child but all to no avail. It was ironic, for the first ten years of their marriage they had religiously used contraception in an effort not to start a family until they had enough money to buy their own home and so provide a good upbringing for their children. Whilst Tom came from a large family Sara was an only child but had always hoped, no expected, to have several children. Even the lottery win couldn't fill the hole that Sara had for this missing brood. Prior to winning the lottery and after exhausting the first two chances provided free by the NHS they had spent all their savings on further courses of IVF but when Sara reached forty the doctors had shaken their heads and said she was just too old to continue. Then early in 1995, the third miracle had occurred and Sara learned that she was going to have a baby. When the baby, a girl, arrived Sara named her Rosie after her maternal grandmother and Catherine after Tom's mother. With Tom and Rosie Catherine Ware - Sara's life was now complete.

This weekend she had planned a lavish party to celebrate her 60th birthday. Money was obviously no object. Tom had taken to being a business man and had grown their lottery win into an even larger fortune. They could now boast about being in The Sunday Times top 1000 British Rich List, although boasting was something Sara had never done. Sara never forgot her old friends and her close family and had always ensured that they shared in her good fortune.

Feeling excited about the weekend ahead Sara headed for the kitchen to put the final touches to the party preparations little knowing that she was about to enter the blackest period of her whole life.

4

Friday 24th January 2014 – 23:00 – Oxford, England

PC Gary Hope was on duty in the Oxford City Police Control Room late that Friday night when the missing person call came in at around eleven p.m. He stretched and yawned as the phone rang lifting him out of the daydream he was, as ever, engrossed in.

Gary was one of life's plodders – though sometimes he barely even plodded. He only joined the police force because that's where all the men in his family worked, his father, uncle and two brothers.

Unfortunately, unlike the rest of his family, Gary didn't have any calling to be a police officer. It was just a job to him. Well paid, secure and with a great pension – if he could only stick it out for the next twenty years or so, which seemed unlikely.

He knew he wouldn't even have been taken on if his Dad hadn't pulled a few strings.

As a result of the good working conditions joining the force had become a profession of choice for many of the graduates streaming out of the myriad of universities that had sprung up in the last twenty years or so. Gary with his five GCSE C-grades, three of which he scraped through on retakes, wouldn't have stood a chance if he'd gone through the normal large scale recruiting channels. Gary knew he wasn't the sharpest tool in the box and was well aware that his nickname around the station had become Gary Hopeless following several embarrassing incidents. He just didn't care. Well, he cared a bit but not enough to up his game much to the chagrin of the rest of his family and his line managers.

'Police, how may I help you?'

'My daughter Rosie is missing,' a distraught Tom Ware reported.

Gary knew that his first task was to assess the risk. A large number of missing persons reports were made every year so they had to be prioritised. Based on the information available it would be

Gary's initial decision as to the level of response the incident would receive. A missing child would result in a Child Rescue Alert being implemented.

'I need you to provide me with some details sir,' Gary said bringing up the COMPACT system that was used to record missing person's details. 'Let's start with her name, age and the circumstances of her disappearance.'

Tom Ware explained that his daughter was Rosie Catherine Ware; she was eighteen years old and had disappeared on her way to her mother's 60th birthday party earlier that evening.

Gary diligently entered all the details into the system. Fortuitously he had recently been on a missing person training course and he knew he had to give consideration to the factors surrounding the person's disappearance when determining the level of risk to apply to the investigation. It didn't take Gary much time to consider this case as a low priority. He himself had lots of experience in getting lost on his way to a party.

'What happens now?' Tom Ware asked – 'will you start to look for her?'

'Not immediately sir. The information will get passed to my supervisor in the morning and he will make an assessment as to the priority of the case.'

'This needs to be the top priority,' Tom replied getting increasingly agitated. 'You need to get a search party out or whatever it is you do to get looking for her straight away.'

'We can't instigate a major crime investigation for every teenager that gets reported missing sir, especially after only a few hours. We get over a quarter of a million missing persons calls every year. The highest statistics are for teenage girls. Most turn up in a day or two. You really shouldn't worry at this stage.'

'I can see I'm not going to get anywhere speaking to the monkey so I'm going to get on to the organ grinder,' Tom responded in his broad Geordie accent slamming the phone down.

Gary shrugged his shoulders and put his feet back up on the desk. He picked up his latest copy of Classic Bike and thumbed through the pages resuming his daydreaming about the Harley Davidson model he was aiming to acquire.

5

Saturday 25th January 2014 – 03:00 – LONDON

DI Dan Brennan woke with his heart pounding and sweat prickling his skin. His mind was racing with 'If-Onlys' and not for the first time. If only he hadn't taken that promotion with the Metropolitan Police. If only he hadn't cancelled their planned holiday. If only he hadn't had an important early morning meeting that fateful day. If only he had given Lucy a lift to her doctor's appointment instead of letting her catch that bus. And if only she had started her maternity leave a week earlier.

But of course trying to change things couldn't bring her back and none of the different scenarios he went through could undo the greatest tragedy of his life. He tried to rationalise his thoughts and tell himself these were just thinking errors. His counsellor always told him that things always seemed worse of a night and this was undoubtedly true. He turned to look at the clock on the night stand. He needn't have bothered. It was three a.m. It was always three a.m. when the panic attacks seized him. He leant over and opened the pill bottle containing the Ativan that his doctor had prescribed to help manage the attacks. He swallowed a tablet and fell back onto his pillow staring off into the darkness knowing that sleep would elude him for the rest of the night but he'd try to rest as best he could.

Lack of sleep can't kill you his counsellor would tell him, your body will always take as much as it needs. Dan felt that he was slowly wasting away with grief. The counselling sessions helped albeit just. Everybody told him that time was a great healer but to Dan, his grief felt as raw today as it had been on the day he had been told that his wife had been killed on the number 30 bus, in Tavistock Square, during the London terrorist bombings of 7/7 back in 2005.

Some people would have resorted to drugs or drink to help dull the pain and help cope with the grief but for Dan, it was work that had helped him through the years. He threw himself into his job volunteering for extra shifts and working every hour of overtime that was offered. He wanted to be busy. It helped him to be busy. His colleagues couldn't understand his addiction to work and tried to make him take compassionate leave but he believed that work was his only salvation and the only way he would ever be able to get through the constant desolation that he felt.

He considered transferring to the Anti-Terrorist Branch to help catch other bastards like the ones that had taken his family and the families of so many other innocents but he knew in his heart that he could never be objective enough and would see only guilt and revenge rather than impartially assessing the facts. So he had stayed with the Metropolitan Police and had even been promoted.

Tommy the baby that he never got to see and hold would have been eight years old now. Lucy his wife was so excited about her impending motherhood. She came from a large family and always dreamed of having several children of her own. Lucy and Dan had been childhood sweethearts. He remembered with a smile the first time he set eyes on her when she started in the fifth year at the local comprehensive, having just moved into the area. She was the most beautiful girl he had ever seen and he turned to his best friend Jack and said,

'I'm going to marry that girl.'

From that day forward they were inseparable. They married at age eighteen. Dan had just started on the force and Lucy was training to be a nurse at the local hospital. Money was tight but they managed to get together enough for a security deposit on a small rented flat on the Lancaster Road estate in their home city of Salford in the North West of England. Lucy didn't want to start a family until they were financially secure so they had waited until she was qualified and Dan had been promoted. It was this promotion that had taken them to London.

Following their move to the Capital they had managed to buy their own place, a two bedroom flat in the Borough of Camden, which of course came with a large mortgage but luckily for them it was just prior to the housing boom where prices had increased hugely, as they have a tendency to do in spurts, particularly in London.

As soon as Lucy found out she was pregnant they had converted the spare room into a nursery. At the three-month scan stage and having decided that they wanted to know the sex of their child, they had been told that Lucy was expecting a boy. They decided he would be called Thomas after Dan's grandfather who had been more of a father to Dan than his real father who was so often abroad on business.

Dan reached out to the empty side of the bed and longed for the warmth of another human body with whom to share the dark lonely nights. He was drifting off down memory lane when his mobile rang. He cleared his throat and answered, 'DI Brennan.'

The dispatcher on the other end of the line told him that the body of a woman had been found in an alley off Saint Katharine's Way near St Katharine Docks. Telling her he was onto it, he swung his legs over the side of the bed, hastily put on his clothes and was out of the flat in a matter of minutes. Much to the relief of his colleagues Dan always volunteered to be on-call during the night.

When Dan arrived at the scene blue and white police tape had already been strung across the end of the alley. A burly PC stood in front of the tape holding back the small group of onlookers that had already formed at the mouth of the alley. London never sleeps - even at four-thirty in the morning there were people about.

'What can you tell me?' Dan said flashing his badge to the PC.

'Good morning, sir. She was found at about quarter to four by the refuse collectors. It looks to me like she's just a down and out who has tried to sleep it off behind one of the dumpsters and has succumbed to the cold,' he replied in the manner of someone who had seen this sort of thing many times before.

The constant, seemingly never-ending increase in demand for social housing because of the influx of eastern Europeans, lately from Romania and Bulgaria, plus the asylum seekers and illegal immigrants, had pushed up the numbers sleeping rough on the streets of cities in the UK, especially London, to an all-time high. The Government had unashamedly turned its back on this tide of human suffering in the knowledge that the voting public had had enough of the UK being seen as a soft touch for too many years already. The austerity measures that had been introduced as a consequence of the banking fiasco had carried a price and in this case, it looked like it was the life of this woman. Dan lifted the tape and walked towards the dumpster behind which the body lay. All he could see at this stage was some long flowing blonde hair.

The paramedics stood to one side stamping their feet to fend off the cold waiting for the signal from the coroner to take the body to the local morgue. The duty coroner sat back on his haunches peeling off a pair of white latex gloves.

'What can you tell me?' Dan asked.

'Not a lot at this stage. Not until we get the body out of here. She's not been dead long. Rigor hasn't set in yet. I'd say about two maybe three hours tops. I can't see any sign of trauma.

'Do you think she died here or was she just dumped in this location?'

'In my opinion, she died here but she could have been placed here shortly after her death. You can see the lividity starting to form in the flesh closest to the ground,' he said raising the woman's jumper a few inches to reveal her torso.

Dan could see the slight two-tone appearance in the flesh. The two inches nearest the ground looked purplish whereas the skin above was milky white. He knew from his induction into the world of autopsies, during his initial police training, that this was caused when the heart stopped pumping and the congealed haemoglobin settled at the lowest point. Even if a body was moved these marks remained and gave away the clue as to how the body had lain at the time of death.

The death looked like natural causes as far as he could tell but something about the circumstances just didn't feel right to Dan. The woman had no ID; in fact she had no personal possessions whatsoever. Apart from the dishevelled old clothing, she looked good, far too good in Dan's view. You would never have classed her as one of the many rough sleepers to be found on the streets of London. Even in death, she had a distinct beauty - but one that perhaps hadn't been appreciated in a long time.

Dan decided to call in the Scene of Crime Officers to forensically assess the death and the associated potential crime scene. He wouldn't be popular if this death did turn out to be natural causes but if any foul play was uncovered at the post-mortem and the scene had been compromised valuable evidence could be lost and that would be even worse.

He returned to the gathering crowd at the alleyway entrance and asked the PC if he had a list of any potential witnesses.

'Only the refuse collectors who found the body and a local prostitute named Val who plies her trade in this area,' he explained whilst consulting his note book. 'Val's probably your best bet; she wouldn't have allowed another woman on her patch so she'll know if the dead lass had been hanging about the area recently. You might also want to chat with the volunteers at the local homeless shelter; they may be able to help with names of people who might have been in the area or they may have known the dead woman if she was indeed a homeless person.'

Dan jotted down the details in his notebook and waited for the forensic team to arrive. He always liked to use the American term John Doe or Jane Doe where the identity of a body was unknown. To

Dan it made the body seem more human. His therapist had once told him that it wasn't actually an American invention at all but an old English term used in law, often for land disputes, which was hijacked by the Americans to refer to unidentified bodies. This somehow made Dan feel better that he was reclaiming the term for Britain.

6

Saturday 25th January 2014 – 06:00 – Oxford, England

DCI Ian McBride was woken from a deep sleep by his mobile phone ringing. He answered it quickly and quietly trying to disturb his sleeping wife as little as possible. Moving deftly out of the bedroom he listened as his Chief Superintendent, Mike Harding, explained that a young girl from Oxford University had gone missing the previous evening. Two things struck McBride as unusual. One that his Super was getting hands on with a case and second that the disappearance of an eighteen-year old student only, relatively, a few hours ago would command serious incident status. Harding explained that the missing girl came from money and the incident was being treated as a kidnapping for ransom. A team had already been sent to the girl's parents, who lived near Newcastle in the North East of England, to monitor any contact, including incoming calls, but so far any kidnappers had not made a move.

'I want you to head this end of the operation McBride. Have a think and let me know what you need?'

'Initially I'll need a standard team of at least eight detectives, a media liaison officer, and a data analyst. Possibly three or four civilian staff to man the Incident Room, that's if we need to appeal for information from the public. I'll let you know how many constables we need once I've established if house to house enquiries will be necessary. Plus I want DS Emma Blakely as my second in command.'

'You've got it. I'll have the rest of the team in place later this morning but you can make a start with DS Blakely by interviewing Rosie Ware's boyfriend, another student at the university. Don't forget tread warily lest any kidnappers get spooked but if we don't hear from them within twenty-four hours we'll have no option other than to go public. I definitely want an ABC approach on this one.'

The ABC strategy was a simple means of ensuring that all aspects of the case were thoroughly investigated. It stood for Accept nothing, Believe nobody and Check everything.

Harding stressed how seriously this incident was being taken. What he failed to tell McBride was that the girl's father was a close friend of the Deputy Chief Constable of Northumbria and it had been an earlier call from him that had effectively jump started the investigation.

7

One hour later McBride picked up DS Emma Blakely from her home and travelled into Oxford to interview Rosie Ware's boyfriend, Ben Tanner a fellow student from Oxford University.

The room door in the Halls of Residence opened before they managed to knock and they were confronted by a tall, dark haired young man kitted out in a rowing outfit. He looked more like a male model than a student standing as he did six feet four inches tall, tanned, slim and yet heavily muscled.

'Sorry, whatever it is it will have to wait I'm running late for rowing practise.'

He attempted to push past but DCI McBride blocked the way holding his ID in front of his face and saying, 'DCI Ian McBride and DS Emma Blakely with the Thames Valley Police, can we come in please – the rowing'll have to wait?'

A look of panic and confusion spread across the boy's face. 'Do you have a search warrant?' he stammered.

'You've been watching too many TV cop shows son,' McBride replied before adding 'We want to talk to you about Rosie Ware. We're not interested in anything else.'

The boy half stepped to the side and they took this as an invitation to enter. The room was typical for a student, every surface was covered with clutter and there was only a narrow gap allowing them to make their way to the small two-seater settee.

'Is your name Ben Tanner?' McBride enquired.

'Yes,' Ben replied though now looking guilty and a little perplexed. 'What's the matter with Rosie?'

DCI McBride sniffed the air and turned to DS Emma Blakely with a look that said – Is that what I think it is?

Filling the silence. 'I only had enough for personal use, I'm not a dealer or anything like that, I'll be thrown out if the Uni gets wind of this, and I'm not the only one who's smoking it,' Ben stammered nervously.

DCI McBride raised his hand, 'we're not concerned about a bit of pot son just Rosie.' Ben's face now changed from panic to worry.

'She was supposed to go to her parents for a party this weekend but hasn't turned up. Do you know her whereabouts?' McBride asked.

'No, the last time I spoke to her was yesterday afternoon just after our lectures finished. She was packing and rushing to catch the ten past six train from Oxford railway station.'

'Do you know how she planned to get to the station?' McBride asked thinking maybe a taxi driver might have abducted her.

'She was planning to cycle there. The station's not far from her digs.'

Ben had a thought and reached into his pocket and took out his mobile phone.

'Don't bother laddie, she's not answering, I've had my men calling her phone every half hour and nobody is answering.'

Ben gave him one of those, don't you old folk know anything looks. 'I'm not ringing her I'm using my Rosie locator APP.'

'APP?' McBride frowned.

'Yes, an APP for the iPhone. If friends, family etc. want to know where a person is and they have downloaded this APP it will show their exact location, iPhones have a built in GPS locator,' Ben explained.

'Useful,' DCI McBride said nodding his head and filing away this piece of information for future use. He felt like such a Luddite sometimes, however hard he tried, which wasn't perhaps too hard, technology raced ahead at a pace he just couldn't keep up with. He wouldn't put it past the hordes of police admin personnel putting this in place to keep track of senior officers.

Ben pressed his phone a few times and turned the screen towards them where it displayed a map with a red dot in the centre.

'There you go she's on the canal tow path or at least her phone is. I can't understand why she's there as there aren't any houses in that area but it is on the way to the railway station so I expect she would have taken that route.' Ben looked worried. 'Do you think she may have fallen off her bike it was very icy last night? Or she might have just dropped her phone. It's really dark along there. If she's lying injured by the canal she could have frozen to death. Have you checked the local hospitals?'

'That's the first thing we do,' DS Blakely assured him. 'Can you come with us and see if we can find the phone and any indication of what might have happened or where Rosie might be?'

Ben quickly changed into jeans and a thick jumper and followed the officers out. He felt the eyes of some of his fellow students on the back of his head as he jumped into the rear seat of the unmarked police car.

Half an hour later they parked on Aristotle Lane in the heart of Oxford's Jericho district. They stood on the road bridge that spanned the canal. The Anchor pub stood imposingly at the other side of the bridge. A path ran down towards the canal between the bridge and a brightly coloured children's play area which sat deserted at this time of the morning. They could see the tow path stretching ahead of them into the distance. Smart house boats were dotted randomly along the edge. Ben pointed to the direction where the app indicated Rosie's phone was located.

'The railway station's just over a mile that way,' he said pointing south along the tow path. 'It's a twenty-minute walk, quicker by bicycle.'

They walked slipping and sliding down to and then along the path. Every few hundred yards Ben rang Rosie's number. After five minutes walking, they reached an area that was more desolate. No buildings were within sight and no houseboats were moored along this stretch.

'Ring her number again,' DS Blakely prompted.

Ben rang Rosie's number once more and they heard a faint ringtone from within the hedgerow. Parting the thick frosty branches DS Blakely leant forward and carefully extracted the ringing phone from the undergrowth. As she did this she noticed a body-like form covered with about a centimetre of snow further under the hedge.

'Sir, I think we have a body,' she exclaimed with shock.

DCI McBride stepped closer, to better investigate the find and gently brushed some of the snow off the body. 'It's a dog,' he stated.

Emma let out a sigh of relief.

McBride sent Ben back to sit in the car to avoid any further contamination of the suspected abduction site. Another track intersected with the tow path at the point where they stood.

'You continue to search in this area and I'll take a look to see what's up there,' he indicated pointing to the track leading away from the canal.

He returned ten minutes later.

'Find anything?' Emma asked.

'There's a secluded turning area where a car could have parked. Unfortunately the ground is too hard for any tyre tracks or footprint impressions to have been made. Have you found anything further here?'

'Only a right handed mitten,' Emma replied pointing to an area further along the path where a forlorn glove lay.

McBride stood in contemplation for a moment. Emma knew better than to interrupt him while he was deep in thought. She had witnessed DCI McBride's, what she sometimes considered to be, almost amazing deductive skills before.

Finally he spoke, 'I think this kidnapping was well planned. The perpetrator knew the time and route Rosie would be taking to the station. I think he parked his vehicle at the end of this access path then lay in wait in these bushes. Having acquired the dog somewhere I believe he incapacitated it to entice Rosie to stop and help it. She couldn't have used her phone wearing thick mittens so she removed the right one to enable her to tap in the number. As she phoned for help he could have come up behind Rosie and grabbed her using something possibly a form of Chloroform to knock her out. Maybe this caused Rosie to drop her phone and the glove. The dog having served its purpose was discarded and he carried Rosie to his car which was parked in the turning.'

'So you're thinking foul play?'

'I am. Remember what the police training manual states – "In cases where the circumstances are suspicious or are unexplained, use the maxim IF IN DOUBT, THINK MURDER."'

Emma gave a shiver. She'd never been involved in a murder investigation before.

They searched for the next ten minutes hoping to find Rosie's bike or belongings but found nothing further.

'Ring the forensics boys will you please and ask them to remove the dog and have a post mortem carried out. I want to know when and how this animal died and how it might have been controlled. It seems too much of a coincidence that the dog is in the same spot as Rosie's phone. Also get them to check if it's been microchipped, I want to know where it came from and who owned it. After you've done that get onto traffic and ask them if there are any CCTV cameras between Rosie's accommodation and the railway station. Then pull any recordings and arrange for them to be viewed.'

McBride was already on the phone organising a team to comb the embankment and an underwater dive team to search and dredge the canal. He expected the bike and rucksack would be found at the bottom of the canal. He was just hoping that Rosie's body wasn't also there. He arranged for a squad of PCs to carry out house to house enquiries, or perhaps more appropriately houseboat to houseboat enquiries given the fact that this seemed to be the only form of accommodation in the area. They would start this the next day once the twenty-four-hour communications embargo had expired. Emma put police tape around the area where they believed the abduction had taken place to preserve the scene until the forensic team could have a chance to look for further evidence. The public would be inconvenienced by having the tow path closed but this couldn't be helped. At least it was quiet today as students wouldn't be in college on a Saturday.

'I'll wait here for the boys. You go back to the car and ask Ben for a list of all Rosie's tutors, close friends, and acquaintances. Then you can let him go,' McBride instructed.

'So you don't think he's involved?'

'There's no evidence to suggest he is, so we've got nothing to hold him on. Better to keep on the right side of him until we know more.'

Once the forensic team had arrived and the search for further clues was underway McBride excused himself and drove towards Rosie's student digs whilst Emma phoned around her closest friends discreetly asking if any of them knew her whereabouts. Nobody admitted seeing her later than the afternoon of the previous day.

The grey early morning had given way to an even greyer mid-morning and the early morning chill at this time of year remained unabated when they pulled up outside a modern looking apartment building. Ben had given them a key to the apartment. McBride didn't expect to find anything there but they would look extremely stupid if Rosie was tucked up in bed having lost her phone the previous night and having decided to forgo the trip to see her parents – albeit this was unlikely.

Knocking first and getting no reply McBride unlocked the apartment door and the two of them stepped inside.

'Well it's nothing like my student accommodation was thirty years ago,' McBride said looking around the modern flat with its expensive looking furniture. As well as the state of the art entertainment by way of a forty-two inch TV and sound system it was the overall space that impressed him.

'I doubt your parents were multi-millionaires.'

'I still don't think you can beat a music centre!' he offered almost by way of an analytic aside.

There were two large white leather sofas facing each other with a low-level glass coffee table in-between. The flat screen television was hung in the centre of the chimney breast. A top of the range sound system sat on the shelving off to one side. Three doors led off the lounge. The first was Rosie's bedroom. A large empty neatly made double bed took up most of the room and there was a desk on which sat a computer screen, a printer, and an empty docking station.

'Looks like she took her laptop with her,' Emma said.

The next door led into a simple bathroom that contained a shower, toilet, and basin. A single pink toothbrush stood in a glass next to the basin. McBride took out an evidence bag and placed the toothbrush inside.

'I'll send this off to the lab for a DNA test. Best to have it on hand just in case.'

'I wonder why she didn't take it with her,' Emma thought aloud.

'She probably has her own en-suite bathroom at her parents or at least a toothbrush at theirs. However better check with the boyfriend that it's not his. I doubt he would own a pink toothbrush but you never know nowadays. I'd hate to capture the wrong DNA.'

The third door opened into a kitchen with granite worktops and white high-gloss fitted cupboards. A matching kettle and toaster stood on one side.

'I'll say this for her she's tidy. I wish my kids were like this,' McBride commented.

They spent the next twenty minutes looking through all the cupboards and the desk but didn't find anything that helped with the enquiry.

A beautiful photographic portrait of Rosie hung on the lounge wall. McBride took it down and removed the photo from the frame.

'This will do as a description of who we are looking for. We'll have a quick look round the outbuildings and the surrounding area but I doubt there's anything here for us to find. I'm keen to get back to the station. The operation team should be in place now and we need to start on a more active search. The sooner the better.'

8

Later that same morning the Oxford PVP (Protecting Vulnerable People) Unit met for their first daily briefing. The PVP unit is responsible for investigations into child abuse, domestic abuse, vulnerable adults, missing people and the management of violent and sexual offenders. The unit had been assigned the Rosie Ware missing person case.

A large whiteboard stood at the end of the room. The glossy portrait photograph that McBride had obtained from Rosie Ware's flat was fixed to the board. Her beauty radiated from the photo. She had shoulder length straight honey blonde hair, gorgeous blue eyes and a smile that exuded a self-confidence that belied her relative youth. She seemed to be gazing at the team with inquisitive eyes as if challenging them to break the case and find her wherever she was.

DCI Ian McBride addressed the assembled officers. 'First off the Chief Superintendent is taking a personal interest and has already given this case major incident status.' It was unusual for a missing teenager case to be treated so seriously so soon after a missing person report was filed. More often than not the teenager turned up a few days later, having changed their plans at the last minute and gone to stay with friends without telling their loved ones. The Ware family must have some clout to get a major incident operation underway so soon. McBride was secretly pleased about this. Although he didn't like to see privilege getting a better police service than the rest of the population he knew that the first forty-eight hours was critical in getting a positive result in any type of case. Further, he was convinced that a teenager leaving home to attend her mother's 60th birthday party and not making it and then not being in touch with anybody was so inherently suspicious as to warrant the relatively early major incident status.

'Second,' he went on, 'the computer has thrown up the following choices for an operation name – Coffee, Blizzard, Burglar, Tractor or

Silver.' The computer was used to randomly generate five names one of which was chosen as the operation name. It used to come up with just one name but after a number of inappropriate selections, the process had been changed so that the police had some discretion about the chosen title.

One of the DCs piped up, 'well given the weather recently it's got to be Blizzard.'

'I disagree,' another officer said, 'Silver is more fitting.'

'Silverware,' he elaborated. More puzzled looks were aimed at him.

'WARE, Rosie's surname SILVER WARE, as in cutlery.'

'It'll do for me,' DCI McBride said 'Operation Silver it is, now let's get on with it.'

'Right, what have we got?' McBride said nodding firstly to Emma Blakely.

Emma cleared her throat and flipped through the first few pages of her notebook. 'The dog's remains have been sent to the Animal Health and Veterinary Laboratories Services as you requested. They are hoping to have their preliminary report back to us in two days.'

'Get back on to them and please stress to them how urgent this is.'

'Yes sir,' Emma replied knowing that arguing with DCI McBride that the Lab would take as long as it took and wouldn't speed up their examination even if the Prime Minister rang them wasn't worth mentioning. She continued. 'We have identified six cameras in the area that may give us footage of Rosie and any vehicles in the vicinity at the time. All the material will be with us for examination by early this afternoon. We know that Rosie didn't reach the train station as the railway police have confirmed that only a middle aged man and a mother with two young children boarded the six ten train to Newcastle.'

'Get them to check the earlier and later trains just to confirm she didn't take a different train irrespective of the destination,' McBride requested.

Emma nodded making a note in her book feeling slightly annoyed that she hadn't already thought to do this. She continued, 'I've managed to contact most of her close friends that the boyfriend gave me and none of them has seen or heard from her later than yesterday afternoon.'

'Pass the task of contacting the remainder of her friends and acquaintances onto DC Bowker,' McBride said nodding towards a female constable seated on the front row. 'I want you with me when we go to visit the family in Newcastle later.'

'Finally, I've searched for any missing Labrador dogs in the area and put out an alert. Nothing has come through yet but I'll keep checking,' Emma said closing her note book.

DC Anthea Bowker who was the analyst assigned to the case spoke next saying she was looking into Rosie's social media sites plus her emails and phone. 'I'm compiling a list of all her friends and any other contacts. It's clear she is a popular girl. She has many friends so this is going to take some time. I've also added Rosie's details to the Missing Persons Database. It will take a few days to get her DNA processed and into the system. The Specialist Search Team has been out since first light searching the tow path where the phone was located but apart from lots of litter nothing has been found so far, that's likely to be connected to the case. There was no sign of the bike or the rucksack she was believed to be carrying. The underwater team thought it unlikely that anything had been thrown into the canal as it had been frozen over the previous night although it could have sat on the surface then sunk when the ice melted, unlikely, but they were going to search it anyway. I also took the liberty of putting a trace on Rosie's credit card and setting up an alert on her bank account. If she uses her card or withdraws any cash we'll know straight away. So far nothing has been reported.'

'Good thinking, Anthea. Keep up the good work,' McBride said encouragingly.

The media officer Cath Powell spoke next. 'I've put together a statement for the press and I've also produced a media strategy for you to look at.'

McBride asked to review the statement before its release the next day. Although the press could be a pain they were also the best way to engage the public who might have vital information in a case such as this. McBride knew that careful management of the media was essential. A balance between giving them enough newsworthy material to engage the public but stopping any interference with the investigation had to be found.

Cath Powell continued. 'The next scheduled showing of the Crimewatch program isn't due to be aired for three weeks but I've reserved a slot on it just in case we haven't made significant progress or even closed the investigation by then.'

This was a disappointment to McBride as running a reconstruction as soon as possible was a great way of jogging people's memories and so stealing a march. He thought the program should run weekly not monthly as it currently did.

'I'm also putting together a televised appeal from the parents and Rosie's boyfriend asking for her release and any information the public may have to offer.'

This reminded McBride of the many appeals he had witnessed where it subsequently turned out that a relative was the perpetrator of the crime. It never ceased to amaze him how these people could sit there appealing for help and crying crocodile tears when they knew full well where the body of the missing person, often a child, was hidden. He must be getting even more cynical in his old age he thought.

Next DCI McBride turned to DS Rod Hartley. 'What's the latest from the parent's home Rod?'

'Nothing to report sir. We've had a local team set up since the early hours and no contact has been made by any kidnappers.' Rod was a fairly servile sort but had a reputation for being ruthlessly efficient nonetheless.

McBride frowned. 'If this was a kidnap for ransom I would have expected contact by now or imminently. Emma, you and I are going to take a drive up to Newcastle and speak with the parents. I want to know about any disgruntled employees or people who might want some kind of revenge against the family as a whole as well as Rosie in particular. And remember we're ABC on this case.'

The briefing was about to wind up when PC Gary Hope put his head round the door. 'Yo boss, we have a body.'

McBride hated the "Yo boss" expression that Gary had picked up from his favourite TV show Breaking Bad. He made a mental note to put a stop to it. The shock of a body being found registered on the faces of the Operation Silver team.

'Is it Rosie?' DS Emma Blakely asked.

'Definitely not,' Gary replied. 'It's an old guy but here's the really interesting thing which you'll like. He should have had a yellow Labrador dog with him but it's missing.'

'Newcastle will have to wait for now,' McBride said. 'I've got a strong feeling this is connected to our case. It could be an important first lead. The rest of you continue with your assignments. I want a plan for all of Rosie's friends and contacts to be interviewed plus the barge owners on the canal. We will start this first thing tomorrow once the embargo has been lifted. Emma, you come with me and we'll take a look at what's happened. Gary, find out who's been assigned the old man's case and get back to me with a name as soon as possible.'

'Ciertamente!' replied Gary.

'Gary – if you aren't Spanish, or even if you are, don't speak it in my presence – understood?' McBride bridled.

'Yes sir,' Gary instantaneously replied, experience having taught him that agreeing was the best way to react to a rebuke before whispering in Rod Hartley's ear as he departed, 'I thought it was French!'

9

The site where the old man had met his death was only about ten miles or so from the canal where Rosie had gone missing. The crime scene was already shrouded in the usual white PVC tent with blue and white police tape strung around the surrounding trees. Several policemen stood around with weatherworn red faces, hugging themselves to try to fend off the cold. The Home Office Pathologist and Scene of Crime Officer both dressed in white protective suits were just exiting the tent as McBride and Emma Blakely arrived. McBride recognised the DI but he couldn't bring his name to mind. He had worked a case with him a few years back and knew him to be a good officer. McBride introduced himself and Emma explaining the potential link to their case and asked the coroner, 'do you have a preliminary cause and time of death?'

'I can't absolutely confirm the cause of death yet but it looks like a single gunshot wound to the head fired from very close range. There are obvious powder burns around the entry wound. I don't know enough about ballistics to tell you the calibre of the bullet. When it's been removed I'll send it to an expert and run a check to see if it's been involved in any other shootings.'

The shooting was a surprise to McBride and Emma, which effectively escalated the Rosie Ware case to another level. Gun crime was still relatively uncommon in the UK and was mainly restricted to gang related crimes in the major cities.

He continued, 'As for the time I'd estimate it at between about four and six yesterday afternoon although it's been so cold the margin for error is that bit greater. Rigor is complete.'

'This fits in with the witness statements we have,' the SOCO added nodding to an elderly woman currently being comforted by a younger woman standing further down the road. 'The neighbour Mrs Burton said that Mr Banks, the deceased, passed her house at about four forty-five p.m. yesterday walking his dog Jasper as he did every day at that time. We do know that this wasn't a robbery as his wallet hasn't been touched and he still has a rather decent watch on his wrist.'

'Do you think he was killed here or was the body just dumped?'

'The lividity marks, hypostasis, suggest he was killed here. It looks like he was shot on the footpath then rolled out of sight into the ditch. This is why nobody noticed him until this morning. I expect the Post Mortem will confirm this.'

'Did anyone in the area hear a gunshot?'

'Nobody we have spoken to so far admits to hearing anything but we still have to carry out house to house enquiries in the vicinity. What's your thinking?'

'That perhaps he used a silencer. Which makes it seem like a professional hit?'

'An old man like Mr Bank's seems an unlikely target for a hitman.'

'I don't think he was the target. The dog was the target and unfortunately, Mr Banks was just in the wrong place at the wrong time. McBride filled him in about his theory that the killer was just after a dog, any dog, to use as a prop in his abduction of Rosie Ware.'

'Seems very elaborate and callous to me,' the officer said.

'It does to us too but we believe we are dealing with a calculating, well organised professional team or even a lone kidnapper,' Emma added.

'Do you mind if we have a word with Mrs Burton,' McBride asked.

'Go ahead I'd be grateful for any help you can give us on this one. Apart from your theory, it's a mystery to me why anyone would so violently target someone like Mr Banks.'

Mrs Burton couldn't add much to what she'd already told the other officers but she did confirm that Mr Banks did have an old yellow Labrador dog named Jasper. She burst into tears again, 'Mr Banks was such a gentleman. He was always kind to everyone. Who could possibly want to hurt him?'

'Have you ever heard the name, Rosie Ware?' Emma asked her.

The woman thought for a moment and shook her head. 'Doesn't ring any bells, do you think she hurt Mr Banks?'

'No, we don't but we think this could be connected to another case we're investigating.'

A black coroner's van pulled up next to the site. Two men climbed out. Opening the double rear doors, they took out a stretcher with collapsible legs and wheeled it towards the makeshift tent. The crowd looked on as the old man's body was taken away. Everyone was silent, some even bowed their head slightly either out of respect or the fear that death sometimes evokes. As the doors of the van closed, the crowd began to disperse like an audience at the end of a show but without the usual applause.

10

McBride and Emma still had time to make the four and a half hour journey to Newcastle to interview Rosie Ware's parents.

As they headed North the landscape turned more rugged and the snow on the hills and hedgerows became deeper. Luckily the snow ploughs had been out, as had the gritters, so the roads were relatively clear. The North-East of England was bleak but had its own natural beauty. It reminded Emma of the book Jane Eyre that she'd read as a youngster. The sky seemed much bigger here and the air cleaner and certainly cooler and crisper. She had wondered why rich people like the Wares had chosen to remain in the same area but now she was here she could perhaps understand why. It did have something of a tranquil and soothing effect. McBride had a Thunder CD playing during the trip which surprised Emma as she never had him down as a hard rock fan. He told her his teenage son played it so often that he had begun to like the group and had even gone to see a couple of their concerts even if he thought that live they were a little too loud. McBride always reminded her of the TV detective Jack Frost but unlike Frost McBride had a happy marriage and two lovely sons, he didn't drink excessively and he worked to live rather than lived to work. Emma liked these qualities and believed it actually helped to get the job at hand done better. The dysfunctional detectives often portrayed in books and films rarely existed in the real world of policing.

The satnav indicated that they had reached their destination. The house seemed to be totally surrounded by a high dense hedge which gave the property complete privacy. An equally high electric gate blocked their progress to the drive and the house beyond. They announced their arrival into the speaker mounted on a post to the right of the gate. Emma noticed a camera blinking in their direction as the gates slowly opened to allow them through. The house still wasn't visible and the car travelled at least a further half mile before it eventually came into view.

'Wow, what a place,' Emma said as an imposing Georgian mansion got bigger as they approached.

The drive split into a turning circle around an ornate fountain, currently dormant for the winter months. The left fork continued on to a five car garage. The doors were open and a young lad was busy polishing a silver Bentley. Three other cars, equally impressive sat waiting their turn for valeting. A green ride on mower was parked redundantly in the fifth garage. This machine would have to wait until spring time before being required for work duty cutting the extensive lawn areas around the property.

McBride parked at the foot of the stone steps that lead to the magnificent double fronted doors. There was no sign of a door bell but there was no need as an elegant middle-aged lady met them at the door as they arrived.

'Mrs Ware?' McBride asked.

'No, I'm the housekeeper Miss Keaton,' she replied.

'I'll show you through, Mr and Mrs Ware are in the lounge but before I do you've got to know that it will destroy them if you don't find Rosie, it will destroy us all. She means everything to us.'

Miss Keaton led them through an impressive hallway containing an imposing staircase which disappeared into the upper stories of the house and on into a large lounge at the front of the mansion. It was tastefully decorated in keeping with the period of the property apart from a large incongruous plasma television in the corner which though on had the sound turned down. Every available surface in the room was covered with family photographs nearly all including or of Rosie from a baby right up to the present day.

Rosie's parents weren't at all what Emma had expected. The mother reminded her of the singer Susan Boyle as she had looked when she first walked onto the stage of Britain's Got Talent. The father was overweight with thinning grey hair and jowly red cheeks. They were older than she had envisaged. Emma admonished herself for thinking how such a plain mother and rather ugly father could have produced such a beautiful child as Rosie Ware. However when Mr Ware started to speak she could understand how he had done so well in business as he had an engaging Geordie accent and eyes that held your attention in at least an interested if not slightly hypnotic way.

'I can offer a reward for Rosie's safe return or for any information the public might have.'

'That wouldn't be helpful at this stage sir,' McBride replied.

Noticing the confused look on Tom Ware's face he added, 'We would get crank calls and sightings from John O'Groats to Land's

End even as far as Australia. We don't want to be overwhelmed at this stage; we need to concentrate on the evidence and information that we already have. Maybe in a few weeks the focused offer of a reward might prove to be helpful.'

'And this evidence you already have, what is it? As far as I can see you have hardly anything.'

'We have a number of lines of enquiry,' McBride responded hating himself for trotting out such an off-pat response. In actual fact they had far less evidence than would normally be the case in a kidnapping or missing person case. All the team had been convinced that this was a kidnap for money but had that been the case they should have heard from the kidnappers by now. Something may have gone wrong but he really didn't want to be alarmist.

The Family Liaison Officer held the lounge door open and the housekeeper Miss Keaton carried a large tray into the room and placed it on the coffee table. 'I thought you might be thirsty after your long drive. Tea or coffee?'

'Tea for me, milk no sugar,' said McBride.

Emma followed suit. She normally drank coffee but thought that tea would be more refreshing.

They carried on through the usual questioning regarding any threats the family had received. Were there any grudges that might be held against them, jealous friends, disgruntled employees current or more likely former, problems with any members of their extended family? Nothing was forthcoming. Indeed Emma had rarely met a couple that seemed to be so well liked and respected.

'Can we take a look at Rosie's bedroom,' asked Emma.

'If you think it might help go ahead, it's up the stairs, the second door on the right,' Tom Ware replied.

They immediately found the right bedroom as a plaque obviously designed for a much younger child was engraved with *Rosie's Room*. Although much larger than most girls bedrooms the layout and content could have belonged to any teenager. A bookshelf held a collection of books on an array of subjects. Rosie obviously had an eclectic taste as there was everything from Caring for Your Pony to Space - Everything You Ever Wanted to Know. A row of DVDs was just as varied with several Disney classics alongside a box set by Professor Brian Cox and another by David Attenborough. They searched the rest of the bedroom for themselves even though the local team had already been through it with something of a fine toothcomb but nothing struck them as unusual or suspicious – and they had even as expected found a toothbrush in her en-suite. They discovered Rosie's diary from the previous year. McBride asked Mrs Ware if he could take it. She was hesitant at first but agreed that if it might shed some light on where Rosie was or what might have happened he could take it – but she stressed she wanted it back. Mrs Ware confirmed that Rosie always kept a diary so they should find one for this year back at her student digs. McBride made a note to look for this but suspected Rosie probably had it with her at the time she was taken as they hadn't noticed it when they searched her apartment that morning.

They spoke with the technicians who had been located in the house from the outset to monitor any incoming phone calls or other contacts. Nothing had been heard from any kidnappers. A Family Liaison Officer had been appointed to keep the Wares appraised of any developments as and when they happened. This appointment was as much to observe the family as it was to support them. They took the officer aside and asked for her views. She confirmed that the Wares were behaving as you would expect any concerned parents to behave. They had cancelled Sara's 60th birthday party telling the guests that she had contracted flu. The officer had spoken with all the staff working at the house and none of them had raised any suspicion as far as she was concerned.

McBride and Emma spent the next couple of hours re-interviewing the staff but learned nothing of note.

11

Sunday 26th January 2014 – OXFORD

Sunday 26th January 2014 – OXFORD

DCI McBride strode through the near empty incident room towards his office. It wasn't that the case wasn't being worked on, quite the opposite. The majority of the team were out interviewing the residents of the canal boats moored in the vicinity of the spot where Rosie's phone had been found. Early Sunday morning was the best time to catch people at home and McBride always found them to be more convivial when they weren't rushing about dealing with their busy weekday lives. He had instructed each member of the interview team to contact him as soon as they located any witnesses who might be able to give them a lead they could follow up. He didn't want to have any of the rookie officers, who had been drafted in to help with the enquiries, carrying out the important interviews. He would be involved with these. Leading a case like this meant being in control, effectively at the centre of everything, assessing all the information as it came in, picking out what was important and discarding what wasn't. The proverbial sorting of the wheat from the chaff. So far no calls had come in but it was still early days. When he got to his office he sat down on his swivel chair and placed the newspaper he had just been out to buy from the local newsagents on the desk in front of him. Their press release had been issued late last night in time to make the early morning Sunday papers. Placing his reading glasses, which he had reluctantly started to wear recently, on the end of his nose he looked at the headline which took up most of the front page.

Millionaire Lottery Winners Daughter Missing see page two
for further details was printed underneath an old picture showing the Wares with their lottery winning cheque from 1994. The paper must

31

have taken this from their archives. He read through the newspaper article that summarised the case:

Police divers search the canal for missing Oxford University student Rosie Ware. She was last seen by friends at 16.30 on the Friday afternoon of January 24th and was captured on CCTV at 17.15 that evening cycling along the Oxford Canal near her student digs in Jericho travelling in the direction of the railway station. Police have refused to comment on speculation that the daughter of Britain's first lottery millionaires Tom and Sara Ware has been kidnapped. DCI Ian McBride who is leading the investigation has issued a statement saying that everyone is concerned about Rosie's whereabouts and is urging anyone with information about this to come forward. Specialist police divers in yellow wetsuits have been combing the Oxford waterway where she was last spotted. A sniffer dog handler with a black Labrador took to the canal on a red dinghy boat to scan it for evidence. Police have trawled through hundreds of hours of CCTV footage and carried out "extensive" searches using specialist officers in the hunt for the missing University of Oxford student. Rosie, aged 18 is white, 5ft 11ins tall, of very slim build and with shoulder-length, honey-blonde hair. She was last seen wearing dark blue jeans and a green jacket and carrying a dark purple rucksack. She may have been wearing denim blue Vans shoes. She was riding a dark blue ladies bike. Police said they were "especially concerned" as it was not in Rosie's nature not to contact her friends and family. Her distraught parents raised the alarm on Friday evening when Rosie failed to show up for her mother's 60th birthday party weekend in her home town near Newcastle. Anyone with information can call police on 020 8358 0100, Thames Valley Police Protecting Vulnerable People Unit on 101 (outside the UK 0044 1865 841148) or the charity Missing People on 116000.

A portrait picture that McBride hadn't seen before was printed alongside the article together with a smaller picture showing the dive team working from a boat on the canal. McBride threw the paper into the bin alongside his desk. He had never had a case with so few clues. Hopefully tonight they would get a breakthrough as the live appeal from Rosie's parents and boyfriend was being aired.

12

McBride liked his superior officer, Chief Superintendent Mike Harding, immensely. He had risen through the ranks starting out as a beat copper. He was a copper's copper knowing when to be hands on and when to take a back seat. What McBride liked most of all was that he was politically savvy and could handle both politicians and the press with consummate ease. They had first met as new recruits twenty-five years ago and their paths had continued to cross throughout the years. For the first twenty years, their lives seemed to mirror each other. They both got married in the same year and both had their kids at the same time although Mike had two girls whereas McBride had two boys. Five years ago Mike Harding's career had accelerated away. There was no envy or bitterness for McBride as in his mind Harding was the better man and well deserved the promotion. As far as McBride was concerned he himself had reached the final rank in his career and would stay in his current position until retirement. It didn't cause him to be any less motivated or dedicated to getting a result on the cases that came across his desk.

Earlier in the day, they had discussed the strategy they would take for the televised press conference. Harding would lead the appeal and McBride would stand in the wings observing the boyfriend and family looking for any tell-tale signs of guilt or contradiction in their stories. A local school hall had been hired for the occasion. A long table covered with a white cloth had been placed on the stage behind which three chairs had been placed. A dark old wooden lectern which McBride suspected belonged to the headmaster for his morning assembly stood off to one side. A crowd of adults instead of school children sat patiently waiting for the proceedings to commence looking rather comical perched on the child sized chairs. Most had notebooks, some recorders and a few had both. With the confidence of an award winning orator Mike Harding strode onto the stage ready for the press conference and appeal to start. Standing behind the lectern he shuffled his papers waiting for the press photographers to finish taking their pictures and resume their seats. Looking towards the TV news camera he gave an outline of the case to date and told the assembled press that he would answer their questions at the end.

An old dark blue bicycle was wheeled onto the stage. 'This is a bike similar to the one Rosie was riding when we believe she was abducted. To date its whereabouts are unknown. We are very interested in locating it. If anyone out there has seen a bike like this possibly abandoned in the Oxfordshire area please contact the police on one of the numbers I'll give out at the end.'

A young police constable came out onto the stage holding a rucksack aloft as if an auction was taking place and the highest bidder would take home this prized possession.

'This is a replica of the rucksack Rosie was carrying. It is also missing. Again if anyone finds or knows the whereabouts of this item please get in touch. An Apple iPad was believed to be in the bag. If anyone is offered an iPad and is suspicious as to its origin again we would like to know about it. We're only interested in matters relating to this abduction – nothing more.' This being the standard code for the criminal fraternity to understand that no other prosecution would ensue, in this case doubtless for handling stolen goods, if the missing iPad were to be offered up.

Next, he introduced Tom and Sara Ware and Rosie's boyfriend Ben Tanner. Tom Ware sat in the centre chair with Sara on his left and Ben on his right. Firstly Ben Tanner rose and addressed the audience. He exuded self-confidence that usually only came from being part of a wealthy family and having attended the top British public schools. He gave a very credible performance with just the right amount of sincerity. He didn't come across in the least bit arrogant and McBride could see those present almost hanging on his every word. This was good because the more the public felt for those at the heart of an investigation the more likely they were to want to help. McBride could not see any sign of guilt or indeed anything untoward from the boyfriend and his story stayed true to the statement he had given the police. As Ben retook his seat Chief Superintendent Harding introduced Tom Ware, Rosie's father, to the audience. Earlier in the day they had sat down together and rehearsed what Tom would say. All had been in agreement that Tom would do the talking and Sara would sit at his side nodding encouragement. McBride didn't need to add that a few tears would help the situation as Sara had been seemingly crying constantly since Rosie's disappearance. All was going well until Tom Ware went off script. The audience stood up as one with questions flying across the room and photo flashes lighting up the hall. McBride held his head in his hands. This was the worst possible direction for the investigation.

13

Eating a rushed breakfast early the next morning DCI McBride glanced at the newspaper headline:

Lottery Winners Offer a Million for Missing Daughter's Safe Return

Last night Rosie's parent's wealthy lottery winners Tom and Sara Ware issued an emotional appeal to help find their missing daughter. Mr Ware said: "We'd like to say to Rosie first of all that we miss you, that we love you and want to know that you're safe. We just want you to come home. Then Mr Ware dropped the bombshell offering a reward of one million pounds for information leading to the release or whereabouts of his daughter. This is the largest reward ever offered in the UK. Chief Superintendent Mike Harding added 'We're appealing to anybody who might have seen her or who may have made contact with her or who may know something about her whereabouts to contact police on 101 or Missing People on 116 000, and to get in touch because we're really concerned about her well-being." Thames Valley Police and Northumbria Police have both provided specialist resources to help with the case.'

His team would be up against it now. Worse than having no leads was to be inundated with too many knowing that most were likely to be spurious. Sorting out what might help and what wouldn't would take time and resources. Both of which he didn't have. After the televised appeal Chief Superintendent Harding had promised thirty additional support staff to man the phones but he knew that every call, every claimed sighting would need to be followed up by one of his officers. All the crackpots and time wasters would be ringing in this morning all wanting a part of the reward money.

As if on cue when he arrived in his office he hadn't even removed his coat when one of his new officers delivered a message. 'Sir, we've had a call from a Peter Tetley who's the chief executive of the charity Missing People to say they can't cope with the volume of calls they're getting in about the Rosie Ware case.'

McBride gave a heavy sigh. This was just what he had expected and what he hadn't wanted. The reward offered by Tom Ware was already generating an excessive number of calls from across the world. 'Ring him back and tell him I'll call in to see him to discuss the problem.' McBride said wearily. He couldn't really spare the time but he knew it was important to keep these charitable groups onboard. They provided a fantastic service to both the public and the police. Protocol dictated that communication links are established between the police and the charity in a missing person case and that any information must be managed within the investigation. Refastening his coat he left the office.

The charity was located above a supermarket on a busy west London street. It had been set up in the wake of the disappearance of the estate agent Suzy Lamplugh twenty years earlier. On the door, a plaque showed their mission statement - Missing People, the charity that helps both the disappeared and those left behind.

Climbing the steep stairs McBride was feeling his age. He told himself that when this case was over he would look to quit his twenty a day cigarette habit.

Peter Tetley the charities chief executive was a tall, slim man with white hair and caring intelligent blue eyes. Shaking hands he showed McBride into a small office and his assistant brought in two cups of coffee. He got straight to the point. 'I wish you had given us some warning about this reward. Maybe we could have recruited some more helpers to man the phone lines. My biggest concern is that our normal callers won't be able to get through to us. As you can see we are only a small operation here and it's all paid for by charitable donations.'

McBride didn't try to defend his position. He knew it was indefensible. 'I can offer you some additional resources to man your phone lines.' Chief Superintendent Mike Harding had already come through on his promise of extra staff to work on the police hotline, now McBride was going to have to divert some of these people to help out here. It was only fair.

Peter Tetley looked dubious.

McBride added, 'don't worry they will be civvies I know you wouldn't want police officers involved in your operation. I'll also contact all the newspapers and ask them to remove your phone number from the appeal.'

'It's not just that, although using police officers would cause us a problem, it's that we don't have the room here to accommodate extra people.'

'What about if we divert your calls to the police hotline - screen them - we will deal with those relating to the Rosie Ware enquiry and we will forward your normal callers back to your staff. Do you think that will work?'

'Seems like a good plan to me. Let's try it out and see how it goes,' Peter Tetley said looking visibly relieved.

For the first time, McBride looked around at the office space. The operation looked like a police incident room. The phones were constantly manned and lists of the missing with where they were last seen adorned the walls.

Seeing his interest Peter Tetley offered to show him around. 'The charity runs three helplines – for young runaways, missing adults, and the families of the disappeared, all manned twenty-four hours a day. We receive one hundred and twenty thousand calls a year. Even before today, we could barely cope with the volume. Every day, thirteen million CCTV cameras track our movements, computers register what we buy, GPS systems on phones and tablets know our location yet the numbers of Britons who disappear each year is at record levels. Over a quarter of a million missing person's reports are made each year. Most people are traced eventually or return of their own volition but as many as twenty thousand are still missing after a year. There are the practical problems like unpaid bills, insurance companies not paying out on policies but for the friends and relatives it is the sense of not knowing that concerns them most.'

'Do you have any insight into the Rosie Ware case?'

'Are you asking is she a runaway? Statistics would tell us no. Ninety-three percent of children who go missing are from single parent households. We know Rosie is from a loving two-parent home. She is, however, a single child which increases the risk somewhat. I can tell you that the parents did everything correctly - Police were swiftly alerted, as was Missing People and local media. Her face is on the web, on posters, and already thousands of leaflets have been printed and are in the process of being distributed. Unfortunately, in this case, Rosie is eighteen years old and therefore classed as an adult and this makes it far less likely to be resolved quickly, if at all. Even if we do trace her eighty percent of the missing refuse to return home and forty-one percent of those located are not prepared to make contact with those who were looking for them.'

'The parents stress that it is totally out of character for Rosie to disappear like this.'

'Do you know how many times I've heard that statement? Parents often don't really know their own children. They don't know the stress they are under. In Rosie's case she has always been a high achiever but what if in attending the University of Oxford she has suddenly met her match and she can't face the fear of failure? Or she may have had a fight with a boyfriend. Something that we may see as trivial may have tipped her over the edge and made her run away. When she sees reason and thinks of the suffering of the family she has left behind she may reach out to us. And we do have some success. Some do return. About ten disappeared persons a week are found through the work of Missing People.'

Ten out of so many. A drop in the ocean McBride thought. With one crisis resolved McBride thanked Peter Tetley and left the building to return to his main objective which was finding Rosie Ware.

14

Monday 27th January 2014 – LONDON

The next time DI Dan Brennan saw the deceased woman she was lying on the cold stainless steel autopsy table under the harsh glare of the strong overhead lights. No matter what other officers might say Dan knew that nobody got used to dead bodies and the feeling they evoked of your own mortality and the time your body might be lying on a similar slab.

The mortuary had a strong smell of disinfectant not quite covering the underlying smell of decay. The place was quiet apart from the low-level sound of an overhead extractor fan.

Dan looked at the woman and wondered what kind of life she'd had that had led to such a final demise. Had she been loved? Would she be missed? Had her life been a catalogue of tragedy and unfulfilled potential? Dan knew that his own life of highs and especially lows gave him an insight into the lives of others. So far no-one had come forward to claim the body and Dan still didn't have a name to give to his Jane Doe.

The Home Office pathologist Dr Ken Atkinson looking like a surgeon, apart from his thick green plastic apron, worked quickly and methodically whilst dictating his findings into the microphone positioned above his head and entering the details of the dead woman's internal organs onto a chart next to the table.

The autopsy revealed death due to hypothermia. Not unusual for someone sleeping rough as London had been experiencing its coldest January in nearly fifty years. This was the fourth such case to have come to light in the past month, where one of the homeless had huddled down in a dumpster hoping to find some extra warmth only to discover the endless sleep of death as their bodies shut down to conserve energy but never managed to reawaken. What was unusual in this case was the fact that the pathologist revealed that judging by the extensive stretch marks and the number of C-section scars this woman had had multiple births over many years; how many he couldn't say. She had been pregnant recently but had suffered complications as she had undergone a hysterectomy in the last few weeks. Dan asked if the operation had been botched but Ken Atkinson assured him it had been carried out by a very competent surgeon and had no connection to her death. The time of death was confirmed as early Saturday morning. Her approximate age was also a surprise, not the age of around sixty that he had originally thought; she was only in her mid to late forties. There were no other distinguishing marks other than the fact she had broken her leg in her earlier years. Dan asked how Dr Atkinson could know this and he explained that it was evident from the bone regrowth that the break had occurred several years before the girl reached maturity. Her teeth had been well cared for in her youth but hadn't seen a visit to a dentist for many years. In Dr Atkinson's opinion, the small amount of dental work had been carried out by a British dentist. He explained that dental work was like a signature and could be attributed to specific countries. This was a relief for Dan, if the body had belonged to a foreigner it would be much more difficult to identify – if not impossible. In recent years this had become a major problem for the Met. as London had become even more cosmopolitan with more and more residents originating from other countries. Dr Atkinson said there was no evidence of recent sexual activity. This put paid to the idea that she might have been a prostitute - at least not recently. Her clothing hadn't been disturbed apart from the fact that one sock was inside out and a shoe lace was undone on her left foot.

Dan always asked the pathologist at a post-mortem for his own personal thoughts. Off the record of course. Dr Atkinson mentioned that his thoughts went to what wasn't in evidence. This woman had no trace of make-up. Her hair hadn't seen a hairdresser for a long time. Her nails hadn't been cared for. She hadn't removed any unseemly body hair for a long time. This led him to believe that she didn't currently have a man in her life. It was as if she had been in prison or some kind of institution. This also linked in with the signs of low levels of vitamin D in her body; as if she had been deprived of sunlight for long periods. It also helpfully proffered that though she had been the victim of hypothermia she was by no means a regular rough sleeper.

Maybe she was one of the thousands of mental patients who had been dumped into the city and ended up on the streets under the Care in the Community banner which had garnered political support and so been prevalent in the last couple of decades. Although this didn't explain the multiple births. Everyone knew the care in the community programme was more about mental health budget cuts but in the politically correct world that we now lived it could be career suicide to voice such an opinion but perhaps, more importantly, it wouldn't help him make progress with his case. The contrary argument that institutionalisation may deny the disabled the chance to live as near normal a life as possible, even if it could put the general public at a marginally increased risk from some of the more unsettled or volatile patients held sway.

In the pathologist's opinion, she wasn't a runaway who had left home for whatever reason and found herself on the streets of the capital in an ever decreasing spiral of descent into drink and drugs. There was no evidence to suggest she was an alcoholic and no needle marks to suggest drug abuse. If anything she was fit and well-nourished, although her stomach had been completely empty so she hadn't eaten or drunk anything for several hours prior to her death. At least if she had such a large family there should be a missing person's report for her.

'One last thing before you go. She isn't wearing any jewellery which is very unusual for a woman her age.'

'Do you think she's been robbed?'

'It's possible but there's no evidence that she had worn any jewellery for a long time.'

Dr Atkinson turned the woman's head to one side and brushed her hair away from her ear. 'See this tiny scar on her ear lobe?' He turned her head to the other side showing the same mark on the other earlobe.

Dan looked closely and could just make out a slight indentation in the skin and the colour was slightly different.

'It looks like she once had her ears pierced but allowed them to heal up many years ago. How many women go to the trouble of getting their ears pierced then let them heal up?'

Dr Atkinson then took hold of the woman's hands and laid them gently on the sheet covering the body. 'Look at her hands.'

Dan looked down at the pale white hands. The fingers were long and elegant like the hands of a pianist the nails trimmed short, blue in death. 'I don't see anything,' Dan said looking puzzled.

'Exactly. If she had been wearing rings I would have expected them to leave marks, indentations. Most women put on weight as they age and their rings tighten on their fingers. If she had been robbed I would expect to see marks or even broken fingers where the thief has struggled to remove them.'

Taking a last look at the body Dan silently mouthed a promise, 'I will find out who you are and I will let your family know you are here waiting for them.'

Dan got out of the hospital by eleven-fifteen. He was due in court at one that afternoon as a witness in a paedophile case he had concluded some months earlier. He just had time for a quick bite and a coffee before the stressful drive across London to get to the Old Bailey.

He hated court appearances as the inevitable waiting made him feel so frustrated when he could be out solving cases or indeed doing any other work which would always be of greater value but it did feel good when he eventually heard the guilty verdicts and that a long sentence had been handed down.

After waiting three fruitless hours to be called, the case was adjourned for a psychiatric assessment. How many times had Dan seen the same ploy by criminals and how many times had the establishment fallen for it, bending over backwards to try and come up with a reason as to why people behave badly. Couldn't they see that for whatever reason there were bad people in this world and to protect the majority they must be put behind bars not sent to a luxury holiday camp as Dan saw it?

It was nearly five o'clock when Dan returned to his office. He typed the Jane Doe details into the missing persons search page which formed part of the HOLMES2 computer system, Age: around forty-five, Height: 5' 10', Hair: natural blonde, Eye Colour: blue, Skin: white, Sex: female, Distinguishing Marks: none and then pressed enter. He decided to take a coffee break whilst the computer churned through all the data but he hadn't even risen from his chair when it pinged back the results. It never ceased to amaze him how quickly a computer can sift through mountains of data. The computer listed a hundred and thirty-four possible matches. None of the women had been reported missing recently. This surprised Dan he had expected a woman with a large family to have been reported missing quickly. He would have his work cut out for him in the next few days even possibly weeks tracking down all these potential leads. A DNA sample from the body was being processed but as the preliminary autopsy report showed death by natural causes the case didn't qualify for fast-track analysis so could take weeks to get done. Likewise, a toxicology report had been requested but this was likely to take equally as long. Dan cursed the cut backs which had slowed down much of the forensic laboratories work. He did have a set of fingerprints which he intended to put in the IDENT1 computer system. If she was in the police system this would quickly identify her or at least rule out the possibility that she had recently been released from prison. He decided to contact the relevant police forces and the recently formed UK Missing Persons Bureau part of the National Crime Agency to ask if they had DNA samples, photos and most importantly dental records for the matches he had identified.

It was a long shot but a team had been set up within the Missing Persons Bureau to gather and record DNA evidence for all old cases. In most instances, nothing remained from the original victims but where close relatives still survived their DNA was taken and entered into the DNA database and their relationship noted. Something to do with familial DNA which Dan didn't start to try and understand. This work had proved a great and simple success in recent years with several high-profile, previously unsolved cases being cleared. The heightened profile of this task force had meant it had survived the recent cuts that were being imposed in many other areas. Even if it didn't identify his Jane Doe it might eliminate some of the hundred and thirty-four matches. He also ordered lists for recently discharged patients from long term care and secure institutions, again another long shot but perhaps worthwhile given that the pathologist had thought she might have been institutionalised.

Dan looked at his watch; it was now nearly six o'clock maybe he would just be in time to catch someone still working at the Missing Persons Bureau. He knew they tended to work regular hours, unlike the unsociable hours he and his colleagues kept. As he waited for the phone to be answered a thought occurred to him about what it would be like to transfer to one of these police jobs with regular hours but he dismissed it almost instantly knowing that it wasn't for him as he would miss the unpredictable nature and even excitement that working for the Met gave him. And he did want to keep busy and he did want to work long hours .... Currently. After the fourth ring, someone picked up at the other end.

'Cathy Grainger, Missing Persons Bureau.'

Dan explained the reason for his call providing the essential information on his case and asked if the Missing Persons Bureau would be able to offer any assistance. Protocol required all missing person's cases to be notified to the Bureau.

'I can't do anything for you tonight. Budget cuts mean no overtime, not that we ever got too much but I should be able to work on it tomorrow. Send over what you have and I'll see what I can dig up. When will you have the DNA result?' Cathy asked.

'I'm afraid that's on the slow track. Unless the tox results show foul play I can't up the priority so it could be weeks,' Dan explained.

'Well, lots of the cases I have here have been waiting decades so a few more weeks won't make a difference. I'll start work with what you've got. I should at least be able to whittle down the list,' Cathy said helpfully.

'I'd be grateful for any help. I'll email the details over. I'm just sorry the list is so long. Give me a call when you have something.' Thanking her for her assistance Dan replaced the receiver.

15

Missing Persons Bureau, Bramshill, Hampshire

Following the phone call from DI Dan Brennan and having received the promised email Cathy Grainger turned off her PC with a heavy heart. This was always the worst time of the day when she had to leave work and return home to her family. For everyone else in the office, it was the other way around. Cathy thought back to how her life had become what it was, there was nothing she could pinpoint directly it had been a slow insidious slide into the abyss. We all make choices and you just have to learn to live with them Cathy told herself echoing her mother's words.

As a child, Cathy had been painfully thin and shy. She was always the one stood at the side of the playground hoping beyond hope that some of the other more popular girls would invite her to join their group, but they never did. She grew into a tall lanky teenager and although she had a pretty face the boys never looked in her direction preferring the girls with budding breasts rather than a flat chested Cathy. Life at home was no better. Her parents only had time for her brother who was bright, good looking and had a personality that attracted lots of friends. I suppose it was her neediness that made her grasp the relationship with Brian when he first approached her at the church youth club. Brian was everything Cathy dreamed about. He was good looking and very funny, he was always the clown at the party and Cathy couldn't believe her luck when he sauntered over and asked her to dance. She had only been at the youth club because her parents had insisted that Andy her brother take her so they could have a rare night out.

Brian asked her to meet him the following Saturday night outside the local cinema. Cathy spent all the next day going round the shops looking for the right outfit and finally decided on a tight pair of flared jeans that showed off her long legs and she also bought a tank top that made the most of her small breasts. Looking in the mirror after doing her hair and applying some make-up even she had to admit that she didn't look half bad. At seventeen she was still a virgin, unlike all the girls she knew at school in her first year at sixth form. By this time she had a couple of friends, who though not exactly best friends, allowed her to tag along with them during school hours.

Brian hadn't stayed on in further education, he had chosen instead to do an apprenticeship as an electrician. This made him even more appealing as he had a small weekly wage coming in.

Cathy didn't even remember what film they had gone to see, all she could think about was Brian's hand slowly creeping up under her tank top until it slowly cupped her right breast. Cathy's nipple hardened and she felt a sensation flow over her that could only be described as lust. Cathy turned to Brian and he covered her mouth with his in a long drawn out kiss. She felt wonderful and knew from that moment on that she would be putty in Brian's hands.

The next day Brian arranged to meet her outside the local park gates. It was a beautiful spring day. He had brought along a rug and picnic basket. They lay together under the warm sun eating and drinking and chatting excitedly. Brian was a wonderful kisser and soon Cathy was caught up in the passion of the moment. In a husky voice, he suggested that they go back to his parent's house. Cathy thought it was a bit soon to meet his parents but didn't want to upset him so she agreed to go along.

Brian's family lived in a nice semi-detached house on a tree lined avenue. Her suspicions should have been aroused as soon as they entered the house and it was so deathly quiet. He showed her into the lounge but before she could even properly sit down he was on top of her and she fell roughly from the settee onto the floor. She was too shocked to even to let out a scream as Brian lifted her skirt and tore roughly at her panties which soon gave way. He then loosened his trousers and took out his erect penis. Pinning Cathy to the floor he entered her forcibly and lasted all of three strokes signalling completion with a satisfied grunt. Brian climbed off and behaved as if nothing more than an everyday common or garden event had taken place.

'Sorry I couldn't last longer, you just turn me on far too much,' he said breathing heavily.

Looking back even this statement put the blame on Cathy and maybe this was the start of the mental abuse he would inflict on her. Cathy just lay there in abject shock. She would have given herself freely to him but never like this. Thoughts whirled through her head – none of them good. She knew she should report it immediately to the police but then she thought of what her parents would say. All her mother would be concerned about was the shame of what had happened, what Cathy might have done to lead Brian on and more pointedly what the neighbours would think. Perhaps Cathy had even encouraged him; after all, she had allowed him to kiss her. And she had dressed so that he'd find her attractive. Brian took her silence as acceptance and returned to enter her a second time. This time he took longer, unbuttoning her shirt and pushing her bra up to reveal her pink breasts, even after the initial assault on her she couldn't stop the response of her body and her nipple hardened as he flicked his tongue across it.

Cathy vowed not to see Brian again. He bombarded her with phone calls and everywhere she went he seemed to be waiting for her. Four weeks after the rape she realised her period was late. She told herself it was nothing; it must be the trauma she had been put through. She couldn't be pregnant after one evening with Brian. She just buried her head in the sand. It was where she wanted to be. After eight weeks the morning sickness started. She sat at her desk in school hoping she could get to lunch time before throwing up in the toilets.

One Saturday she took the bus to the next town and walked into a large chemist. She purchased a pregnancy testing kit. She remembered sitting in a toilet cubicle at a nearby KFC restaurant holding the testing stick in her hand willing it to come up negative but knowing in her heart it would be positive.

She didn't have enough money to pay for an abortion. She didn't even know if you could get one free on the NHS. She daren't tell her parents. She made a decision, probably the worst in her life, to ask Brian for help.

'Brian, it's Cathy.'

Silence.

'I need to speak with you. It's important.'

'We are speaking. What do you want?'

'Not on the phone. I need to speak with you in person.'

'OK meet me at the park gates. The one where we had the picnic. Two o'clock tomorrow afternoon.'

The next day Cathy told him she was pregnant and the baby was his. Brian's reaction hadn't been what she expected. She thought he would be mad at her. She thought he would insist on her having an abortion. He was the opposite. He seemed really pleased she was pregnant. He wanted to marry her immediately. When she told him she didn't want the child - she wanted to finish her 'A' levels, he insisted that he would give up work and look after the baby so she could complete her education.

Together they went round to Cathy's parents to inform them of the pregnancy. Cathy felt a sense of pride in the way Brian defended her and insisted to an angry Mr Smith that he would do right by his daughter.

So two months later they were married. It was just a simple register office wedding. The only guests were Cathy's parents, her brother and a couple of friends from school. Nobody from Brian's family attended. This didn't seem to faze him. Cathy had never seen him so happy.

Ryan was born the following January. True to his word Brian gave his notice in and looked after the baby whilst Cathy continued with her 'A' levels. The Local Authority found them a three-bedroomed council house and the Social Security office paid them a weekly supplementary benefit payment. Money was tight but they managed. Cathy found it hard to study. She felt guilty that Brian had been with the baby all day so allowed him to go out with his mates in the evening.

Ryan wasn't an easy baby. He was demanding. Cathy got the feeling that Brian let him sleep during the day so when it came to evening time he was full of energy. She often sat with Ryan in one arm and a book in the other; sometimes falling asleep in that position.

She managed to get through her exams and she did reasonably well; not as well as she would have done pre-baby but she got good enough results to get accepted into the admin. side of the local police force.

She now had a small wage coming in each week. The Benefits Agency topped this up with something called Family Credit aimed at helping low-income families. This gave them a reasonable income. They had enough spare to take a week's break to the Butlin's holiday camp at Minehead in Somerset. It was during this holiday that Cathy found out Brian was seeing someone else. It was a girl from her old school. She overheard him on the phone telling Sharon how much he loved her and how much he missed her. Cathy felt angry and confronted him. His face turned red with fury. This was the first time that he hit her. He ranted on about what he had given up to look after her and the brat. He pushed her roughly back onto the bed and raped her for the second time in their short relationship. This was how Todd, their second child, was conceived.

Coming back to reality she walked across the car park and got into her car for the depressing drive home.

16

Before going home Dan wanted to visit the homeless shelter to ask around for any potential witnesses then he wanted to check out the prostitutes in the area where the body was found and hopefully find the woman named Val.

From the directions the PC at the crime scene had given him he easily found the shelter which was tucked away down one of the side streets, a block away from the site where the body had been found.

A large room was split into two by a row of screens which had notices haphazardly pinned to them. One side contained a number of chairs, settees and coffee tables set out in front of a large flat screened TV. The other side comprised of a kitchen area, serving station and four long trestle tables with wooden benches down each side.

It must have been feeding time as the lounge was empty but the dining area seemed full and had about thirty men and women of all ages noisily chatting and eating. Dan was struck by their various states of appearance. One would be dressed in a shabby coat but expensive looking shoes; another would have long dirty hair but clean stylish attire. Several seemed to be students with book bags slung over their shoulders.

At the top of the room, two men and three women worked feverishly dishing out plates of steaming hot food. As he approached the serving area the food smelled so good he started to salivate realising he hadn't eaten since that morning. The nearest woman looked up and nodded that he should take a plate.

Dan shook his head. 'I'm not here to eat. I'm looking for potential witnesses to a suspicious death that occurred in this area early

48

Saturday morning,' he said pulling his warrant card out of his pocket and showing it to the woman.

'Put that away,' the woman replied sharply, 'you'll clear this place faster than a fire alarm if these people know you're police.'

Dan put his warrant card away and repeated his question asking who might have been in the area early Saturday morning.

'It's too cold for anyone to sleep out in this weather. A person would freeze to death. This is our busiest time of year,' the woman said nodding to the rag-tag group of people in the dining area. 'We can only take in a maximum of thirty homeless. We are full every night.'

'What happens to those you can't take?' Dan asked thinking his Jane Doe might have been turned away.

'We refer them to other shelters. If they can't take them then they end up sleeping in hospital waiting rooms or even get themselves arrested so they can spend the night in the local Police lock-up. Each year the number of homeless grows. The message across the world seems to be that if you can get yourself to the UK you will be given a free council house and social security payments for life. As you can see that's a fallacy. Social Services only start to be interested if you have kids.'

Dan took out a photo of the dead woman and passed it around the shelter staff. Each one looked at it carefully and shook their head saying they had never seen the woman before.

One of the men said, 'you could speak to Lawrence he was here Friday night but we had to throw him out at around two in the morning as he had sneaked a bottle of whisky into his room and was somewhat inebriated. It's one of our rules - strictly no alcohol,' he explained pointing to one of the notices pinned to the nearest screen that had RULES printed in bold capital letters across the top followed by a long list of dos and don'ts.

'And where could I find Lawrence?' Dan asked.

'He's sat at the far end of that table, looking rather sheepish and trying to avoid eye contact with us. No doubt hoping we will let him stay tonight.'

'And will you?'

'Of course, we aren't cruel but they have to know that we have rules for a reason and they have to suffer the consequences if they break them.'

Dan thanked the team and threaded his way towards Lawrence where he sat at the end of one of the trestle tables.

'Ever seen this woman?' Dan asked placing the photo in front of Lawrence.

Lawrence's eyes jumped nervously from the photo to Dan.

'How much is it worth?' Lawrence replied.

Dan let the question hang for a moment then thumped his fist down on the table making the plates and cutlery jump into the air.

'You've been watching too many American cop programs. We don't pay for information in the real world.' Dan knew this wasn't actually true, the police paid informers all the time, but he was annoyed that this man would want to sell information just to enable him to buy more alcohol and get drunk again.

Dan continued, 'I only have to put in one call and we could haul your sorry little arse away for withholding information and aiding and abetting a criminal.' Dan didn't know if a crime had even been committed but he felt good venting his anger.

Lawrence put his hands up in surrender. 'OK, OK, I'll tell you what I know.'

Without Dan even noticing the area surrounding them had emptied as if these people had a sixth sense that he was trouble.

'Yes, I saw her early Saturday morning but she wasn't dead; dead drunk but not dead.'

'What did you see?' Dan prompted.

'Not a lot. She was walking with her arm around some guy. He was holding her up otherwise she would have fallen into the gutter. Drunk as a skunk she was. A sight worse than I was. They turned down one of the alleys for what I assume was a bit of hanky-panky. That's the last I saw of them. Too cold a night for hanging about, I made my way to one of my cosy little dens under the arches to sleep it off.'

'Did they speak to you?'

'He didn't. She tried to say something but it all came out slurred. I hate women who drink,' he added with righteous condemnation.

'Which direction did they come from?' Dan asked.

Lawrence ran his fingers through his thinning greasy hair whilst thinking, 'St Katharine Docks I expect. There are lots of restaurants and bars around there. I sometimes get some decent leftovers from the staff.'

'Can you describe the man?'

'Tall, slim, salt & pepper hair, mid-fifties, dark overcoat, gloves, shiny black shoes, wealthy looking. I think he was European.'

'I thought you said he didn't speak?'

'He didn't.'

'What makes you think he was European?'

'Well, he had one of those man bags over his shoulder like European men always carry.'

'Did you see anyone else around?'

'No apart from Val, she's always knocking about around there. Although I can't imagine any punters would be out in that freezing weather.'

'Do you know where Val lives?'

'No idea but wait until after ten o'clock and you'll find her on the corner of Vaughan Way and The Highway plying her trade.'

'I might need you to come to the station to make a statement so stay in the area,' Dan said as he got up to leave.

'Do I look like I'm heading for a fortnight on the Costa Blanca?' Lawrence said sarcastically.

Dan reached into his pocket and threw a ten pound note on the table. 'Don't drink it all at once,' he warned.

It was only ten to eight so he had a couple of hours to kill before Val would be around to speak to. He decided to take a walk to St Katharine Docks and maybe get a bite to eat and keep warm. Although it was slightly warmer than the previous two nights there was still a biting cold wind blowing.

St Katharine Docks had been transformed several years earlier into an up-market trendy area full of bars and swanky restaurants. In the centre, expensive boats, housed in expensive berths, bobbed up and down rhythmically. Dan looked at a few of the restaurant menus but soon realised they were well out of his price range. As it was Monday night many of the bars and restaurants were closed so the area was quiet. He decided to canvass the establishments that were open to see if anyone recognised the woman or had any other relevant information. It always seemed to be the Chinese and Indian restaurants that stayed open; the Asian people came across as grafters with a good work ethic in Dan's opinion.

Trade had been pretty quiet since New Year he was told by most of the places he visited. All of them had closed before midnight and nobody had seen the couple. Dan asked about the boats in the dock. It seemed most belonged to rich city workers who only used them in the summer months. He made a note to himself to contact the Thames river authorities to find out who owned the boats.

It was only nine o'clock so he still had an hour to wait before Val would be making an appearance. He made his way back to the alley where the body had been dumped and noticed a small café one hundred yards further down the road. He was relieved to find it still open. It could have seated about thirty people and was set up with tables for four down one side and tables for two down the other. Apart from him, there were no other customers in the place. He lowered himself into one of the many vacant seats, facing the door and hungrily looked at the menu. A young waitress approached from the kitchen at the back.

'What can I get ya?' she asked in a distinctly Australian accent.

'What would you recommend?' Dan asked.

51

'The spag bol is good, the chef is Italian and it's his grandmother's recipe.'

'Then I'll have one spaghetti Bolognese and a coke please,' Dan ordered.

'No worries,' the girl said as she turned and quickly went towards the kitchen as if the café was busy.

When the girl returned with his drink Dan showed her the photo and asked if she knew the woman.

'I've never seen her around here,' came the now expected reply.

Dan asked what time the café stayed open 'til.

'It depends on how busy we are but at this time of year we normally shut before eleven o'clock,' the waitress told him with a smile.

Fifteen minutes later a large steaming bowl was placed in front of him.

'Parmesan?' the waitress asked.

'Please,' Dan replied as she liberally sprinkled cheese over his meal.

It was the best spaghetti Bolognese Dan had ever eaten and suitably prepared him for his next trip into the cold night.

At just after ten p.m. and with the bitter cold wind biting into his flesh Dan made his way back along the street.

As promised Val stood forlornly on the street corner stamping her feet and rubbing her hands together dressed in a short skirt and leather jacket. Dan couldn't help but think that there must be better ways to make a living.

'Val is it?'

'Who wants to know?' came the cautious reply. 'You from the Vice Squad?'

'CID,' Dan said showing her his ID. 'Actually, Vice is now called Serious Crime Directorate 9: Human Exploitation and Organised Crime Command, or SCD9 for short. A bit of a mouthful I know.'

'Well I know all about mouthfuls – came the instantaneous retort before she added in a more considered and reflective manner ... Can't a working girl be left in peace to make a living? I'm not harming nobody.'

'I'm not from SCD9. I just need to know if you have ever seen this woman before. Has she been working this area?'

Val looked at the photo. 'Is this the poor cow they found Saturday morning?'

'Yes, it is. Do you know her?'

'Never seen her before in my life.'

'So she's not working the streets?'

'Well, she's certainly not working these streets. This is my area and any girls that wander in here are history,' she said slicing her hand across her neck.

As soon as she said this she thought of the implications and immediately tried to backtrack. 'That's only a figure of speech. I wouldn't harm no-one.'

Dan believed her that she hadn't harmed the dead woman.

'I've been told you were about at the time in question. Did you see a man and woman in the area early Saturday morning?'

'I got a lucky break Friday night and one of my regular Johns' paid for a four hour sesh. I didn't get back out until three in the morning. Just before the bin men found her. So I didn't see nothing. That witness who said he saw me must have been mistaken.'

This was a disappointment for Dan and he wasn't sure but he felt she was holding back telling him something. He gave Val his card and asked her to phone him if she remembered anything or heard anything on the streets.

Next Dan decided to visit one of the many pubs he frequented to ask his contacts if there was any word on the streets about the dead woman.

One of the good things about criminals is that in most cases they are stupid. It never ceased to amaze Dan the cathartic need they had to confess their crimes to other criminals. Whether they wanted to be absolved of their sins or boast about their conquests Dan wasn't sure but they almost always did it. What he did know was that it was a good thing for him. There is no truth in the adage, "honour among thieves". By their very nature criminals are inherently dishonest and in his experience will happily sell out their fellow lawbreakers for a few quid every time. Dan obtained most of his intelligence from the group of snitches, or registered informants as he sometimes had to call them, that he had accumulated over the years.

Dan walked into The Flying Scotsman in King's Cross. It was still as dingy as the first time he remembered but since the smoking ban there wasn't the dense fog hanging in the air and the smell had abated although not completely. This made the stained discoloured walls more visible. It wasn't an improvement. Dan found himself wondering if it might look better if they allowed the smoking to return.

He saw Henry, his snitch, sitting on his usual stool at the end of the bar. Henry was an information magnet. In another life, he would have made a top journalist but he hadn't had the best of starts. He had got in with a bad crowd in his teenage years. After several convictions for petty crimes, no self-respecting employer would entertain giving him a job. So he stayed hovering around the underworld picking up small illegal jobs, keeping his ears open for gossip that he could sell on. He had one of those quiet, contemplative, reflective personalities where you couldn't help but open up to him. And in turn, Henry expertly sucked you dry of anything worth its salt. Dan always had to check himself from possibly relaying information to Henry when it was his intention to elicit it from him.

'Can I buy you a drink?' Dan asked.

'Sure, the usual,' Henry replied.

Dan beckoned the bartender over and ordered a neat whisky for Henry and a pint for himself. He waited for the barman to place the whisky and a pint of London Pride on the bar in front of them and move away before continuing.

'What are you working on?' Henry asked.

'An unidentified body that was found early Saturday morning near St Katharine Docks,' Dan replied.

'Oh that woman who froze to death,' Henry replied.

'You know something about it?' asked Dan.

'Only that. And that in itself might be suspicious. When a dead body is found normally the criminal network is buzzing. In this case, there's nothing. No gossip, no confessions, no knowledge of the woman, absolutely nothing. It makes me think that this is either a suspicious death perpetrated by a true professional or just as it seems on the face of it - natural causes.'

'So you think it could be a suspicious death then?' Dan probed.

'Don't you?' Henry enquired before adding. 'Otherwise, you wouldn't be here.'

'I do, but I'm not sure others will see it the same way,' he said thinking that his boss wouldn't want him spending time investigating what had been cited as a death by natural causes by the coroner.

'I do have some info' on that paedo case you investigated a few months back though,' Henry offered.

He gave Dan the names of four other men who he believed were part of the group who had been grooming under-aged girls and then passing them around for sex.

Dan reached into his wallet to pull out a note to pay Henry for the information. Henry held up his hand. 'You can have that one on me Guv,' he said. 'I hate those kiddie fiddlers more than I can tell yer.'

Thanking Henry, Dan finished his pint and set off out into the still icy night.

Lying in bed that night Dan assessed what he had found out so far. Something about the autopsy findings was niggling him but he couldn't put his finger on it. As he drifted off to sleep it came to him what had been bothering him. Lawrence had said that the dead woman had been drunk but Ken Atkinson the pathologist had said that her stomach was empty, that she hadn't eaten or drunk anything for several hours.

A sleepy Dr Atkinson answered his phone on the third ring. 'This had better be important,' he said.

Dan explained his thinking adding, 'don't you think it's suspicious?'

'Absolutely. There was no evidence of needle marks on the body but I agree with you that this looks suspiciously like she was drugged. I'll go over the body again first thing in the morning,' he promised. Before also offering, 'but I have to say that your witness hardly seems of impeccable standing.'

17

Tuesday 28th January 2014 - LONDON

Early the next morning Dan was drinking coffee and eating a slice of buttered toast in his small kitchen when the phone rang. It was Ken Atkinson.

'Did I wake you?' he asked.

'Wake an insomniac, hardly,' Dan responded with a laugh.

'I've found something. Do you have time to call in at the hospital on your way into work?'

'Sure, give me thirty minutes and I'll meet you in your office.'

The pathologist worked out of one of London's many large hospitals. As always seemed to be the case the morgue was tucked away out of sight deep in the basement. Little natural light made its way into the area and old flickering fluorescents marked a dim yellow path from the elevator to the office Ken Atkinson used to write up his reports and conduct the admin aspect of his coroner duties. Dan passed the grim viewing room where countless bereaved families must have experienced their world falling apart. Beyond this was the large refrigeration room where the bodies were stored until being claimed for burial.

Dan could hear Dr Atkinson dictating in his office. He tapped quietly on the door. Everything about the area seemed to demand silence; like being in a church.

Dr Atkinson looked up and motioned Dan to enter the room whilst he finished off his dictation. When he'd completed the recording he put down the Dictaphone and asked Dan if he wanted a coffee.

'No thanks,' Dan replied. 'This place never makes me want to eat or drink.'

Ken looked slightly hurt but this gave way to an easy pleasant smile as he gestured that Dan should follow him into one of the examination rooms.

Once more the Jane Doe lay on the cold steel table covered by a green sheet. Dr Atkinson raised the bottom end to reveal her feet. Putting on a pair of surgical gloves he parted the big and first toe on her left foot and nodded that Dan should look.

Two puncture wounds were clearly visible. 'It looks like she has been injected with something. One of the needle marks is clearly earlier than the other. You can see it has already started to scab over. My guess at this stage is that she was injected with some form of GHB to incapacitate her but still allow her to be walked to the disposal site. Then the second dose was administered which put her into a deep sleep. The cold would have taken care of the rest.'

'GHB - That's the date rape drug isn't it?' Dan asserted.

'Gamma-Hydroxybutyric. Quite. You will know it as the date rape drug or liquid ecstasy.'

'So are you now changing your verdict to murder?'

'Not at this stage, it's still only my hypothesis. The cause of death is still hypothermia. This new evidence does make the death suspicious so I've increased the priority for the toxicology testing so we should get the results back in a few days.'

'This would also explain why her sock was inside out and her shoe lace undone,' Dan added.

'Yes, I expect it was dark in that alley so the suspect would have struggled to see what he was doing. Was a syringe found in the area?'

'No, SOCO didn't find anything relevant at the crime scene.'

'Could we look for any fingerprints on the body? He must have needed to take off his gloves to do the injection.' Dan asked hopefully.

'Unfortunately, the body has been washed so if there was anything it's gone now. I've bagged up her clothes and shoes for you to check if they have any prints on them,' he said reaching over to a table and passing Dan a clear plastic bag containing a pile of clothes and a pair of blue and white trainers. 'You might even find some useful trace evidence.'

Dan left the morgue carrying the only evidence they had managed to secure. He breathed in deeply as he escaped into the fresh chilly January morning. Dr Atkinson had promised to phone him as soon as the toxicology test results arrived.

Dan turned on his phone and it beeped to indicate that he had voicemail. The gravelly voice of Henry his snitch came over the line, 'It might be nowt guv but that prossie Val you mentioned last night is splashing the cash. Buying drinks for everyone.' The call ended abruptly, Henry never wasted words.

Dan thought that Val knew more than she was letting on. After dropping of the Jane Doe's shoes and clothing at the lab he decided to pay her an early morning visit. She lived in the worst block of flats

57

on a run-down council estate. The road approaching the block was potholed with litter gathering in the gutters. Obviously, the council didn't risk venturing into the area. A car with smashed windows and no wheels stood forlornly alone with each axle placed on three house bricks. Dan hoped his car fared better whilst parked in this dump of an area. At least it had a chance at this time of the morning as nobody was around. The place was like a scene out of an apocalyptic movie where all the inhabitants had succumbed to a mysterious virus.

The lift was out of order but Dan doubted he would have used it had it been working. She had to live on the top floor didn't she he cursed. He climbed the stairs and counted the doors leading out along an open passageway. Only a few of the flats displayed a number. Number fourteen was the last door. It took several raps on the flimsy paint peeling pale blue door before it was finally opened by a young girl of about fourteen with bed tousled hair and sleep encrusted eyes wearing a mans oversized jumper and a pair of tight white cotton briefs.

'I'm looking for Val. Is she here?'

'She don't work mornings,' came the reply, 'Come back later.' The door started to close.

Putting his foot into the closing gap, 'This isn't a social call I'm with the police. Now I'll ask again, is she in?'

'Ma you have a visitor,' the girl shouted as she sauntered back into the flat leaving the door open and Dan standing there.

After several more minutes with still no sign of Val, Dan crossed the threshold and made his way into the dingy flat. To the left was a small kitchen. Dirty crockery and pans were strewn across every available work surface. It didn't look as if anyone had attempted to do the washing up in weeks. To the right, there was a lounge filled with an oversized three-piece suite and a brand new flat screened television - the cardboard packaging still leaning against the nearby wall. The next room from what Dan could make out was a grubby windowless bathroom. Beyond this, Dan presumed the two doors were bedrooms. Both were shut. He opens the one on the left. The girl who had let him in was sprawled across a single bed fast asleep. The room was decorated for a young child with pink elephant wallpaper adorning the walls. Obviously, no-one had bothered to re-decorate as the child grew older.

'Shouldn't you be in school?' Dan said shaking the teenager awake.

'What's the point? You don't need qualifications to get on the dole,' she replied pulling the bed covers over her head.

Dan turned his attention to the second bedroom. Opening the door and looking inside he thought at first the room was empty but then he made out a shape beneath the covers. Turning on the light he poked the shape beneath the blankets with his toe. 'Val wake up I need to speak with you.'

'Go away it's the middle of the night.'

Dan noticed a glass of water standing on the bedside table. He poured the water slowly onto the bed at the point where he calculated her head lay. It had an immediate effect. Val shot upright like a rocket the covers falling to her waist. Her sagging breasts swung like pendulums across her chest. She made no effort to cover herself. Screaming she pointed towards the door, 'get out of 'ere y'bastard else I'll sue you for breaking and entering and police harassment.'

'Val Froggot I am charging you with aiding and abetting a crime, perverting the course of justice and wasting police time. You do not have to say anything but it may harm your defence if you do not mention when questioned something which you later rely on in court ....'

Interrupting Val looked terrified, 'I ain't done owt what ya talkin about. Who's going to look after my Tiffany in I get banged up?'

'Maybe I can drop the charges if you come clean about what you know about last Friday night.'

'I told you everything I know I didn't see a thing.'

'We both know that's not true. You found that woman, didn't you? You pinched her handbag and all her jewellery and sold it.'

Val was crying now, old mascara streaked tears ran down her cheeks.

'Maybe if you come clean and help with our enquiries I can get the charges dropped,' he repeated.

'Ok, ok. Let me get decent and I'll tell you what I know.'

Five minutes later Val came into the lounge where Dan was perched on the edge of the settee, not just the cleanest part but the only clean part of any of the furniture. He couldn't believe the transformation from the woman he had seen minutes before. Her hair and make-up were perfect and she wore a black suit and high heels. She looked more like a high flying city worker than a hooker.

'You scrub up well,' Dan commented.

Val looked pleased. 'Would you like a drink?' she asked.

Thinking of the dirty kitchen Dan declined. 'No thanks, just tell me what you know and if I believe you I'll leave.'

'Everything I told you about that night was true I just missed a couple of things out. I didn't see the woman alive but when I returned to the streets after my sesh with Dev around three fifteen I saw the woman's body behind the rubbish bin. She was already dead. She'd been dead a while.'

'So you decided she didn't need her handbag, phone or jewellery anymore so you relieved her of them - took the rings from her dead fingers?'

'No, she didn't have a bag or a phone and she didn't have any rings. All she had was a pendant. It looked expensive. Solid gold like. I thought she wouldn't miss it so I took it. Honest that's all I took.'

'So you never saw the woman alive and you didn't see the man she was with?'

'Well I think I might have seen them from a distance earlier but I couldn't have described them. They turned off the road before they got near me.'

'What time was that?'

'Around two .... Yeah just after two in the morning.'

'Which direction did they come from?'

'from down the docks.'

'And you didn't see them again until you discovered the body?'

'Well, I did see the man. I hoped he would come my way but he went back towards the docks about ten minutes after I saw him with the woman.'

'What did you do with the locket?'

'I pawned it at that shop on the High Street.' She passed a receipt to Dan. It had the name and address of the shop and an amount showing £450.

'I assume you spent the money on this he said pointing to the new television?'

She nodded, 'and I bought a couple of rounds of drinks for me mates last night. Will I have to give it back?'

'I think you have more to worry about than repaying the cost of a television. I need you to come down to the station and make a formal statement. Then we will decide whether to take this further.'

Meekly Val followed Dan out of the flat.

Leaving Val with the booking sergeant Dan drove to the pawn shop and presented the receipt for the locket to the elderly woman sitting behind the wire mesh screened counter.

'That'll be six hundred pounds mate,' she told Dan holding up the locket just out of his reach.

'What one hundred and fifty pounds increase in less than a week? That's daylight robbery.'

'That's business. Take it or leave it.'

'I'll take it but I'm not paying,' Dan replied showing his badge to the woman, 'This is stolen property.'

'I can't afford to lose four hundred and fifty quid.'

'You should be more careful who you buy from then.'

'The woman looked so respectable. She said it had belonged to her dead mother.'

Dan gave the woman a police receipt for the locket and told her to take it to the station. 'I can't promise you will see your money again but you might get a new television out of it.'

Dan left the puzzled woman in the shop and left with the locket in an evidence bag. He doubted there would be any usable prints on it but he would get it dusted.

The outside of the locket had revealed no usable prints and the inside only had prints that belonged to the dead woman. Dan opened it to reveal two small photographs. The one on the left was of a strikingly handsome elderly couple. The one on the right showed a pretty young girl, aged about twelve, with waist long straight blonde hair stood in front of a couple Dan assumed were the parents. Judging from the age of the photos the girl could have been the deceased woman as a child. This photo didn't seem to be sitting flat inside the locket. Using a pair of tweezers Dan gently removed the picture. A small lock of very fine blonde hair fell onto the table. It looked like baby hair. Dan placed it inside an evidence bag and sent it off for analysis. He sent the photos to be enlarged.

He asked a jeweller for his opinion on the necklace. The results didn't add a lot to the enquiry. It was 18ct solid gold manufactured around the turn of the 20th century in London and valued at about five to six hundred pounds.

Dan looked at the locket, 'I thought you were going to be my breakthrough on this case but you've told me nothing.' He signed the locket into the evidence locker.

18

Tuesday 28th January 2014 - Missing Persons Bureau, Bramshill, Hampshire

Cathy Grainger had arrived at her desk that morning with a happy heart. She loved nothing better than having a body to try and match against her missing persons' list. She loved logic, the meticulous sorting of facts, of solving a puzzle, this was her world. Not that she relished the thought of telling a relative that their loved one was dead but she knew that every one of them would prefer closure rather than the not knowing. She had seen it on so many faces; it was as if they had stopped living on the day their son or daughter had gone missing, unable to move forward - just living in the past. One mother had described the not knowing as paralysing.

In the early 1990s, Cathy had seen an internal advert asking for volunteers to take an aptitude test to be considered for the recently formed police computer department. Bored with her then current job she had decided to take the test, plus if she passed and got taken on the job paid an extra allowance and more money was always good - especially when she was the only wage earner. She had passed the test. She went on a six-week training course to learn COBOL which was the computer programming language of its day. She had fallen in love with writing computer programs. She still used these skills today even though the programming jobs had long since been outsourced to India where the staff costs were much cheaper.

She had taken the older cases from the list, leaving Dan with the more recent missing person cases. Her expertise was with the long term missing; those who had been gone more than two years. The split left her with eighty-five cases and Dan with the remaining forty-nine. The information he had already provided was good. The fact that the body belonged to a natural blonde with blue eye colouring narrowed down the list of missing persons considerably. Had the body had dark hair and brown eyes the list would have been in the thousands.

Cathy had taught herself SQL, XML, Microsoft Access and a range of other computer software products which enabled her to search the many databases belonging to the police and other Government departments. It used to be the case that Government Departments weren't allowed to share information but as a consequence of the rising levels of fraud being committed the law had been changed and data sharing and data matching was now much more common. It amazed her how often a missing person appeared on one of the Department for Work and Pensions databases now living a new life. She then had to delicately inform the relative that the person was safe but didn't want to contact them for whatever reason.

There is a massive amount of information held about a missing person but it took someone with Cathy's computer skills to be able to interrogate the Missing Persons Database and extract what was relevant. Cathy was good at using Microsoft Access and quickly put together a search criterion. She didn't rely on the search Dan had provided her with just in case he had missed something. It was one of Cathy's failings that she didn't trust other people's work.

The fact that the body only had one broken bone was a good clue for narrowing down the search. Although the broken leg could have occurred after the missing person report was filed it would be impossible to un-break a bone so this allowed her to exclude all the reports where the missing person had previously broken an arm, finger, left leg etc. This immediately reduced her list to seventy-eight.

The next exclusions came from the dental records. Like the bones, it is possible to lose a tooth or fill a tooth after a person goes missing but it was impossible to regrow a new one or un-fill a tooth. Where available all dental records from the time the person went missing had been recorded in the database. It gave the police a snapshot in time. So it allowed Cathy to do a comparison between the unidentified body lying in the morgue and the dental records of the missing persons. Cathy had long ago written a programme that quickly compared dental records. It didn't take her long to enter the details of the Jane Doe's teeth. This information allowed her to eliminate another thirty-five cases.

Next, she worked on the fingerprints. She already knew that the unidentified body didn't have a criminal record but she re-checked this anyway. She confirmed what Dan had already told her that the woman didn't have a record. This allowed her to exclude all the cases where the missing person did have a record.

She was now down to twenty-one possible matches. She was just about to request the files of these remaining women when the phone rang. It was a very excited Dan Brennan.

'I've just got the preliminary toxicology report back and she had a large amount of Gamma-Hydroxybutyric in her system. So the death is now being classed as suspicious. The Home Office pathologist said he was surprised she could even walk. He now thinks that she was deliberately put in that alley and left to freeze to death. He's re-examined the body and found two needle marks between her toes. Apparently, this is a favourite spot for drug addicts to inject as it's not obvious to anyone doing an examination that they are using. The DNA evidence is now being rushed through and I hope to have it with you in a few days.'

Cathy told him about the work she had done so far and said she would get the twenty-one case files out of storage and see if she could narrow it down further. He sounded impressed and said that he hadn't made as much progress on his list. In fact, he hadn't made any progress. Cathy offered to take over his missing persons list and he gratefully accepted. She thought maybe she should have offered sooner but didn't want to appear presumptuous by taking over what was in effect Dan's case. But the quicker they could identify the body the better chance they had of catching the murderer.

Dan explained about the lock of hair and the pictures he had found in the locket. 'I'm still waiting for the hair sample to be analysed but I'll send you a copy of the pictures.'

Cathy had to admit that working on Dan's list was more difficult as the information was spread out around the country as they were all under two years old and therefore active cases. The first thing that Cathy did when a case was passed to her unit was to contact the relatives. Often the missing person had got in touch but the relative was so relieved all thought of updating the police went from their mind, so the case remained open. Where the person was still missing the relative anxiously asked if there was some news. Cathy would gently tell them that the case had been passed to her unit but the investigation was still ongoing.

Sometimes only the basic information had been entered on the central police database. Data often sat in in-trays up and down the country just waiting to be processed. To find out more about the women on Dan's list it would entail her ringing round the various police departments where the initial missing person report had been made. This took time. By the end of the day and after a lot of cajoling Cathy was happy that the database held the up to date information. Applying the same criteria to these cases Cathy had managed to reduce Dan's list of forty-nine women to a more manageable twenty possible matches.

The next step was to ring each of the relatives. Out of these, she managed to contact thirteen, she made a note to try the others seven again later when they may have returned home from work. Out of the thirteen there were six who had now located their missing relative. Cathy made a note to contact the relevant police force and have them update their records. She hated it when cases weren't closed off properly. So she now had seven relatives to ring back and fourteen still on the *possible list*. When she spoke to each relative she checked if a DNA sample from the missing person was in the system. Where it was missing she arranged for the closest relative to have a swab done at their local police station. This would allow them to narrow down the list further once Dan had the DNA results back from the murder victim.

The next day she had the cold case files in front of her. She had managed to contact a further five people from Dan's list and exclude another two. So she had her twenty-one cases plus Dan's twelve which made thirty-three possibilities allowing for the fact that their unidentified body was in the Missing Persons Database. If the person had never been reported missing in the first place then they were at a dead end.

Unlike Dan's list most of Cathy's cases were old. Some were getting on for nearly thirty years missing. Rather than worry the relatives unnecessarily she decided to wait for the Jane Doe DNA result to come through. This would provide conclusive proof of a match or not. In the meantime, she checked through her list to ensure that a sample of DNA was available to compare against. Ten samples still hadn't been taken so she used the time to arrange for this to be done. Even if it was fruitless in this case she knew that it would speed things up the next time a body couldn't be identified.

The pictures Dan had emailed her weren't much use. The one presumed to be their Jane Doe was too grainy and the potential difference between a child and an adult in their forties was far too great for anything other than the most circumspect of conclusions to be drawn. Aging software could be used on the photo and Cathy would carry this out if the DNA analysis didn't throw up a match.

19

Saturday 25th January 2014 – Early Morning – Location Unknown

Rosie awoke to pitch darkness. Her body seemed to have stirred before her brain. She lay still for several seconds trying to understand where she was and what had happened to her. As the shock realisation about what had been done to her flooded through she started to shake and catch her breath. This was reality and not some horrific nightmare. She sat up abruptly only to hit her head on the low ceiling. In the darkness, she put out her hands and felt around taking in her prison. She was in some sort of big box or crate, or was it a large coffin? Her first thought was that she had been buried alive and panic momentarily seized her. She had always had an irrational fear of being buried alive but now she noticed a gentle swell as if she was on water and she could also hear gulls crying out in the distance as they cavorted together in the air. She must be on some kind of boat. Her head spun and she wanted to throw up. Rosie tried to compose herself and take control of her mind that seemed to be racing in all directions. She knew it would be better to allay panic if not fear. The box was hot and stuffy she guessed that she had been unconscious for several hours as her mouth was dry and her muscles stiff from being in one position for so long. She tried to recall her last memory.

She had been cycling towards the railway station with the cold icy wind biting into her face. She noticed a yellow Labrador dog lying beside the canal tow path that she had been riding along. At first, she thought it was dead but as she approached she saw it stir slightly and let out a small whimper. Maybe it had been hit by a car and crawled down here to lick its wounds. People drive so fast down the country lanes. Rosie had always been an animal lover. Her family had always owned dogs and she had been brought up with them.

Before going to university she had volunteered one day a week at the local RSPCA near her parents' home. There was no way she could leave the stranded animal to die alone on such a cold night – if indeed it was badly injured. She stopped and dismounted. The dog lifted its head and looked at her forlornly with sad large dark brown pleading eyes. It attempted to lick Rosie's hand as she stroked its head offering words of comfort and encouragement but the effort was feeble and it gave up the struggle and lay back down on the cold ground. Although wary of the gloomy woodland to the side of the path she had removed her mitten and reached into her pocket for her iPhone hoping that she could get a signal in this remote area. She was in luck and had two bars showing. Before she could dial for help she was grabbed from behind and her phone flew out of her hand landing in the nearby undergrowth. Rosie tried to scream but a strong hand smothered her nose and mouth, she tried to kick out, run – to do something but her assailant held her tightly. Totally helpless she felt a sharp pick in her thigh and sank into a dark oblivion. This was the last thing she remembered before waking up here.

Think Rosie, think, she told herself, before subconsciously considering what the heroines in the movies do, they either cry and scream and act stupid invariably winding up dead or they use their cunning and brains to find a way out of their impossible situation. This was the only point of reference that Rosie had to her current predicament – Hollywood. She had never experienced anything akin to this before nor knew of anyone who had. Rosie knew that the former course of action would be futile so she decided she would follow the latter. Her first thought was 'why her?' If it was a sex attack she would probably have been raped and even murdered at the scene. This hadn't happened. The only other reason she could think of for her abduction was possibly in the hope or expectation of a ransom from her parents. Her parents were very wealthy and it had always been a worry that any one of them could be targeted by kidnappers. Rosie wasn't worried that her parents would fail in their attempt to come up with the money demanded but she wasn't naive enough to think that this would necessarily lead to her release. She didn't know how much the kidnappers would be asking for her release – what if they wanted more than her parents actually had – what then? She kept herself in check – she was getting carried away and this really wasn't going to help.

She had read or heard about so many cases where the parents had co-operated with the kidnappers only to be devastated when their child had been found murdered. These too had featured in films that she'd seen. What she did come to realise was that her abduction had been carefully planned. Someone must have known her plans to go to her mother's for the weekend, the route she would follow and also the fact that she wouldn't have passed the injured dog. Also, the crate seemed to have been made to measure – or was this only her imagination. She felt in her pockets but everything had been removed; she was hoping to find her keys and be able to use them to exploit any weakness she found in the crate. She felt around her surroundings in the darkness again. This time she touched a small ledge above, nearest to her feet. Struggling to turn around in the tight space she managed to feel along the ledge and her fingers found a soft muslin bag. Eagerly she pulled it towards her and opened it. Inside there was a bottle of water, a bar of chocolate, a small pen light and some paper. She fumbled with the torch, her fingers stiff with lack of use and a little cold. The torch gave off a surprisingly strong beam of light. She could now see that there was a grill at the back of the ledge which allowed air into her prison. At least she wasn't going to suffocate. She unscrewed the bottle and took a long swig of water. She was still thirsty but she wanted to conserve the remainder of the bottle as she didn't know for how long it was expected to last. She focused the torch beam onto her watch which was still strapped to her left wrist. It showed the time as seven o'clock. Given how stiff she felt Rosie didn't think it had only been an hour and a half since the attack but she had no way of knowing whether it was the following morning or even the following night, hell she couldn't even be certain as to which day it was. It could have been days since her abduction. She unfolded the paper which was a type written letter.

Dear Rosie,

> *Firstly apologies for the ordeal you are going through. It is not my intention to hurt you as long as you fully co-operate with my plans. The journey to your new home will take about two days. Unfortunately, I can't allow bathroom breaks so you will have to rough it for now. Everything will be explained on your arrival.*

> *Regards,*

> *P.*

The words 'new home' brought a shiver of fear. If this was a kidnap for ransom the kidnapper wouldn't be referring to a new home with the implied permanence that such a phrase conjured up. In Rosie's mind at the very least this referred to something much more long term – why had she been kidnapped? Why her? and what for? More questions; fewer answers. Perhaps it was a kidnap for sex after all – but why her? Maybe she was being sold to one of those Arabic harems – worry and panic began to consume her again. These came over her now like waves. She had to confront and address them or else she'd lose control and maybe miss an opportunity for escape. But now she doubted that such an opportunity would present itself. 'P' seemed to have covered all the angles. Rosie wept at how powerless she was and the fact that neither her intellect nor the family wealth could get her out of this mess.

All sense of calm left her and she pounded on the roof of the box and screamed for help until her fists were bruised and her throat raw. Exhausted and defeated she fell back and sank into a deep fitful sleep.

20

Monday 27th January 2014 – OXFORD

The autopsy report on the dog came back from the Animal Health and Veterinary Laboratories Services late on Monday afternoon and gave them their best evidence to date. The dog's spinal cord had been deliberately severed to debilitate it rather than kill it. This confirmed McBride's thinking that the injured dog was used as a lure to make Rosie stop on the path where the kidnapper or kidnappers were waiting to abduct her. The cause of death was confirmed as hypothermia. The poor dog unable to move had been left to suffer a long slow painful death. The concern now was that this was a well-planned and, having regard to the dog and the dead old man, callous crime. The dog hadn't gone down without a fight, human DNA had been found trapped in its teeth. This had been sent for further analysis and for comparison against both Rosie's and the dog owner's DNA. McBride asked for a nationwide alert to go out to hospitals asking them to report any adult patients presenting with a need for a tetanus injection as a result of a dog bite on the day or the days after the kidnap. The dog had been microchipped and as expected this confirmed that it belonged to the late George Banks.

The CCTV recordings had shown Rosie cycling towards Aristotle Lane but the next camera along her route hadn't sighted her which added to the likelihood that the tow path where the phone and dog were found was the abduction site.

The trains to all destinations from Oxford station had been checked for the hours around Rosie's disappearance but no trace of her was found.

The search of the canal by the underwater team hadn't resulted in anything useful. Neither had the extensive search of the canal path nor the surrounding area.

Most of the narrow boat residents had now been interviewed but none of them had seen or heard anything suspicious on Friday night. This wasn't a great surprise as the stretch of the canal they were interested in was devoid of both houses and boats. It was a very well thought out location to snatch Rosie.

Anthea Bowker had looked through Rosie's Facebook page. Three weeks earlier Rosie had made an entry about travelling to Newcastle that Friday night to attend her mother's 60th birthday party. Maybe this was how the kidnappers had known her intentions that night. Like so many Facebook users Rosie hadn't secured her profile and it would have been an easy task to monitor her life. Why youngsters found the need to publicise their lives remained a mystery to McBride. He made a mental note to check up on his own children to ensure that their profiles had been secured. Rosie had hundreds of friends and it would take days maybe weeks to interview them all. McBride doubted that the perpetrator of this heinous crime would turn out to be one of Rosie's friends. All his instincts told him he was looking for an older experienced professional criminal. He had asked the team to draw up a list of offenders who had been involved in previous kidnaps of this type especially those targeting children of wealthy families.

No activity had been reported on either Rosie's credit card or her bank account.

All the CCTV footage had been rigorously screened. A dark coloured Range Rover had been seen in the area but it was too gloomy to make out the occupants or the registration number. Even if this had been possible McBride suspected that the car would either have been stolen or be using false plates – he was now increasingly accepting that this had been a very well planned, organised and executed abduction. But why hadn't the kidnappers made contact? Had something gone wrong? In his experience, only the death of the victim would stop them demanding a ransom. He didn't want to accept this might be the case but he was beginning to believe this might be the logical conclusion.

21

Monday 3rd February 2014 - Just Outside OXFORD

Like many farmers, Stan Bowtell was a very early riser and had been for, what seemed to him, all his life. Farming had to follow nature and nature demanded an early start. The cows needed milking at the same time each morning and evening. They didn't know nor did they appreciate that the clocks moved backwards or forwards. Most farm jobs had to be done when there was light so farmers worked long days during the summer and short days in the winter. Stan preferred the longer summer days purely because of the extra warmth. Stan's workload had been easy throughout December and January as the frozen ground had stopped him ploughing his fields. Today the ground had definitely thawed, if only a little, but enough for him to start ploughing up the field on the South side of his farm. The morning milking had taken place and his cows turned out on to the pasture land. He would have breakfast before getting his tractor out of the barn. He always liked to start work after a hearty breakfast, especially in the winter. Stan's wife Mary had already collected a batch of fresh, free range eggs from their hen house and Stan could smell them frying in the kitchen as he returned to the farmhouse. After eating a hefty if not healthy meal Stan made his way to the barn and unlocked the large double doors. He remembered the days when he could leave his tractor outside with the keys in the ignition if he chose. But not nowadays. All farm machinery had to be securely locked away as it was a target for the many thieves often organised criminal gangs who stole it to order and had the resources to have it hidden in a freight container on its way to mainland Europe within a matter of hours.

With Terry his loyal black and white border collie sitting at his side, he travelled down the quiet country lane towards his field. Today was a good day, bright winter sunshine, a clear blue sky, without a hint of wind. A rare combination in early February though bitingly cold first thing. Still as Stan often said 'there's no such thing as bad weather, just wrong clothes.' He would get a good day's work done today. Stan loved being a farmer, loved the fresh air, loved the peace and quiet, loved doing something that mattered but most of all he loved being his own boss. Like his father and grandfather before him who had tended this land, he wouldn't swap his life for any other. Though he'd be the first to admit that his knowledge of other jobs wasn't just fairly limited but non-existent. He was a farmer born and bred and his main goal in life was to pass on his farm as a going concern to the next generation of Bowtells. It had come as something of a shock when his only son Alan had announced that farming wasn't for him and he was going to work in the city. This was the reason Stan was still working at the tender age of seventy-seven. Fortunately, he enjoyed very good health and was as slim, fit and as strong as he had been thirty years ago – or so he felt anyway. Recently his motto was - "every day's a bonus". He couldn't bring himself to sell the farm that had been in his family for three generations – over one hundred years.

He would actually be seventy-seven next week. His birthday was on Valentine's Day. It had always been a bit of a joke in his youth when his pals had compared the number of cards they had got, more often none, to those Stan could claim to have received - dozens. In reality, he hadn't received one Valentine card in his entire life; not even from his wife. He smiled to himself remembering many years ago when she had said that she would only send him one card only on that day. His choice – Valentine with a birthday greeting or vice versa. He didn't mind in the least indeed he probably wouldn't have wanted to marry her had she been too soppy. Hardy is the requirement for a good farmers' wife.

Their son had done well in the city. Albeit Stan didn't fully understand or appreciate what he did. He had married and given them three strong healthy grandsons. It had come as a most pleasant surprise when the eldest of these Richard had proclaimed that he wanted to become a farmer. He was currently studying at one of those new agricultural colleges. Stan understood that farming was changing and becoming hi-tech. His grandson wanted him to invest in one of those new satellite navigation systems that could take control of your tractor and plough the fields without any assistance from the farmer. Stan remained sceptical. Soon, along with so many other occupations, farmers would be redundant but not now, not today. Hopefully, Stan could continue farming in the way he knew, with perhaps just a little change, until he decided to retire and hand over the reins to Richard. Though he accepted that retirement might not be that far away.

Reaching the large green iron gate Stan stopped the tractor and swung down from the cab. Terry raced in circles at his feet in almost palpable excitement. Taking the key from his pocket he unlocked the padlock and swung the gate inwards. Stan turned the tractor with plough in tow into the field. A sense of annoyance burst the bubble of euphoria he had felt earlier. An old dark blue ladies bike lay directly across his path. Some idiot had thrown it over the hedge into his field. If they didn't want it why didn't they just leave it against the hedge on the road – why throw it into his field? Stopping the tractor once more he jumped down onto the cold, damp brown earth. He was about to lift it out of the way when he remembered the police appeal from the television news he had watched the week before last. Weren't the police looking for a bike similar to this? The thought crossed his mind to just move the bike to one side and get on with his ploughing but his strong sense of duty meant that he knew that if he didn't do anything he'd just feel guiltier as the day progressed. After all, it was to do with the abduction of a young girl and so reluctantly he removed his mobile phone from his pocket. He couldn't remember the special enquiry line number given out by the police at the end of the television appeal so he just dialled the emergency services on 999.

22

'I think we may have a lead sir,' Rod Hartley said poking his head around McBride's open office door. 'A local farmer name of Stan Bowtell has just rung through to say he has found a ladies bike abandoned in one of his fields down at Woodford Farm, which isn't far from the abduction site. The colour and make of the bike matches the details of the one Rosie owned.'

'At last, we may have something,' McBride replied. 'I want a team sent down there immediately and the whole area searched and I mean thoroughly searched. We have to consider that we might be looking for a body in the vicinity. Give me the address and I'll meet you down there. I don't want anyone outside the station getting wind of this. The last thing we want is a bunch of reporters trampling my crime scene or just getting in the way as they have a tendency to do.'

McBride parked his car in a lay-by several hundred yards from the field and walked back along the narrow country lane. Two police transit vans were already stationary on the grass verge their occupants milling around awaiting detailed instructions. It was a good day for doing a search. The sky was clear and bright so visibility was good and the wind calm.

Clearing his throat McBride addressed the men and women gathered in front of him. 'I want every inch of this area thoroughly searched. Anyone finding anything at all is to stop, blow their whistle and raise their arm. We'll decide if it's of interest. You are not to touch or move the object, is that understood?' The assembled group gave a cursory nod of their heads in unison having done this type of exercise many times in the past. 'Let's get to work then.'

McBride walked into the field to examine the bike which lay forlornly on its side a few feet from the hedge. DS Hartley was standing over it whilst a forensic technician dusted it for prints. 'What do you know?' McBride asked.

Rod Hartley took out his pocket book and glanced at the notes he had already made. 'I've interviewed the farmer a Stan Bowtell who found the bike early this morning. He hasn't been to this field since Rosie was taken so the bike could have been here undisturbed since that night or could have been dumped any time since. He hasn't noticed any suspicious activity in the area. He told me that this lane is rarely used but since the growth of satellite navigation there had been an increase in traffic trying to join the A34. Taking this lane would most likely be the quickest route from the canal to the main exit route out of Oxford.'

The sudden sound of a whistle pierced the air. All heads turned to an officer with his arm raised in the air about a hundred feet further down the field. McBride couldn't see what the man had found but it didn't look big enough to be a body. They made their way to where he was standing. A broken black leather dog collar lay on the ground. A silver disc glinted brightly in the early morning sun with the name *Jasper* clearly engraved in Cyrillic writing.

'The name of the dead dog,' the DS stated.

'and Mr Banks home address and phone number inscribed on the back,' McBride pointed out after carefully turning the disc over with the tip of a pen to ensure evidence contamination was avoided. 'Photograph it in situ then get the techie to dust it for prints and bag it for further analysis.'

The day wore on, the search was concluded but nothing further of any significance came to light. The team were slightly disappointed but at least they hadn't found a body so there was still hope the Rosie Ware was still alive somewhere.

23

The bike had been confirmed as belonging to Rosie. Apart from her fingerprints, no other forensic evidence had been found.

The same applied to the dog collar. There was a small spot of blood but it turned out, following laboratory analysis, to be from an animal and was not human.

Rosie Ware's DNA had been obtained from her toothbrush and entered in the Missing Persons Database. This would mean that all unidentified bodies that were found in the future would be automatically compared to check to see if the corpse belonged to Rosie.

The DNA results from the dead dog's mouth had come back and wasn't a match to either Rosie Ware or George Banks so the working assumption was that it belonged to 'the' or one of 'the' kidnappers. The DNA was being run against all the police databases but so far nothing had been found. They had even sent it for a search against the Interpol database, which gave them access to forty-nine separate countries, in case it was a foreign criminal with whom they were dealing. This wasn't standard practice but they were pulling out all the stops given the high-level interest and the professional yet brutal approach taken in this case.

As the names of suspected and actual dog bite victims arrived each incident was remotely investigated but so far nothing of note had been received to warrant further action.

Anthea Bowker had put together a short but comprehensive list of offenders who had carried out similar abductions in the past. This list contained the names of four men. Their number one suspect was a rogue named George Coates. He had been involved in the brutal kidnapping of a young girl in the Oxford area twenty years earlier. After the ransom was paid the terrified girl was released but missing two fingers. The kidnapper was shopped by his ex-girlfriend after he dumped her for a younger prettier model. At the subsequent trial, Coates had been found guilty and detained at Her Majesties pleasure for fifteen years. He had been released the previous year so was seen by the team as good fit for the abduction of Rosie Ware. Anthea tracked down his parole officer and arranged for McBride to visit him. It turned out that George Coates was back on remand as he had been involved in an altercation with the bouncer of a night club over the Christmas holidays and had had his parole revoked. Obviously, an unreformable character and back where he no doubt belongs McBride thought. The other three men on the list had also turned out to be dead ends. One had died five years ago. Another was still locked up in Broadmoor. The third had been involved in a road traffic accident and was paralysed from the neck down.

Just after ten p.m. DS Emma Blakely was just about to pack up and go home for the day when an email pinged into her inbox. It was short and to the point –

> *Tom and Sara Ware are not Rosie's biological parents. You need to investigate further.*

Emma showed DCI McBride the email.

After reading it through he said, 'I think we need to go and have another chat with the Wares. If this is true I don't understand why they haven't given us this information already. In such a case the primary suspect could be the real parents or at least one of them. I'll also want to know what else they might not be telling us. I'll pick you up at seven o'clock in the morning – sharp.'

24

This time when they arrived at the Wares house they were met with at least a dozen paparazzi standing either side of the entrance gates. Microphones and cameras were thrust into DCI McBride's face as he tried to announce his arrival into the intercom system. A barrage of questions assailed them mainly asking if Rosie or even a body had been found or seeking information about the primary direction in which the investigation was going. As well as asking specifically why they were visiting the Wares with the perennial -

'Are you treating them as suspects,' thrown out not so much as a genuine question to be answered but more to prompt a reaction, stinging or otherwise from either officer.

McBride quickly closed the car window and locked the doors, making several 'no comment' declarations whilst looking directly ahead at all times. His experience allowed him to be seemingly unfazed by everything the press threw at him even if deep down it did rile him a little. He rang the house from his mobile and told the housekeeper they were stuck at the gate. Once again the camera blinked in their direction then the gates slowly opened and he drove slowly through them being careful not to run over any members of the press, as tempting as it might be on this occasion. Nobody followed him in which was a relief but he knew that attendance of the Police from Oxford at the Wares home on a second occasion would be reported widely not least as they didn't have anything else to report about the case but they would want to keep it in the public eye to repay in part at least their investment in time and effort.

Once again the housekeeper led them through to the lounge. Mr and Mrs Ware were sat in the same position as on their last visit; indeed if it hadn't have been for a change of clothes it would have looked as if they hadn't moved at all during the last week. The only addition to the room was a number of daily newspapers spread out on the coffee table. McBride couldn't blame them for searching for any snippet of information about their missing daughter but he knew they wouldn't gain any knowledge from these rags. The only other addition to the scene was a large dog laid with its head on Tom Ware's knee. It wagged its tail slowly and followed their progress into the room with its soulful eyes but didn't attempt to raise its head or leave its master's side as if caught up in the sombre atmosphere of the dire situation that the family found itself in. Mrs Ware looked at them hopefully.

'Any news?'

'No, I'm sorry we still have very little to go on,' McBride replied. Before adding

'As you know from your family liaison officer we've confirmed that the bike found was Rosie's.'

He hated the desperate look in a parent's eyes when their child went missing and they wanted news, any news; he felt such a burden of responsibility to find them alive and safe. He couldn't even feel angry towards Tom Ware and his misguided offer of the reward money. Desperate parents do desperate things.

'Then why are you here,' Mr Ware asked. 'You should be out searching or doing something more constructive than driving up to Newcastle for the day.'

'We've had an anonymous piece of information,' Emma said placing a copy of the email in front of the Wares. 'We can't see the relevance but if it's true we thought perhaps someone from Rosie's biological family may have abducted her.'

Mr Ware read the email, stood up, said nothing and went to a desk at the far side of the lounge. Returning he placed a copy of a birth certificate on top of the email. It showed Rosie Catherine Ware born 16th August 1995 in Brighton, mother Sara Ware and father Thomas Ware.

'This proves Rosie is ours.'

The document certainly looked authentic but Emma made a note of the details so that she could check them against the relevant entry at the Brighton Register Office where details of all Births, Marriages and Deaths for the area were held.

'Can I just ask,' McBride enquired, 'why was Rosie born in Brighton?'

Mr Ware looked wistful as he thought back to the time of Rosie's birth.

'Nothing but the best for my girls. As soon as we found out Sara was expecting we registered with the top gynaecologist in the country a Dr Frederick Simpson. We didn't want to take any risks due to Sara's age. He has his practice on Harley Street, you know, in

London. We booked Sara into St Mary's hospital Paddington for the delivery; if it's good enough for royalty then it's got to be the best right? A week before the due date we booked a holiday cottage in Brighton so that we would be nearer to London. As they say "the best laid plans of mice and men aft gan awry", Rosie decided to make an early appearance; she's always been ahead of the game our Rosie. They always say a first birth takes ages but Rosie couldn't wait for a hospital or even the midwife to arrive.'

'Are you saying you delivered Rosie?' Emma asked.

'I am young lady,' Mr Ware replied proudly. Then he dropped his head into his hands and sobbed, 'you've got to find her, please we will do anything, pay anything, just bring her safely back to us.'

'Well either the Wares just produced an Oscar winning performance or they are telling the truth,' McBride said as they left the house.

'I'll follow it up with checks at the Register Office but I have to admit I agree. It makes me so mad that someone would send such a malicious email at a time like this. There are some really evil sods out there with nothing better to do.'

25

The first job when Emma arrived in the incident room the next morning was to ring the Brighton Register Office. As expected they confirmed that the details in their register matched those printed on the birth certificate.

'Before you go,' Emma asked out of curiosity, 'how easy would it be to forge the register?'

'Perhaps not nigh on impossible but at least very difficult,' the clerk replied. 'A doctor or midwife has to confirm the birth and complete the necessary paperwork. A copy is given to the mother and a copy sent directly to us by the attending health professional. When the baby is registered we check the details match.'

'What if it was a home delivery and the baby was delivered by the father?' Emma added.

'A doctor or midwife still has to examine the mother and baby as soon as possible and confirm that a birth has taken place.'

'and fill in the paperwork,' Emma added.

'That's right,' came the reply, 'Got to have the paperwork.'

'What if the child is adopted? Will the certificate show the biological parents or the adopted parent's details?'

'When the baby is born it will be registered just like any other child, with the name of its birth mother and, if available, birth father. However, if the child is to be adopted, after the appropriate court order has been received by the General Registrar, an updated registration will be made, that will include the details of the adoptive parents. This certificate will be linked to the original one which will be held in a confidential index, accessible by the child in question once they've reached the age of eighteen.'

'What about registering a baby conceived after fertility treatment or surrogacy?'

The woman who has the baby, including a surrogate mother, is recorded as the child's mother. The man regarded as the father will usually be the husband or partner who received treatment with the mother i.e. the biological father. In the case of a surrogacy arrangement, the 'commissioning parents' – the couple who arranged for the surrogate mother to carry a child for them - can apply to the courts for a Parental Order that allows them to re-register the birth and be named as the child's parents. On issuing a Parental Order, the court notifies the General Register Office automatically, who re-register the birth. This new record will supersede the original.'

'Would you know that the original birth certificate had been superseded?'

'The Register Office would know but it wouldn't be evident to anyone looking at the birth certificate.'

'Am I allowed to ask has the birth of Rosie Ware been re-registered or superseded?'

There was a long pause at the other end of the phone then the voice returned speaking in a hushed manner, 'no you aren't allowed to ask but you can apply for a court order and we will release the details but to save you the time, effort and expense I can tell you now that you would be wasting your time.'

'Thanks, you have been most ....,' the receiver at the other end clicked in place before she had finished her sentence but Emma already had all the information she needed as she put the phone down.

Emma put her head around McBride's office door. 'Dead end, as we expected, in my opinion there's no way the Wares could have forged the birth certificate they are definitely Rosie's biological parents.'

26

Tuesday 11th February 2014 - LONDON

It was two weeks later when DI Dan Brennan rang Cathy Grainger at the Missing Persons Bureau to let her know that the Jane Doe's DNA had been entered into the database so she could begin the comparison with the DNA held on the Missing Persons Database. Disappointingly this hadn't resulted in a match being found. Their last resort was to wait for the final DNA samples from the relatives of their list of potential matches to be analysed and stored on the system. If this failed to find a familial match it could be years before the body was identified or worse still never.

The hair from the locket had been another dead end. Because it had been cut it didn't have any roots so no DNA could be extracted. All the lab had been able to tell them was that the hair was probably from a new-born baby. The colour was natural blonde and it didn't have any chemicals on it. Likewise, the trainers and the clothing from the dead woman hadn't revealed anything significant. The only fingerprints had belonged to the deceased and no trace evidence had been found. The clothes had been purchased from Primark in the preceding twelve months and the trainers could have been bought from any number of outlets.

Dan had been back to canvass the remaining restaurants at St Katharine Docks. All confirmed that they had been closed for at least a couple of hours when the victim had been seen in the area and yet again no-one recognised the dead woman's photo. It had been a long shot anyway as Dan thought it was highly unlikely that she'd been to one of the restaurants given the fact that her stomach was empty but maybe she had visited one of the restaurants on a previous occasion.

All the residents in the vicinity of the dump site and along the route from the docks had been interviewed but as was now the norm for big cities nobody had seen or heard a thing.

27

Wednesday 12th February 2014 – OXFORD

A week after receiving the first email a second one arrived in Emma's inbox from the same anonymous source. This time it had several attachments. Emma scanned the attachments before opening them as she had learned through bitter experience that this could be an effective way of delivering malicious viruses into the police computer systems.

Opening the attachments she discovered that they were scans of a batch of medical records. She immediately recognised the name of Dr Frederick Simpson the Harley Street doctor that Mr Ware had mentioned. The patient name and address belonged to Mrs Ware. Emma knew she was looking at the pregnancy records for Sara Ware. They certainly looked genuine as the type face used on the computer printouts dated them to the '90s, the time of Rosie's birth. Emma started to feel annoyed. Why send these she thought? Didn't it just add more weight of proof to the fact that Sara Ware had given birth to Rosie? Further, and perhaps more importantly, one thing this definitely did mean was that these emails weren't just from an uninformed malicious individual as she had first thought but rather from an informed source. It was a matter now of whether they were meant to help or from someone with an axe to grind.

The attachments gave details of each visit Sara had made to the gynaecologist in London. Starting at around four months into the pregnancy, then every six weeks with one four weeks prior to the birth and the last one six weeks after, five visits in all. Everything about the pregnancy seemed normal. The mother had a rare blood group AB+, the baby was expected to be on the large size, the mother didn't want to know the sex of the child. A handwritten note had been added in the margin – *"boy"*.

Emma just sat there staring at the note. It couldn't be possible; the Doctor must have got it wrong. Something niggled at the back of her mind. Was this why she had been sent the medical evidence, was this what she had been meant to see. And, if so, what did it mean exactly?

Different scenarios went through Emma's mind. She wondered if maybe the Ware baby had died and whether they had stolen another one to replace it. She ran a search for missing babies from around the date when Rosie had been born but nothing of even the remotest interest came up. It would have been a national news event if a baby had gone missing and hadn't been found. She decided to discuss the email and its contents with McBride as he was older than she and would have maybe remembered if not a case such as a baby abduction, then some other event that might provide a link to a case like this.

Walking across to his office where the open door indicated he was accepting interruptions, 'sir, can I have a word?'

'Certainly, come in, take a seat,' he said putting down the report he was studying.

'I've just had another anonymous email from the same source as before regarding the Rosie Ware case. I don't think perhaps we should be so keen to dismiss it.' Emma explained about the medical reports and what she had found.

McBride thought for a moment. 'Sexing a baby in the womb has never been an exact science; the Doctor must just have got it wrong. Made a mistake. There's no harm done so long as the baby is healthy.'

Emma interrupted, 'There's also the statement that the baby was expected to be on the large size. We know from what the Ware's told us that Rosie was tiny only 6 lbs. Even back then this would be considered small for a new-born. Can we find out Mrs Ware's blood group?'

'Not without asking her and I doubt she would give us this information without an explanation.'

'So where do we go from here?' Emma asked.

'See if you can track down Dr Simpson but be discreet. It's been eighteen years but he may remember something.'

'Won't we be tipping him off if he's involved in a scam?'

'Maybe but I don't know where else we can go with this currently. We can't speak to the Wares again until we have some concrete evidence. Also, speak with our techie guys and see if they can trace the email sender. I want to know who is sending us this information and more importantly what their game is.'

28

Thursday 13th February 2014 – Dr Simpson's Residence

Emma opened the garden gate which creaked loudly on its hinges. An elderly lady raised her head from the flower border she was kneeling beside.

'Mrs Simpson?' Emma asked.

The lady nodded in response putting down her trowel and removing her gardening gloves and greeting Emma with a broad smile. She rose and shook Emma's hand saying, 'you must be the police officer who phoned earlier?'

'Yes, I wanted to speak with your husband Dr Frederick Simpson.'

'Come this way. You are lucky; you have called on a good day.'

Emma looked puzzled, 'I don't understand,' she said.

'My husband has terminal cancer; he doesn't have much longer to live.'

'I'm so sorry Mrs Simpson.'

'Please call me Lena. I always think of King Edward VIII mistress when people call me Mrs Simpson,' she smiled again.

Emma followed her up the winding garden path to a beautiful chocolate box cottage with ivy growing up the front of the whitewashed wall.

'You have a lovely home here.'

'Yes, we love this place. We have lived here for over forty years. We raised our five children here. It has so many happy memories.' Tailing off her recollections leaving a sadness in the air she beckoned Emma to walk with her.

Lena opened the door and Emma followed her into a comfortable lounge where an elderly man sat in an armchair next to the coal fire wrapped in a paisley woollen rug.

'Fred, this is the police officer I told you about who wants to discuss one of your patients.'

Dr Simpson looked at Emma with clear perceptive and intelligent eyes. He certainly didn't look like a criminal to Emma but then again neither did Dr Harold Shipman, Britain's most prolific serial killer, with over 250 victims, some say as many as 284. He was a family GP, adored by his many patients, who practised in Hyde near Manchester. A town that's previous notoriety was linked with the infamous child murderers Brady and Hindley, it was well used to negative publicity but nothing prepared the inhabitants for the shock of knowing this monster had lived and practised his deadly trade within their community for almost twenty-one years.

Emma snapped out of her day dream as Dr Simpson replied in a surprisingly clear and articulate voice. 'I'm not sure how much help I can be. I retired over ten years ago and I'm still bound by patient doctor confidentiality DS Blakely.'

He placed the book he was reading face down on the side table next to him. It was entitled When I Die: Lessons From The Death Zone by Philip Gould. Not the cheeriest of reading material but in the circumstances ….

He noticed her looking at it. 'This is a wonderful book, DS Blakely. I hope I can die with the same dignity when my time comes.'

Emma didn't know how to respond so she carried on regardless. 'We don't need to know any personal details about your patients,' Emma explained. 'I just need for you to confirm some things written on one of your patient's medical notes.'

Emma took out printed copies of Mrs Ware's medical records from her bag. She pointed to the word 'BOY' written in the margin. 'Is this your handwriting Dr Simpson?'

He looked down at it, 'yes, that's my writing. I always used to make a note of the babies sex just in case the parents changed their minds about wanting to know.'

'Could you have got the sex wrong?' Emma asked.

'It's possible but I've never got it wrong before - well not to my knowledge.'

'Could you have got it wrong in this case?' Emma asked.

Dr Simpson looked down at the patient's name and thought back over eighteen years. 'I do remember this case as it was one of the few where I didn't actually deliver the baby. The baby arrived a week early when the mother was on holiday. I think it was somewhere like Brighton. I remember the father ringing me saying that Mrs Ware was having very mild contractions but they were about thirty minutes apart. It sounded like Braxton Hicks contractions which are a false alarm and very common in late pregnancy. I suggested that he take her to the local hospital but he said that she adamantly refused to go saying she was sure it was nothing. Mr Ware said he was very concerned and didn't want to take any risks and asked if I could arrange for a local midwife to call round to the house and examine Mrs Ware. I made the arrangements and two hours later I got another call from Mr Ware saying that the baby had arrived and mother and baby were doing fine. He asked me to cancel the room he had booked at St Mary's hospital Paddington.'

'So you never actually saw the baby. So you don't know if it was a boy or a girl?'

'That's correct I wouldn't have any reason to see the child. Once a baby is born its care immediately moves on to the relevant paediatrician.'

'Would you have seen Mrs Ware again?'

'Yes, I would have seen her at her post-delivery six-week check-up.' Dr Simpson skimmed through the pages to the bottom of the last page. 'Here,' he pointed, 'I signed her off at the check-up, she was doing fine.'

'Do you happen to remember what Mrs Ware looked like?'

'Not really,' the Doctor replied, 'I don't spend much time looking at their faces,' he smiled.

'One last question,' Emma asked. 'You stated in the medical records that the baby was expected to be on the large size but the birth weight was only six pounds.'

'Now that is strange. I could have got the sex wrong but there is no way that I would be that far out with the birth weight. I would have been expecting a baby of at least ten pounds so it should have weighed more than six pounds even if it was born a little prematurely.'

'Thank you Dr Simpson you have been most helpful. I won't keep you any longer I can see you aren't well and I don't want to burden you.'

Emma rose to leave thinking that this was still something of a mystery that needed further investigation and hopefully some clarity.

As she was leaving Emma asked, 'You don't happen to know the name and address of the midwife you engaged to visit Mrs Ware?'

'Not off hand but I can speak to someone at the practice and try and find out. We may have used her again for some of our other patients in the Brighton area.'

Emma needed to speak with that midwife as her gut told her that something wasn't quite right about this case but how it connected to Rosie Ware's kidnapping she couldn't fathom. Keep digging she thought.

29

Gary almost gleefully called Emma over as soon as she entered the room the next morning.

'Emma I have a message for you from a Mrs Lena Simpson. She asked me to tell you that the midwife's name is Stella Hodson and the last known address they can give us is on Southampton Street in Brighton.'

'That's great Gary can you contact her and arrange a visit so we can question her, please? Anytime this afternoon will be fine. Failing that just as soon as is possible.'

'Who, Mrs Simpson?' Gary enquired.

'No Gary, Mrs Hodson,' Emma replied exasperated before adding - 'It's Stella Hodson I want to see!' as if to reinforce her requirement.

Luckily Stella Hodson still lived at the same address in the Brighton area. She had been named Stella Halsall at the time she had been involved with the arrival of Rosie but as she had done further work for Dr Simpson's medical practice they had her change of surname in their records.

It took Emma just under two and a half hours to drive the one hundred and ten miles from Oxford to Brighton. Luckily the traffic wasn't too bad and even the M25 ring road around London hadn't had the usual hold-ups. At three that afternoon she rolled up outside a pretty whitewashed terrace cottage. The door was opened by a petite middle-aged lady with a pleasant smiling face.

'Mrs Hodson, my name is DS Emma Blakely and I'm with the Thames Valley Police, my colleague contacted you about a case we are currently working on.'

'Yes, he was quite evasive, so I have no idea what this is about.'

'It's about the delivery of a baby that you were involved in eighteen years ago in Brighton. I know you can't discuss anything confidential but this is regarding the possibility that the registration of the birth had some irregularities.'

'Goodness me that's rather a long time ago. I sometimes struggle to recall what I did yesterday, but I'll do my best. It must have been one of the first Brighton births I was involved as I had only just moved here after I got married to a local based journalist for my sins.'

Hearing the word journalist Emma felt some concern. She didn't want this story getting into the press as they were making these enquiries behind the backs of the Wares.

Stella Hodson saw her unease. 'Don't worry luv he's long gone. Ran off with a twenty-year old hooker he was doing a story on.'

'I'm sorry,' Emma said.

'Don't be I'm well rid of him. I've remarried since and have two lovely kids.'

Emma got out Mrs Ware's medical reports and passed them over to Mrs Hodson.

She carefully read through them. 'I can't tell you much but you have a couple of things wrong in some of your reports. One is the sex of the baby and the other is the weight.'

'Can you tell me about the actual birth?'

'That's the funny thing and it's why I remember the case better than most. I got the call from Dr Simpson asking me to check up on Mrs Ware. He didn't sound at all concerned but I didn't want to take any chances as this was one of my first solo deliveries so I rushed around to the holiday cottage where they were staying.'

'And what did you find there?' Emma prompted.

'The baby had already been born,' Stella replied. 'I know some births can happen quickly but this was super quick, especially for a first birth. Even the afterbirth had already been passed as I recall. I examined Mrs Ware and the baby girl. Everything looked fine. I remember thinking how easily she had been able to deliver her first baby. No vaginal tearing. She was lactating normally and the baby was happily suckling at her breast.'

'She had definitely just given birth,' Emma clarified.

'That's a strange question to ask. Yes, her abdominal muscles were still split. It can take days or even weeks for these to fuse back together. In my opinion, she had given birth shortly before my visit.'

'When you say shortly are we talking hours or days?'

'Well from what I had been told I would have said within hours but if you are suggesting the birth occurred earlier then I suppose the baby could have been born a day or two earlier but that wouldn't have made any sense. Thinking back there were another couple of strange things. The cord had been cut and tied off with cotton thread but the wound didn't look as fresh as I would have expected but back then I wasn't so experienced. I re-tied it. Mr Ware had done an impressive job for an untrained first-time parent. Secondly Mrs Ware refused to go to hospital. I didn't push it as everything else seemed fine. Both mother and daughter were quite well.'

'Mr Ware didn't insist?' Emma asked thinking back to the conversation she had had with Dr Simpson where Mr Ware had seemed so keen for his wife to go to the hospital.

'On the contrary, he agreed with Mrs Ware that they remain at the cottage.'

'So you remember Mr Ware?'

'Oh yes, who could forget him. He was so handsome and so polite and well spoken. He reminded me of that Dr McDreamy off the TV show Grey's Anatomy. What's the actor's name? .....Patrick Dempsey, that's it.'

Emma thought that the Mr Ware she had met could never have been described as handsome and bore no resemblance to Patrick Dempsey. Still, it was over eighteen years ago but then again nobody could have gone downhill that fast even in eighteen years, could they?

'How would you describe Mrs Ware?'

'Ordinary, dark hair, dare I say a bit common sounding, not what you would have expected for such a handsome well-spoken husband but then again what woman looks her best just after giving birth. I did think she looked a lot younger than the birth date on her records but women who can afford Dr Simpson's prices have the money to spend on plastic surgery and a multitude of anti-aging products if they desire.'

Stella Hodson confirmed she had supplied the necessary paperwork to enable the Wares to obtain the required birth certificate.

'I visited her again the next day and that was the last I saw of the family as they planned to travel home the following day. I had no concerns as all was well and I never heard from them again.'

On her return to the station Emma reported her finding to DCI McBride. 'The facts just don't seem to add up. It's as if the birth parents aren't Mr and Mrs Ware, indeed it only really makes sense if you assume the parents in attendance at the birth weren't Mr and Mrs Ware and the baby they were expecting wasn't Rosie but I can't understand what anyone had to gain from this kind of deception. It's not illegal to use a surrogate mother to have a baby for you. With the money the Wares had they could certainly afford the expense,' Emma summarised before adding 'but why go to so much trouble to hide it?'

'And I still have the additional nagging doubt around the expected sex of the child. I can't believe such an experienced and gifted or at least highly paid member of the medical profession would make such a mistake …. But he could have I suppose. So it looks like we have one birth mother and two babies a boy and a girl. We know the Mrs Ware that Doctor Simpson treated wasn't expecting twins so we are missing a birth mother. We also don't know what happened to the baby boy, assuming Simpson wasn't wrong about the sex,' McBride added.

'So what if the Mrs Ware Dr Simpson and the midwife saw wasn't the real Mrs Ware? What if this was an imposter just provided to give provenance to Rosie's birth in the UK to obtain a birth certificate and passport? This theory backs up the statement from the midwife that Mrs Ware looked a lot younger than the date of birth on her records but as I said she put this down to cosmetic surgery or anti-aging products. What if the baby girl was stolen from abroad?' Emma added.

'That's possible and it would be very difficult to prove given the number of East European children that get snatched each year but we know that this baby had been born very recently, within hours or at most a couple of days prior to the midwife seeing it. It would be difficult to abduct a child of the right age and get it into the country that quickly. And why go to all this effort? There was nothing to stop the Wares adopting a foreign baby legally,' McBride said.

'It would be difficult to bring a new-born into the country immediately after birth but maybe not impossible. Back then it was a lot easier to travel with undocumented infants. The UK only introduced passports for new-borns a few years ago but as all babies look alike apart from perhaps their colour who's to say the baby coming into the UK is the same one as on the passport even now. Plus when someone leaves the UK they aren't logged out. In other words, somebody could bring a baby into the UK, leave it here and return home alone shortly thereafter with a babies passport in their pocket completely undetected. They could do this over and over again, one passport, multiple babies. There could be a racket of babies being trafficked into Britain. Let's think this through. We take a rich childless couple who are desperate for a child, the Wares, and for a price, someone offers them the chance to get a baby. We then find an expectant mother and pay her to assume the identity of Mrs Ware. This imposter attends Dr Simpson's clinic posing as Mrs Ware but also sees her own doctor under her own name. This provides two mothers but only one pregnancy. The real mother gives birth to her baby in hospital under her own name. The traffickers abduct the baby from abroad. Leaving her baby in the hospital the Mrs Ware imposter slips out and pretends to be Mrs Ware having just given birth to the stolen child.'

'It all seems too messy. Maybe the baby wasn't stolen but bought to order.' McBride posed – thinking out loud. Also, how do you guarantee the babies are born so close together? I just think that too many things could go wrong with this scenario. So where do you want to go with this? Do you want us to re-interview the Wares?'

Now it was Emma's turn to be cautious, 'I think we need to do a bit more digging first. Let's assume that the medical records are correct and follow the facts. We know the Mrs Ware the Doctor met was having a boy that weighed ten or more pounds and was born in the hours or days prior to 16th August 1995; plus we also know from her medical records that she had a rare blood group. I think we need to locate the mother of this baby boy and interview her first.'

'Where do we start with that? She could be anywhere?'

'I keep thinking why Brighton. Why would the Wares go to Brighton? Surely it made more sense to go to London to be as close to St Mary's hospital as possible. The only reason I can think of is this is the area where the Mrs Ware impostor lived and expected to give birth. If she had just given birth then she had to be close to the holiday cottage where the Wares were staying. I think we can narrow down our search to the Brighton area.'

'I'm still not sure where this lead might take us and how it could be connected to Rosie Ware's kidnapping but I'll give you some leeway. It's the only lead we have at the moment. And Emma – you've done really well. Engage the help of that Data Analyst, what's her name? The one the chief has assigned to the case.' McBride said looking on his desk for the name.

'Anthea Bowker,' Emma replied thinking how tired McBride must be to forget one of his team's name.

'That's the lassie,' McBride said as if he had solved a puzzle.

Emma headed off to see Anthea with a spring in her step after McBride had set such store by her opinion. A pat on the back, indirectly or otherwise, was always better than a financial bonus as far as she was concerned – though she wouldn't have rejected the latter out of hand. She didn't know where this lead was taking them but it was better than anything they had managed to uncover so far and her gut feeling was that this was in some way linked to Rosie Ware's kidnapping.

Emma sat down with Anthea and explained that she wanted to know if it was possible to find records that showed the following details:

- Births of boys on 16th August 1995 and the preceding four days in the Brighton area weighing more than ten pounds
- The names and addresses of the parents
- Mothers of these babies with an AB+ blood group

'How urgent is this? Do you want me to drop what I'm currently working on?' Anthea asked.

'Make this your top priority and get back to me immediately you have anything. It doesn't matter what time of the day or night it is.'

30

Monday 17th February 2014 - OXFORD

It was mid-morning the following Monday when Anthea Bowker contacted Emma and asked her to come to her workstation.

'Pull up a chair,' Anthea indicated as Emma rounded her partition screen. 'I've been in touch with the main maternity hospital for the Brighton area. We are in luck that they do keep statistics showing the date, sex and birth weights of the babies born there and have records going back to the early '90s.' Anthea pulled up a graph onto her computer screen. 'On the day and four days prior to Rosie's birth date, there were twenty male births at the main Brighton maternity hospital. On only two of the dates had any babies over ten pounds been born. Fortuitously this rules out twelve of the births leaving only eight to consider. Unfortunately, it doesn't include any home births or any from the smaller cottage maternity hospitals in the Brighton area so we might be missing the birth you are looking for. Also further bad news the data has been anonymised. This means that all personal information has been removed so the chart doesn't show the names of the babies or mothers so we have no idea which of the eight births matches the weight we are looking for. This got me to thinking that we could obtain these details from the Birth Register. A birth has to be registered in the area where it took place. Thanks to the advent of computerised Birth, Marriages and Deaths I've been able to draw up a list of names for the eight male births from the two dates we are interested in. To get more information we need copies of the actual birth certificates. I rang the Brighton Register Office and spoke with a Mrs Barry. She confirmed that the birth certificate holds the parent's information including their home address at the time of the birth. I was hoping that the baby's birth weight might be recorded on the register but unfortunately it isn't. We can order a copy of the certificates for each of the eight babies but they take about a week to get delivered. Alternatively, someone can visit the Register Office and get them straight away.'

'I don't want to wait a week. I'll drive down to the office myself.'

'I thought you would say that so I took the liberty of making an appointment for you to see Mrs Barry this afternoon.'

It was a beautiful crisp February afternoon when Emma drove down to the famous seaside resort of Brighton which is located on the south coast of England. She stopped off for a sandwich and coffee bought from one of those roadside take away vans you see dotted along the British 'A' roads where the main customers tend to be long-distance lorry drivers. Arriving at her final destination it brought back childhood memories of a holiday she had spent there with her parents during happier times before the untimely death of her father. With the Rosie Ware kidnapping case stalled and no other leads to follow it had been a no brainer to take the two and a half hour drive from Oxford to get copies of the birth certificates. It would be laborious work tracking down all eight birth mothers but if she was lucky her target might be one of the first she investigated. Identifying which of the eight was the one she was looking for would be more difficult. The impostor wouldn't be likely to admit her involvement in the scam.

She parked up and walked the short distance to where the Brighton Register Office was located inside the town hall. It was certainly an impressive building fronted by a portico made up of giant fluted columns. Unfortunately as so often is the case a modern carbuncle had been attached to the rear of the building to provide additional office space. Entering the place was like walking into a cathedral. The place was deathly quiet. A young girl was seated behind a reception desk. Emma stated her name and said she had an appointment with Mrs Barry at one o'clock. She was ten minutes early but always preferred to be on the right side of the appointed time something that McBride had instilled into her over the years. The young girl politely asked her to take a seat and rang through to presumably inform Mrs Barry that she had arrived.

Whilst she waited Emma checked her emails and voicemail but nothing significant had arrived, just the usual internal office emails that seemed to proliferate on a daily basis.

'Mrs Barry will see you now,' the young receptionist indicated, 'the second door on the right just along that corridor,' she pointed.

Emma walked down the corridor and knocked on the door that had Mrs Barry's name printed on it. Patricia Barry was exactly how Emma expected her to be. Tall, slim, elegant with an easy but authoritative manner.

'How can I be of help DS Blakely?' she asked.

'I actually came to obtain copies of eight birth certificates you have registered here.' Emma said passing the list across to Mrs Barry.

'Short or full?' came the rather curt and impatient response.

'What's the difference?' Emma asked.

'Apart from the cost, the information recorded is more detailed on the full certificate.'

Mrs Barry passed Emma a leaflet that showed the details contained on both types of certificates:

Birth Certificates

There are 2 types of birth certificate:
- the short version, which contains only the baby's details
  - date and place of birth
  - sex of the child
  - the forename(s) and surname that the child will be brought up with
- the full version, which also contains the parents' details
  - **Mother's details (at the time of the birth):**
    - full name (and maiden surname, if relevant)
    - date and place of birth (Registrations made before 1969 do not include details of the parents' place of birth)
    - occupation (only certificates after 1984)
    - usual home address
  - **Father's details (at the time of the birth):**
    - full name
    - date and place of birth (Registrations made before 1969 do not include details of the parents' place of birth)
    - occupation
    - usual home address

Emma pocketed the leaflet for future reference and requested full birth certificates as these contained the mothers' details that she was after.

Mrs Barry took the list and lifted the receiver from the phone on her desk. After no more than three seconds an uncontrolled angry outburst started, 'Come on! Come on! Come on! Answer the damned phone. I haven't got all day.' After it rang out no more than half a dozen times she slammed the unanswered phone down exasperated. 'What's wrong with you people?' she said addressing the inert phone.

She looked apologetically at Emma, 'you just can't get the staff these days.' Then she rang what Emma presumed was a different number. This time the phone was answered on the second ring.

'Harry, I have an urgent request for a number of birth certificates. Could you do a search for me and print off the details?'

'My assistant will locate the relevant documents for you but it may take him a while to find them. I suggest you come back in a couple of hours. Is there anything else I can help you with?'

Before Emma could answer a grey haired, middle aged man, knocked and came into the room taking the list from Mrs Barry. Emma presumed this was Harry.

Emma gave the man her mobile number and he promised to phone her as soon as he had the certificates. She wandered off towards the sea front whilst she waited for his call. Picking up a leaflet at the nearby tourist information kiosk Emma read how Brighton had taken off as a Georgian seaside resort and became a popular destination for day-trippers and holiday makers from the capital London. Its two most iconic landmarks are the Royal Pavilion and its pier. Looking to the right she could make out the neglected West pier that had been closed in the 1970s and since ravaged by storms and fire. To the left was the grand Palace pier, the one shown in all the holiday brochures. Between the two was a long sandy beach deserted at this time of the year. She turned to the left and walked along the promenade enjoying the solitude and break from her normally hectic life. Reaching the pier she looked at the small map on the back of the leaflet and realised she was only a short distance from the famous Royal Pavilion so she turned inland and made her way across the main road. The palace looked anything but an English royal residence. It looked as if it had been spirited from the Indian continent with its complex arrangement of domes, towers and minarets. Its architect John Nash must have been dreaming about the Arabian nights when he drew the plans for this exotic building. Maybe the Prince of Wales had wanted to create his own Taj Mahal for the mistress for whom it was built. It certainly created a romantic vision of splendour. Today wasn't the day for touring this magnificent building Emma had more important things on her mind. She had a young woman to find and a kidnapper to bring to justice. She must make time to bring Becky and her mother here for a summer break sometime in the future. Turning away from the grand building she started to make her way back towards the Brighton Town Hall.

It had taken only an hour before Harry the assistant rang Emma to inform her all the certificates were ready for her to collect and the bill came to a total of £240. This was far more than Emma had expected and she hoped it wouldn't take her over her credit card limit. Harry picked up the shock in her voice.

'Sorry I should have warned you that it costs £30 each for an express while you wait birth certificate. We normally insist on payment upfront but I knew you would be trustworthy.'

Hopefully McBride wouldn't quibble when she put in her expenses for this impromptu trip to Brighton.

Ten minutes later Emma was back at the Register Office with the certificates in her hand. Harry had helpfully pointed her in the direction of a room available to the public which had access to the online records if she needed them but he added that they couldn't give her any more details than she already had. It would though give her a quiet space if she needed to make any private phone calls.

She now had the names of the babies plus the name and address of the mothers. Now all she had to do was contact the mothers and find out which of the babies had a birth weight of over ten pounds. Of course she didn't know how up to date the information was as a lot can change in over eighteen years.

To speed things up she phoned Anthea back at headquarters in Oxford and asked her to try and find current phone numbers for the mothers she was interested in. Anthea came up trumps again finding five of the mothers straight off; she promised to continue to track down the remaining three.

Emma knew that more than one baby had weighed more than ten pounds as this had been shown on the statistics table that Anthea Bowker had shown her so she had to try and ascertain the mother's blood group to identify the correct woman she was looking for. Although rare there could be more that one of the mothers who was AB+ but the chances that more than one woman was both AB+ and whose child had been born weighing more than ten pounds was remote. She decided on a little bit of subterfuge to narrow down her search. Emma made a start on the list she had.

'Mrs Rhodes, this is the Brighton Blood Transfusion Service. We have a shortage of your blood type AB+ and we wondered if you would be willing to give a blood donation?'

Mrs Rhodes replied. 'You must have your records wrong luv, I'm O+ which I thought was the most common blood type?'

'Sorry my mistake,' Emma responded putting a cross next to baby Rhodes name.

'Miss Davis, this is the Brighton Blood Transfusion Service. We have a shortage of your blood type AB+ and we wondered if you would be willing to give a blood donation?'

Miss Davis replied, 'I've no idea what my blood group is but there's no way anyone's sticking a needle in me.'

'Thank you for your consideration,' Emma politely responded putting a question mark next to Miss Davis's name although she expected it wasn't the right mother as people with a rare blood group tend to know about it.

She got no reply from the next two numbers and wrote *"ring back later"* next to their names as well as noting the time of her call when they didn't answer.

With the next call she believed she had hit the jackpot.

'Miss Barras, this is the Brighton Blood Transfusion Service. We have a shortage of your blood type AB+ and we wondered if you would be willing to give a blood donation?'

'I regularly give blood as I know I have a rare blood group. I only gave some two weeks ago but if you are desperate I can come in again maybe later in the week,' she said.

'That won't be necessary if you've only donated recently,' Emma replied putting a tick next to Miss Barras's name. 'We don't want to bleed you dry. Whilst you are on the phone can I just check some details with you? Your address is in Moulsecoomb, Brighton and you have a son born 14th August 1995 who weighed over ten pounds?'

Irma Barras didn't seem in the least bit phased by these somewhat unrelated questions.

'Yes I have a son born on that date, I have five children, three girls and two boys and yes our Jason was a big bugger he weighed eleven pounds two ounces would you believe it? He was my last thank goodness. You've got my address wrong though I moved from Moulsecoomb about fifteen years ago. I now live at 88 Downland Drive in Hove. I got myself a lovely four-bedroomed council house,' she said proudly.

It never ceased to amaze Emma how easily people parted with their personal information. The registrar's assistant Harry had told Emma that it was possible to search for all births belonging to a particular maiden name. As Irma Barras was an unusual name it didn't take long for her to identify the five births and the fact that each of them had a different father.

Emma decided that a trip to interview Irma Barras was in order especially when she was already in the area. As an apparent single mother with so many children she would have been tempted to participate in any organised deception for financial gain. The thought crossed Emma's mind that maybe Irma Barras had perpetrated the baby scam five times.

Hove is Brighton's near neighbour and it was only a few miles to the address she had been given. Emma located the council house which was surprisingly well appointed and opposite a lovely piece of open parkland. She knocked on the door which was opened by a heavy set woman in her early fifties with dyed blonde hair with about three inches of dark root growth.

'Miss Barras,' Emma asked holding up her police ID. 'DS Emma Blakely from the Thames Valley police Protecting Vulnerable People Unit, would it be OK if I ask you some questions?'

Shock registered on the woman's face. 'I bet it was that nosey Mrs Brocklehurst next door that's dobbed me in to the social. I've told them there's no way I'm paying any bloody bedroom tax. I need my spare rooms for when the grand kiddies stay over.'

'I'm not here about your social security payments,' Emma clarified 'I'm here to ask you some questions about your son Jason.'

'Oh, what's he got himself into now? That boy is nothing but trouble.'

'No, he's not in any trouble. It's about his birth. Can I come in?'

Irma Barras looked a little sheepish and Emma's detective gut instinct told her she was onto something.

She opened the door and gestured Emma to enter the house.

Emma took note of how surprisingly neat and tidy everywhere was. She was expecting far worse.

'It doesn't look like you have five kids living here?' she said by way of intended praise.

'I've only got Jason at home now; all the others have their own places. I've got ten grandchildren and two more on the way,' she said proudly. 'A real brood' she added

'So Jason is the youngest?' Emma confirmed.

Irma Barras seemed more reserved now. Emma had to decide whether to play at being a good cop or bad cop. She plumped for good cop thinking of her previous conversation with Miss Barras and how forthcoming she knew she could be.

'You're not in any trouble and if you co-operate we won't be bringing any charges against you, so I want you to answer some questions for me and I want you to answer them honestly, please. A young girl's life may depend on you being truthful today. Do you understand?'

'....................Yes,' Irma Barras replied after something of a prolonged pause.

'I am not interviewing you under caution so nothing you say here can be used against you, do you understand?'

'Yes,' Irma Barras replied.

'Is it true that when you were expecting Jason you assumed the identity of another woman called Sara Ware and attended the office of her gynaecologist a Doctor Frederick Simpson using that name?'

'..........Yes,' Irma Barras replied after another hesitant pause.

'Is it true that after giving birth to Jason at the Brighton maternity hospital you went to the Sea View Holiday Cottages and pretended you had given birth to a baby girl?'

'Yes,' Irma Barras replied quietly.

'I want you to tell me in your own words everything that happened?'

'I didn't hurt anyone,' Irma wailed.

'I know,' Emma said patiently and reassuringly, 'just tell me what happened in your own words. You're not in any trouble.'

Irma began her sorry tale softly, slowly and hesitatingly. 'I already had four kids under the age of ten and I found out I was expecting again. I was only thirty-four years old. I was at my wits end and even considered having an abortion. I was a single mother living in a two bedroomed flat in a rough part of Moulsecoomb. I barely had enough money to feed and clothe me and the kids as it was.' Emma didn't interrupt but she took note of the then nearly ten year age gap between Irma and Sara Ware.

Irma continued picking up pace as she settled into her story 'It's not true what the telly and newspapers say about living in luxury off state benefits. It's hard, damned hard. I'm not good with men; I always seem to pick the wrong-uns. As soon as Steve, Jason's dad, found out I was pregnant he didn't want to know and that was the last I saw of him. He left me quicker than the others mind. At least they hung around a bit longer .... If not much. The only thing I was ever good at was getting pregnant. Too good my Mam says. I was three months gone when I received a phone call out of the blue from a man who was offering me the best medical treatment and ten thousand pounds if I would just pretend to be another woman for a short time. At first I thought he wanted to buy the baby and I was so desperate I even offered to sell Jason to him. How bad a mother am I? Anyway, he seemed a little aghast with my suggestion and said this wouldn't be necessary. He paid me five thousand pounds up-front, gave me Mrs Ware's details and a phone number to ring as soon as I went into labour. As instructed I visited Dr Simpson, a lovely man, every six weeks. When I went into labour I rang the number and was told to ring again after the birth. When I rang the second time I was told to wait two days then go to the holiday cottage by taxi, it was all paid for, but to leave my baby behind at the hospital. When I arrived at the cottage a strange man was there with a baby girl. Beautiful little thing she was. The man told me that a midwife would be arriving shortly and I had to pretend that I had just given birth to the baby girl. After this was done I would get the remaining five thousand and a taxi straight back to the hospital to collect Jason and I would never see or hear from him again.'

'Did you ask where the baby had come from?'

'Yes, I was very concerned but he said that it was an unwanted pregnancy by a university student who was terrified of telling her parents. She didn't want to go through the authorities so he had found the baby a perfect home where she would be loved and want for nothing. There was a slight change to the plan as the midwife insisted that she visit us both the next day. The man offered me an extra five hundred pounds to slip out of the hospital for a second time. The midwife seemed to be fairly new to the job and so was really just pleased everyone was alright. She did frown from time to time but didn't ask me anything I couldn't easily answer or explain away. After that day I never saw the man, baby or midwife again. I just returned to see Dr Simpson for my six-week check-up.'

'Do you think the man was Rosie's father?'

'Who's Rosie?'

'The baby girl,' Emma replied annoyed that she had let Rosie's name slip.

'I never knew her name. I've often thought about what had become of her. Oh my god is she the girl who was kidnapped a few weeks back?'

'Yes,' Emma said 'but you must keep our conversation confidential. I need to remind you that if this story gets out my boss will insist on bringing charges against you. And this could mean jail.' Emma didn't know what charges they could bring or if the offence was too historic for punitive action but she wanted to stop this information from getting into the hands of the media.

'Anyway the answer to your question as to whether the man was the father is that I don't think so. He was dark with lovely almond eyes. Not dark as in black but maybe Mediterranean, olive skinned like. The baby was blonde with beautiful blue eyes and had very fair skin. He was also in his thirties which I thought was a bit on the old side for dating a university student but then again you do hear about professors and the like going after young girls don't you?'

'Do you think the man you met was the same man you spoke to on the phone?'

'Yes, I do. They both spoke good English but with a slight foreign accent.'

'One last question,' Emma said. 'Do you think either Doctor Simpson or the midwife was involved in the scam in any way?'

'No, I don't. It was them two that I had fooled,' Irma replied proud of her acting skills.

'We may need a sketch artist to work with you on a photo fit of the man you met.'

'Well you can if you want but I don't know how accurate I'll be able to make it after all this time,' Irma offered.

As she was letting herself out Emma remembered another question. 'You don't happen to still have the man's phone number do you?'

'I kept it for a few years but threw it out when I moved. I can't remember what it was but I know it wasn't a local number.'

Thanking Irma for her help and re-emphasising the need for secrecy Emma returned to her car none the wiser as to how this information might necessarily help them in the Rosie Ware kidnapping case. However, she now had enough ammunition to return to Mr and Mrs Ware for further questioning and ask why they had lied.

31

McBride was still in his office when Emma got back. She recounted the story if not verbatim then in plenty of detail.

'I want another chat with the Wares in the morning. But this time don't let them know we're coming. Just check with the Family Liaison that they'll be at home – one of them at least. Also get onto our techie people and find out if they have traced where those emails are coming from. Someone out there knows something but for some reason doesn't want to come forward,' McBride said.

'Yes, sir.'

'When you've done that go home and get some rest you look shattered. I'll pick you up at eight in the morning and we'll see what the Wares have to say this time around.'

Emma returned to her desk and fired off a second email to the techie team attaching the two anonymous emails she had received asking them to urgently trace where they had come from as well as supplying any other information that may prove to be of use .... or at least interesting. She phoned the Family Liaison Officer assigned to look after the Wares and confirmed that both would be at home the following day. Then she packed up her things and set off home.

She was looking forward to having dinner with her mother and daughter as she hadn't had time for more than a fleeting chat with either of them in the last couple of weeks such was the nature of her job. She phoned ahead to tell her mother she was on her way home and to lay an extra place at the table. She thought about how lucky she was to have such an understanding and supportive mother. So many mothers she met in her line of work disowned their daughters when they found out they were pregnant at eighteen but Emma's mother had taken it all in her stride even taking early retirement to look after the baby so Emma could carry on with her studies. Emma had always been a Daddy's girl. When her father died suddenly of a heart attack, when she was just fourteen, she had really gone off the rails. She put her mother through hell. Getting involved with the wrong crowd, being picked up for minor offences like shop lifting. All attention seeking reactionary stuff that she now better understood through her work. She was lucky she never got charged and saddled with a criminal record. It took up until she found out she was pregnant before ridding herself of the anger at an unjust world. The baby's father didn't want to know and went off to Canada, effectively vanishing but Emma's mother was always there and always able to help pick up the pieces. Becky her daughter was only a few years younger than the missing Rosie and this gave Emma a degree of empathy when it came to understanding what the Wares were going through. She shivered at the thought of what she would do if Becky ever went missing. This thought seemed to make her drive faster to get home.

32

Tuesday 18th February 2014 - NEWCASTLE

The next morning when they returned to the Wares house it was as if they had never left. Mr and Mrs Ware sat on the same settee in exactly the same position. This time it didn't even look as if they had changed their clothes. They just looked thinner and more drawn as if they hadn't eaten since Rosie's disappearance. They did seem more on edge than on the previous occasions – whether this was fear at what might have been uncovered in the interim or just the extent to which they had been worn down …. only time would tell.

McBride went straight in for the kill. 'You've been lying to us.' He said looking back and forth between Mr and Mrs Ware but finally settling his steely gaze upon Sara Ware. 'We know that you aren't Rosie's biological mother.'

They still didn't know if Mr Ware was the father and had decided to stick to the facts they knew rather than conjecture and thus losing their advantage.

'This is your last chance to tell us the truth, otherwise, I will have to arrest you both for obstructing a police enquiry,' McBride added.

There was an uncomfortable pause then Sara Ware turned to her husband and quietly said, 'tell them Tom; it can't make things any worse than they already are.'

Tom Ware let out a sigh, collapsed down on to the sofa and reflectively mumbled, 'Where to begin? We've been living the lie for so long it's almost become the truth for us.'

McBride changed into the caring concerned police officer Emma knew him to be.

'Take your time Mr Ware and just tell us in your own words the whole story.'

'It must have been about four weeks after we won the lottery. We were wishing by this point that we had asked for our names to be kept secret. We were receiving so many begging letters. Old friends and relatives who we hadn't seen for years kept coming out of the woodwork. We even had to change our phone number and go ex-directory. Anyway, it was a Sunday afternoon and the phone rang. I don't know how he had got hold of our number. I thought it was just a crank call and was about to put the phone down but something about the man made me continue the call. He said that he knew the one thing we really wanted was a baby and he was in a position to provide the most perfect baby we could ever wish for. He couldn't say whether it would be a boy or a girl but if we wanted blue, brown or green eyes with blonde, black or red hair he could pretty much guarantee it. One thing he was sure about was the child would be exceptional whether a boy or a girl in both looks and brains. I asked how much this would cost us thinking by now it was most definitely a scam. There will be some expenses but apart from the doctors' bills, you won't have to pay anything upfront he told me. After you get the baby you will make four payments of five hundred thousand pounds at six-monthly intervals. After that nothing more and you'll never hear from me again. I do have one rule he had said. You must never tell anyone, including the child, about this arrangement. If you do the child will be taken away from you .... by one means or another. Is that clear he reiterated? I asked where the child would come from. He said that it was a beautiful university student who'd been involved with her professor and who, for religious reasons, didn't want an abortion but also didn't feel able to bring up a child. As her parents were very strict she didn't want them to know about the baby hence the secrecy and the reason why it had to look like Mrs Ware had given birth. He also added that the child would legally be ours and that our names would appear on the child's birth certificate so the real mother couldn't return and claim the child at a later date. I asked what would happen if the student changed her mind. He repeated the deal that I wouldn't pay the money until after we had had the child for six months but categorically assured us the student wouldn't change her mind. I asked him, why us? He told me we had all the qualities to bring up a child and that he was very choosy about his clients. I thought at the time that I had nothing to lose so I agreed to discuss it with Sara and let him know. We settled on his terms thinking nothing more would come of it but three months later we received a medical bill from Dr Simpson's practice on Harley Street. We received a second phone call from the man telling us everything was set for an August birth and to be ready for further instructions. Sara had to tell all her friends and relations she was expecting and increase the size of her stomach as the months went by. She was to tell them that she hadn't told them until she was three months gone so as not to tempt fate. She was also to tell them that she had to rest a lot and so would be taking it easy and be out of circulation until after the birth. Early in August we were contacted again and told to be ready to collect the baby from a holiday cottage in Brighton. When we arrived at the cottage, the door was unlocked. We went in and there was our Rosie lying in a carry cot gurgling happily, looking at us with her beautiful blue eyes. Next to her was the documentation to enable us to register the birth. We made an appointment with the Brighton Register Office to get the birth certificate the next day then we brought her back here. I made the payments as agreed and we haven't heard anything from the man since.'

McBride asked, 'so you never met the man and the baby was on its own in the cottage?'

'That's correct. We never met anyone involved in person. We thought it strange the baby had been left on its own but I was pretty sure that there would be someone nearby making sure that everything went as planned.'

'And the money. How was that paid?' McBride asked.

'We were sent a key for a left luggage locker at Newcastle central railway station and told to place the money in cash there on the specified dates,' Tom Ware explained.

'We used the intervening six months to gather it all together by one means or another using business and private funds. It's not that hard really when you're focused on the task at hand.'

'I have a couple of questions,' Emma said, 'you mentioned that the man said you could have a choice of eye and hair colour, didn't that strike you as strange?'

'I just thought he was joking,' Tom Ware replied.

'What eye and hair colour did you ask for?' Emma continued.

'Well I said a blue eyed blonde would be nice but I didn't actually care.'

'We would have loved any baby,' Sara Ware added.

'But you did receive a blue eyed blonde baby?'

'Yes, we did, I just thought it was a coincidence,' Tom Ware answered.

'And she was as exceptional as he promised she would be.'

Mrs Ware joined in with the over enthusiasm of a proud parent, 'Rosie was always more advanced than any of the children her own age. She had an insatiable thirst for knowledge. By the time she was seven she could speak three languages more or less fluently, she had been accepted into MENSA, the genius society. Not only was she highly intelligent she also excelled at sport. She could have been selected to swim for GB but she didn't want to jeopardise her academic career. She always wanted to be a marine biologist ever since we took her to Sea World in Florida when she was eight. She also played piano and violin and could sing like an angel. Though I accept we might not be impartial in making that assessment.'

'You mentioned that he told you that he was very choosy about his clients,' McBride reminded him. 'Wouldn't that imply that he had done this sort of thing before?'

'Maybe. I don't know. We didn't really think about it at the time. As I said I never expected it to be real.'

'So you just went along with it?' McBride admonished.

Tom Ware now took control, 'All this may be interesting for you but it doesn't help explain who took Rosie or why. We never broke our promise. We didn't tell a soul about where Rosie came from. We really didn't know ourselves.' He looked for confirmation from his wife who nodded her head in support.

'So Rosie didn't ever suspect you weren't her biological parents?' Emma asked.

'I think she always suspected something but she never ever raised the subject with us,' Sara Ware said.

'Could she have spoken to someone else?' Emma asked.

'Possibly but she wouldn't have found anything out. Not even our closest friends or family knew and all the paperwork confirmed that Sara had given birth to her,' Tom Ware said.

Emma thought that someone knew and that someone was the person who had sent her the anonymous emails. She had to find out where they had come from.

'You say you never met the man but is there anything you remember about his voice or what he said?' McBride asked.

'He had a very clear precise enunciation. I thought he might be foreign, you know how they often talk in a very clipped British accent but I can't be sure,' Tom Ware said.

'I'll need you to make a statement about what you have just told us,' McBride informed the couple rising from his seat and nodding for Emma to follow him.

'Do you think this information will help you find her,' Sara Ware asked.

'I don't know but it certainly gives us another line of enquiry,' McBride replied not wanting to admit that he didn't have a clue as to how the information he had just acquired would help him solve this case. 'Anything else you remember please get in touch or let your Family Liaison Officer know.'

On the drive back to Oxford they discussed the case and what their next course of action would be.

'This new information doesn't get us much further, does it?' Emma said.

'No, but it does give a motive. I think we need to go back to the University and talk to the staff and her friends there. See if Rosie confided in any of them. We will speak to the boyfriend first then her tutors. Also get back onto the techie people and see if they have traced those damned emails yet.'

When Emma got back to the office she rang the technical team. She was told there was no way to trace the emails. They had been sent from a new Hotmail account which had been set up a couple of weeks earlier. The information given for the account was all false and the emails had been posted from an internet café in central London. They suggested she contact the internet café and find out if they had surveillance cameras as the emails contained the exact date and time they had been sent. They also suggested that she just reply to the emails to ask who they were from. Emma wondered why she hadn't already done this and immediately fired off a reply. A simple one liner – Who are you? She then rang the internet café. It took some persuasion and a few threats but they finally confirmed they would still have the footage from the date when the second email had been sent but the video file from the first date would have been overwritten by now. They promised to email her a copy of the recording.

33

Emma viewed the internet café video footage the next day, then viewed it twice more - she couldn't believe her eyes. The film was in black and white and rather grainy but the image clearly showed what appeared to be Rosie Ware sending the emails to her. She called the rest of the team to her desk and they gathered round whilst she ran through the video footage again. They all agreed that it certainly looked like Rosie although there wasn't a clear image of her face almost as if she had known where the camera was located.

'Print off a still picture and we will take it to show the boyfriend Ben Tanner when we interview him again this afternoon,' McBride told Emma.

'Why would Rosie fake her own disappearance?' Emma asked.

'Maybe she was suspicious about her origins and wanted us to investigate her family. Which is exactly what we have done,' McBride replied.

'It seems a bit over the top and totally out of character for Rosie. It just doesn't seem right,' Emma said.

When they arrived on campus Ben was already seated in the small meeting room they had arranged for the interview. He looked carefully at the photo they placed in front of him.

'It certainly looks like Rosie but it's not her,' he said.

'How can you be sure?' Emma asked.

'Well, this girl's hair is longer. Even given the few weeks Rosie has been missing it wouldn't be this length. Also and what makes me absolutely certain is that Rosie had a little tattoo of a dolphin on the top of her shoulder. This girl doesn't have a tattoo.'

'Nobody mentioned Rosie having a tattoo,' Emma said.

'She only had it done at the start of term. It was my Christmas present to her.'

'Why didn't you mention this earlier?'

'You didn't ask,' Ben replied.

'Is there anything else you haven't mentioned to us?'

'Like what?'

'Like the fact that Tom and Sara Ware weren't her biological parents and she was trying to find her real family?'

Ben looked shocked, 'Rosie never mentioned anything like that. She really loves her parents. She always said how close they all were and how much I would like them. She never even hinted that she was adopted.'

Emma and McBride believed him and if she hadn't confided her suspicions with Ben then it was unlikely she had discussed it with anyone else. This gave them yet another dead end and dispelled the motive for kidnapping her.

'I'm sure she would have mentioned it if she had thought she was adopted and was searching for her family,' Ben reiterated.

'Quite right Ben. Forget what I said about her family,' Emma said closing down the conversation.

Together with McBride, she left the campus.

34

Thursday 20th February 2014 - OXFORD

Operation Silver met for their daily briefing. McBride addressed the team. 'We now have confirmation that the girl who sent the anonymous emails, despite appearances, is not Rosie Ware. Given what we know and how similar she looks we now suspect that she is maybe related to Rosie perhaps even her biological sister. It's feasible she saw Rosie's picture on TV or in the newspapers and suspected she was related,' McBride told his team.

'Why send an anonymous email, why not come straight to us with the information,' Rod Hartley asked.

'That we don't know. Maybe she wanted us to get the proof for her before coming forward. Or maybe she's fearful of the people involved in this baby selling scam,' McBride replied.

'So you think she will come forward now that we believe her and it's been confirmed by the Wares?'

'Maybe, we still don't know who she is or how to contact her. DS Blakely has replied to her email but hasn't received anything back yet.' McBride looked across at Emma who confirmed this was still the case.

Emma added, 'I had the tech. team take a look at the computer she used at the internet café to see what sites she accessed but it had been wiped clean. They tell me she used a software tool that overwrites the hard drive. There's no way they could recover any useful information.'

McBride continued, 'we now have the full definitive list of all Rosie's known friends and associates, I've split up the list between you all. I'd like you to interview any we've missed previously to see if there's anything we might have overlooked. Let's see what we can shake from the tree if needs be.'

Turning to the media officer Cath Powell, 'How are you doing with the reconstruction that's due to go out on Crimewatch this week?'

'Everything's ready. We've found a girl who looks similar to Rosie and we have filmed the reconstruction taking the route along the canal that we believe Rosie followed on her way to the station the evening when she was abducted. We've got our slot on the programme tomorrow night. They have asked if you can appear on the programme to tell the public the details we know so far.'

'Tell them I'm happy to appear. Get me the details and I'll be there.'

Letting his eyes drift around the assembled officers, 'Is there anything else?'

The resounding silence gave him his answer, 'well back to work then.'

35

Friday 21st February 2014 - OXFORD

The third anonymous email arrived just after Emma returned from her lunch break –

20140125FIU1

That's all it said but Emma didn't know what it could mean. The first part looked like a date in reverse 25th January 2014 but she had no idea what FIU1 stood for.

She asked around the office but nobody could come up with an explanation. Some thought it could be the reference number of a book. Others thought maybe an employee ID.

She decided to reply to the email even though her previous attempts hadn't elicited a response.

I don't understand what this means???????

Almost immediately a reply arrived –
Guy's Hospital

So it looked like it was some form of hospital employee or patient identity. Thinking it looked more like a patient ID Emma rang the hospital and asked to be put through to the patients' records department.

An overly cheerful male answered the phone asking how he could help. Emma explained that she was looking for the identity of a patient with the reference number 20140125FIU1.

'So are we, so are we,' he replied laughing.

'I don't understand are you saying this isn't a patient?' Emma asked.

'I wouldn't describe her as a patient, I mean she won't be getting better and walking out of here. This number refers to an unidentified body in the morgue. The first part is the date the body arrived here, the F stands for female and the IU is Identity Unknown. I expect the number one just means it's the first unidentified body of the day just in case they get another.'

Emma's first thought was that the unidentified dead woman must be Rosie but why hadn't this been picked up? Her team had an alert out at every hospital and morgue in the country. She asked if he would put her through to someone in charge of the morgue. She was glad to be ending her conversation with this irritating man but at least he had given her some useful information in a relatively short space of time without her having to pull teeth as happened from time to time.

After ringing half a dozen times another male answered the phone but this time he seemed to be older and a more serious type altogether. Emma introduced herself and explained the case she was interested in.

'I'm Dr Ken Atkinson and I carried out the post-mortem on this victim. I can assure you that the body definitely doesn't belong to your missing teenager. This woman was in her forties. At first, I thought it was death by natural causes but I have since changed my opinion.'

He couldn't explain how this woman was linked to Emma's investigation but he gave her all the details he had about the case and suggested she get in touch with DI Dan Brennan who was heading up the investigation.

Emma phoned the number Dr Atkinson provided.

'Hi, is that DI Dan Brennan? This is DS Emma Blakely from the Thames Valley Police, Protecting Vulnerable People Unit. I've just been speaking to a Dr Atkinson at Guy's Hospital and I wonder if you could give me some information about the murder of an unidentified female victim that you are currently investigating. I think your case may be linked to a kidnapping case I'm currently working on.' Emma went on to explain about the anonymous email she had received with the cryptic message linking the two cases.

Dan said that all the details were on the computer system and he gave her the access code so that she could view all the information.

'I've no idea how the two cases might be connected but my victim was murdered shortly after Rosie Ware was kidnapped,' Dan said.

'I've no idea either but the information I've had from my source previously has been accurate so I intend to find out how these cases are linked,' Emma explained.

36

Monday 24th February 2014 - Bramshill, Hampshire, England

As each DNA sample came in from the close relatives of the potential matches they had compiled from the Missing Persons Database, Cathy Grainger was able to compare each of them with the DNA from the unidentified body. It was a long drawn out task as the relatives of the missing women were scattered across the whole of the country and it had been a job and a half to get the local police forces to locate them and then arrange for the DNA samples to be taken. As the DNA would only be from a close relative there wouldn't be an exact match but a trained eye could spot the likelihood of a high percentage match and so establish a relationship. Cathy always thought of ITV's The Jeremy Kyle Show on these occasions where fathers were shocked to find out they either were or weren't the biological parent of a particular child or sometimes even children. She always preferred using a mothers DNA given the number of times it turned out that the dad wasn't actually the biological father of a child. After a few disappointing non-matches, Cathy finally believed that she'd made a breakthrough. She rang Dan immediately. 'Dan I've got a match, I've identified your Jane Doe. Her actual name is Jennifer Shepherd. You won't believe it but it looks like she's been missing since August 1986. That's nearly twenty-eight years.'

'That's great news' Dan said. I've also got some news. We think this case is linked to that recent kidnapping case of Rosie Ware. You've probably seen it alluded to on the news. Although we've no idea what that link is.'

'Interesting ....I've got the contact details for Jennifer's mother in any event. It's a Mary Shepherd. Her father died a number of years ago in a road traffic accident but her mother is still living at the same address. Do you want to come with me to break the news to her?'

'Yes, I'd be interested in speaking to her and trying to find out where Jennifer might have been for all these years. Could you email her file to me please?'

'Sure, I'll do that straight away. Are you free tomorrow to visit Mrs Shepherd?'

'Where does she live?' Dan asked.

'Somewhere called Lytham St Annes in Lancashire. I believe it's a town on the coast near Blackpool, Lancashire in the North West of England. A long drive but it's a nice part of the country.'

'I know it well,' Dan replied. 'We used to go to Blackpool for our holidays and it's just a bit further down the coast. Arrange for us to see her early tomorrow afternoon if you can. We will need to stay over. We can call in at Oxford on our way home and talk to the Operation Silver Team who are investigating the Rosie Ware kidnapping. I don't know how these cases are connected but I really do want to find out.'

37

Tuesday 25th February 2014 – Lytham St Annes, Lancashire, North-West England

Mary Shepherd lived in a quaint terraced house overlooking the whitewashed windmill that stood on the green that ran along the sea front at Lytham. Lytham and St. Annes on the sea, to give the latter its full title, are actually separate towns but as they were physically adjoined so over time so had their place names.

As soon as Mrs Shepherd opened the door Dan could immediately see the likeness to her dead daughter Jennifer.

They introduced themselves showing their warrant cards to the bewildered old lady. She invited them into the warm cosy kitchen and they sat around a large oak table whilst she busily prepared tea and coffee for her guests. French windows looked out onto a small courtyard. A bird table stood a few yards away and a number of birds squabbled amongst themselves for the choicest titbits. An overly large clock ticked noisily on the wall above the old fireplace. It seemed to mesmerise them all and no one spoke for what seemed like an age.

Dan let Cathy break the news about Jennifer. She was much more experienced in dealing with the bereaved. Mrs Shepherd didn't look shocked, if anything she looked relieved. She just gazed out at the birds whilst silence hung heavily in the air. After a few minutes, she broke the silence and slowly began to speak.

'She was only just eighteen when she disappeared. I've always known she was dead. There's no way my Jennifer would have just disappeared and never have got into contact with us. She was a good girl.'

'Can you please tell us again exactly what happened when Jennifer first went missing,' Dan asked sensitively. He had read the file but he wanted to hear the details directly from Mrs Shepherd.

'It was the day she got her 'A' level results. 'She went to the school to pick them up and that's the last we saw or heard from her. At first, we thought she hadn't got the results she needed to get into university but we later found out she had straight As. Jennifer was very clever she took after her father's side of the family.'

Mary Shepherd had always assumed that Jennifer must have been murdered around the same time that she disappeared and was visibly shocked to find out that she had only died a couple of weeks earlier. She was even more shocked to find out that Jennifer had been a mother and to possibly more than one child.

'You mean I have grandchildren?' she said with renewed hope in her eyes.

'That's certainly a distinct possibility,' Dan said 'but at this time we have no idea where Jennifer has been for the last twenty-seven and a half years or where any of her family might be. No one has come forward to report her missing. In fact, the missing person report you lodged with us was the last we've heard from anybody family or otherwise.'

'She must have been held somewhere against her will,' concluded Mary, 'but for such a long time. Why would someone do that?'

'If this is the case it really does beggar belief,' countered Dan.

'My Jenny would never have left me just like that. Definitely not without saying anything. We thought the world of each other.'

'Maybe she was pregnant and that's why she ran away,' Cathy suggested sensitively.

'I can't say that she wasn't pregnant but she didn't have a boyfriend, her school work was everything to her. She worked so hard. She had passed the entrance exam to attend Cambridge University. If she attained the right grades in her A levels, which she did, then she was guaranteed a place there. Why throw that all away? I even checked to see if she had enrolled. I went to the University and watched the students for weeks on end just in case she turned up but she had just disappeared off the face of the earth. If she had been pregnant she would have told us. She knew that we wouldn't have cast her out. We're not like that. She was our daughter when all said and done. Jennifer was my only child. After Bert my husband died I had no family left.' Looking towards Dan as if for confirmation she continued. 'For a man, there is always the hope of a long lost child turning up out of the blue but for a woman she always knows how many children she has, she knows that if her only child dies that's the end of the line. Since Jenny went I've had to accept that finality so please don't get my hopes up about the possibility of grandchildren.'

'Did Jennifer have her ears pierced?' Dan asked changing the subject.

'Yes, she had them done for her last birthday before she went missing. She had been pestering me for years to get them done but we wouldn't allow it until she finished her exams.'

'So she had her earrings in the day she went missing?'

'No, the school didn't allow students to wear jewellery so she didn't have them in that day although Jenny did wear a gold locket that my mother gave her. She could hide that under her blouse.'

'So she was wearing the locket the day she disappeared?'

'Yes, I told the police all this at the time. Have you found it? The locket I mean.'

'Can you describe it?' Dan asked deliberately not answering her question.

'It was solid gold – eighteen carat I think. Quite valuable. It opened and it had a picture of my mother and father - Jenny's grandparents. On the other side, Jenny had placed a picture of the three of us.'

'Did it contain anything else?' Dan didn't want to specifically mention the lock of baby hair lest it was to get Mary's hope up of the existence of a grandchild .... which she'd already said she didn't want.

'Not when I last saw it.'

This described exactly the locket Jennifer had been wearing when she died.

It was as if Jennifer Shepherd had been frozen in time from the day she had disappeared to the day she had been found dead. Still without her earrings but having kept the locket that meant so much to her for nearly twenty-eight years.

'Jenny would never have sold it. She thought the world of her grandmother and it was the last thing she gave her before she died.'

'She didn't,' Dan finally answered. 'I have it safely in London.'

'Could I have it back? It's the only thing I have to connect me to her missing years.'

'Of course. As soon as our enquiries have been completed we will let you have it back.'

Cathy could see that Mrs Shepherd was getting tired. She had been subjected to something of an emotional roller coaster over the last hour or so.

'I think that's all we need for now Mrs Shepherd. We'll be in touch if we find out anything further.'

Mrs Shepherd looked at Cathy. 'When can I get my Jenny back? Her body I mean. I want to bring her back home and bury her next to her father.'

'We can't release the body until we have finished our investigation but as soon as we have we will be in contact so you can make the necessary arrangements.'

'And you will let me know if you find or hear anything about any of my grandchildren won't you?' she asked hopefully.

'Of course,' replied Cathy reassuringly.

Dan and Cathy were booked into the Clifton Arms Hotel on the promenade at Lytham. They were given charming rooms overlooking the seafront. A benefit to staying mid-week on a cold February night was that the hotel was quiet. They decided to get a drink in the lovely Victorian town centre.

They found a pub called The Taps just around the corner from their hotel and managed to get a couple of comfy seats next to the roaring log fire. Cathy thought how nice it was to spend an evening away from home with not just a good looking fella but someone who was so easy to talk to and treated her as an equal. For Cathy, it was as novel as it was pleasant.

'I don't know how you can do this job,' Dan said. 'It must be so difficult breaking bad news to people all the time.'

'I think your job is much more difficult. It must be a huge shock when relatives find out someone they love has been murdered. For the relatives I deal with it's been such a long time since they last saw their loved one that they welcome the news .... even if it's bad. It gives them closure. It allows them to bury a body.'

'Have you ever had cases like this before where someone has been missing for nearly twenty-eight years then been found .... Dead or alive?'

'Yes, it happens quite often but usually they have set up a new life somewhere with a new family and the death is by natural causes. You would be amazed about the secrets and lies within families. Parents think they know their children when in reality they know little or nothing about them. If a child thinks their parents will disapprove of a decision they've made sometimes they cut off all ties to their families instantly. Or a wife or husband runs off with their lover never to be seen again. But saying that I've never had a case where someone hasn't been seen for this long and then turns up murdered. This really does stand alone in my experience.'

38

Wednesday 26th February 2014 – OXFORD

Early the next morning they set off for the four-hour drive from Lytham St Annes to Oxford. Luckily the roads were quiet and it was motorway all the way there, so they were able to do the journey in a little over three and a half hours. Dan and Cathy arrived at the Thames Valley Police Head Quarters in Kidlington near Oxford and asked to see DCI McBride and DS Emma Blakely.

After the introductions Dan got straight down to business.

'So why do you think the two cases are linked?' Dan asked the detectives.

Emma explained in more detail about the emails and about the anonymous informant who had helped them so far.

Cathy had been looking at the headline information from the Rosie Ware case. 'There are lots of similarities between the two cases,' she explained. 'First we have the appearance. They could be twins based on Jennifer's photo of when she was Rosie's age, they do look so alike, and then we have their ages when they both disappeared. Jennifer was just eighteen and about to start university; Rosie was just over eighteen and in her first year at university. We also have the fact that both girls were academically brilliant. Rosie had been accepted to Oxford University and Jennifer would have gone to Cambridge University if she hadn't gone missing. Do you have any DNA from Rosie?' Cathy enquired.

'Yes, it's on the database.'

'Can I borrow a terminal to check something?' Cathy asked.

'Certainly,' Emma said pointing to a nearby desk with a PC on it.

Cathy logged on and quickly typed some details into the computer. A few minutes later she turned to the group and said, 'I know what links the two cases. Jennifer is Rosie's biological mother.'

The team were stunned into silence. This was a development none of them had ever contemplated. McBride was the first to break the silence.

'So it looks like whoever kidnapped Jennifer nearly three decades ago decided, for whatever reason, to dispose of her and replace her with her daughter Rosie. We now have to assume that our kidnapper murdered the mother which escalates this case to an even higher severity level. It would be too much of a coincidence that Rosie is kidnapped and then her mother Jennifer is murdered hours later and the crimes not be linked. We have to ask the question - Why does there seem to be such a fixation with this family line? McBride posed.

'It certainly looks that way,' Dan agreed.

'So who do you think the girl sending the anonymous emails is and how did she manage to link all this information before we did?' Emma asked.

'I think you are right with your earlier thinking that she is Rosie's biological sister and this makes her another daughter of Jennifer's,' Cathy said before adding, whilst pointing at the still photo of the girl taken from her session at the internet café and now pinned on the evidence board behind them, 'Just look at the likeness between these three women.'

The post-mortem on Jennifer said that she'd had multiple births. I think she could be someone who has been in a similar position to Rosie certainly in terms of her birth. If she's as clever as Rosie or Jennifer then she may have found out that her parents aren't who they claim to be. That is not her biological parents.'

'Why would she be so secretive and how has she put the pieces of the puzzle together?' McBride asked before adding '.... And more importantly what else does she know that we don't?'

'Maybe she didn't want to upset her adoptive parents or maybe she's afraid the kidnapper will come after her. Whichever it is she's one clever lady,' Cathy said. 'Give me a few minutes to interrogate the database and I'll try and find out how she managed to piece all this together.'

Cathy feverishly typed away whilst the rest of the team had a brainstorming exercise to try and move the cases forward.

Cathy finally said, 'she really is one very intelligent lady. She's been searching for her real biological family members for over two years. I'll try to explain how I think she did it. Firstly, she extracted her own DNA and entered it on the police Database under an assumed name. Then she wrote a clever Trojan programme.'

'What's a Trojan?' McBride asked

'I was just going to explain that,' Cathy continued. 'This Trojan is a small packet of code that hi-jacks the computer every time a new DNA sample is entered into the database. It didn't do any harm but it compared every sample entered with her own DNA looking for a high percentage of common markers. Nothing happened until Emma here entered Rosie's DNA into the Database. As soon as this happened the system sent out a message to your friend with the details of the individual.'

'But how was she able to put a Trojan into our computer system?' Enquired McBride wanting to understand exactly what had been done.

'There is a myriad of ways this might have been done,' Cathy explained '.... It could have been attached to an email similar to a virus; she could have hacked the programme; she might even have inserted it directly into the server housing the Database. The thing is it's unlikely to have been unearthed given that it didn't do any damage to the data stored. It just gave the Trojan owner a message when something of interest came to light and nothing more.'

'So from this she was able to find out that she was related to Rosie?' Emma said.

'Exactly,' Cathy said. 'I bet you didn't get your first email until after you entered Rosie's DNA information onto the system.'

'I didn't,' Emma confirmed. 'It was about a week later. But why wait a week she must have known straight away?'

'She may have wanted to find you some more information before passing it on. I suspect she may have also been born via Dr Simpson's practice so could have already managed to access his computer medical records looking for her own details and possibly others. Someone with her intelligence wouldn't have found it difficult to hack into the doctor's computer system and find Rosie's birth records.'

'But if she already had a link to Dr Simpson before she became aware of Rosie wouldn't she already have hacked the good doctor's records,' countered Dan. 'It seems more likely to me that her mother wasn't Dr Simpson patient and part of the one week delay was spent tracking down Mrs Ware's medical records.'

'Until we speak to her we are only guessing about some of her actions but we know that once she had this information she noticed the discrepancies and sent the antenatal medical reports to you Emma. The next piece of the puzzle was when Dan entered his Jane Doe DNA details into the system. Again the Trojan ran and identified a close match and sent a message to your informer giving her the details of the unidentified body at the morgue. She had no more idea as to the identity of the body as we did but she did know the body was closely related to both her and Rosie and it was highly likely she was their mother. She put all the pieces together and sent Emma information questioning the true parentage of Rosie and providing the record number for the unidentified body. That put Emma and Dan together and got you working on both cases. The final piece of the jigsaw was when I entered Jennifer's mother's DNA into the system. The Trojan will have sent out a further message so your informer will now know the identity of her grandmother.'

'Is there any way we can track where the Trojan sent the messages?' Dan asked.

'No. I've already checked. They get bounced around the world through numerous servers. It would be impossible to trace where they ended up. This lady really knows her computers.'

'So the next question is, do we think she will try to contact her grandmother in Lytham?' McBride said.

'I think she might,' Emma said. 'This may be the reason for what she's done so far which is to try to identify members of her real family.'

'So if we set up surveillance on Mrs Shepherd in Lytham then we might just catch her,' McBride said.

'I think it's our next logical step,' Dan said believing that even a short time with the anonymous informer could result in meaningful progress on both cases.

'I'll try and get the budget agreed for this but I think I can swing it not least as it's in furtherance of investigating a kidnapping and two murders if we include the old man Mr Banks,' McBride said, exhilarated about the sudden leap forward in the enquiry and keen to keep up the momentum.

Cathy said, 'I agree that finding Jennifer's other possible daughter might not lead us to Rosie but she may have vital information for us.'

'Dan, Cathy - 'I'll have a word with your superiors and ask if you can both have a temporary transfer to my team. Let me have their details. We'll then pursue both cases simultaneously working together. Is that OK with you both?'

The latter being more of a rhetorical question. Cathy and Dan both nodded their heads by way of agreement and McBride said he would ring later that day to discuss the final details for the surveillance operation. He stressed that he just wanted the four of them involved.

'You're coming with us on a surveillance op sir?' Emma asked surprised as such work was way below a DCIs paygrade.

'You're right I wouldn't normally get involved in this sort of work but I think we need to keep the existence of this secretive woman as quiet as possible. I don't want her getting spooked. I also want to get the first chance to interview her if we do manage to apprehend her. If she lawyers up we might not get anything.'

Speed had to be of the essence. Given her past performance, it wouldn't take their anonymous source long to track down Mary Shepherd to her home in Lytham St Annes.

39

Thursday 27ᵗʰ February 2014 – Lytham St Annes, Lancashire, North-West England

Early the next day the team comprising of Dan, Emma, Cathy and McBride were on their way up the M6 motorway towards the Lancashire coast. This was not just their primary lead it was their only lead. The technical team from the Lancashire constabulary had agreed to provide the surveillance equipment for them to use. The local council had allowed them to set it up in the old disused windmill which was located on Lytham Green directly across from Mary Shepherd's house. The windmill, now a sightseeing attraction, was only open to the public a couple of times during the year. So it was an ideal location to observe the house undetected. They relieved the two local Bobbies who'd be in place since the previous evening, just in case their target made an early appearance, but they reported that everything had been quiet. They decided to split into two teams, Cathy and McBride would cover the morning shift six a.m. until three p.m. with Dan and Emma covering the afternoon shift three p.m. until midnight.

Their hotel was only across the road so it was easy to take toilet breaks and grab a bite to eat. A tap had been put on Mary Shepherd's phone. It was heart breaking to hear the calls she made to her friends to explain that her beloved Jennifer had been found at last. The team felt embarrassed about eavesdropping on her grief but knew that she would forgive them if it led to her granddaughter's release. There were no calls from their target. Boredom was setting in and bottoms were getting sore from sitting in the cold abandoned windmill.

Emma had been secretly pleased to be paired up with the ruggedly handsome Dan Brennan. She discreetly looked across to where he sat. He was tall, dark and well-muscled, just how she liked her men.

She was well aware of how attractive she was and the ability she had to attract men which in most cases was unrequited on her part. She had a healthy sex drive but living with her mother and teenage daughter gave her little chance to invite men friends back home. Her job took care of the rest of her time. On the drive north, she had a vivid daydream of Dan slipping into her hotel room in the middle of the night and them making mad passionate love. Thinking of it now helped keep her warm. She smiled unknowingly.

After endless hours sitting in the cold dark windmill, she had come to the conclusion that he was either married, had a girlfriend or was gay. In any event he hadn't even remotely flirted with her never mind anything more. Emma had always been direct so on the first day she decided to just ask him -

'You married?'

'Nope.'

'Girlfriend?'

'Nope.'

'Gay then?'

'Nope.'

'You don't say a lot, do you?'

'Nope,' he said returning to his damned Gameboy.

Emma gave up on the conversation, if it could have been called a conversation – more of an interview she thought and not a good one at that. He was a challenge, that was for sure - but then again there was nothing Emma loved more than a challenge.

It was now the second day and Emma focused her binoculars on the people walking along the sea front. There were couples and single people, some with dogs, some with children, all were wrapped up warm against the cold wind coming off the Irish Sea. At least it wasn't raining today. Emma wondered if she should get a dog, it was a good way to meet people and she quite fancied the thought of long walks in the Oxfordshire countryside. She dismissed the idea. She was kidding herself. When did she have time to walk a dog? She barely had enough time to spend with Becky her daughter who was growing up so fast. She sometimes thought Becky saw her more as an older sister than a mother. She had to face the fact that her own mother had perhaps been more of a mother to Becky than she had. She loved Becky with all her heart and she was sure that the girl knew this. Like many working mothers, Emma felt like there wasn't enough of her to go around and she let down people at work and at home as a result. Time for herself was a luxury she couldn't afford.

Suddenly Emma jumped out of her daydream having noticed a young woman matching the description of the girl from the internet café walking down the path to Mary Shepherd's house.

'I think we have a visual on our suspect,' she announced.

Dan put down the Gameboy he was playing and picked up a pair of binoculars. 'I agree it looks like her. Give Cathy and McBride a ring.'

Ten minutes later the four of them stood together next to the windmill. A middle-aged man with a young boy of about five years of age had seen them leave the windmill and stopped to ask them if it was open to the public today.

'Not today, I'm afraid,' McBride told them. 'We are just carrying out a structural survey.'

The young boy looked very disappointed. 'But Dad why have the people got those binoculusses?' unable to get his mouth around the long word.

'I expect it's so they can see the high up places, Ben,' the father explained as he dragged him away smiling apologetically at the group.

'Do we go in now or wait until she comes out?' Emma asked.

'I think we will wait until she comes out. I don't want to upset Mrs Shepherd. Dan and Cathy, you go around the back and Emma and I will wait out the front. Be as discreet as you can. We will apprehend her and take her back to the hotel for interview,' McBride directed.

'Don't forget if she asks she's being detained on suspicion of transgressing the Computer Misuse Act,' McBride added.

It was two long hours before the girl appeared at the door. Mary Shepherd had tears streaming from her eyes but she looked a very happy woman. McBride and Emma waited until the girl turned to walk down the path and then they walked towards the house arm in arm looking like a loving couple taking a stroll along the sea front. They reached the gate at the same time as the girl and separated either side of her.

'Police,' McBride said, 'We have some questions for you.'

The girl was surprisingly calm. 'I'm surprised it took you so long to find me,' she replied.

Politely McBride escorted her back to the hotel ringing Dan and Cathy on the way arranging to meet them back in the small meeting room they had secured for the interview.

'What's your name?' they asked the girl.

'Laura Webb,' she stated.

The story Laura told was more or less the same as the one Cathy had come up with. The only exception was that Laura's mother hadn't been a patient of Dr Simpson. Dan smiled thinly when he heard this.

'That would have been too easy,' Laura said. 'These people you're up against don't do easy.'

'How did you find out you were adopted?' Emma asked.

'My parents, my adoptive parents, were killed in a car crash when I was twenty-one. There was a letter with their Wills explaining that they weren't my biological parents. They said how sorry they were that they hadn't been able to tell me but the man who had arranged the adoption had been very specific that if they ever told anyone, including me, then I would be taken away from them. I'd just finished university when they died. They were very well off and I inherited a lot of money. It meant I didn't have to work straight away so I decided to take some time off and try and find my real mother. I went through all the adoption agencies, the Salvation Army and the churches. Nobody had any record of an adoption. That's when I had the idea to look on the police DNA database. I was really disappointed when nothing came back. I left the Trojan there to message me if anything of interest came in. You know the rest.'

'So you hacked into the police computer system?' McBride said more as a statement than a question.

'Yes, but I didn't damage anything or harm anyone, did I?'

'Let's not worry about that whilst we're trying to solve an abduction and a double murder,' replied McBride.

'Why did you choose to remain anonymous?' Emma asked.

'Well for one hacking is a criminal offence. Also from what I'd found out and from the letter my adoptive parents left I had the impression I was potentially dealing with a very dangerous group with tentacles that were very far reaching. All I wanted was to find my family. I now know my biological mother is dead but I now have a lovely grandmother who I have just met for the first time and I suspect I have other siblings out there. The pathologist's report did say my mother had had multiple births. I intend to continue my search for the rest of my family.'

'So you also managed to get your hands on the autopsy report?' McBride enquired.

'Oh yes, I am quite good with computers.'

Cathy knew this to be true in fact it was an understatement. The young woman that was sat in front of her had abilities way beyond those that she possessed. She also didn't mind breaking the law. She thought how useful she could be tracking down some of the many missing persons on Cathy's books. Pity about the illegal aspect otherwise...

'What makes you think this is a group and not just one person?' Dan asked.

'I can't be sure but given the sheer number of girls that have been reported missing over the years how could one man keep something this big a secret? My mother wasn't the only one. This group or organisation has been in operation for at least twenty-eight years from what I've found out.'

McBride looked shocked, 'you're saying there are other girls that have been taken. How do you know?'

'I don't know for certain but logic and deduction tells me this is true.'

Laura began to tell them about the research she had done so far. 'He or they only take girls between the ages of eighteen and twenty. All of them are beautiful, talented and exceptionally bright. Until my mother's body turned up no trace of any of them has ever been discovered.'

'Surely the public or the police would have noticed this link,' Emma said.

'Do you know how many young girls go missing every year?' Laura said.

'Thousands,' Cathy confirmed.

'Exactly. If they had been children then a link would have been made but lots of young women disappear and sixteen to eighteen years old is the most common age for this to happen. The Missing Persons Database registers things like skin and hair colour, height, sex, distinguishing marks or features. It doesn't hold information like academic ability, talents or how beautiful a person is.

'That's true,' Cathy admitted, thinking that maybe these attributes should or at least could be included. 'So how did you make the link?'

'By chance really and I haven't finished searching yet. I always thought I was an only child but when I read the pathologists report it got me thinking. What if there was an organisation out there providing designer babies for wealthy couples.'

'That fits in with what the Wares told us,' Emma recalled. 'Do you remember the man gave them a choice of hair and eye colour.'

'That's right he did. The Wares thought he was joking but what if it was actually true,' McBride said.

'It also ties in with our thoughts that he had offered babies to other couples,' Emma added.

'So if the Missing Persons Database doesn't hold this information how did you find the identity of these missing girls?' Dan asked.

'I went about it the same way as I thought the kidnappers would have,' Laura explained. 'First they were looking for exceptionally bright girls and they also needed to be over eighteen years of age, so their disappearance would not arouse suspicion. Also this is the best age to start having children. So I hacked into the 'A' level results database and selected the brightest 1% of girls from each year. Then I cross referenced this list with your Missing Persons Database. This gave me a short list of possibilities. I was just in the process of checking their appearances, a kind of beauty assessment, but I can confirm that my biological mother and sister, Rosie, are both on the list.'

'Do we need to look for a similar list of boys?' McBride asked. 'Someone must be fathering these designer babies, or do you think that the man who kidnapped the girls might also be the father?'

'At first I thought some form of cloning might have been involved but looking at pictures of myself and Rosie we are very alike but not identical. Also the procedure hadn't been perfected back in the 1990s. The DNA does show that Rosie and I have the same biological father. That said we must be looking at the possibility of multiple fathers otherwise the designer options offered wouldn't be feasible. For example to guarantee a blue eyed child both parents would have to have blue eyes. Or maybe they are using gene manipulation. However, this again has only been possible in recent years and wouldn't have been available when I was conceived.'

'So we might need to look for kidnapped boys who also match the criteria?' McBride added.

'Unlikely given the higher risk from more abductions and the readily available alternatives. They could be using sperm donors,' Emma considered.

'Laura you have been really helpful. I can't condone the illegal methods you have used but if you can keep us in the loop about anything else you find I'd be grateful. But I have to tell you not to do anything illegal.'

'OK,' Laura acknowledged. 'So you're definitely not going to arrest me then?' she clarified.

'Not on this occasion. We would never have made this breakthrough without your help. Can you send the list of missing girls to Cathy and we will take things from here? We will get back to the office now and hold a briefing to update the other team members,' McBride instructed.

Dan volunteered to drive on the long journey back to Oxford. Each of the team was deep in thought as they headed back down the M6. It was getting late when they arrived at the station this time the journey had taken nearly five hours due to heavy traffic around Manchester.

McBride decided to postpone the briefing until the next morning. 'Go home and get some sleep. It will be better if we look at this with fresh eyes in the morning,' McBride told them.

40

Saturday 1st March 2014 - OXFORD

McBride looked at his investigative team as they streamed into the briefing room. When they had taken their seats he addressed the group.

'I spoke with Chief Superintendent Mike Harding last night and he agreed to let us have a couple of extra bodies to help with the spade work. So I'd like to introduce PC Gary Hope and WPC Chrissy Prendergast to the team.'

A couple of groans came from the back of the room as Gary turned to face the group giving a long low bow.

Cathy a little concerned at the thought of having to work with someone like Gary quickly said, 'sir, I'd rather work alone if you don't mind. In my line of work, it's often much better.'

'OK Cathy, you start work on the potential additional missing girls that Laura Webb has identified. Also continue the search for others and include males matching the same criteria though I accept there might be no males but we still want to identify the fathers wherever possible,' McBride said.

McBride relayed the details of what they had discovered. The team sat almost open mouthed in astonishment. He left Laura's name out of the details not wanting to get her in trouble as he was well aware that she had broken numerous laws. He would have to consider what to do about Laura at a later date but for now she was far more useful to the enquiry working as a free if rogue agent. Although he'd instructed her to stop any further investigation he doubted she would abide by his request. Finding Rosie was their priority and if Laura could assist them then McBride decided to turn a blind eye to her activities for the time being.

After bringing them all up to date he said, 'we now have lots of work to do so I suggest we split the tasks as follows – Dan – You continue with the investigation into the murder of Jennifer Shepherd....'

'I'd like to go back to London and follow up some leads that I have sir,' Dan said.

'That's fine with me but make sure you keep us informed. Use Emma as your point of contact,' McBride said nodding towards Emma.

'Sir, I'd also like to suggest that we get a psychological profile done on this guy we're looking for. I know a very good clinical psychologist who has provided the Met with profiles in the past.'

'Good idea,' McBride replied. 'DC Bowker - can you let Dan have a copy of all the information we hold, once you've updated it with the new additional details.'

'Certainly sir. I should be able to have it with you by the end of the day,' she indicated to Dan.

'Emma I want you to work with Gary looking into the sperm bank angle. We need to find the male source of the parentage of these designer babies.'

Gary looking thoughtful. 'My cousin breeds champion Cocker Spaniels. She gets sperm shipped in from all over the world. They never meet - the dogs and bitches. Shame they don't get the fun bit. I often wonder what would happen if they got human sperm mixed up with the dog sperm, would you get a very intelligent Cocker Spaniel or on the other hand a woman who barks and snarls. Still that might explain my current girlfriend perhaps her father was an Alsatian,' he said laughing to himself. Others who heard his comments merely looked askance .... And not for the first time.

'I think the DCI was referring to human sperm banks rather than animal ones,' Emma replied dismissively; wondering what she had done to deserve being paired up with Gary Hopeless.

'DS Hartley I want you to start looking into locations where these women could be being held. It's unlikely this location is overseas since Jennifer's body was dumped in London. I expect the place is remote and very secure. If nobody has escaped over the last couple of decades it must be impregnable. Start with remote islands and old hospitals and mental homes that have closed prior to or around the date Jennifer Shepherd was abducted.'

'This is assuming she was the first, we may find that there were others abducted prior to this date,' DS Hartley added.

'True better make it from ten years prior to when she was abducted. Check with the Land Registry to find any suitable buildings that were sold around this time and haven't changed hands since.'

DS Hartley wished he had kept his mouth shut. He'd just made his task a whole lot bigger. Although a conscientious worker he liked to keep his work load to the minimum possible.

'The rest of us can start work on gathering more details for the missing people once Cathy has been able to identify them. Also list what you've been able to rule out and why. We will meet here again Monday morning. Dan and Cathy, you can both teleconference in. I assume you have the equipment back at your offices?'

'We do Sir,' they both replied.

'Right well let's all get to work. We have a lot to do. Good hunting to all of you.'

41

Saturday 1st March 2014 - Bramshill, Hampshire

As promised Laura Webb sent Cathy the list of twenty women she had already identified by cross referencing the top 1% from the 'A' level results database against the police missing persons database. Cathy being the perfectionist she was rechecked Laura's results. Rather puzzling one name, a girl called Jacqui Bates, hadn't appeared on her database and she wondered why Laura had included her, she made a note to ask someone from the Operation Silver Team to follow this up. Laura hadn't got around to checking the appearance of the women to consider if they would be classed as beautiful. After looking at the photos in the missing person files she ended up with ten highly likely candidates, three possible and six definitely not.

Another startling observation was that all ten from the highly likely list had disappeared between August and October at the age of eighteen. This couldn't be a coincidence in Cathy's opinion and added to the suspicion that the girls had been snatched before taking up their place at university. It would attract far less suspicion if like Jennifer Shepherd youngsters were abducted prior to accepting a place at university. The University would assume that they had decided not to take up the offer of a place, either preferring a course at another university or choosing not to go to university at all. Cathy wondered why Rosie Ware was different. She had been abducted during her first year at Oxford University.

Next, she decided to continue the search for more names using similar methods to those used by Laura. When Cathy thought about it, she concluded that university students came to the UK from all over the world. Many hadn't taken 'A' levels here so wouldn't be included in this database. Also, a lot of public schools used different examination boards so they also wouldn't be included either. It was going to be a hard slog collecting then going through the data from all the examination boards and even then she felt it wouldn't give a full picture. She didn't have the resources to cover the whole world.

She decided to take a different approach and concentrate on the top universities and medical schools admission records where she expected to find the youngsters with the highest IQs. She phoned the Universities and Colleges Admissions Service. Luckily February was their quietest month so they agreed to help search through their records.

Oxbridge was the logical starting point as the universities of Oxford and Cambridge attracted the cream of the further education student intake each year. They also held entrance exams and interviews which would allow Cathy to measure and assess the students' personalities as well as their academic ability.

Cathy set up a spreadsheet to store the information for each year. From what they had learned already the kidnapper would only be interested in the top students so she wrote a search programme to select those applicants who had come in the top ten percent of the Oxbridge entrance exams. The university admission records had only been computerised since 1998. Prior to this, they were held by the individual universities some on microfiche some still on paper. The woman who had assisted her from the admissions board gave her a list of contacts for each university. To continue the search prior to 1998 would entail Cathy visiting each university and trawling through their records.

This was going to be a mammoth task. Really Cathy should ask McBride for some assistance but she couldn't let even a small part of her enquiries be farmed out to someone else. In Cathy's opinion it was just too important to trust to others but then Cathy's opinion was always clouded by her perfectionist nature.

By the end of the day, Cathy had managed to add a further eight girls to her list of ten making an amazing eighteen in total and this was only the start.

42

Dan decided to follow up with his enquiries into the murder of Jennifer Shepherd by looking more closely at the boats moored in St Katharine Docks. Based on what the coroner had said Jennifer was near incapable of walking so couldn't have moved very far on foot especially at the pace she was travelling. Her companion would have wanted to have been exposed for the shortest possible time. The man must have had transport to get her from the facility where she had been imprisoned into that part of London. If it had been by car why not take her directly to the alley where she was left. So maybe he had indeed transported her by boat, moored in the dock and walked her the short distance to the disposal point. What Dan couldn't understand was why bring her from a remote location and dump her in the centre of the capital. Surely this couldn't have been his original plan. Something must have happened to change things. He intended to find out what this could have been.

As promised DC Anthea Bowker had sent him the case summary for him to forward on to the profiler he had recommended to McBride. He decided to speak with the psychologist Dr Darleen Clutterbuck before looking into the boats at St Katharine Docks. He knew how busy her case load was, given the demands made on her time and how difficult she would find it to fit in additional work but he hoped she would be sufficiently intrigued by this case to provide the necessary commitment.

Dan knew Darleen's number by heart. It had been his lifeline in the early days following the loss of his wife and unborn baby. Dan had never met anyone as patient or as supportive as Darleen. Even when he rang her in the middle of the night, which had only happened once during a panic attack, she had patiently listened and talked him through it until he calmed down. He still had monthly therapy sessions with her but could now better manage the panic attacks himself.

'Dee, it's Dan Brennan.'

'Hi Dan, what can I do for you mate?' Darleen replied in her usual Aussie twang. Even though Darleen had lived in London since the 1970s she hadn't lost her accent or the easy friendly manner with which she dealt with people whether they be patients, colleagues or friends.

'I've got a case that I'm working on and I wondered if you could take a look at the details and perhaps put together a profile for us?' Dan asked.

'Sure Dan, email it over and I'll take a look and give you my thoughts on it.'

'Thanks Dee. We have an appointment a week on Monday. Perhaps you will have something for me by then?' he asked hopefully.

'I'll certainly try. There's not much else for a girl to do on these dark cold British nights so I'll have a look and do a bit of work on it when my last patient leaves later.'

Dan could never understand why anyone would give up the hot sunny shores of Australia to live in the cold damp miserable weather that the United Kingdom has to offer but Darleen had fallen in love with London and never wanted to leave it.

'That's great Dee, I'll see you soon then.'

Dan tapped a few keys on his keyboard and the files were sent on their way to her. He closed down his computer, pulled on his jacket and left the building.

After several fruitless calls trying to find the people responsible for boats on the river Thames Dan was directed to The Port of London Authority (PLA) head office based in Gravesend in Kent. He thought they would have been based on the river itself but apparently due to the cost the head office had been moved out of the city. Luckily they provided a 24/7 service so worked during the weekend.

A helpful lady explained in a spiel that sounded as if it was lifted directly from an operational manual that the PLA operations covered ninety-five miles of the River Thames working to keep commercial and leisure craft users safe, protect and enhance the environment and promote the use of the river for trade and travel.

She proudly even keenly offered to send Dan a copy of The Tidal Thames Recreational Users Guide telling him it had only recently been updated and would remain current for the next couple of years. It gave a two-sided waterproof map of the River Thames and was free-of-charge so long as Dan didn't require more than two copies. More to keep the woman on side Dan gave his home address so she could post the guide to him. He told her he was looking for information regarding the boats moored at St Katharine Docks.

'You need to speak with Mike Robson. He's a bit of an anorak when it comes to the Docks. He even gives guided tours once a week. There isn't anything he doesn't know about the place. The next one's later today.' She gave him the time of the next tour as well as Mike's contact details.

When Dan arrived at the Docks a small group of tourists was already milling about at the pre-determined meeting point. The man leading the tour looked like a clone of the seafarer from the old Captain Birdseye fish fingers commercials. He appeared to be dressed in a kind of captain's outfit. A white beard and moustache covered much of his face. Equally white hair, curled from beneath the cap he wore. Dan suspected that this guise was perhaps more for the benefit of the tourists than anything else. It probably increased the tips from the Americans who seemed to like this sort of thing.

Beginning the tour Dan tagged along at the back. He had his notebook ready to record any facts that he thought may be useful at a later date.

Mike Robson began, 'St Katharine Docks is one of the best kept secrets in Central London. It is situated on the River Thames next to two of the most famous London landmarks; Tower Bridge and The Tower of London,' he was pointing to the two sites in question.

'The Docks are built on a site thought to be over one thousand years old and full of the most dramatic history. The actual history of some of the buildings on today's site can be traced back to the tenth Century when King Edgar gave thirteen acres of land to thirteen Knights with the right to use the land for trade. There is evidence of there being a dock on this site since around the year 1125. Throughout the ages, it has housed amongst other things a hospital and a monastery. The first use of the name St Katharine Docks has been traced back to Elizabethan times. At that time the area around the hospital was thriving with many busy wharves. By the end of the eighteenth Century, St. Katharine's was a prosperous settlement with its own court, school and alms houses. The immediate area housed around three thousand people. When the Industrial Revolution came to London, the River Thames became the superhighway of its day for the rapidly growing city. London's existing docks could not handle the ever burgeoning amount of trade so Parliament authorised the construction of new, purpose built docks. In 1825 The St Katharine Docks Bill was passed. The staggering sum of £1,352,752 was granted for the upgrading of the docks.'

'Quite cheap then given the cost of the London property prices nowadays,' a man at the back piped up.

141

'Depends how you look at it,' Mike the guide replied. 'If we used the Retail Price Index to convert this into today's money the amount would translate into a mere ninety-one million pounds but if we use the amount as a share of the country's GDP then it converts into nearly four billion pounds.'

'Wow, that's a lot of money!' the man replied.

'What's GDP?' his son asked.

'I'll explain later,' the father said not wanting to interrupt the talk further.

Mike continued with his talk. 'Enacting the bill the whole area was cleared to make way for the new centre. Around 1,250 slum houses in colourfully named roads, that could have been lifted from a Dickensian novel, such as Dark Entry, Cat's Hole and Pillory Lane, along with a church and St Katharine's Hospital itself were demolished to make way for six storey warehouses with cast iron window frames and extensive vaults to store thousands of casks of valuable wine and other luxury goods.'

Dan made a note of the *extensive vaults* in his book. Maybe the missing women were actually being held here right under their noses.

'You may have heard of the designer a man named Thomas Telford one of Britain's most famous civil engineers. He worked with the architect Philip Hardwick to create his vision. St Katharine Docks gained a reputation for handling valuable cargoes from Europe, the West Indies, Africa and the Far East such as sugar, rum, tea, spices, perfumes, ivory, shells, marble, indigo, wine and brandy. The docks thrived with the bustle of commerce.'

A voice at the front said, 'it doesn't seem very bustling and thriving now,' indicating the tranquil surroundings.

'That's very true young man. Between the two world wars, the World's trade ships grew too large for St Katharine Docks and it was instead employed in war work. Although the site was a victim of The Blitz, Telford and Hardwick's vision can still be seen today. The modern office blocks such as International House and Commodity Quay house internationally renowned businesses. They sympathetically mirror the architecture of the imposing warehouses that stood on the site before them. Ivory House, built in 1852, still stands with its distinctive clock tower and today it houses luxury warehouse apartments, offices, smart restaurants and shops.

Some one hundred and eighty-four years on from its opening as a busy, noisy and colourful industrial site St Katharine Docks, at first glance, looks to be a haven of tranquillity, nestled attractively in the heart of the City of London. The Marina houses up to one hundred and sixty luxury yachts and historic barges, much of the international trade that the Docks was always famed for, now goes on inside the commercial buildings on site. You don't necessarily need to be a boat owner to enjoy the picturesque setting of St Katharine Docks. Situated next to The Tower of London, and immediately next to the beautiful Tower Bridge, visitors are welcome to enjoy the stunning views of the River Thames, saunter along the docks and enjoy the fantastic waterside restaurants, shops and cafes. It can be reached via its own pier, Royal Mint Green, Orton Street or through the entrance at Ivory House where I expect most of you arrived today. You may have noticed the two elephants guarding the entrance. A symbol of the once lucrative ivory trade.'

The group walked round to the river entrance of the dock.

'As you can see there is a lock that allows boats access to and from the river. Many of you won't know this but the Thames is tidal from Teddington to the North Sea; that's ninety-five miles of river and estuary.'

'I've heard of Teddington Lock,' someone commented.

'So a boat can only get in and out of the dock at certain times?' Dan asked.

'Yes. The lock can only be used around high water. The winter season operational times run from November through to March. The lock operates from two hours prior to high tide to an hour and a half after it. As you will know there are two tides each day but the lock is only open during the daytime from eight in the morning until six in the evening. In the summer this is extended to eight thirty.'

This timeframe didn't make sense to Dan. If the murderer had to have docked before six how could he be kidnapping Rosie in Oxford at the same time? Did he have a partner? Also, the risk of keeping the woman imprisoned in such a busy area seemed madness and the same question came back to him now like a stuck record. Why bring her here? Why not dump her in a remote spot. Maybe his earlier thought was correct maybe the women were imprisoned right under his feet but somehow this didn't feel right. So if a boat containing Jennifer Shepherd had docked prior to six o'clock then others must have perpetrated the kidnapping of Rosie Ware. A group, not a one man band.

'Is there no exception to the opening times?' Dan asked, again to puzzled looks from some of the other tourists not understanding his obsession with opening times.

'There is one exception and that's if the Thames Barrier is closed. If there is a particularly high tide and there is a risk of flooding to London then the barrier is closed. On these occasions we allow boats to moor back in the docks otherwise they can be stranded out on the river as they can't sail beyond Blackwall Point. Staying out on the river all night is dangerous.'

'Did this occur on Friday night on 24th January this year?'

'I don't know you would need to contact the St Katharine Haven they coordinate such operations via VHF Radio. You can contact them on Channel 80 during scheduled locking times. Their call sign is "St Katharine's".'

Dan made a note in his book.

Turning his attention to the boats in the dock Mike explained, 'As I mentioned earlier the Marina now houses up to one hundred and sixty luxury yachts and barges. They can only be docked here; we don't allow the vessels to be used for residential purposes. Many are owned by rich business men, multi-national corporations and embassies. They are mainly used in the summer months for entertaining clients.'

Mike in his tour guide guise as Captain Birdseye finished off his talk and tour by telling his audience that they may wish to combine their trip with a visit to the Tower Bridge Exhibition or go to see the Crown Jewels at The Tower of London. Also across the road is the historic Royal Mint, and just a short walk across the bridge are The Design Museum, City Hall and More London. He could provide tickets to anyone wanting to go on to these destinations. For those seeking refreshments, he could recommend a lovely historic pub called The Prospect of Whitby. Alternatively Thomas More Square was just a one minute walk away where they could find some local shops and perhaps, more importantly, a Waitrose supermarket. Everyone smiled. A bit cheaper than the restaurants here he added. He liked to end with a humorous remark as it seemed to make the world of difference to his tips.

Dan assumed a little unkindly that he was on commission for any tickets he sold. He hung back and waited for Mike Robson to collect his tips and sell other tourist destination tickets as well as dispensing more advice. When everyone had gone he made his approach holding out his badge.

'I thought you might be a copper what with the interrogation and all.'

'Sorry about that but I'm investigating a murder that occurred nearby and I have reason to believe that the perpetrator may have used a boat to bring his victim here. Have you got time for a few more questions?'

'Sure, shoot away. I've got all day. Better still let's go to that pub I just mentioned. My fee for answering your questions will be a pint of best.'

'How far is it?'

'Twenty-two minutes if we walk, or six minutes if you drive. I don't own a car,' he added.

'I think we'll drive there then. My car's parked over here.' One of the advantages of being a copper was that he could park almost anywhere in this congested city.

The pub, as they approached it, was crowded in on both sides by much taller more modern double fronted apartment blocks. It looked strangely out of place as if it had been caught in a time warp.

Seeing Dan's surprise at the location of the building. Mike helpfully explained, 'It's a listed building. Otherwise, it would have been re-developed long since like almost everything else in this city.'

A pub sign with a picture of a ship on it hung lazily above the door, swinging to and fro gently in the fresh breeze that seemed to be picking up. Mike pointed up at the sign.

'Do you know why British pubs always have their name depicted by a pictorial sign?'

'No but I'm sure you're going to tell me,' Dan said smiling now getting used to the constant history lessons with which this fascinating man was able to regale him.

'Well, in 1393, King Richard II passed an Act making it compulsory for pubs and inns to have a pictorial sign in order to identify them to the official Ale Taster. Back then very few people were able to read and write. Ever since then, inn names and signs have reflected and followed British life at the time. And it's now tradition.'

'Why "The Prospect of Whitby"? I thought Whitby was in the North-East?'

'It is. The pub is supposedly named after a Tyne ship named The Prospect of Whitby that used to be moored next to the pub.'

Dan noticed a hangman's noose hanging by one of the windows. 'What's the noose all about?'

'An infamous judge named Jefferies lived nearby and frequented the pub. He was famous for the number of criminals he sentenced to hang. He was known to the locals as Hanging Judge Jeffrey's.'

'Is there nothing you don't know about the history of London?' Dan asked.

'Oh, there's plenty. That's why I love living in this great city. I'm still learning all the time but this part of the city is where I excel.'

Getting out of the cold damp air they walked into the bar. The nautical theme continued inside the pub with old barrels and ships' masts built into the structure. The room had a flagstone floor and Mike Robson told him it had a rare pewter-topped bar. They found a quiet table tucked away in the far corner but with great views overlooking the river Thames. Dan ordered the drinks along with a plate of assorted sandwiches. Mike excused himself and went to the toilets. When he returned Dan hardly recognised him. Gone was the hat along with the white hair and whiskers. Now a clean shaven grey haired man, in his late sixties, sat down beside him.

'The captain look is only for the tourists,' he explained.

Whilst they waited for the refreshments to arrive Dan took out his note book. 'You mentioned that there are extensive vaults built under the docks. Would it be possible for someone to be living down there without anyone else knowing?'

'I think it unlikely but I suppose they could be. The vaults were mainly converted into car parking in the 1970s. I suppose it could be possible for a section to have been sealed off. I suggest you look at the plans at the town hall. They have detailed copies of all the different configurations of the docks going right back to when they were first built.'

'You also mentioned a radio station The St Katharine Haven. Where are they based and who could I speak with there?'

'They are based further up the river. You need to speak with a man called Neil Brooks he runs the operation. It comes under the remit of the Thames River Authority.'

The drinks and sandwiches arrived. On the whole English pub food had improved immeasurably over the last couple of decades. The offering laid before them didn't disappoint. Dan tucked in hungrily.

'So do you have information about the boats moored in the docks?'

'I know about all the boats. Give me a name and I'll tell you who owns it, where it was built, what the class is.'

'I don't have a name yet but if I need some further details can I call you?'

'Sure,' he said passing a business card across to Dan.

Dan was surprised to read on the card that Mike worked for the Government.

'The tours are only a hobby I do at the weekend or if I have a day off. I have a passion for history and like to share my knowledge and try to entertain .... If only a little.'

Dan thanked Mike and said his goodbyes and made his way to the Thames River Authority and asked to speak with Mr Brooks. Unfortunately, he wasn't in the office as he was working nights that week. His assistant was very helpful and gave Dan the information he asked for. He was able to confirm that the Thames barrier had indeed been closed on the evening in question and that only three boats had docked during the extended time that the docks had been open. The three boats were called The Dark Serpent, the Felix and the Perfection. Of the three only two of them had left the next morning. The Dark Serpent had continued on its journey to France, through the now open Thames Barrier, returning to St Katharine Docks two days later. The Perfection had turned back up river. It was a week

146

before that boat returned. The Felix hadn't left the Docks since arriving that night so was still there.

Armed with the details of the boat owners and contact details Dan decided to do a bit more digging before he arranged to interview the three owners in question.

Giving Cathy Grainger a ring he asked if she could do some background checks on the boat owners. She told him she would get onto it as soon as she had finished her current job. He also left a message with Mike Robson asking him for more details about the three boats.

Dan made his way back to St Katharine Docks and slowly walked around looking for the boats. He wasn't a boat person and they mainly all looked the same to him. He found The Dark Serpent first. It was an old fashioned boat comprising of varnished wood and brass with a tall mast. Dan thought it would have looked more at home on Lake Windermere. He was expecting something sleek and black to live up to its name. Nobody was on board. The rigging vibrated and the halyards slapped non-stop against the mast in the light breeze. The boat dipped lazily up and down in the slight swell of the dark murky water. Dan jumped onto the boat. At the stern, there was a covered wheelhouse with a door and two portholes on either side of the cabin. The door was locked. Cupping his hands around his eyes he peered through one of the portholes. A steep wooden staircase disappeared into the bowels of the boat. A large glass window allowed the skipper to see ahead and let light into the cabin. Several yellow sou'westers were hung from brass coat hooks along one side. A desk with what looked like navigational charts sat beside the large wheel. Dan would have loved to get a look below deck but without a search warrant, it just wasn't an option. He shouldn't even be on the boat at all. Jumping back onto dry land he searched for the next boat on his list of three.

His mobile rang. It was Mike Robson returning his call. 'Sure I know about the three boats,' he told Dan. 'The Dark Serpent is owned by a man named Miklos Orban. It's a thirty foot motorised sail boat capable of crossing the channel to Europe but you wouldn't take it across the Atlantic. Orban runs an import and export business out of a suite of offices based in Ivory House. He's Eastern European. Not from the current wave; he came here as a boy with his parents shortly after World War II, grew up in the East End. From all accounts he's a bit of a hard case.'

'Ivory House that's actually located at the Docks?' Dan said remembering Mike's talk on the tour.

'Yes, that's right.'

'What about the other two?'

'Now the Perfection that's one expensive and beautiful boat. Not too big so it can navigate most rivers and canals but capable of going almost anywhere. It's owned by the Austrian embassy. They use it for the entertainment of visitors, guests etc. A man named Max Rainer seems to be in charge of it. A nice chap. Very posh. If he's not on the boat now I expect you can get in touch with him through the Austrian embassy.'

'Your third boat Felix is a Catamaran. A retired couple in their fifties are planning to sail it around the world,' he laughed. 'They didn't even make it into the English Channel. They hit one of the bridge stanchions and it's now laid up waiting for some parts to be flown in from Germany to repair it.'

Thanking Mike for the information Dan continued his search for the other two boats.

The Perfection was more like the boat Dan had expected the Dark Serpent to look like. It was sleek, black and very expensive looking. It had a row of red lights across the stern and a flag that Dan assumed was the flag of Austria comprising of three equal horizontal bands of red, white and red again with a coat of arms in the middle. The coat of arms seemed to depict a golden crowned black eagle holding a hammer in one talon and a sickle in the other. A broken chain dangled from each of the talons. A shield also in red with a white band across the centre sat across the bird's body. A metal gang plank was incorporated into the stern of the boat. Dan guessed this was operated electronically. There was no way he was going to be able to gain access to this boat not to mention the diplomatic repercussions if he was even discovered near it never mind on it, so he continued his search for the third boat.

The Felix he found nearest to the dock entrance. A couple on-board were in a heated debate or just full blown argument as only man and wife can. The woman seemed very upset and given the extensive reddening around the eyes had clearly been crying.

'If you don't want to come then go back home,' the man shouted 'I'll go on my own.'

Dan coughed discreetly to gain their attention. Both stopped their argument and looked embarrassingly towards him. 'I'm a police officer. I'd like to ask you some questions about the night of Friday 24th January if I may.'

'I told you we'd be in trouble for hitting that bridge,' the woman wailed once more. 'How much is that going to cost us? This boat has already taken our entire retirement fund and we haven't even left England yet.'

'It's got nothing to do with the bridge. It's about a murder that happened near here on that night,' explained Dan.

This seemed to calm the couple down if only a little. From their reaction and body language Dan doubted they had been involved in the murder but then again professional killers could produce Oscar winning performances when they needed to.

'Tell me about that night,' Dan asked.

The woman started to tell the sorry tale about them picking up their new boat from Lots Ait boatyard fifteen miles further up river and how they had been warned not to take it out whilst the tide was coming in but the husband had decided not to heed the warning. Apparently, he had been sailing all his life and could manage a simple river system. The man took up the story.

'The power of that tide. I couldn't believe it. The river patrol gave us a tow and we have been here since that night.'

The wife chipped in again, 'You were told to purchase a copy of that book The Mariners' Guide to Bridges on the Tidal Thames but oh no you didn't want to waste your money. Now look what it's cost us.'

'Oh shut up woman,' the husband retorted.

Dan wondered how this couple could have managed a trip around the World together.

'With hindsight, I should have read the book as it provides an overview for navigating London's bridges, and highlights the safety issues but I didn't and we ran into Tower Bridge over there. I never realised that the river Thames was such a challenging environment.'

'Did you see anything suspicious when you arrived here?'

'It was very quiet as it was quite late. We did see a man loading some packages off that boat over there,' he said pointing in the direction of the Black Serpent. He seemed to have a bad leg. I went over and offered to help but he got quite shirty so I left him to it.'

'Can you describe him?'

'Tall, well built, dark hair. He had a slight foreign accent but spoke very good English.'

'What was he wearing?'

'Jeans and a leather jacket I think it was.'

'Why do you say he had a bad leg?'

'Well he seemed to be limping slightly. He definitely favoured his right leg.'

Dan wondered if this could be from a dog bite. Maybe he had a lead at last ... but would it work with the timings that Mike had mentioned earlier – maybe?

Dan decided to leave before the marital howling recommenced but in doing so he posed the throwaway question – 'why did you call your craft Felix?'

In unison as if rehearsed Mr and Mrs Price shouted 'Felix ... the cat - catamaran!'

It was time for Dan to pay Miklos Orban, the owner of the Black Serpent, a visit. Dan made his way to Ivory House. The reception area was very plush. A list of about thirty businesses was etched in brass on a plaque on the wall with the accompanying details of the floor on which they could be found. Glancing down the list Dan found the company name he was looking for and made his way up to the second floor. He didn't know if anyone would be there as it was late on Saturday afternoon but as he approached the office he could see a young woman seated behind the reception desk. Showing his badge he asked the glamorous receptionist if he could speak to Mr Orban. She didn't look surprised as if a visit from the police was a regular occurrence. Buzzing through to her boss she announced Dan's arrival and directed him through. The office was on the corner of the building giving the occupant stunning views across and down the river Thames. The business must be doing very well to afford premises like this. Dan put the guy at about mid to late sixties but he looked very fit for his age as if he worked out regularly or did some kind of manual labour. This was borne out when they shook hands as Dan could feel the aged callouses on his right hand. He wore a shirt with rolled up sleeves. A tattoo of a black snake ran down the length of one arm and back up the other. There was only one word that could describe Miklos Orban and that was menacing. He seemed to have suppressed anger in his voice even though he spoke quietly. Dan felt a primordial fear prickling his spine as if he had walked into a lion's den.

Dan thought back to the description Lawrence, the homeless man, had given him of the man he had seen with Jennifer Shepherd the night she was murdered and compared it to the man facing him. He was certainly tall, dark and European but could never be described as slim given that he was a thickly set big man. Maybe Lawrence had got it wrong. Or maybe two different men were involved as he had suspected earlier; one abducting Rosie and the other disposing of Jennifer. Or maybe he had nothing to do with it.

'How can I help you, DI Brennan?' Mr Orban enquired.

'I'm investigating a murder that happened near here early in the morning of Saturday 25th January. I've been informed that you docked your boat here late on the preceding Friday night. Did you see anybody in the vicinity of the docks that night?'

'I saw a couple aboard a Catamaran. They docked just after I did. You couldn't miss 'em they were arguing so loudly. I can understand why he'd do 'er in, I felt like finishing her off meself. Unfortunately, she's still breathing as I noticed them still arguing first thing this morning.'

'You didn't see anything else suspicious that night?'

'No nothing. I docked the boat and went straight home.'

'I understood you unloaded some packages from your boat. Can I ask what was in them?'

'You can ask but I'm not obliged to give you an answer. I don't see what it has to do with your murder investigation.'

'You're right it doesn't. I was just curious what you would be unloading at that time of night.'

'If you must know it was a delivery I was making to France. I had to abandon the trip as the Barrier was closed by the time I got down river. I don't like leaving valuables on the boat overnight so I unloaded it before going home. I have a storage area in the cellars under this building. Satisfied?'

Dan placed his business card on the desk. 'If you remember anything else let me know.'

Miklos Orban followed Dan to the door. Noticing his limp Dan asked, 'How have you injured your leg?' before quickly adding 'you haven't been bitten by a dog recently have you?'

The man looked genuinely puzzled, 'no I slipped on my boat a couple of weeks ago. Just cracked my knee. It takes time to get better when you get to my age.'

When Dan left the office Miklos Orban picked up the business card, read it and dropped it into the waste paper bin. He keyed a number into his phone and issued an instruction to the person at the other end, 'I've got work for you. I need you to make someone disappear.'

Leaving the building Dan noticed a tourist casually taking pictures of the boats in the dock. He could have sworn that he had snapped Dan's photo as he emerged from Ivory House but dismissed this as nonsense. Was he becoming paranoid?

It was getting late so Dan decided to head straight home rather than go back to the station. He would report his progress first thing Monday morning. He was thinking of how he could obtain a search warrant for the cellars under Ivory House. Mike Robson had said how extensive they were. Maybe the women were being held there right in the centre of London but maybe not. It would certainly explain why Jennifer Shepherd's body was dumped in the area but would anyone bring such unwanted attention on to the actual location of their operation? It seemed unlikely.

Walking back to his car he had a sixth sense that someone was watching him. Paranoia again? He turned quickly but the street behind him was deserted. His footsteps echoed on the cobbled pavement. Every few steps he stopped to listen but heard nothing.

The man following edged a glance around the corner where Dan had disappeared moments before. He was speaking quietly into his phone. 'He's just ahead of me. I think he suspects someone is following but he hasn't spotted me. Do you want me to take him now?'

Dan had parked on the forecourt of a disused warehouse. There were no houses at this end of the street and most of the lighting was out. He was glad when he got to his car. He'd just put the key in the door when a voice from behind said, 'place your hands on the car roof, don't turn round, I have a gun pointing at your back.'

A black hood was pulled roughly over his head and his arms pulled painfully back and secured with a plastic tie wrap. Dan heard a car squeal to a halt next to him and he was manhandled into the back seat. He was driven around for what seemed like ages but was probably only a matter of minutes. When the car came to a stop the questioning started. Who was he? Why was he snooping around the Black Serpent? Dan decided to be honest. He didn't know who his abductors were so there was no point lying. When he mentioned that he was a police officer making enquiries about a woman's murder his two abductors went quiet. He felt one of them go through his pockets and take out his identification.

'He's telling the truth. He's a copper.'

The car started and he was driven about once more. The next thing Dan knew he was bundled out of the car onto the cold damp floor. His restraints were cut and he was left rubbing his wrists.

'Don't try and follow us,' one of his captors said. With this he heard the slam of car doors and the squeal of tyres. As he lifted the hood from his head he saw the red brake lights of a car turning the corner in the distance without its lights on. It was too far way to see the registration number.

Dan looked about. They had left him across from where his car was still parked. He still had no idea who the two men were but suspected Miklos Orban had had him followed to check out whether his story was true – but why? Luckily his keys were still dangling from the car door. Getting in he sat there trying to regain his composure and work out what had happened and why but to no avail. He contemplated reporting the incident but what could he tell the police. He had no idea who the men were.

43

Monday 3rd March 2014 - LONDON

When Dan arrived at his office Monday morning there was a note for him to see the Chief Superintendent immediately. Being summoned to see the Chief Super. was never good especially when he had no idea what it was about. He thought about trying to put it off but reluctantly decided he was best getting it resolved sooner rather than later. The Super's temper was legendary. He made his way up to the top floor of the building and along the corridor constantly racking his brain as to what might have caused this impromptu summons until he came to a door with a brass plate and the name Chief Superintendent Danny Hughes printed on it. He mindlessly thought about the term *'Top Brass'*. Was this because the boss always had the room with the best view and had his name etched in brass on the door? He would Google it when he got home. He was always intrigued with the origin of such sayings.

Knocking on the door Dan hoped that he wouldn't get an answer but was disappointed when an authoritative voice bade him to enter.

'Sit,' his boss ordered indicating a chair across from his large desk.

The Super. wasn't alone. The man sitting opposite him turned. Dan felt a vague sense of recognition but couldn't place him. Maybe he had met him on a job somewhere. Laid out on the desk were photographs. Several of Dan on The Black Serpent, another of him leaving Ivory House, another of him talking to the retired couple on the Felix. It suddenly twigged with Dan where he had seen the man.

'You're that tourist who was taking photos at St Katharine Docks on Saturday?'

'No...I'm DCI Chris Holman an undercover police officer from SOCA and I've been carrying out surveillance on Miklos Orban for the last six months. And YOU – you're the man who's single-handedly managed to blow our whole operation.'

Dan knew that SOCA stood for – The Serious Organised Crime Agency – It had been set up five years ago as Britain's equivalent of America's FBI. It was an amalgamation of the old National Crime Squad and National Criminal Intelligence Service, along with parts of the Customs & Excise and the Immigration Service. It had its own Act of Parliament, budget and extraordinary powers. Its remit was to target criminal gangs, drug smugglers and people traffickers. It was staffed with over five thousand hand-picked officers. Dan remembered being slightly disappointed that he hadn't been selected.

'I don't understand … was I on the right track? So Miklos Orban was involved with the abduction of Rosie Ware and the murder of Jennifer Shepherd?'

'No…he definitely isn't involved with your murder investigation nor any kidnapping for that matter. We've been watching him constantly. Nearly every night he sails to France with bundles of cash, collects a consignment of drugs and goodness knows what else and brings them back to the UK. We had a team ready to bust him yesterday when you turned up. We only delayed an arrest as we wanted to catch all those involved in one fell swoop and we thought that you were an additional player. Now it seems he's scarpered, left the country. We had his phone tapped and he made a call to a fixer just after you left. He wanted someone to disappear. That someone was him. He's probably holed up in his villa in Spain right now and planning to vanish to some tin pot country that we don't have an extradition treaty with.'

'Was it your team that abducted me?'

'Sorry about that,' Holman said raising his hands by way of an apology. 'We did think you were one of his gang. We needed to bring down the entire crew at the same time so they didn't warn each other. We've managed to arrest six of his men. He literally slipped out the back door before we could make the arrest.'

Danny Hughes now stepped in. 'That's enough. What have I told you before Brennan about working on your own and overstepping the boundaries?'

Dan shifted uneasily in his chair, 'How was I to know Miklos Orban was under surveillance. As far as I was concerned he was just a potential witness in my murder enquiry.'

Hughes slammed his fist on the desk and glared angrily at Dan. 'Murder enquiry! What murder enquiry! It hasn't even been established that it was a murder, has it? You've got other cases far more important. Now you might want to drop this wild goose chase and start doing some real police work. Or convince me otherwise and that's likely to take some doing I can tell you.'

Dan thought about his other cases - a series of bag snatchings at Euston underground station and a suicide case. Hardly important in his book. He couldn't understand why his boss was being so obstructive about this case. He seemed to have totally forgotten that Dan had been seconded to the Operation Silver investigation and that he'd agreed to it.

'Yes sir,' he mumbled getting up and backing out of the room. Dan realised that with all the recent excitement with the Rosie Ware and Jennifer Shepherd cases he hadn't got around to bringing his boss up to speed. Dan had always been criticised by his colleagues for his isolated method of working and the fact he never wanted or felt the need for a partner. I'll arrange for you to receive a briefing by lunchtime. He always said lunchtime and not twelve noon as it effectively gave him an extra couple of hours. Always useful when under pressure.

DCI Holman actually looked like he felt sorry for Dan.

A red faced Dan left the Super's office. This would be all around the station in no time. He still had three-quarters of an hour to kill before he had to dial into the Operation Silver briefing teleconference. He decided to go out for a coffee to clear his head. His phone rang as he stood in line at the busy coffee house down the road. Looking at the caller ID it was Cathy.

'I've got some information on the boat owners you asked me to look into. First off the owner of The Dark Serpent is a man named Miklos Orban. He runs an import export business out of a suite of offices based in Ivory House. He's got a rather shady past but up until six months ago he'd been off the police radar for a good twenty years or so. His name came up in an undercover operation about a drugs syndicate that is believed to be importing drugs from France. He served two terms in prison for three years and eight years respectively back in the 1970s and 80s. He seems to have been clean since then. Both convictions were drug related but the second involved a lot of unnecessary violence. The two drug mules involved were found dead with their stomachs cut open. Obviously, someone didn't want to wait for the drugs to be passed naturally. There's a red flag against his name. Apparently the Drugs Squad have had him under surveillance for the last six months. You can't approach him. You must go through a DCI Chris Holman. I'll text you his number.'

'Right,' Dan said wishing he had known this yesterday.

'The second boat is owned by the Austrian Embassy. It is used for entertainment purposes. The person to speak with is the Austrian Embassy Liaison and Security Officer a man named Count Maximilian Schütte-Rainer III known by the shortened version of Max Rainer to his friends. The boat is used by many different people but he will be able to give you the details. I've arranged for you to meet

155

the Count at his home tonight at six o'clock,' Cathy said reeling off the address. 'Don't be late he's a stickler for punctuality so I hear.'

'The third boat belongs to a couple called Jim and Margaret Price. They recently took early retirement from the Civil Service and have plans to sail around the world. There's nothing in their backgrounds that would suggest they had anything to do with our case. Anyway I've got to dash as we have the conference call in ten minutes.'

Dan was rushing back with his coffee for the dial-in when he had a thought. If the Drugs Squad had The Black Serpent under surveillance they may have unwittingly witnessed something from that night of 24th January. They may even have photos relating to Jennifer Shepherd's murder. He made a mental note to contact DCI Holman and ask if he could speak to his team and perhaps take a look at the intel they had.

44

Monday 3rd March 2014 - OXFORD

The Operation Silver Team arrived for their daily briefing.

'Morning team, Do we have Cathy and Dan on the line?'

'Yes sir,' came the joint response from the speaker at the front of the room.

'We will start with your update just in case we lose the connection which has been known. Go ahead Cathy.'

Cathy told the team that she had received, as promised, the list of suspected female abductions and had already managed to identify ten of the girls who matched the profile and three who were possibles. She also provided details about the one case that wasn't on the police missing persons database but had been on Laura's list for the woman named Jacqui Bates. She went on to explain her analysis and how it had occurred to her that many UK university students came from overseas or took equivalent examinations so they wouldn't show up on the 'A' Level results list that Laura had been using. To make the search as comprehensive as possible she was now going through the top universities' entrance exam results and checking the best rated students to see if there were any matches with the Missing Persons Database. Cathy went on to tell them that the entrance exam data was only available electronically from 1998 and prior to this they would need to contact the individual universities.

'Do you want me to come with you to interview the university admissions staff?' McBride asked sensing her reticence.

If the team could have seen Cathy they would have noticed how visibly relieved she was to receive the offer of help. Cathy loved dealing with computers but dealing with people especially intellectuals was another matter. 'That would be great sir.'

'Send me the contact details and I'll arrange for these meetings to be set up,' McBride said.

Next Dan Brennan gave his update telling the team that he had sent the case notes to the psychologist and she hoped to have a profile for him the following week. He said that he was now following up the possibility that Jennifer Shepherd had been moved by boat. He didn't mention the cock-up regarding the drug investigation but he would mention it to McBride separately and copy him into the briefing he was preparing for his Chief Super.

'Good thinking Dan, let us know what you find out,' said McBride.

Turning to Emma Blakely and Gary Hope McBride asked, 'what have you managed to find out about the sperm banks?'

Emma took the lead not trusting Gary to give the concise update required. 'Well sir, not a lot. Sperm donation in the UK is highly regulated. Also, stocks are surprisingly low. It seems that men aren't too keen to become fathers to unknown offspring. Parents are allowed to choose characteristics similar to their own for example skin colour but they are not allowed to choose traits like intelligence although many sperm donors are student doctors who get paid for their contributions, so they usually do have a high IQ.'

Uncomfortable sniggers went around the room more out of embarrassment Emma thought. It always made her smile that these hard, often crass men, who loved to mock the female species couldn't handle the subject of making babies.

'What about sperm banks from abroad?' McBride asked. 'I saw a programme on television a couple of months back in which it said that in the USA you can select an Einstein to father your child.'

'This is true they are much more liberal over there. That's our job for today to find out what the process is for getting a sperm donation from abroad.'

'You and Gary carry on with that line of enquiry.'

'Do we have any updates regarding dog bites presenting at A&Es?' McBride asked DS Rod Hartley.

'Yes sir, you wouldn't believe how many. Most are children so we can rule those out. I've got a list of twenty-seven who received bites around the time of Rosie's abduction. We have eliminated twenty-two already. They either have alibis for the time and date or we have the dog in custody.'

Another snigger went around the room.

'It wouldn't be difficult for the kidnapper to finger the wrong dog, would it? The dog's hardly likely to refute the allegation. I want you to check the whereabouts of every victim and that includes any women as well. We think the offender is a man but we can't rule out a female at this stage,' said McBride. 'DC Bowker I want you to look into that odd case that Cathy identified. The woman named Jacqui

Bates that was on Laura's list of missing women but for whom we don't have an open missing person report.'

'I'll get onto it straight away,' said DC Anthea Bowker. 'Also sir I had another idea. We think that Rosie had her Apple iPad with her. Well similar to the iPhone the iPad also has a tracking device in it which can be activated if the owner reports it stolen. I spoke with Rosie's boyfriend Ben Tanner and he confirmed that it had been set up. I contacted Apple yesterday and they were able to identify Rosie's computer and turn on the tracker. Unfortunately, there isn't a signal coming from the computer so it's either switched off or has been destroyed. They will continue to scan for it and they will let us know as soon as a signal is received. This will pinpoint the machine to within a few yards.'

'Good work Anthea. Let us know immediately if you hear anything positive from Apple.'

McBride looked down at his checklist. 'How are we doing with the Interpol search for a match with the suspects DNA?'

'Still nothing found,' Rod Hartley confirmed to the team.

'The Crimewatch programme. Any leads from that?'

'We've had a couple come forward who state they were walking their dog along the canal tow path ten minutes prior to the time we estimate Rosie was there. They are certain that the injured dog wasn't there when they passed the spot. They also think but can't be certain that Rosie rode past them as they crossed the bridge by the Anchor pub. They definitely seem believable but it doesn't tell us anything new. We've also had numerous sightings of both Rosie and her missing rucksack. The most numerous reports have been about people with suspected dog bites. We are following all these leads up but I have to say nothing looks credible.'

McBride looked disappointed. He had pinned great hopes on the response to the Crimewatch programme. In other cases it had provided the pivotal clue to the arrest of the criminals involved in the crime. He didn't want the rest of the team to catch on to the despondency he felt so he gave a rousing close to the meeting telling them to carry on their good work.

45

With two of the boats now ruled out Dan was down to his last and perhaps most unlikely lead which was the boat named Perfection owned by the Austrian embassy. As expected Count Maximilian Schütte-Rainer III lived in one of the most expensive areas in London. The house must have been worth upwards of five million pounds. Dan doubted his job at the Austrian embassy paid for the house. It didn't look as if the Count relied on his embassy salary alone to pay for his lifestyle given the deluxe style in which the house was presented. Either he had family money or he was making it elsewhere.

Count Maximilian Schütte-Rainer III – a name suitable for a successful middle-aged businessman but who gives a child a name like that? Dan thought as he waited for a response to his three loud taps using the Jacob Marley-like knocker on the large all black gloss painted front door.

The Count was in his late fifties, sporting an expensive deep suntan gained from hours on the tennis court no doubt and holidays sailing in sunny climes. He had thick blond hair and exuded wealth. Dan's father had always told him that the sign of a wealthy man was his shoes. Looking down at the man's shoes they didn't disappoint.

'Hand made by Barker Black,' remarked the man noticing Dan's interest.

Dan like many of the working class often found contact with titled people distinctly uncomfortable.

'Call me Max,' the man said confidently holding out a strong muscular hand for Dan to shake, 'all my friends do.'

The man was well spoken and his English was word perfect but with a slight hint of a guttural accent, Dan assumed from years of speaking German as a first language.

Dan was led through the enormous Edwardian terraced house into a large conservatory at the rear of the property which of itself had about the same floor area as the whole of Dan's apartment. He could hear children's laughter from somewhere deep within the house.

'Would you like a drink? Whisky, wine or perhaps beer?' with the word beer being delivered as a derogatory addition or was it just Dan's heightened sense of paranoia in such august company.

'Not whilst I'm on duty, sir.' He'd never said that before but often seen it on TV.

'Oh I'm sorry I forgot. Maybe tea or coffee; or perhaps some water?'

Dan knew the man hadn't forgotten for a moment that he was a serving police officer and on duty. He was testing Dan to see if he was willing to bend the rules.

'Water will be fine - thank you,' Dan said trying to recover the situation.

Max pressed a button concealed beneath the table next to where he was sitting. An uncomfortable silence hung in the air until a butler appeared in the doorway.

'A glass of water for our guest and my usual Wilson.'

Without saying a word the butler crossed the room and poured a glass of water for Dan and a whisky for his master. He returned and placed the drinks on the table and disappeared in the direction from which he had come. How much easier it would have been for Rainer to get the drinks himself Dan thought but he felt sure he just wanted to add to Dan's feeling of discomfort showing him that he was intruding into a world where he really didn't belong.

Dan looked around the expensively furnished room. Several family photos were prominently displayed on the low-level contemporary sideboard. All consisted of Mr and Mrs Schütte-Rainer with their three children, two boys and a girl. They looked like the perfect family and wouldn't have looked out of place in a fashion magazine. All the children had the same white hair and bright blue eyes as their father.

'Do you have children, Detective Brennan?'

'No, I don't.'

'I always feel sorry for people who don't have children. What's the point in life if you can't enjoy the growth and company of your offspring as they develop and also have somebody to whom you can pass on your wealth?'

'Money isn't everything. To some of us other things are more important,' Dan said trying to get the upper hand.

'Nothing is more important than having children. To continue your bloodline is what life is all about. Anyway I digress as ever, it's a personal failing of mine. To what do I owe the honour of this visit by a member of the Metropolitan Police? How can I help you?' he said with a sickly sweet smile.

Dan took out his notebook and thumbed through the pages even though he knew by heart the information contained within and exactly what he wanted to know. He just wanted to give himself time to get composed.

'I want to know about a boat that you have moored in St Katharine Docks called Perfection?'

'It's not actually my boat. It belongs to the Austrian embassy as I expect you already know.'

'Yes, but I believe you are responsible for its upkeep and control. You authorise its use. You know where it goes and when and more importantly who is on it at any one point in time so I'm given to understand.'

'True it does come under my remit as the Austrian Embassy Liaison and Security Officer. What do you want to know about it officer?'

'I want to know who had use of it on the night of Friday 24th January and where did it sail to on the days before and after this time?'

'I'm afraid that information is classified. We allow many prominent and influential guests to use that boat. They wouldn't want their details disclosed nor banded about. As you will understand some of them use the boat for what you might call clandestine activities,' he said making quotation marks in the air with the first two fingers of each hand. You understand what I mean I'm sure.'

'I can get a warrant that will force you to disclose the information.'

'I don't think you can Detective Inspector Brennan. Haven't you heard of diplomatic immunity?' he laughed if not dismissively then with at least a derisory intent so Dan believed.

He stood up signalling the end of the interview.

'You think that the rich and privileged don't have to work hard don't you Detective Inspector Brennan?'

'Well I bet your children will never want for anything …. sir.' Added as a precautionary after thought. Dan was keen to avoid generating a complaint from a country's embassy only days after cocking up a long term undercover operation. Not a good career move.

'Follow me, Inspector.'

He led Dan into a large kitchen. Around a central island, three children sat happily chatting with a huge pile of pea pods in front of them. Each was deftly popping the pods and sliding their thumbs inside to free the peas which slid into a bowl that each of the children had sitting before them.

'I'm winning Papa,' one of the two boys shouted as he saw his father standing in the doorway.

162

'You see Inspector I teach my children that enjoyment can be found in the most menial of tasks and that all jobs have value. How much easier it would be to take a packet of peas from the freezer but how much more satisfaction we get from eating the fruits of our own labour. This is why so many children of the nouveau-riche go off the rails. They haven't had generations of wealth to teach them true values. They think that once they have money they can sit back and let others do all the work for them. It's what they come to expect. It's what they see from their parents. It's learned behaviour.'

'Then why do you have a butler?' Dan asked unable to hold back his own opinion.

'Touché Inspector, touché. What can I say other than when you get to my time of life you can relax a little and let others take some of the burden. And I must also add it's in part for show and in part an acknowledgement of where I reside, living as I do in a country that employs more butlers than the rest of the world put together.'

Dan wasn't convinced. He didn't think this man had ever had to suffer the hardship of normal men and women.

The butler seemed to have appeared again from nowhere.

'Wilson, please show Detective Inspector Brennan out.'

Dan knew he wouldn't get any further and followed the butler to the front door. Although he didn't match the description of the man who had been seen with Jennifer Shepherd shortly before she died he did think that given the Counts physical attributes he could have been the sperm donor for Rosie. Though he acknowledged this to be a bit of a stretch and may just want the Count to be up to no good ... as he just didn't like him. He could also see him being the man who had overseen the abduction of Rosie Ware but perhaps for similar reasons. He had to think of a way of getting a DNA sample from the Count. He'd then either make progress or draw a line under this avenue of enquiry.

46

Tuesday 4th March 2014 – OXFORD

McBride had arranged an interview for the next day with Ms Frances Prescott the Director of undergraduate admissions at Oxford University. She had been fully apprised of the reasons for the interview in advance to save time. Ms Prescott was a strikingly handsome woman. She was in her mid-forties, smartly dressed and spoke in an upper-class accent as you would expect for such an elite establishment like Oxford University.

'What can you tell us about Rosie Ware?' McBride asked.

'Well, she was exceptional,' she began.

That word again McBride thought.

'All our students are bright but Rosie was one of the brightest.'

Bright or just rich parents who bought their children a place at Oxford McBride thought again. It always annoyed him how the privileged could use their influence to gain access to the best education. Some things just never changed in this country.

It was as if Frances Prescott had read his thoughts.

'It's not like it used to be,' she continued defensively. 'The admissions process selects students based on their aptitude alone. Oxford is committed to recruiting the best candidates, irrespective of their age, colour, disability, ethnic origin, marital status, nationality, national origin, parental status, race, religion or belief, gender, sexual orientation, social background or educational background. Privileged hopefuls who might have been given preferential treatment a generation ago now struggle to win a place here. We now weed out the *thick rich* applicants who might have been offered a place in the past. Tougher testing is the key to differentiating between deserving students and those who have been schooled to make it through the interview process for the prestigious universities. The thing that really links our students together is that they are all selected on their academic merit; they've demonstrated that they can cope with the tutorial environment and they're all really smart. The Government has stressed that we're supposed to be identifying students with real potential for success, irrespective of social background. That's what we strive to do. Rosie was at Oxford because of her intellect and because she earned her place to study here.'

McBride thought that she sounded like she was quoting from a political pamphlet. She had clearly made this speech on more than one occasion. He thought she was just saying what he wanted to hear rather than what she truly believed or perhaps what really happened.

'You can't tell me that intelligence isn't mainly genetic. Surely parents who are doctors are much more likely to produce intelligent children rather than two semi illiterate unemployed parents living on your average council estate?' McBride asked.

She smiled a knowing smile and added, 'that's not for me to question; I just look at the results. These youngsters have already been moulded into what they will become long before we get them. What is the quote from Aristotle - "give me a child until he is seven and I will show you the man"?'

'And what about Rosie Ware? She came from rich parents who could have schooled her to pass the entrance exams.'

'True, they had the money but nobody could be schooled to come top in the entrance exams.'

'Could pupils cheat?' McBride asked.

'I suppose they could have got hold of the written papers, but it's exceedingly unlikely and in any event no one can get through the oral interviews unless they pay for a substitute to stand in for them. This didn't happen in Rosie's case. Are you suggesting Rosie cheated? Is that what you really think? I very much doubt this as she came top in her first term exams and all her tutors say how academically gifted and what a wonderful girl she is.'

'No, I don't think she cheated to get into Oxford. I just wanted to gain your impression of her,' McBride said. He always liked to get their hackles up, like he had just done with Ms Prescott. It reminded him that the upper-class and the council estate residents weren't that much different. Get someone on the defensive and they tend to speak from the heart ... less sticking to a pre-arranged agenda.

'Have you ever heard the name Jennifer Shepherd?' McBride asked.

'No, I've never heard that name but then again I've had thousands of girl's names through my office over the years. Was she a student here?'

'No but she would have been if she hadn't been abducted in August 1986,' McBride said.

'That was before my time. I only started here in 1987,' Ms Prescott said.

'We will need access to all your admission records prior to them being computerised in 1998,' Cathy said.

'Of course,' I'll ask my assistant to give you access to the records in the University's central administration but they do go back hundreds of years.'

Cathy didn't tell her that she was only interested in the previous few decades. The less she had to converse with this woman the better. Cathy felt an unease that she couldn't put her finger on around this woman. Was it the inherent officiousness, some degree of pomposity or just a seething superiority that gave Cathy the impression that she delivered every word through clenched teeth ... Despite the occasional narrow smile.

After the police left her office Frances Prescott removed a laptop from her bottom desk drawer. She logged into her encrypted email account and started typing:

> *I've just had the police here. They know about the link between Jennifer Shepherd and Rosie Ware. I warned you not to take Rosie. You know this is a golden rule never to take the offspring of one of the breeders. They are now delving into the university admission records looking for other missing students. They don't suspect my involvement. I'll keep you posted as and when I hear anything more.*

When she had completed the email she saved it into the draft folder, logged off the internet and closed down the computer.

She then picked up the phone to speak with Eddie Etherington the doddery old University records keeper to tell him about Mrs Grainger's impending visit.

As they walked away from the office Cathy asked McBride, 'why did you mention Jennifer Shepherd's name? She didn't apply to Oxford and Frances Prescott couldn't have possibly known her.'

'It was just a hunch,' McBride replied. 'Did you see the flash of recognition when I mentioned Jennifer's name? I think Ms Prescott may know something.'

McBride wished that he could put a tap on Frances Prescott's phone and monitor her email transactions but no judge would grant him this based on just a hunch and nothing more at this stage.

'I'll arrange interviews with the other key University Admissions Administrators and let you know the times. In the mean time you crack on with looking through the records,' McBride said. 'The sooner we can identify who has definitely been taken the sooner we'll be able to assess what links them and where they might have been or are being held ... and perhaps as importantly by whom.'

McBride stopped in front of a notice board that had a flyer advertising a talk entitled *Future of Our World* presented by *Frances Prescott* the following week in the lecture hall.

Interesting McBride thought and put a note of it in the organiser on his phone.

At the bottom of the stairs they split up, McBride heading back to his car and Cathy making her way to the building where the records were stored.

47

The records were kept in a large room stacked floor to ceiling with boxes clearly marked with the year. The age and style of the boxes changed as they went back through time and Cathy noticed some as early as the 1600s.

An elderly grey haired man with a stooped back approached her, 'nearly as old as me some of those boxes,' he laughed, 'they date right back to 1214 when the University first formally opened for business but teaching has existed at Oxford in some form since around 1096. You must be Mrs Grainger. I've just had a call from Frances telling me to expect you and to give you any assistance I can. Edward Etherington is my name but everyone calls me Eddie,' he smiled holding out his hand towards Cathy.

Cathy took an instant liking to Eddie and soon found out that he shared her love of books and delving into history. Cathy would have liked to spend hours looking through the boxes of ancient documents but she had to focus her time on the 70s to 90s decades alone. Cathy explained that she was looking for the results from the entrance exams for each academic year. She was mainly interested in the women but would also like to see the details of the male applicants.

'Do you know the first women's colleges were only founded in the nineteenth century, and women were only allowed to become full members of the University with the right to take a degree in 1920? There was a quota that limited the number of female students to a quarter that of men, a ruling which was not abolished until 1957. Shocking isn't it?' Eddie remarked.

Eddie began to bring boxes of documents for Cathy to look through. 'It's good that you don't have to search the recent years manually. Last year we had more than seventeen thousand people applying for undergraduate study and over twenty thousand people applying for graduate study entry. We only have around three thousand two hundred undergraduate places and approximately four thousand five hundred graduate places per year.

As Cathy sorted through the records it soon became clear that the number of women applicants reduced as she went back in time. It also became clear that there was a bias towards accepting men over women some of whom had clearly scored much higher in the entrance exams. In some cases men, usually with a title in front of their name, had been accepted following dismal exam results. This bore out some of the spiel that Frances Prescott had given them earlier about what used to happen at least.

Due to the records being so well kept it didn't take her long to identify the boxes containing the top scoring students from the thirty years she was interested in. Eddie asked if she would like a cup of tea. She gratefully accepted. The dusty records were making her throat dry. Whilst she sipped the tea with Eddie he talked about the University which he clearly had a great passion for. Cathy wished that she had been clever enough to attend such a wonderful centre of learning but in her heart she knew that even if she had been she just wouldn't have had the self-confidence to see it through.

'Do you think kids today are cleverer than in the past?' Cathy asked.

'It depends how you measure clever,' he replied. 'Do they know more? Yes. Do they have the mental capacity to learn more? No. I doubt the human brain has changed much for hundreds of thousands of years, never mind in the last hundred or so. There's just a lot more to learn now than there used to be and of course knowledge is a lot easier to access nowadays. Think about all the progress man has made in the last one hundred and fifty years. Probably a thousand times more than all the progress that was made prior to that date. The kids today have all this to learn. And every day more and more knowledge is being added. No wonder they feel so stressed sometimes. As time goes by history gets bigger.

Cathy had never thought about it in this way. How much simpler life must have seemed back in Isaac Newton's day.

'Some people believe that the ability to pass on information is probably our species greatest asset. Building on the achievements of our ancestors,' Eddie said.

'How does the saying go ... "standing on the shoulders of giants," Cathy quoted. 'Isaac Newton I believe?'

'Well he certainly used the phrase in a letter he wrote to his fellow-scientist Robert Hooke, acknowledging the debt he owed to other scientists but the earliest recorded use of the expression was by the 12th century theologian and author John of Salisbury who used a version of the phrase in a treatise on logic called *Metalogicon*, written

169

in Latin in 1159. Translations of this difficult book are quite variable but the gist of what Salisbury said is:

> "We are like dwarfs sitting on the shoulders of giants. We see more, and things that are more distant, than they did, not because our sight is superior or because we are taller than they, but because they raise us up, and by their great stature add to ours."

'Did you know the Newton version of the quote is engraved around the edge of the current British £2 coin,' Eddie added.

'No I never noticed.'

Cathy would have loved to chat with Eddie all day but she pulled herself up short and refocused on the task at hand.

The discussion with Eddie gave Cathy a thought.

'Do you get many students from abroad?'

'Yes. Last year the split was about eighty-two percent from the UK and eighteen percent from abroad.'

Who needed a computer when you had access to Eddie?

'How do you assess the foreign applicants? They won't sit the 'A' level exams.'

'We accept their equivalent qualifications and they still have to sit the entrance exams and go through the interview process, although nowadays it's all done via the internet. You have all the results for the years in question in front of you. We sort them on how well they performed but if you want any other statistics I can get them for you but it might take me a bit longer.

'No this is exactly what I need thank you.'

After a few hours Cathy had noted down a list of the most likely candidates from each year including their country of origin to compare against the Missing Persons Database. She was fortunate that a colour photograph accompanied each application. Based on the image she made an assessment on the appearance of each person giving them a score out of ten. A useful pen picture giving an overview of the applicant was provided so she could also see their sporting ability and other interests. Eddie provided photocopies of any relevant documents and also gave her a list of the students who had taken up the offer of a place at the University for each of the years. This allowed Cathy to identify those students who hadn't accepted their place. These were the ones she was most interested in. Of course they could have chosen to go to another University or even dropped out of further education altogether but these were the students who would be least missed in her view.

48

It was late, around seven in the evening, by the time Cathy walked into her three-bedroomed semi in High Wycombe. She could hear the TV on in the lounge. She walked past the door and upstairs to the master bedroom where she changed out of her work clothes. She carefully hung up her jacket and skirt and threw her blouse into the laundry basket. She then dressed in a scruffy tracksuit, instantly transformed from smart business woman into the role of downtrodden wife and mother her family expected her to portray. She was now like one of the many women on her estate that lived a life of drudgery and abuse both mental and physical. Without her work life she did wonder what other options she might be faced with ... but she didn't dwell on this for long as such an exercise depressed her. She tried to put a smile on her face as she walked slowly back down the stairs and opened the lounge door. Three heads turned in her direction. All three had opened beer cans in their hands. Several more empty ones were scattered about the floor.

'Where've you been? We've been sitting here hours waiting for us teas?' Ryan her eldest son said.

'I'm sorry I had to work late,' Cathy tried to explain. The other two merely continued to watch the TV.

She walked over the cluttered floor towards the kitchen. The house had originally had two separate rooms, a lounge and a dining room, but sometime in the seventies, like so many similar semis, they had been knocked through to provide a long single room. Lots of residents had since seen the error of this action as it took away the sanctuary of a second space where a person could escape the constant noise and intrusion of the television and just enjoy the solitude even if only for a moment. They had either re-built the wall or put in place dividing doors that had the additional advantage of allowing the large room to be split or opened up into one large space as circumstances demanded. As with the whole of their house no work had been carried out on it since their first child Ryan had been born in 1989.

An empty can flew across the room in the general direction of small bin provided by Cathy but as so often happened it missed and lay with others on the floor. She didn't look back, she was devoid of reactions.

'Hurry up and make something, we're fucking starving here,' her younger son Todd shouted after her.

Cathy's husband didn't speak. He just continued watching the TV. No greeting to his wife. No asking how her day had been. No reprimand of his unruly children.

Cathy with tears in her eyes entered the small kitchen and turned on the light. It looked like a bomb had gone off in the room. Dirty cups and plates were strewn around covering every surface. Empty crisp and biscuit packets littered the floor ... again near but not in the bin.

She turned on the electric deep-fat fryer and removed a bag of potatoes from the cupboard. They had to be hand cut chips. Brian wouldn't entertain those frozen oven chips. As she peeled the potatoes she thought about her home life. There had been a price to pay for choosing her career over the role of being a mother. A big price. Brian true to his word had given up his job to care for the kids. Though his take on the meaning of the word *care* left a great deal to be desired. He had moulded them in his image giving them all his values without even trying .....because he hadn't tried. Both boys had left school at age sixteen without a qualification to their names. They had gone straight on the dole and showed no interest in finding work. Her earnings went towards their idle lifestyle providing the alcohol, cigarettes and satellite TV that occupied their every waking hour. None of them lifted a finger to help around the house. They expected her to work all day then slave over them each evening. She often asked herself why she put up with it. Why didn't she just leave? She thought the answer was borne out of guilt and that it was her fault, in part at least, they had turned out this way. If she had been maternal she would have wanted to stay at home and look after them properly. Had they sensed her resentment? Had they known that she didn't love them? Maybe this life was her penance for being a bad mother.

Her own parents had stopped talking to her years ago. They thought she should have walked away from her family. How many parents would suggest such a thing? Likewise Brian's parents had fallen out with them and rarely came round. He just wasn't a nice person. Indeed far from it. Always on the cadge, always on the take, always putting himself first and to hell with the consequences for anybody else. When they did show their faces the distasteful look about the untidy house and their constant praise for the successful life Brian's sister had achieved made their departure, usually not too long after their arrival, a relief. It was like they turned up to rub her nose in what could be achieved if you really wanted something badly enough. Cathy knew from personal experience that this wasn't necessarily so.

Cathy made a decision that as soon as the boys left home she would leave Brian. Sometimes it was this thought alone and this hope for the future that sustained her. That day couldn't come soon enough but lately she did wonder if her boys would ever leave home. They were in their mid-twenties now and neither of them showed any sign of leaving.

As she put the chips in the fryer she looked forward to getting back to work in the morning.

49

When McBride returned to the office he ordered a background check on Ms Frances Prescott.

He then phoned Laura Webb, 'I've got a favour to ask, it's not legal and you can say no if you want to?' He went on to explain that he wanted her to hack into Frances Prescott's computer and telephone and see what she could find out.

'I've got no problem with that. No one will ever know I've been in. I'll get back to you with the results in a couple of days.'

McBride emphasised 'This task must remain wholly between us two, nobody else must ever know about it.'

'Of course,' Laura acknowledged.

Putting the phone down he turned to his next task which was to confirm their visit to Cambridge University the following day. He had agreed with Cathy that they would concentrate their efforts on Britain's two leading universities. With Oxford now completed they planned to carry out the same process at Cambridge.

Thirty minutes later he had arranged a time to see the Director of Undergraduate Admissions early the next morning. McBride suggested he pick Cathy up from her home which was on his way but she was adamant that he should collect her from the office where she worked.

The University of Cambridge is very much like Oxford. Both are old established centres of learning that have served the country's elite for over a millennium. Visitors to either city couldn't fail to be impressed by their grandeur. It was hard to tell if the universities were in the city or the cities were in the universities as they were so closely woven together. The two universities had a friendly rivalry which was contested each year by a famous boat race along the river Thames.

Their visit to Cambridge was like Deja vu. The same lecture from the Director of Admissions regarding the now fairer admission policy and the same dusty files in the extensive records department. As before McBride left Cathy to do the analysis work whilst he returned to the office to work on other matters. Cathy said she had no problem catching the train back.

After another long day and an even longer return journey it was even later than the previous day when Cathy arrived home. Anticipating the abuse from her family she had phoned ahead to their local Italian restaurant and arranged the delivery of two twenty inch pepperoni pizzas, their favourite, putting the cost on her credit card. All was quiet when she walked through the front door. The family were happily munching their food with the usual beer cans in hand. She even received a welcoming hello from her two boys. Maybe things were looking up. She was feeling excited about the work she had planned for tomorrow.

50

Cathy Grainger was tired but elated to be back in her comfort zone. She had arrived early in the office as usual, before any of her colleagues. She loved the sanctuary the office gave her. She had worked in the same building since moving to the IT department in the early 1990s. She had however changed rooms several times. Her latest location was at the back of the building overlooking the car park. Not a great view but then Cathy never spent any time gazing out of the window so the view didn't matter. She always had too much work to do which she liked. The building had changed little over the years. Every once in a while painters would arrive and re-paint the walls in the same boring anonymous off-white colour. They just painted over the dirt and dust carrying out little if any preparation. That's professionals for you she thought, a by-word for sloppy in her opinion. The office furniture had changed with the times. In the early days it had been bright orange and muddy browns, the mid-1990 it had changed to bright purples and blues, now it was charcoal greys and blacks. The linoleum floors had long since been covered with cheap, plain carpet.

Another constant change which irritated Cathy was the name of her team. Currently called the National Policing Improvement Agency's Missing Persons Bureau previously under the Serious Organised Crime Agency (SOCA) but now under the remit and forming part of the National Crime Agency (NCA). Cathy preferred to call her team the Cold Case Unit as she felt it reflected what she did which was to deal with older cases that had been consigned to the archives of unsolved investigations.

Some of the changes to her working life had been a great improvement. One of them was computerisation. Back in the 1980s personal computers hadn't been invented. Computer code had to be hand written in pencil on coding sheets. This, in turn, was sent to the typing pool where it was converted into punch-hole tape which could be fed into the enormous mainframe computers. This took days and any errors had to be painstakingly corrected and the whole process gone through again. The 1990s when Cathy had joined the team had been an IT revolution. All staff had been issued with their own Personal Computer. The coding sheets and punch girl staff had been assigned to history. This innovation allowed a programmer to write and run a program in a matter of hours rather than days. Since the 1990s, however, nothing much had changed in the Government IT world. Yes, computers had got faster but the public would be amazed to learn that the majority of the large scale IT systems paying out their weekly benefits and managing their taxes were the same ones that had been written some twenty years earlier.

Probably the biggest step forward, particularly in the field Cathy worked in, was the discovery of DNA. This had revolutionised not only crime solving but had enabled the missing to be easily identified. As so often seems to be the case the tenacity of a single British man had led to a great scientific breakthrough. This is what happened when Alec Jeffreys believed he could create a genetic fingerprint to identify criminals, in this case, the murderer of young women around his home town. The rest is history and the technique spread around the world. The UK National DNA database used to be the largest in the world and has been accredited with aiding the detection of hundreds of thousands of criminals including many for murder and rape. Unfortunately the UK fell foul of article eight of the European Court of Human Rights and was ordered to delete many of the records. If Cathy had her way the entire British population would have their DNA registered on the database but due to civil liberties this was never going to happen. The latest innovative introduced by the Forensic Science Service, was in the use of familial searching. This was the area Cathy had been diligently working on. She was going through the painstaking process of gathering DNA samples from the close relatives of the missing and entering them into the database.

Cathy made herself a cup of tea then lowered herself into her chair and took her laptop out of her bag, clicked it into the docking station on her desk and readied herself for the start of another long day. She brought up the spreadsheet she had started whilst at the University of Oxford and added to yesterday when she visited the University of Cambridge. Next she merged the data with the information she had previously gathered from the records that had already been computerised. She tapped a few keys and the data was transformed into a graph showing each year with girls names allocated to each column followed by the much longer list of the boy names. She then wrote a program to compare the names against those on the Missing

Persons Database. Sure enough each year showed a corresponding one or two names from the Oxbridge entrance exams candidates also listed as a missing person. What stuck Cathy and what could not be explained as a statistical anomaly was the fact that not one boy showed up on both lists, all those missing were female. Not enough to cause anyone to notice the link but over a period of twenty-seven years around thirty girls had gone missing. All the missing girls had scored ten on Cathy's appearance rating and all, except for Rosie Ware, had disappeared prior to taking up their place at university. Next she added the information she had already extracted from the 'A' Level results data. Many of the names were the same but in the early years the numbers taken immediately after their 'A' Level results were greater. After 1987 this switched to girls being taken after their Oxbridge entrance exam results were available and included several foreigners. The total number of missing women, by the time the final draft was complete, had grown to an astonishing thirty-eight women and spanned the period 1984 to 2014. It seemed that this group had been at work for the last thirty years and no-one, including Cathy, had noticed a thing. Another thought struck Cathy. She had only covered the Oxbridge entrance exam. The figure could be even higher if the group had targeted women from other universities as well.

Next Cathy followed up on the idea she had had whilst at Oxford University and logged onto the Internet and accessed one of a growing number of social media sites called LinkedIn. This one was aimed at business people and was mainly used for networking. She entered Frances Prescott's details and read through the brief biography that appeared under her name. During her early career she had worked for the AQA Board of Examiners based in Manchester in the North-West of England before moving to her current post as Director of undergraduate admissions at Oxford University in 1987. The post oversaw the Admissions Testing Service which organised the Oxford entrance exams. This would have given Ms Prescott the perfect opportunity to identify the cream of the crop from each year's academic hopefuls from around the globe. Was it just a coincidence that the choice of girls taken seemed to coincide with her job move? Cathy didn't think so. Maybe it was a female mastermind that they were searching for after all or maybe it was a couple.

Cathy checked to see if the Director of Admissions at the University of Cambridge had a similar career background to that of Frances Prescott. He didn't. In fact he had only been in the post for two years and had moved into the job from an area outside academia. Cathy made a note to ask Eddie Etherington if Frances Prescott had access to the Cambridge entrance exam results. She expected that she would have or that it would take little effort for her to find out.

Cathy typed up her findings. She always preferred doing a written report rather than a verbal one. This allowed her to get the message just right. When she was happy with the result she attached it to an email and sent it to DCI McBride. She would leave it to him as to whether the rest of the Operation Silver Team should see it. It was beyond her pay grade to cast aspersions about Frances Prescott a highly respected public servant, renowned author and public speaker.

Most of the files belonging to the missing women were in storage so Cathy put in a request to retrieve them. The next task for the Operation Silver team would be to reinvestigate each case and try and find a link between them.

Happy with her morning's work Cathy turned her attention to her other missing person cases.

51

Two days later Laura phoned McBride. 'I'm afraid you will be disappointed. I've checked all the emails Frances Prescott has sent and all the telephone conversations she has made. There's nothing remotely suspicious. It's all just routine university stuff and chats with friends and colleagues nothing more.'

'Thanks for checking Laura,' McBride said replacing the receiver but with just a deep seated feeling of disappointment.

He had also had no luck with the associated background check. Prescott didn't even have a parking ticket against her name. She was an advocate for 'saving the planet' and an avid campaigner for reducing the world's population. She had given lectures on the subject around the world; she had even had a couple of books published. This was hardly someone who would be involved in a human breeding program. He remembered that she was due to give a lecture at the university next week. Maybe he would just go along and get a better feel for the woman.

Maybe I misread her reaction to Jennifer's name he thought. Maybe the link Cathy Grainger had uncovered was just a coincidence. He had the feeling he was clutching at straws with this case and he didn't like it. He always liked to drive an investigation forwards. Drive, enthusiasm and commitment were words McBride wouldn't mind appearing on his grave stone. He told himself to ease off before he got himself and possibly others into serious trouble. What had he been thinking deliberately involving Laura in a criminal offence? This smacked of desperation.

52

Monday 10th March 2014 - LONDON

Dan always loved visits to see his therapist Dr Darleen Clutterbuck. He liked the fact that although she had every qualification going she didn't see the need to display a bunch of letters after her name. Initially, he had refused a psychotherapist. Like many other officers on the force, Dan saw the need to discuss his problems as a sign of weakness. He kept it all bottled up but eventually even he realised that if he didn't find someone to talk to he would go mad.

Darleen worked from home, which was an old mansion set in a large garden, in the London borough of Islington. Developers had offered millions for the property but Dee, as she was known to her friends, had refused them all. She didn't want it and she didn't need it. The house had been in her family for generations and had stood through the blitz; there was no way she was going to let it fall into the hands of unscrupulous developers who would no doubt demolish it in favour of a high rise. Dee had inherited the house from her Aunt in the 1970s. She remembered when she received the phone call in Sydney from the family solicitors 'Whittle & Whittle' to tell her that she was the sole beneficiary of her Aunts will. At the time she had expected to make a flying visit to London to settle the estate and then go straight back to Australia. She hadn't intended to stay in London but she had fallen in love with the place. She loved the vibrancy of the City particularly the café and wine bar culture which in her mind underpinned a sense of social cohesion. She adored the museums and galleries in terms of size, scale and content and she worshipped the fifty plus theatres accessible from her new home. In Sydney she'd be lucky to find more than a couple. But as an archetypal Australian what really appealed to her was the sheer variety and diversity of the sports events that frequented the capital. With more than a dozen professional football teams, two world class test cricket venues, Wembley stadium, and the legacy stadia from the 2012 London Olympic Games the range of sporting facilities was fantastic. And all this before she examined the history of the place which oozed out of every pore and which Australia, given its relative youth as a country, just didn't have. The English capital may not have the weather but it certainly had a lot more to compensate it for this one shortcoming.

Darleen had set up her office so that as one patient left from the back door so the next sat in the waiting room and then entered via the front door. The idea was that patients would never meet. It ensured and protected their privacy often at a vulnerable time of their lives. This system had always worked in the years Dan had been attending her practice. He couldn't think of one occasion when he had seen or heard another soul here.

'Come in, come in Dan, lovely to see you,' Dee enthused.

Darleen didn't live up to her surname Clutterbuck, her office was always immaculately tidy.

The room was set out like an archetypal shrinks office with a couch long enough for the patient to lie on and a high backed winged chair where Darleen could observe her prey.

'How have you been? Any more panic attacks?' Dee asked as Dan got comfortable on the couch.

'I've only had one attack since our last session,' Dan replied.

Darleen gazed at Dan. He could see his loneliness reflected in her eyes. He was haunted by memories … but he did manage them better nowadays.

'It's time to move on Dan. You know you are using your grief as a comfort blanket. If you are already hurting you can't be hurt again. If you don't look for a new life or a new love you can't lose it. You can't build a brick wall around your emotions. I know it's frightening but you have to make that step back into the real world. You are ready for it, you just need to be convinced and take the next step.'

'But I don't want to. I like my world. In my world Lucy is still alive or at least real. I go out to the park and play football with Tommy our child. We go on holiday together and walk hand in hand along the beach. We have a golden Labrador named Bruce. I throw sticks into the surf......'

Interrupting Dan's ramblings Darleen tried to bring him back to reality. 'None of it is real Dan. You know this.'

Dan felt some anger bubbling to the surface. He didn't like change. 'How can you appreciate my life and what I have been through? That day, the day of the bombing is like a film playing over and over in my head on a continuous loop …. Just playing over and over again.' Dan held his head in his hands and his anger died away. He wasn't angry with Dee he was angry with the world and how it had dealt him this fatal blow.

Dan had been seeing Darleen since Lucy died. Immediately after the bombing, he had been almost catatonic. Now he could at least function. His brain had managed to compartmentalise. Only at night did everything sometimes get mixed up and on those occasions he woke in panic and confusion. He had reduced his therapy sessions, following Dee's suggestion, to just once a month.

'Do you think you could have saved them?'

'Maybe.'

'How?'

'Well, I could have dealt with the day differently. I could have taken her to the Doctors.'

'Did you ever take her to the doctors for other appointments?'

'No.'

'Then why would you have taken her on that day?'

'I don't know.'

'You do know. If the bombing hadn't happened you wouldn't have thought there had been anything wrong with your actions that day. It would just have been a day like any other. You still wonder if you could have saved them, don't you? Everyone thinks about going back in time and changing an action that took place but that's just not possible.' Darleen was covering old ground she knew but she wanted to challenge Dan's misconceptions as and when they arose. He was less vehement these days in his efforts at self-criticism which Darleen noticed and regarded as progress .... Even if Dan didn't.

'Everyone like you has many cross roads in their life where a different decision would have changed the course of their life but we can't go back in time, we can only move forward. And without blame. I'm not telling you to forget Lucy and your unborn child. Far from it. What I'm telling you is to stop all the inappropriate, unhelpful, punishing self-recriminations and to perhaps take a risk with the rest of your life. Maybe you will love and lose again .... but just maybe you will find a new love and keep it. And to be allowed to love again without guilt is what's needed. It won't be the same relationship you had with Lucy but humans aren't meant to live their lives in solitude. I don't want you to leave this place today and start a new relationship. I just want you to accept that you can. Nothing more.'

Dan didn't answer. He was thinking. He thought more now in the sessions with Dee. Initially, all he did was to react, or explode might have been a more apt description. He wanted Darleen to stop talking even though her voice became quieter and mellower as she spoke and her delivery slowed. He relaxed. He knew what she was saying. He knew it made sense but he still couldn't stop blaming himself. Though maybe now he didn't blame himself as much. Progress?

Finally, he broke the silence, 'I will try but I just don't feel ready at the moment.'

Darleen sighed and smiled. She felt like she has been going in the same or similar circle with Dan for some time. She doubted her sessions with him were achieving a great deal now but she didn't want to let go. She felt like she was keeping the head of a drowning man above water. Sometimes she wondered if she should let him go. Would he sink or swim? But she didn't want to risk it just yet ... but she was getting closer. She told him that she would see him again next month or maybe extend their sessions to six weeks rather than the current four weeks.

At the end of his session, Dan switched seamlessly from patient to policeman and as if to reinforce this moved to the comfy chair at the other side of the office facing Darleen.

'Have you had time to read the case notes I sent you?' he asked.

'Yes, I have a profile for you,' Darleen replied taking a folder from her desk drawer.

'So what are we looking for; a male white supremacist?'

Dee shook her head, 'male most likely, supremacist definitely but white supremacist certainly not. The person who you are looking for is a perfectionist; someone who wants to breed the best, skin colour wouldn't be a factor to this person.'

'So we are looking for someone who is producing designer babies?' Dan asked.

'You could explain it like that but it would always be a baby to his design - beautiful, intelligent, talented, a great personality. He would allow the adoptive parents to choose the hair, eye and skin colour, that wouldn't be important to him. Have you heard of the word eugenics?'

'I think so. Isn't it something to do with genes?'

Darleen pulled a large dictionary from her bookshelf and leafed through it until she found the appropriate page and placed it in front of Dan so that he could read the entry.

> *"Eugenics – the study of methods of improving genetic qualities by selective breeding (especially as applied to human mating)".*

'So he's playing God?'

'Some people may see it that way.'

'Why give the babies away, surely he would want to keep his creations close to him to admire them?'

'Good question. I believe that he knows that to create the ultimate human being children need to be nurtured and cared for within a loving family. He would choose the adoptive parents very carefully. They would be wealthy not just in order to pay for his services but also to provide the best upbringing for the child. They would also be a couple in a strong solid loving relationship. Think of him as a cuckoo placing his offspring into another's nest.'

'So you think he's the father of these children?' Dan queried.

'Not biologically speaking no, in fact, I'd say definitely not,' Dee replied. 'I doubt he would consider himself the ultimate specimen to breed from. He'd be more self-critical than that. He'd only want the best. The choice he is offering the adoptive parents means that effectively he needs to have a range of super humans to readily call upon as the fathers.'

'So who fathers these children, would it be sperm donors?'

'Yes, but not necessarily voluntary ones. He would choose the fathers as carefully as he chooses the mothers. It would, therefore, be highly unlikely that they are all voluntary sperm donors.'

'So how might that work then? Should we be looking for young clever, talented good looking males who have also been abducted?'

'He wouldn't need to abduct them; he would only need to steal a sperm sample. One sperm sample could be used for multiple inseminations.'

'How can you steal a sperm sample ... and do it without the man knowing?'

'Easy, just knock him out and pass an electric current through the right body parts and a male will ejaculate. He'd be a bit sore but completely unaware of what had really happened to him. Then it's just a matter of freezing the sperm and having it on hand when the woman is ready to conceive. The father could have been selected months or years before the mother. Whereas the women are all young and in their prime the fathers are more likely to be older around forty to fifty years old so as to have demonstrated their academic achievement and so allowed them to prove their relative superiority.'

'So this would be the reason Rosie and Laura have the same father even though they were born five years apart?'

'Yes and I expect that they could have many other siblings,' Dee added.

'So I am looking for beautiful, intelligent, talented young women with great personalities who have been abducted and also men who have been assaulted and had their sperm stolen,' Dan clarified.

'Yes, but the men won't necessarily be aware that they have had their sperm stolen. They'll just have been the subject of an assault where they were unconscious for a short time and perhaps had nothing of value taken. In which case they might not even report it to the police. Another point I've put in my report - if you want to find more of the offspring look for wealthy parents with unusually gifted children. Concentrate on parents who only have one or two children.'

'Coming on to Jennifer Shepherd, why kill her?' Dan asked.

Dee looked sad, 'because she was past child bearing age, she was no longer any use to him. As you will have read in her autopsy report she had recently had a hysterectomy – her child bearing days were well and truly over. Think of him as a horse or dog breeder. The aim is to produce a champion, win the Derby, win Crufts. Once an animal is past its useful life it can be disposed of.'

Dan was thoughtful for a moment, 'but why destroy the promising lives of all these women?'

'He is sacrificing one life to produce many … and many of perfection in his eyes. He sees these women as tools, not individuals and will use them accordingly. To this extent sociopathic tendencies are demonstrated. These women will be producing multiple offspring over time. This is their *raison d'etre* and nothing more. They will have a breeding life of twenty years plus with one and possibly, with the use of fertility treatments, two or even three births every year.'

'So do you think he will strike again?'

'Normally I would apply predictive profiling to my assessment. This includes predicting when and where a serial offender might commit his next crime. We know he normally takes girls aged eighteen and we know he normally takes them after they receive their offer of a place at a prestigious university. So there is a window over the summer months where the likelihood of an abduction increases. You could follow the same selection criteria as your offender and then put a round the clock watch on any of the candidates. However, in your case, I doubt he will take another victim this summer. This man is ultra-cautious which is why he has eluded you for so long. He will be well aware of your investigation into the disappearance of Rosie Ware and I expect him to keep a very low profile. You are also in the unfortunate position of not having a living witness to interview. It's amazing what can be gleaned from talking to a victim, for example, a recollection of the attacker's words, smell, mannerisms, and other identifiable traits.'

'Great. So we've got nothing?' Dan said disappointedly.

'No you have a great deal and it was an amazing stroke of luck or great detective work to have been able to link the murder of Jennifer Shepherd with the abduction of Rosie Ware. I'm just saying that catching this person is not going to be easy.'

'So what about this man? What more can you tell me about him?'

'I think you are looking for a wealthy, highly intelligent, white male who is utterly ruthless. He will live a solitary life and I expect he will be single with no children of his own. But don't think of him as antisocial, he will be quite the opposite. In company he will be engaging, likeable and even charming. I expect him to be a popular individual, particularly within academic circles. Assuming he started out on this criminal career around twenty-five or thirty years ago and he was in his late twenties when he started he would be mid to late fifties now. To have so much money at such a young age he would probably have inherited wealth. He would need a very secluded location to hold these women securely for so many years, some place very difficult to escape from.'

'Wouldn't he need medical personnel to run a large maternity clinic like this?'

'Yes, but not many .... maybe he himself is a Doctor or has had some form of medical training. I suspect he would keep the number of staff employed to an absolute minimum. This man likes to keep control and to do this means the fewer people who are involved the more control he has. He might even use the women themselves to run the facility. Remember these are highly intelligent individuals. They could be trained to carry out all the necessary procedures.'

'Why would they be complicit, surely they would rebel?'

'He must have some sort of hold over them; I can't really answer that without more information. There's one more thing. He took a big risk abducting the daughter of one of his victims. As you know this has given you the only lead in this case. I think that Jennifer was very special to him and possibly he couldn't bear losing her lineage. It's a bit like an animal breeder keeping the best of the litter to continue breeding from. Maybe his discipline is slipping from that high or perfect pedestal that it's been on all these years. This makes him potentially more volatile and unpredictable.'

'So you think Rosie has been abducted to breed from?'

'I do. He thinks he has what he considers to be a perfect specimen and will want to continue the line. To increase the chances of producing an intelligent, blue-eyed blonde child he will have selected a father with the same attributes. I suggest you look for a very smart, blond, blue-eyed male that has been chosen to father her children. Look at assault cases from the last couple of years especially where nothing of value was stolen.'

'Thanks Dee, your profile and insight have been really useful, as expected.'

All that Dee had told him only strengthened his belief that Maximilian Schütte-Rainer III was somehow involved with this case all apart from the fact that Rainer was married and had children which Dan chose to overlook. In his view Dee had described Rainer's personality down to a tee. He had to find a way of obtaining a DNA sample to compare against that found in the dog bite.

53

At the next morning briefing for the Operation Silver team, Dan reported back on the profile that Darleen had prepared for them issuing brief bullet pointed hard copies to inform the team as well as utilising the evidence board to record and talk through each of the key traits she'd identified.

McBride was pleased with the provision of this insightful additional information and the new leads this gave them.

'Cathy, can you just concentrate on female kidnappings from now on. The male line doesn't appear to be getting us anywhere as we haven't identified one male who meets the selection criteria who has been abducted. I want the rest of you to look into assaults on males who are highly intelligent, white skinned, have natural blond hair, blue eyes and are aged between thirty-five and fifty-five. Particularly those where there was no motive found. If we can find the man selected to be the father of Rosie's children it may give us some new leads,' McBride told the group.

'Dr Clutterbuck suggests that we look for exceptionally bright children. Any ideas about how we can go about this?'

'I'll look into it,' said Anthea Bowker.

McBride held Anthea in his gaze, 'Have you heard anything back from Apple about the location of Rosie's iPad yet?'

'They got back to me but only to confirm that it hasn't been used since Rosie went missing. I think we have to assume that it has been destroyed or disposed of. Another dead-end I'm afraid. They'll keep monitoring and let us know if it does come back online.'

'Any update on the Jacqui Bates case, the woman on Laura's list who wasn't on Cathy's list of missing persons.

'Yes sir. It was closed about two weeks ago. The girl, Jacqui Bates, went missing in 2001. It turns out that she returned home after three weeks. She ran off with some bloke and he seems to have dumped her after a couple of days. It must have taken her the rest of the time to pluck up the courage to go home. Nobody thought to inform us and the case stayed open. Miss Bates applied for a job with the Home Office recently and a Criminal Records Bureau check was carried out on her. She was flagged up as a missing person case. The error was corrected and the case closed. That's why Cathy didn't have it on her database but at the time Laura compiled her list it was still an open active missing person's case. I don't think her disappearance is connected to our case. There are similarities but also some marked differences.'

'And what are those?'

'Well, she certainly met all the criteria to be kidnapped. She was beautiful and very intelligent. She was studying for a PhD at Cambridge at the time. However, she was older than the other victims. She was twenty-two when she disappeared. She went willingly with this man and he allowed her to return to her home safely after they split.'

'We know that Rosie was also an anomaly. She was also older than the other girls. She was the only one who was actually attending university at the time of her abduction. It might not lead us anywhere but I want to know why this other girl met all the criteria and wasn't taken. Let's just dig a bit further if we can to make sure there really isn't a connection. Arrange an interview with her will you please.'

McBride changed his focus of attention to Rod Hartley. 'Any progress with the dog bite victims?'

'All of them have been followed up and eliminated. Of course, we are getting new ones reported every day.'

'Cancel the request. If he hasn't presented himself to a hospital by now I doubt he will. We have to assume that either the bite wasn't too severe or he has access to his own medical treatment. Given the insight Dr Clutterbuck has given us I expect he has the resources and ability to treat his own wound.'

'What about the search for where these women could be being held?'

'I'm flying to the Isle of Sky in Scotland this afternoon. I'm following up on a lead regarding an old mental hospital that was closed down in the 1960s. The local police have received many reports over the years from locals claiming that the place is haunted by screaming women and crying babies.'

'If there's any truth in the reports let me know immediately.'

On the table at the front of the room sat a large pile of dusty files, some looking more aged than others. 'These are the missing person files for the women Cathy has identified so far.' Nodding towards WPC Chrissy Prendergast and DC Anthea Bowker, 'I've asked Chrissy and Anthea to go through all the files and make copies of each woman's photo profile and add them to the whiteboard. When we have them all together we can try and identify common traits by which this man is selecting his victims. I will go through the details of each associated investigation and try and identify any useful links.' Going through thirty-eight files would mean burning a lot of midnight oil but McBride felt that the task should fall to one person else clues might be missed. As the rest of the team were already fully occupied and had their own tasks to concentrate on he felt he was the only choice for this job. Mrs McBride wouldn't be happy about him working even longer days but sometimes the job just had to come first.

54

McBride removed his reading glasses and rubbed at his tired eyes. It was two in the morning. He had been reading the missing persons files for the last eight hours with just a short break to grab a bite to eat. He currently had file number five open in front of him. A stunning redhead gazed sexily from a ten by twelve inch photo, caught forever in the moment of blowing a kiss in the direction of the photographer. She oozed class. She wore a long emerald green evening dress that clung to her tall willowy figure and perfectly matched her bright intelligent eyes. A cliché but she truly was the picture of happiness. McBride turned the photo over. On the back was printed Kelly O'Connor, Aged eighteen, St Mary's School Summer Ball August 1984, Belfast, Northern Ireland. According to the police report, this was the last night anyone had seen Kelly. One minute she had been dancing at the ball. The next gone. Disappeared. Similar to the other girls from the previous four files he had read through. No clues - nothing.

In McBride's experience, for most crimes, the victim knows their assailant. Either a family member or an acquaintance, a work colleague, a friend of a friend, often the association is distant and unrequited, but it is there – the link. This is what gives the police investigation the clues to follow. They can delve into a person's life, into their past, follow the threads until it brings them to that link and the motive because there's always a motive, whether it be jealousy, greed, love, hate or even cruelty. McBride had seen it all. What struck him about the five case files he had read was not just that all the women were young, beautiful and intelligent but that the link wasn't there. Not one suspect had been identified from any of the cases. When a victim is targeted by a complete stranger the police have nowhere to go they can only rely on the bad luck of the criminal. In these cases the abductions had gone off without a hitch. Either the person they were looking for was very lucky or extremely clever. Nobody's luck held for over thirty years. McBride's belief that they were looking for a criminal mastermind was strengthened. This didn't give him a warm feeling and he felt he was letting these women down. They were out there somewhere, waiting, hoping that someone like him could free them from their prison, from their anguish. So far he had failed but he wouldn't give up.

Replacing his glasses McBride closed the file and took the next one from the pile. It was going to be a long night.

When Jane McBride looked for her husband the next morning she found him fast asleep face down on top of the file he had been reading. She returned ten minutes later and placed a cup of coffee on the table next to him and gently shook him awake. She knew her husband wouldn't thank her for letting him oversleep. When a case like this came along it consumed him one hundred percent. Over the years Jane had learned to be patient, his work was his mistress and he wouldn't return to his family until he had either caught the criminal or exhausted all leads in his quest for justice.

Smiling at his understanding wife McBride carried the steaming coffee through the patio doors and into the garden breathing in the still frigid - dew filled air. Ignoring the early morning chill he sat on a wooden garden bench and lit a cigarette, hungrily sucking in the smoke eager to get his first nicotine fix of the day. The first cigarette of the day – always the best in his opinion. He had cut down on his habit over the years but couldn't give up this morning ritual much to the chagrin of his family. Taking his habit into the garden had been his only concession.

So what had he learned from the files last night? Not a lot. Nothing that would give them the lead they were looking for.

55

Tuesday 11th March 2014 - LONDON

Dan was up early. He stood in a doorway across and down the road from Maximilian Schütte-Rainer III's house waiting for him to appear. He didn't have to wait long; Max was also an early riser as he suspected he would be given the emphasis he'd placed on the value of having a work ethic. It was only a twenty minutes stroll from Max's house to the Austrian embassy where he worked but Max didn't hang around. He seemed to want to get his early morning fix of aerobic fitness.

Dan followed discreetly, keeping a safe distance, as Rainer strode confidently towards the embassy. He didn't go straight there. He stopped at a small café en route and sat at one of the outside tables drinking what looked like a coffee whilst speaking on his mobile phone. Dan wished he could get close enough to hear the conversation but the café was too small for him to enter unnoticed. He sat for a further ten minutes reading his newspaper in the light coming from the café window then he picked up his briefcase and continued his journey.

As soon as the coast was clear Dan made his way across to the café and sat in the seat that Rainer had just vacated. Pulling an evidence bag from his pocket he carefully pocketed the coffee cup Max Rainer had used. The waiter approached to take his order and clear the table. He looked puzzled at the saucer sitting alone on the table but didn't ask Dan where the missing cup had gone. Dan pretended to answer his mobile and breaking off from the call told the waiter that he had an urgent errand to run and couldn't stay after all.

On his way to the station, Dan deposited the porcelain coffee cup at the lab and asked them to look for a DNA sample and fingerprints.

56

Wednesday 12th March 2014 - LONDON

McBride had asked Dan if he would interview Jacqui Bates as she worked in London not far from his office. Now in her mid-thirties, she hadn't lost any of her good looks. Dan felt like a young schoolboy as he gazed across the desk at her. She was tall, slim with sleek black hair. She had large almond shaped eyes in a shade of hazel he had never seen before.

'I understand this is about the time I ran away from home but I don't understand why? I was just a silly young girl back then. I became infatuated with an older man. My parents wouldn't have understood. I had my whole life in front of me - a place at Cambridge University. Why throw it all away for a man? But I would have given it all up to be with him. I loved him. Really loved him.'

'So what went wrong?' Dan couldn't believe any man would walk away from this woman and so quickly after they appeared to have run away together.

'I mentioned that I couldn't have children. I have a rare condition. I was born without ovaries. It was as if a switch went off between us. I didn't think he would be that bothered. He was older than me in his forties. I thought he would already have had a family but it's not something we discussed in any detail before we went off together. I couldn't have been more wrong. He was so angry. I'd never seen him like that before. He told me we were finished. I never saw him again. I stayed in the cottage we had rented for the three weeks. When my money ran out I returned to my parents. You know the rest. I tried to trace him but everything he had told me was a lie. He didn't live or work where he told me. He was just an enigma.'

'I'd like you to work with a sketch artist to give us a description of the man. Also, I'll need a detailed statement. Maybe not all he told you was a lie.'

'But why are you so interested in him now after all this time?'

'He may be involved in another missing person only this time the decision to go away together may not have been mutual.' Dan left it at that.

57

Dan looked at the face drawn by the sketch artist. It bore no resemblance to Maximilian Schütte-Rainer III. The man featured in the sketch had dark hair and brown eyes. It did, however, bear an uncanny likeness to the man the women in Brighton had met during the scam surrounding Rosie Ware's birth. He had a copy of the sketch scanned and emailed to the Brighton police headquarters and asked them to show it to Irma Barras and the midwife Stella Hodson to get confirmation that this was indeed the same guy.

The good news was that the results from the coffee cup had come back. The lab had found DNA from Count Maximilian Schütte-Rainer III, to give him his full title. The bad news was that it didn't match the DNA taken from the dog bite. So it cleared him of the Rosie Ware abduction. His finger prints didn't match anything on their systems. Not a good result.

Everything seemed to be a dead-end as far as Max was concerned but Dan couldn't get away from the thought that Max Rainer was somehow involved in this case. Was it just a copper's gut instinct? And more importantly was it right or was it just wishful thinking on Dan's part as he so disliked the man?

He had spoken with DCI Chris Holman earlier and arranged to meet him at an office overlooking the St Katharine Docks. His team were clearing out their surveillance point and DCI Holman had graciously allowed Dan to look at their reconnaissance from the stakeout. Dan received a frosty reception from the team but was given a box containing hundreds of photographs that had been taken around the docks with the date and time on the back of each. Luckily the photos were well catalogued and sorted in chronological order so he could go straight to the time around which Jennifer Shepherd's body had been found. He slowly scanned each photograph. Most showed Miklos Orban and his comings and goings on and around The Black Serpent. When he came to the jackpot photo he nearly missed it but then he saw in the top right-hand corner a couple with their arms around each other. The woman had long blonde hair and had her head resting on the man's shoulder. The man, dressed as Lawrence the down-and-out had described, seemed to be supporting the woman as they walked along the quay away from the boat Perfection. Bingo – at last he believed he had evidence that Jennifer Shepherd had been brought here by boat. Now he should be able to get his search warrant to look for evidence that she had indeed been on the Perfection.

He spent a further two hours carefully looking through the rest of the photographs but they didn't reveal anything else of significance. There was no trace of the man returning alone to the Perfection. Taking the single snapshot he decided to send it to Photographic Services to ask them to enlarge the relevant section. Maybe they could get a better image of their suspect and establish a few other relevant parameters such as height, weight and age.

'No, no, no. I won't sign a request for a search warrant for the boat Perfection. Do you want to cause a diplomatic row?' Chief Superintendent Danny Hughes said slamming the photo down onto his desk. 'This photo may prove Jennifer Shepherd was at St Katharine Docks but it in no way proves she was brought there by boat never mind on that boat. She could just have easily been staying in The Tower Hotel next door or have been in one of the restaurants.'

'But sir she must have been. They could only have been walking away from one of the boats. There's nothing else along that side of the quay. I've already established that only three boats docked that night and I've already ruled out the other two. The Perfection is the only one left. I've spoken with all the restaurants and all of them had long since closed by the time in question. I've also checked the video footage and guest list from the hotel and no-one left around that time.'

'If the boat was owned by anyone else then I'd sign the request but I'm not putting my reputation on the line for another one of your hunches. I need more, much more.'

'So you are saying that some people are above the law, sir?'

'That's exactly what I'm saying. Now drop this. Unless you get something more compelling I don't want to hear anything more about it. Not that I'm convinced we'd get access to the boat in any event without some level of international wrangling.'

58

Thursday 13th March 2014 - OXFORD

The enlarged photo of the couple leaving the dock area was pinned onto the Operation Silver crime investigation whiteboard alongside the sketch drawings provided by Irma Barras, Stella Hodson and Jacqui Bates. The obvious likeness dispelled any doubt that this was the same man.

'Why didn't he eliminate these three witnesses?' McBride asked more to himself than to the team. 'We know how ruthless he is from the fact that he killed the old man just to get a dog.'

Emma Blakely gave her thoughts. 'I don't think he wanted to draw any attention to Irma Barras and the midwife Stella Hodson. Any police investigation might have led to the unlawful acts surrounding Rosie Ware's birth being uncovered. He probably thought it highly unlikely that we would ever find out about the scam. He would have been right too. It's only because he abducted Rosie that we found the link.'

'What about Jacqui Bates. Why didn't he kill her? We know from what she told us that he had covered his tracks and she couldn't find any trace of him. Why not eliminate her just in case?'

'I suspect for similar reasons. For one thing, she couldn't give any useful information about him as everything he had told her was a lie. For another it would have instigated a heavy police investigation. He believed he was safe. I also wonder whether he might not have been able to bring himself to destroy such a beautiful young girl. We know how much he prizes gorgeous women. Well, that's just my thoughts on it sir,' Emma said. 'Sir. Isn't there anything you can do to assist Dan in getting a search warrant for that boat?'

'I've raised it with Chief Superintendent Mike Harding. He's going to see what he can do but he doesn't hold out much hope. It seems diplomatic immunity trumps everything no matter what justification for a warrant we might be able to cobble together. In the mean time, I suggest that we just carry on with the investigation as best we can.'

McBride looked towards Anthea Bowker, 'How's the search for parents with exceptionally gifted children going?'

'Slowly,' she replied. 'It's really difficult to identify child prodigies. I've been concentrating on two areas. One is applications to join MENSA for people under the age of sixteen. I've hit a brick wall there as they won't release details of their members without a court order. The second is the annual Child Genius competition. This is a competition where parents pit the intelligence of their children against others from around the country. The next competition is being held in Appleby next week. I thought I would go along.'

'Good idea. Take Detective Sergeant Hartley along with you.'

Turning back to the assembled team he asked for their progress on the case.

Assaults on males that matched several of the key points of the profile were numerous but none of them seemed to match all the criteria. They had one really hopeful lead but it turned out that the guy, a top neurosurgeon dyed his hair and was not a natural blond. The vagaries not just of youth it seemed.

Thinking back to Gary's stupid comment, and there were many to choose from, about the dog sperm got Emma thinking. 'Maybe we have to widen our search,' she said. 'Surely it's possible that the sperm donation came from abroad. It could have been frozen and dispatched to the UK from anywhere in the world just like they do for livestock inseminations.'

'Good thinking,' McBride agreed. 'Now we just need to find a way to identify the most brilliant male specimens in the world and see if they have ever been assaulted. Where do you suppose we start with that?'

'We could look at Nobel prize winners,' someone suggested.

'That would be a start but perhaps a little too obvious, get on to it see what you can come up with,' McBride directed with a heavy sigh.

DC Anthea Bowker replaced the telephone receiver and let out a whoop of delight. Her fellow officers stopped what they were doing and looked in her direction. 'That was Apple. Rosie Ware's iPad has just come online.' It had been several weeks with no activity and now, at last, they had a lead. The guys at Apple had even managed to activate the camera on the machine and had agreed to email a photo of the person who had used the iPad. The team now stood anxiously around Anthea's PC waiting for the promised email and photo to arrive. They didn't yet know if it was a male or female or if it might be Rosie herself. As soon as the email pinged into her inbox Anthea ignored the text, most of which was taken up with the normal corporate small print relating to copyright infringements, and opened the single attachment. The photo started to slowly display on the screen starting from the top and infuriatingly adding only a few lines of detail at a time but the quality was excellent. When the hair came into view they knew immediately that it wasn't going to be a picture of Rosie Ware. The hair was dark peppered with grey. Could this be their suspect? As the face gradually appeared it revealed the lined and weathered face of an elderly gentleman with a look of intense concentration on his face.

'Well he doesn't look like a criminal mastermind who could pull off a high-profile kidnapping,' DS Rod Hartley said. 'Does the email give us a location from where the transmission was sent?'

Anthea went back to the text of the email, 'It gives an address – Bennett Crescent over at Cowley.'

'I know that area it's near the BMW Mini factory on the outskirts of Oxford,' Chrissy Prendergast added. 'It's a cul-de-sac containing apartments and town houses. I had a boyfriend once who lived there.'

McBride now stood behind the team attracted out of his office by all the excitement. They discussed the next steps. Should they obtain a search warrant and go round to the house all guns blazing or just casually visit the house and question the old man? The man could have innocently come across the iPad or on the other hand, he could have Rosie locked up somewhere within the building.

'Can you get up Google street view to give us an idea of the layout of the area? I want to know if we can seal it off if this man decides to make a run for it.'

Two minutes later they had a view of the area. There was only one entrance into the crescent. The road ran in a circle with apartments in the centre and three-storey town houses around the edge. Number eighty-six where the signal had come from was one of the town houses. It was located just off to the right of the entrance road.

'It looks easy enough to seal off,' McBride commented. 'Anthea, can you find out who lives there?'

Anthea logged onto the electoral register for the Cowley area. 'There seems to be a number of people living there but only one man around the right age. His name is Michael O'Shea.'

'Check if he has a record. Also, check the other people living there. I want to know what we are up against before we go in.'

Nobody living there had a criminal record in the UK although a couple of the occupants had foreign sounding names so the team couldn't be sure if they had committed any crimes back in their homeland. Anthea checked Michael O'shea's photograph from his driving license held by DVLA and confirmed he was indeed their man.

With the evidence they had McBride made the call to take a softly-softly approach. Taking two cars containing eight officers they made their way along the A4142 Oxford ring road. Just past the BMW car factory, Chrissy Prendergast told the lead car to take the slip road onto a large roundabout. The second car followed closely behind. A large Tesco superstore was off the first exit, the second would take them back onto the ring road. They continued round to the third exit and came off onto another main road.

'Go straight across the first roundabout then at the traffic lights turn right and Bennett Crescent is first left,' Chrissy explained.

The two cars pulled into the entrance to the Crescent and parked abreast blocking off the access. The officers piled out of the cars and split into pairs. The operation had been coordinated before they left the station and the officers silently went to their preordained positions. All the officers wore stab vests under their plain clothes. McBride and Emma Blakely had been elected to approach the house. A silver Toyota Yaris sat on the gravel drive which indicated that perhaps someone was home. McBride rang the bell. The door was opened after only about thirty seconds and McBride and Emma came face to face with the man they had seen in the photograph. He was smaller than they expected and didn't look at all threatening.

'Are you here about my spare room?' he said eyeing Emma up and ignoring McBride completely. Seeing their confusion, 'you have come about the spare room I advertised on Gumtree?'

'No, we are here about a stolen iPad you have been using,' McBride said showing Michael O'Shea his identification. 'Mind if we come in for a moment?'

O'Shea looked more disappointed that Emma wasn't going to take his spare room than worried that he was in possession of stolen property. Reluctantly he opened the door and ushered them through the hall and kitchen and into a sunny conservatory at the rear of the property. The furniture was all a bit tatty and consisted of two settees and a low coffee table that needed a good clean as it was covered in cup rings and stains. At the end sat the iPad which was plugged into a nearby socket. Michael O'Shea went to pick it up but McBride stopped him. He didn't want even more contamination of the forensic evidence they may find.

'So who lives in the house with you?' Emma asked.

'Mainly young professionals but there is one student. They are all legal if you are implying I've broken the law. I check all their credentials. You can't be too careful these days. I was alone in this large house when the kids left home and my wife died so I let out the spare bedrooms. I've currently got a nice bunch of youngsters and they keep me company. It's so hard for people to buy their own homes these days. This country has gone back to the Victorian days where lots of people have to share one home. Shameful really.'

'Would it be OK if DS Blakely takes a look around?' McBride didn't think O'Shea was lying but he didn't want to take any chances. For all he knew Rosie Ware could be gagged and tied up somewhere.

'Be my guest but you won't find anything. Well, you won't find anything as far as I know; I can't vouch for what my lodgers get up to in their rooms.'

'Are any of them at home at the moment,' Emma asked.

'No, they're all at work or college.'

Emma got up and went to take a look around.

'See what you think of my spare room. It's the first one on the left at the top of the stairs,' O'Shea added hopefully.

McBride turned to Michael O'Shea. 'Tell me where and when you got the iPad.'

'I found it a few weeks ago. It was just sat on the grass verge next to the A40. It looked as if someone had thrown it out of a car window. I thought at first it was broken as it wouldn't turn on but one of the lads here thought the battery was just flat. I didn't have a charger so I had to order one off eBay. It arrived this morning and I plugged it in. I don't really know how to work these sort of things but I thought it might be useful to Skype the grandchildren. They are always on at me to get online. I have the internet here for the lodgers. You can't rent rooms without it nowadays.'

'Didn't you think to hand it into the police?'

'Well, I wanted to see if it worked first. No point getting it back if it isn't claimed if it's broken is there?'

McBride gave him the scathing look this lie deserved. He was sure he had no intention of handing in the iPad to the police. McBride knew this would be impossible to prove and he suspected O'Shea did also. He wouldn't have forked out for the charger if he hadn't intended to keep the machine. He probably had no idea it could be traced. Even McBride had no idea this function was available. 'Didn't you see the appeal on the news asking for the whereabouts of an iPad relating to the Rosie Ware kidnapping case?'

'Appeal? Rosie Ware kidnapping case? No,' he repeated McBride's words.

Emma returned shaking her head to indicate that she hadn't found anything suspicious in the rest of the house.

'Bag that up and we'll take it with us,' he said nodding towards the iPad.

Emma donned plastic gloves and took a large evidence bag from her pocket and carefully wrapped the iPad.

'You won't take the charger will you?' O'Shea asked. 'I did pay for that I've got the receipt if you want to see it.'

'No you can keep the charger but it won't be much good without a machine to charge,' McBride replied sarcastically.

'Won't I get it back if it's not claimed,' he asked hopefully.

'No you won't get it back as we know who it belongs to,' McBride said with some satisfaction. 'Now we just need to take your fingerprints so we can eliminate them. Did anyone else touch the iPad to your knowledge?'

'No I kept it locked away. You can't be too careful these days.'

'I also need to know exactly where you found it on the A40. If I bring up a picture on Google maps do you think you will be able to pinpoint the exact location?'

Now resigned to the loss of his find and the expense he had incurred O'Shea nodded his head. Emma took out her own iPad and brought up a map of the area. O'Shea indicated exactly where the iPad had been. She then logged into the fingerprinting system and asked O'Shea to place his hand on the machine as it scanned in his prints.

As they left the house and collected the rest of the team McBride asked Emma to organise a search of the area where O'Shea had found the iPad. It was a long shot but perhaps other evidence might be found. Rosie's backpack was still missing.

McBride read the forensics report and thumped his fist on his desk in frustration. The only useable prints belonged to Rosie Ware and Michael O'Shea. Another dead-end. The search of the area where the iPad had been found hadn't turned up anything either. He felt they were doing everything right but getting nowhere. He was running out of ideas. He decided to run it past the rest of the team maybe someone could come up with something.

'At least it shows the direction he was heading in,' DS Rod Hartley said. He made three marks on the map of Oxfordshire that was pinned on the wall. The first showed the location where Rosie was abducted. The second where the bike and dog collar were found at Woodford Farm. The third where the iPad was located. 'It looks to me that he's heading north.'

'I can see why he didn't leave the bike and rucksack at the abduction site. He would have wanted to delay the start of any investigation as long as possible but why didn't he throw the rucksack into the field along with the bike and the dog collar. Why hang onto the iPad and leave it in another location and why keep the rucksack?' McBride pondered.

Emma gave her thoughts. 'We know he was bitten by the dog; perhaps he'd got blood on the rucksack so he didn't want us to find it.'

'That's a possibility but it doesn't explain why he would dispose of the iPad separately.'

'Maybe he got disturbed whilst he was throwing the bike and dog collar away and didn't have time to get rid of the rucksack,' Chrissy Prendergast suggested.

'Again a possibility,' accepted McBride still thinking.

Anthea Bowker came up with the most plausible scenario, 'I think he wanted Rosie to keep some of her possessions like her diary and the photo of her parents. He only disposed of the iPad because he knew its location could be traced.'

'It still doesn't answer the question why he left it where he did,' McBride said. 'Maybe it's like a trail of breadcrumbs leading us in the wrong direction. If we think he's gone north we will look in that direction but maybe he doubled back and actually headed south. We already know how careful he is – he doesn't make mistakes. He might expect us to find the bike and iPad eventually so he has used these to his advantage - as a red herring.'

'So we thought we had the idea that he went north but now we think he may have gone south but we aren't sure,' Rod Hartley said despondently.

'Errm.. seems so. Which puts us right back to square one.'

59

McBride slipped on his coat. Tonight was the night Frances Prescott was due to give her lecture. Although he had told himself Frances Prescott wasn't involved maybe her life was just a smokescreen for her criminal activities. At two million a pop this designer baby racket was potentially big business. It wouldn't do any harm to keep her under investigation. He was also quite interested in what she might have to say. She had the perfect opportunity to identify the girls that met the desired criteria and she had worked in the right jobs at the relevant times. Too much of a coincidence in McBride's book.

McBride stood at the back of the lecture hall. He reckoned it could have held about five hundred people seated but the number attending was more like six hundred with the overflow standing at the back and sides of the room. She was obviously a very popular speaker or her subject matter was. Frances Prescott walked out onto the stage and a polite ripple of applause greeted her arrival. She strode confidently to the centre and stood behind a clear plastic lectern placing her notes down in front of her. She acknowledged those attending with a slight smile and took a few confident moments to arrange her notes. A vision in a long flowing flaming red evening gown, she was dressed to be seen as if fearing that had she worn monochrome attire she might have just blended into the plainness of the stage on which she stood. He half expected her to produce a violin and start playing The Storm by Antonio Vivaldi. Clearing her throat she welcomed her audience and the chattering from the onlookers dwindled to a discreet hum.

She immediately threw a question out to her listeners, 'What do you think is the greatest risk to human life on this planet?'

A young girl of Chinese origin put her hand in the air. Frances Prescott nodded for her to answer.

'Well, it has to be global warming.'

'No it isn't,' came Frances's response quickly and dismissively to the crestfallen student. 'The earth has warmed and cooled throughout its history. This obsession scientists have with global warming is just that – an obsession and nothing more.'

'The earth being invaded by aliens,' a lad shouted from the back causing a ripple of laughter.

Keeping to the space theme another lad called out, 'Being hit by an asteroid.'

'What you personally or an asteroid like the one that wiped out the dinosaurs,' his mate sitting next to him added. More laughter filled the room.

Other answers followed including the deadly Ebola virus spreading around the world, a nuclear holocaust and an Islamic backed uprising by the Middle Eastern countries.

McBride was impressed by how engaged the undergraduates were.

All your answers are a distinct possibility but none of them represents an immediate threat. The answer to the question 'What is the greatest risk to human life on this planet? Is Homo-Sapiens.'

'What us?' someone shouted. 'How can that be? Why would we want to destroy the planet?'

'Have you ever heard of the saying "the world is paved with good intentions"? The fight against AIDS, malaria, starvation; the introduction of IVF, the extension of the human lifespan. You can even include antibiotics in the list. All have primarily achieved an increase in the world's population. Behind her a screen had descended and a slide flashed up on the display showing a graph. She turned to the graph and with a pointer indicated the horizontal line at the bottom. 'This shows the years from 1600 to 2060.' Pointing next to the vertical line, 'this shows an estimate of the human population for each of the years. Pointing to the red line starting on the left-hand side, 'as you can see for the first few hundred years there is very little change to the total human population. War, disease, hunger kept the population in check.' Pointing to 1960. 'This is where it started to go wrong.' The graph clearly showed a rapid rise. By 2060 it had gone off the top of the graph.

Now pointing to the top right-hand side of the chart, 'When it reaches this level mankind is doomed. The world can no longer sustain the population.'

A second slide replaced the first. This showed a flattened map of the world. Along the top, on the left, it showed the date followed by the total human population followed by the total number of major life forms on the planet. 'The red dots on each country indicate the human population. Next, you will see a simulation showing the future of the planet if nothing is done to slow the relentless growth of the human population,'

The date on the left climbed ten, twenty, thirty years as did the human population figure in the middle whilst the figure at the end predicting the number of other life forms on the planet reduced at an alarming speed. The red dots spread across the different countries, some faster than others. When the date reached 2060 the human population total started to drop alarmingly.

This is the time when all food resources have been consumed and the human population starts to starve to death. All the forests, oil, coal and minerals have gone. By this time the only thing left to eat is other humans so mass cannibalisation commences. Is this a future you want your descendants to experience?'

The room was hushed. Some students seemed to be genuinely intrigued by the severity of the potential outcome even if on the alarmist side.

'Surely scientists can invent new food sources?' one student asked.

'Yes, productivity in food production has increased massively in recent years. It will slow down the reduction in the world's food stocks but it can't reverse it. Only one thing can prevent this outcome and that's control of the world's population. Before it's too late we have to put safeguards in place.'

'What like the Chinese did with their one child policy?'

'Yes, that's one solution. We have to get away from people thinking it's their right to breed.'

'Didn't I read that the population of most European countries is actually falling?' another young man stated.

'Yes, this is true but the human population is increasing much more than this in other areas.'

'So we will be OK if we stay in Europe?' the same young man asked.

'For the time being but what happens when Africa, the Middle-East and America run out of food. Do you think they are going to sit there and go hungry? No, they are going to take from the countries that have the food. The tide of humanity flooding into Europe will be like a tsunami. It could be likened to a plague of locusts destroying everything in its path. It will be like the tide coming in. Once it starts it will be unstoppable and I believe irrecoverable. It will consume everything in its path. With this mass movement of humanity, anarchy will rule, the weak will be crushed and civilisation as we know it will be at an end. It will be the modern equivalent to the end of the Roman Empire but on a much larger global scale. A new world order will dominate and it won't be for the better. The new Dark Ages are likely to begin.'

'But we don't hear of famine nowadays apart from those in Africa. There hasn't been anything like that since the potato famine in Ireland,' one student stated.

'Would it surprise you that since the Irish Potato Famine there have been seven others around the world that would dwarf the number of people who died in Ireland?' As if Frances Prescott had anticipated the question she projected another slide onto the screen.

'This is a list of the worst ten famines on record. Would it shock you to learn that seven of these occurred during the 20th century? It certainly surprised me. Until I did this research, like you I'd only heard of the Irish Famine.'

Great Chinese Famine 1958 to 1962
Forty-Three million dead
In China during 1958 as part of their "Great Leap Forward", the owning of private land was outlawed. Communal farming was implemented in an attempt to increase crop production. More relevant, however, was the importance the Communist Regime placed on iron and steel production. Millions of agricultural workers were forcibly removed from their fields and sent to factories to create metal.

In addition to these fatal errors, Chinese officials mandated new methods of planting. Seeds were to be planted three to five feet under the soil, extremely close together, to maximize growth and efficiency. In practice, what little seed sprouted was severely stunted in growth due to overcrowding. These failed policies, teamed with a flood in 1959 and a drought in 1960, affected the entire country. By the time the Great Leap Forward had ended in 1962 an estimated forty-three million Chinese had died from the famine.

Chinese Famine of 1907
Twenty-Five million dead
East-Central China was reeling from a series of poor harvests when a massive storm flooded forty thousand square miles of lush agricultural territory, destroying one hundred percent of the crops in the region. Food riots took place daily and were often quelled through the use of deadly force. It is estimated that, on a good day, only five thousand were dying due to starvation.

Chalisa famine - 1783
Eleven million dead
The Chalisa famine refers to the year in the Vikram Samvat calendar used in Northern India. Occurring in 1783, the region suffered from an unusually dry year, as a shift in the El Nino weather system brought significantly less rain to the region. Vast swaths of crops withered and died, and livestock perished due to lack of food and drinking water. The tumultuous year killed eleven million Indians.

Soviet Famine of 1932-1933
Ten million dead
Incredibly, the severity of this famine was not fully known in the West until the collapse of the USSR in the 1990s. The main cause was the policy of collectivization administered by Josef Stalin. Under collectivization, large swaths of land were converted into collective farms, all maintained by peasants. Stalin went about implementing this by destroying the peasants existing farms, crops, and livestock, and forcibly taking their land. Reports of peasants hiding crops for individual consumption led to wide-scale search parties, and any hidden crops found were destroyed. In actuality, many of these crops were simply seeds that would be planted shortly. The destruction of these seeds and the forced collectivization of land caused mass starvation, killing an estimated ten million people.

Bengal Famine of 1770
Ten million dead
This horrific event killed a third of the population. Largely ruled by the English-owned East India Company, reports of severe drought and crop shortages were ignored, and the company continued to increase taxes on the region. Farmers were unable to grow crops, and any food that could be purchased was too expensive for the starving Bengalis. The company also forced farmers to grow indigo and opium, as they were much more profitable than inexpensive rice. Without large rice stocks, people were left with no food reserves and the ensuing famine killed about ten million Bengalis.

Bengal Famine of 1943
Seven million dead

With World War II raging and Japanese imperialism growing, Bengal lost their largest trading partner in Burma. A majority of the food the Bengalis consumed was imported from Burma, but the Japanese suspended the trade. In 1942, Bengal was hit by a cyclone and three separate tidal waves. The ensuing floods destroyed three thousand two hundred square miles of viable farmland. A fungus then struck destroying ninety percent of all rice crops in the region. Meanwhile, refugees fleeing the Japanese from Burma entered the region by the millions, increasing the need for food supplies. By December of 1943, seven million Bengalis and Burmese refugees were dead due to starvation.

Russian Famine of 1921
Five million dead

The early 20th century was a tumultuous time for Russians, as they lost millions in World War I, experienced a violent revolution in 1917, and suffered from multiple Civil Wars. Throughout the wars, the Bolshevik soldiers often forced peasants to sacrifice their food, with little in return. As such, many peasants stopped growing crops, as they could not eat what they sowed. This resulted in a massive shortage of food and seed. Many peasants had taken to eating seeds, as they knew they could not eat any crops they grew. By 1921, five million Russians had perished.

North Korean Famine 1994 to 1998
Three million dead

This famine was brought about by a combination of misguided leadership and large scale flooding. Torrential rains in 1995 flooded the farming regions and destroyed one and a half million tons of grain reserves. Politically, Kim Jung II implemented a "Military First" policy, which placed the needs of the military above the needs of the common people. The insular nation already suffering from a stagnating economy was both unable and unwilling to import food. As such, the childhood mortality rate rose to ninety three out of one thousand children, and the mortality rate of pregnant women rose to forty-one out of one thousand mothers. Over a four year period, nearly three million people perished due to malnutrition and starvation.

Vietnamese Famine of 1945
Two million dead
As a protectorate under France, Vietnam was under colonial rule for much of World War II. As Japanese expansion began in Indo-china, Vietnam was taken by the Japanese, and the French influenced government collaborated with the Japanese. Agricultural focus shifted from food to war-materials, specifically rubber. The Japanese invading forces commandeered most of what crops remained. This teamed with a severe drought followed by massive flooding caused mass starvation across much of Northern Vietnam. The resulting famine killed two million Vietnamese.

Great Famine Ireland 1845 to 1853
One and a half million dead, two million emigrated
One of the most famous famines in history, the Great Famine was caused by a devastating potato disease. Over a third of the Irish population relied on the potato for sustenance, and the onset of the disease in 1845 triggered mass starvations that lasted until 1853. The large Catholic population was suppressed by British rule, and left unable to own or lease land or hold a profession. When the blight struck, British ships prevented other nations from delivering food aid. Ireland experienced a mass exodus, with upwards of two million people fleeing the country, many to the United States. At its conclusion in 1853, one and a half million Irish were dead, and an additional two million had emigrated. In total, the population of Ireland shrunk by a resounding twenty-five percent.

McBride had heard enough. He couldn't have been more wrong about Frances Prescott. It was highly unlikely that a woman who held such beliefs could be involved in a baby breeding programme. It would have flown in the face of her strongly held ideology. He backed slowly out of the room. On the steps outside he stopped to light up a cigarette. One of the students had had the same idea.

'Pretty intense message wasn't it?' McBride said.

'You can say that again. I feel really depressed now. There doesn't seem any point going on.'

'Maybe that's Ms Prescott's plan. Get everyone so depressed we all commit suicide. That will reduce the population.'

The student laughed at the black humour. 'I'm thinking maybe I should change my subject. Perhaps philosophy will be more enlightening.'

'I doubt it,' McBride said stubbing out his cigarette and walking back to his car.

60

Friday 14th March 2014 – Appleby in the North of England

DS Rod Hartley felt grumpy, grumpier than he normally felt first thing in the morning. They had stayed overnight in a local bed and breakfast. His bedroom overlooked the town square which when he first walked into his room he had thought was a good thing. The best rooms are always at the front he thought to himself. Anthea had been given a smaller room at the back of the building. Obviously, the B&B owner had regarded him as the senior officer. He soon realised his room location wasn't the best when the town hall clock chimed right outside his window and continued to chime throughout the night; on the hour every hour. He hadn't slept well. As soon as he got to sleep the clock woke him up again. On top of this, the mattress had been lumpy, he could feel every spring and the shower had been lukewarm with an unenthusiastic water pressure. The traditional English breakfast was a bonus. Rod ordered everything and a large plate arrived with two Cumberland pork sausages, three rashers of middle back bacon, grilled tomatoes, mushrooms, two fried eggs and a large slice of black pudding. Rod got through four slices of buttered toast and mug of hot strong black coffee. Anthea on the other hand just had a continental breakfast consisting of one croissant which came with a small pat of butter and one of those tiny jars of jam where it was nigh on impossible to get the lid off. She ordered a large pot of tea and sipped it slowly as Rod wolfed down his enormous meal.

The annual Child Genius competition was being held in a local hotel. Hopefuls had already been put through their paces via written and internet tests. Extensive questionnaires had been completed and studied by child psychologists in order to weed out any families who might have psychological problems. The cream of this year's entries, which consisted of the children from twenty families, had been invited to pit their wits against each other in order to be crowned Britain's Child Genius of the year 2014.

The first day of the competition was well under way when they arrived.

Anthea thought it was the epitome of pushy parents. It reminded her of an Agricultural show with children being herded along hoping to win best of breed.

Two children stood out immediately to Anthea. She nudged Rod beside her. He looked up from the book he was engrossed in. 'Look at those two over there.'

Rod glanced towards a boy and girl aged around fourteen years old. They looked very alike. Both had jet black hair, large almond eyes with a healthy olive complexion. They were tall for their age. They reminded Rod of young colts who would grow into winning race horses. Rod liked horse racing and always prided himself on being able to pick a winner just by looking at the physique of the horse. He had no doubt these children would grow into stunning looking adults. 'Identical twins,' he said.

'Not identical, fraternal. Identical twins have to be the same sex. Look at the mother. Although she's dark skinned and of Arabic origin, she looks nothing like them.'

Rod looked at the mother. She was small, dumpy with a sallow yellowish pock marked complexion. More like a cart horse than a race horse he thought.

'I'll go and sit next to her and try and get her talking,' Anthea said. 'You hang around here and see if you can see any other likely candidates.'

Anthea made her way towards the woman and asked if the empty seat beside her was free. The woman nodded in a curt manner. This wasn't going to be easy Anthea thought.

'What are your kids called?' she asked.

'What's it to you?' she replied in a heavily accented voice.

'Just making polite conversation.'

'We aren't here to make polite conversation we are here to win, aren't we darlings?'

The two children nodded in unison.

'And we will win,' the boy added.

'Only one of us will win. You will be second. You know I have the greater intelligence,' the girl responded.

The boy looked sullen and defeated as if he had spent his life coming second to his precocious sister.

'You have two beautiful children,' Anthea continued. 'Were they born in this country?'

'They are British if that's what you mean. As British as you are.'

'Is their father here today?'

'No, he's working.'

'What does he do?'

'He works at the Iranian embassy. He's a diplomat there. You ask a lot of questions. Where are your children?'

Anthea nodded towards Rod who was conveniently standing outside the toilets as if waiting for someone.

'One child. A boy. He's with my husband over there. I think the competition has got to him a bit. He has spent most of the morning in the toilets. I think he's nervous.'

'Is it your first time here?'

'Yes, this is the first time Ollie has qualified,' she said enjoying elaborating about her fictitious child.

'You don't have a chance of winning. My two have come first and second for the last three years.'

Leaving the woman Anthea walked over to the large gold cup sitting on a table at the side of the room. The names of the previous winners were engraved on the trophy. Looking at the years 2011, 2012 and 2013 she could see that the same girl had won each time. Anthea assumed that Yasmine was the name of the girl she had just been speaking with. She made a note of the girl's name in her notebook. Another woman now stood beside her.

'She wins every year. The mother hothouses those kids. She doesn't let them go to a normal school. Home schools them. It doesn't seem right not letting them mix with other kids.'

'Do you know the family?'

'Nobody really knows the family. The rest of us,' she said indicating the other families in the room 'treat this competition as a bit of harmless rivalry. We wouldn't let our children compete if they didn't enjoy it. But Mrs Pahlavi has to win. She never mixes with the other parents. I'm surprised you got the time of day out of her. Stuck up cow.'

'Does she have any other children?'

'Not that I know of. As I said none of us really know much about her. I know her husband is some kind of political refugee and they come from money. I did hear they were related to the Shah of Iran. You know the one who got ousted by that Ayatollah Khomeini bloke. They came here in the 1970s seeking political asylum. Brought a load of money with them.'

'So he's not a diplomat?'

The woman chuckled, 'I doubt that very much.'

A bell sounded which announced the start of the next session which was the spelling round. All the families filed into the adjacent room where the competition was being held. Six children, including the son of the Iranian woman, sat at the front. Anthea and Rod sat beside the helpful woman they had spoken with earlier.

'So what happens now?'

The woman paused and frowned surprised by the question as if any conscientious parent would know the format of the competition already.

'We are thinking of entering our child Oliver next year. We've just come along to see if he's up to the high standard expected,' Anthea added trying to recover the situation even though it meant changing their cover story.

'He wouldn't get this far if he wasn't highly intelligent.'

At least the woman seemed less suspicious of Rod and Anthea than she had a minute ago and now seemed happy to answer their questions.

'Each child has to stand on the podium and spell the word given to them by the judges. This is one of the cruellest rounds because an incorrect answer terminates their turn. At the end of all the sessions, the four children with the lowest score are eliminated.'

A girl of about nine had made her way to the front. A woman judge said 'please spell the word SESQUIPEDALIAN.'

The young girl looked terrified.

As she spelt out the word it was displayed on a screen behind her with the correct spelling underneath so the audience knew immediately whether the answer was correct:

'S-E-S-Q-U-I-P-A-D-A-L-I-A-N'

S-E-S-Q-U-I-P-E-D-A-L-I-A-N

'I'm afraid that is incorrect.'

The girl broke down at the podium.

'This means she's out,' the woman beside them said.

'I don't even know what it means never mind how to spell it,' Rod Hartley commented.

'It means the unnecessary use of long words,' the woman responded.

'Seems appropriate for this competition,' Rod retorted.

They sat through the rest of the session. The rest of the children did much better with scores around eight or nine out of a possible twelve marks. The boy, however, got eleven correct before faltering on the last word.

The next group of six children contained the daughter of the Iranian woman.

Rod was interested to see how she would perform. He was amazed. She sailed through the round managing a perfect score of twelve marks, she showed no hesitation in her answers.

'This afternoon it's the maths round. At least it isn't sudden death like the spelling,' the woman stated as she rose to leave.

'Where do you fancy going for lunch?' Anthea asked Rod.

Rod was still suffering the effects of heartburn from the greasy breakfast he had consumed earlier. 'I think I'll skip lunch I'm not very hungry.'

'OK, you hang around here and see what else you can find out. I'll nip out for a sandwich and check in with the team.'

It was Rod's intention to try and collect forensic evidence from the Iranian family. If he could get a sample of their hair or saliva he would be able to check their DNA and prove that the mother wasn't related to the children. The problem he had was how to gather this evidence without raising alarm. Getting a hair sample from one person would be easy but from three people it would look highly suspicious if he pushed past each of them and tried to yank out a strand of hair. No, he had to be covert in gathering the samples. He thought his best chance would come during the lunch break. He could watch the family and collect any discarded cups or cutlery that they used. Of course, none of this evidence would be admissible in a court as it wouldn't have been gathered legally but it would at least allow them to confirm or disprove that this woman was the biological mother and therefore make the decision to pursue further enquiries or drop the case.

Most of the families chatted amiably amongst themselves but the Iranian family, Rod could never accept their British status, stood apart. At no point did the mother partake in the food offered by the hotel as if it might in some way be drugged and interfere with her offspring's performance. Maybe her fears weren't unfounded. Rod looked at the other parents and thought it not beyond the realms of possibility that one of them would nobble a competitor to give their child an edge. Mrs Pahlavi had a carrier bag from which she took a series of food and drink items, which Rod could not have named, to feed her children. She didn't even discard the food wrappings but folded them carefully and placed them back in her bag. Even if the woman had known Rod's intentions she couldn't have been more guarded.

He had to admit defeat and waited for Anthea to return.

Trying to look inconspicuous by reading a book Rod suddenly became aware of a presence near him. Looking round he found the Iranian girl was sat to his left and the boy to his right. The mother was nowhere in sight.

'Where's your mother?' Rod asked concerned she may notice him talking to the children.

'Oh, she's gone to find out what time we are on later this afternoon. Why are you watching us?' the boy asked.

Rod was taken aback, surely his surveillance wasn't that obvious but somehow his cover had been blown.

'I wasn't. I'm just waiting for my wife and son to return,' Rod mumbled hoping the two kids didn't ask him to elaborate. He wasn't in luck.

The girl took over the questioning. 'You may have your wife with you but your kid doesn't exist. We make a point of checking all the competition and you don't have a child entered in the competition. Who are you?'

Rod wasn't used to having the tables reversed on him and certainly not by a couple of kids. He decided the best course of action was to be evasive so he trotted out the same explanation that he had given earlier about him and his wife considering entering their son in next year's competition. This may have fooled the woman but it didn't fool these kids.

'We don't believe you. Are you private investigators?'

'What makes you say that,' replied Rod surprised and a little intrigued.

'We thought maybe our real family had sent you to find us.'

'Are you saying the woman you are with isn't your real mother?'

'Does she look like our real mother?'

'Not really,' Rod admitted.

'We know she isn't our real mother. We always suspected we were adopted. We arranged for a DNA test last year and this confirmed that we aren't related to our parents but we are related to each other.'

'And have you asked your mother about this?'

'Yes, but she won't tell us anything. We can't ask for our birth records to be opened until we reach eighteen but we suspect these won't tell us what we want to know.'

'And what's that?'

'Who our parents really are. Where we came from.'

'So are you a private investigator?' the girl asked again.

'No but I am a police officer and you are right we are investigating where you came from.'

'See I told you I was right,' the girl told her brother.

Rod gave the girl his card with his contact details on. He told them not to mention the investigation to their parents and stressed the importance about keeping the enquiry quiet.

'You will let us know if you find anything out about where we came from?' the boy requested.

'I promise you as soon as I find something about who your real parents are I will let you know.' If Rod could save these two children from a ruined childhood he would.

When Anthea returned for the afternoon session Rod steered her out of the hall and told her about the illuminating conversation he had had with the two children.

By three that afternoon, they had seen all the youngsters from the competition and concluded that only Ali and Yasmine Pahlavi were of interested to the investigation. There was nothing further they could do so they set off back to headquarters to report the important break they had made. Things couldn't have gone better.

61

As the officers arrived for the daily morning meeting of Operation Silver they noticed a stranger stood beside DCI McBride studying the white board containing the evidence they had gathered to date.

The woman was tall and broad wearing a brightly coloured blouse and white trousers. She looked more suited for a meeting in a Jamaican beach bar than in a serious crime investigation room on a cold English day in March.

As the team assembled and took their seats the two turned to face the group.

'I'd like to introduce you all to Dr Darleen Clutterbuck. You may remember she is the psychologist who produced the profile of the suspect we are searching for. She has kindly agreed to come on board as a consultant on the case. Her time is limited and we must use it wisely. I've been going through the evidence with her and she has some interesting observations for us. I'll now pass you over to Darleen.'

'This is one area that piqued my interest,' she said pointing a long brightly painted finger nail towards a picture of a beautiful young woman pinned to the board.'

'That's Jacqui Bates,' Rod Hartley said 'she's the victim that managed to escape because she had a gynaecological problem and couldn't have children.'

'But she didn't escape he let her go,' Emma Blakely said correcting Rod.

'Exactly,' Darleen Clutterbuck said. 'We know how ruthless this man is yet he let her go. He could have easily disposed of her but he didn't. What does that tell us?'

'That he has progressed to become more ruthless over the years,' DC Bowker said.

'Maybe he has but it tells me that he really loved this girl. He didn't want her to add to his collection. In this instance, he was looking for a wife and a mother for his own children. If we look at the MO we can see that he behaved in a totally different manner. He took the time to woo this girl. He didn't just snatch her. She went with him willingly.'

'If he loved her why didn't he stay with her?' Emma Blakely asked.

'She was flawed. She couldn't have children. Although he loved her he could never bring himself to marry someone who wasn't perfect but he couldn't bring himself to harm her. I think we need to have another chat with Miss Bates she knew this man better than anyone else could ever have known him.'

'Do you think he's married someone else?'

'It's possible but I doubt it. We know this man is very calculating and extremely ruthless. It was probably a chance in a million that he fell in love with one of his intended victims.'

'How does this help us?'

'We know that by the time he got together with Jacqui Bates he had already abducted several women. He still had to care for these women so he would need to be in a location within easy travelling distance from them. I suggest you search for a facility close to where he hired this cottage.'

'Thank God for that,' Rod Harley piped up 'I'm sick of travelling to remote wind swept islands off the coast of Scotland. Do you know how many desolate places there are up there?' Rod's recent trip to Sky hadn't resulted in anything of interest. The myth about babies crying and mothers screaming had been exactly that – a myth.

'Oxfordshire doesn't seem a likely location to be hiding all these women,' Emma Blakely said.

DCI McBride thought the same but he didn't want to puncture the aura of expertise that the eminent doctor had brought to the case by openly decrying her theory. He did think it was a good idea to interview Jacqui Bates again. Darleen was right the MO for that case had been completely different from the others. He made the decision to travel to London and interview Jacqui Bates himself. He would ask Dr Clutterbuck to go with him. Maybe she would be able to extract something relevant.

'How did you get on at the Child Genius competition,' McBride said looking towards DC Bowker and DS Hartley.'

'It was very interesting,' DC Bowker replied. 'I think we have found two children who match the profile. Ali and Yasmine Pahlavi, brother and sister, fraternal twins, born in 2000. The parents came to the UK in 1980 fleeing Iran after the uprising. They were granted political asylum in 1985 and given British citizenship in 1992. Mrs Pahlavi was unable to conceive when miraculously she became pregnant aged forty-five. They brought money out of Iran. A lot of money. Neither of them works even though the woman told me her husband had a job at the Iranian embassy. They seem to spend most of their time bringing up the two kids. He was a scientist working in the nuclear industry back in Iran. She was the niece of the late Shah of Iran. Unfortunately, we failed to get a sample for DNA testing to confirm our theory but I think DS Hartley has come up with something better.

Rod Hartley detailed his conversation with the children and explained that they had suspected they weren't related to their supposed parents. 'Would you believe it, they arranged their own DNA test and confirmed the Pahlavi's weren't their biological parents but they did establish that they were siblings. When they confronted the parents they couldn't get anything out of them.'

'So do you want us to formally interview the Pahlavi's,' DC Bowker asked.

McBride looked towards Darleen Clutterbuck for guidance.

'Not yet Anthea. If they are anything like the Wares we won't get anything from them unless we have some leverage. Remember they will be in constant fear of their kids being taken if they reveal where they came from. I expect this is why they home school them and seem so over protective,' Darleen replied.

McBride agreed with the doctors thinking. 'Dig a bit further into their backgrounds. I want to know the history surrounding those births. Get the birth certificates. Find out where they were delivered; who the doctor was. I want to know if Dr Simpson and Stella Hodson were involved.'

'Have you any more thoughts on where and how he's getting the fathers for these children?' McBride asked Darleen.

Darleen pointed to the pictures of the missing women stuck to the whiteboard. 'If you look at the traits of the women we think he has abducted you can see that they cover a wide variety of races, we have Chinese, Japanese, Asia, black, white in fact every race on the planet. If we look at when and where these women were taken you can see that initially he only selected white women from the British Isles. Later he started selecting different races as he grew his clientele. This enabled him to make the perfect ethnically matched child for parents to adopt. To enable him to provide the promised skin, hair, eye colour choices offered to the buyers he would need to be able to choose the fathers from a large pool of ethnically diverse men. I doubt he would want to risk selecting these men from many different countries as he would want to keep his operation as small as possible. So I'm asking myself where would I find a pool of very intelligent, high achieving, handsome and ethnically diverse men? The only answer I can think of is the United States of America.

221

This is my answer to the WHERE but it is only my opinion, I may be wrong. As to the HOW it's common practice to ship donor sperm across the world this would be the easiest part of the operation.

'Well it's the best idea we have had so far and seeing as we haven't had any success finding the sperm donor for Rosie's babies here in the UK I suggest we move the investigation over to the USA and make some enquiries there. They have a large population including every race and creed so I agree with Darleen that it makes sense they would have men that meet the criteria. I suspect that being an English speaking country would also be attractive to our perpetrator.'

'The USA is so big and their law enforcement is so disjointed. Unless it's a murder or kidnapping the FBI wouldn't be involved and the CIA mainly look for terrorists,' Emma said.

McBride was thoughtful for a minute before saying, 'This is also an advantage for our perp. It makes it more likely that his operation will go unnoticed. I suggest we concentrate on areas like Silicon Valley, Washington and New York where successful men would be attracted to. I also think we will do better if we approach our law enforcement friends across the Atlantic face to face. Emma and Dan I'd like you to go over there and make enquiries. I'll clear things with the Chief Superintendent first. The chief won't like the hole it will make in his budget but needs must.'

The rest of the team tried to hide their disappointment about not being assigned this dream job.

62

Tuesday 18th March 2014 - OXFORD

When Emma arrived at the station the next day she found a post-it stuck to her computer screen. It asked her to see McBride as soon as she arrived. She knocked on his door. He asked her to come in and take a seat. He pressed some buttons on the phone in front of him. After two rings Dan Brennan answered. McBride had the phone on speaker so Emma could hear the conversation.

'Hi Brennan. It's McBride here. I've got Emma Blakely with me. I thought I'd get you both together to discuss the idea that came up yesterday about you going to the USA to look for the possible sperm donors. I'm afraid the Chief Superintendent spoke with the Chief Constable but he refused to sanction it. You know how it is with budgets these days?'

Emma could hear Dan's disappointment and her own face must have shown the same feeling of regret.

'However, I have been given permission to use some spare funding that we have in one of those corporate accounts that the bigwigs use for entertaining. You know how it is "use it or lose it". If it doesn't get spent before the end of the tax year it just disappears. I've been told that we have to keep it very hush-hush which is what they always say … but bear this in mind. Top of the office doesn't want us to let other Departments know that there is spare money knocking about. So any expenses claims can't go through the normal route.'

He passed Emma a black credit card from a bank she had never heard of. It had the name TSW Entertainment Services printed on the front.

'I'm giving Emma a credit card. You can use it to book all your flights and hotels plus you can get cash out on it. I must stress nobody must know about this and Dan, don't tell your boss at the Met where you are going. I don't want him asking questions. He knows you're seconded to Operation Silver so he shouldn't be asking after you for the next couple of weeks.'

Emma thought this was all a bit suspicious but if it allowed their US visit to go ahead who was she to worry. Dan didn't seem to have a problem. Maybe it was more common in the Met to have slush funds hanging about.

'I want you to leave as soon as possible. Emma, you can use my office to make the arrangements. I suggest you start your enquiries in New York as it has the shortest flight time. Let me know when you expect to arrive and I'll arrange for someone from NYPD to meet you at the airport and help you with that end of the investigation.'

With that, he got up and left the room. Emma was left gazing at the credit card wondering what the spending limit on it was. Dan said he would book the flights if she sorted out the hotel. Emma agreed and gave him the credit card details to use.

63

Thursday 20th March 2014 – New York, USA

Emma had only been to the USA once, four years ago. Her mother, having come into a small inheritance from an uncle, had paid for herself, Emma and Becky to have a two week holiday in Orlando, Florida. They had done all the usual touristy things including visiting all the theme parks. Emma had instantly fallen in love with the place. She loved the brashness and the general 'over the top' lifestyle. So she was thrilled about going back even though this trip was only work related. She had always wanted to see New York ever since watching the film Breakfast at Tiffany's with Audrey Hepburn. Going with Dan was also a bonus. Maybe she could work on their relationship and move it up to the next level.

The visit didn't get off to the best of starts.

'I'm afraid with it being a last minute booking they couldn't get us seats together on the plane,' Dan said.

The flight was uneventful but passed quickly. Emma watched a couple of films that she had wanted to see for ages but had been too busy to find time for. The story of her life. She could see Dan further up the cabin. He seemed to be asleep for most of the journey.

Dan only had carry-on luggage but Emma had packed a large suitcase as if she was going on a major holiday. Not knowing what she might need she had thrown in anything and everything. Still having space, on a last minute impulse, she had thrown in even more. She regretted this now as she waited by the baggage collection carousel. Dan with his bag in hand looked decidedly pissed off as he was keen to get going on their assignment. They then had to get through the endless queue at immigration. Since the 9/11 terrorist attacks on the World Trade Center, anyone entering the USA had to give their fingerprints and have a retinal scan. An officious immigration officer asked what the intention was for her visit. When

225

she told him she was on official UK police business his manner instantly changed and he welcomed her to New York and hoped that she had a pleasant stay. As she had paved the way Dan got through the questioning in half the time. When they eventually emerged from the entrance into the arrivals hall a large black man was holding a cardboard sign aloft with the names BRENNAN/BLACKLY scrawled in black pen.

'I assume that's us,' Dan said to Emma smiling at the fact her name had been misspelt.

'Hi I'm detective Geoff Lawson,' he said introducing himself. 'I'm acting as your liaison whilst you are here in New York. I understand you are booked into the Excelsior Hotel, 45 West 81st Street. I'll take you there first so you can drop off your luggage,' he said looking bemused at the size of Emma's case. 'Then we can carry on to the precinct and start work - if you aren't too tired?'

Emma felt the colour rising in her face and thought again what a mistake it was to have brought so many clothes. The hotel turned out to be clean and functional rather than luxurious but it had been cheap and was in a good location. Disappointingly it didn't live up to the pictures and description she had seen on the internet when she'd booked it. She hadn't known how much to spend on the corporate credit card so had sided on the economical. In any event, they didn't expect to be in it much so it wasn't too important. On the other hand, things were looking up when the receptionist passed them their keys and she noticed she had the adjoining room to Dan.

After a wash and quick change of clothes, she met Dan and Detective Lawson in the hotel lobby. She noticed Dan had also changed and was looking smart and fresh. Maybe she should have slept on the plane rather than have spent her time watching films.

When they arrived at the precinct Emma outlined what they were searching for.

Detective Lawson looking perplexed told them straight, 'well you will have your work cut out. Do you know how many muggings and assaults we have in New York? It's around a hundred or more.'

'Is that a week or a month?' Emma asked.

'That's a day, young lady,' Lawson replied. 'This isn't like peaceful little old England.'

'That might have been true a few years ago,' Dan said. 'I bet London could give New York a run for its money nowadays on the crime front.'

'Well things are certainly better since Mayor Rudy Giuliani put in place his zero tolerance policy and we got the funding from Homeland Security to install surveillance cameras everywhere like you have in Britain. Crime figures were five times higher back in 1990.'

Dan thought about the call back home to take out many of the cameras around the cities of Britain. It was a policy he just couldn't understand. The idea of privacy was fine but when a major incident occurred the press and politicians were up in arms if the crime hadn't been captured on camera.

'Still, if you are looking for muggings from the last two years you will be getting on for ninety thousand cases in New York alone. Multiply that up across all the states and you are talking hundreds of thousands if not millions. Do you have a saying about needles and haystacks and how difficult they could be to find? Also, more importantly, the information we have tends to describe the perpetrator rather than the victim.'

Emma thought how stupid they must look. Of course the crime report wouldn't state the victim was a handsome blue-eyed blond male with a high IQ. It would only describe the man who had committed the crime. The person the police were looking for. How much would they actually be able to find out on this visit she now wondered?

'Maybe we can look at it from another angle,' Emma said thinking about the method they had used to identify the kidnapped women back in the UK. 'Can we put together a list of the most successful intelligent men in the USA who match our criteria, then cross-reference it with the names of men who have been mugged or assaulted?'

'You won't find a list like that here but I think I can put you in touch with someone who might be able to help you. There was a piece in Condé Nast magazine recently entitled America's Most Wanted. It wasn't about criminals as you might expect, it was about the most successful American business men that companies would want to headhunt. One of the other detectives here is dating the reporter who wrote the article. I'm sure he will be able to get you an interview with her.'

'That would be great,' Emma said glad that they hadn't had a wasted trip.

'You go and get something to eat and some sleep. I'll set up the meeting hopefully for tomorrow and leave a message at reception for you.'

Dan reminded Detective Lawson that they'd still be on British time so would be awake early and available as soon as the reporter was free to see them the next day 'Anytime six a.m. onward will be fine for us,' as much to demonstrate their professional attitude as their keenness and commitment.

Dan and Emma got a yellow taxi cab back to their hotel. Across the road was one of those deli's that so often featured in American movies and TV shows. From the front, it looked really small but when you entered it seemed to go back forever .... and it was busy which is always a good sign. They found a table for two near the window. Both decided to have the house special of the day mainly to overcome the delay of having to consider the twenty-two page A5 menu in the form of a booklet which was positioned in the centre of the table. The special consisted of a pastrami on rye sandwich. When they arrived Emma wished they had got one to share. The sandwiches were enormous as were the mugs of coffee they had ordered to go with them. Emma only managed to get through half her sandwich. Dan finished off all of his. Emma asked for a doggy bag to go. They settled the check and left a hefty tip for the waitress as tradition dictated in this part of the world. Emma looked at Dan questioningly. Dan merely offered the excuse 'When in Rome ....'

Once they were outside though it was dark, cold and time was getting on Dan asked, 'Do you fancy a walk around Central Park? It's only down the road,' he added.

'Sure that would be great.'

So they ended up walking through Central Park on a beautiful early spring evening. To others, they must have looked like any other young couple. Emma thought how romantic the horse drawn carriages were. She was just thinking about her and Dan spending their honeymoon here when he brought it all crashing down.

'Lucy and I spent our honeymoon here,' he said.

'Oh, I didn't know you were married?' Emma stammered.

'I'm not now. I'm a widower.'

'I'm sorry I didn't know.'

'Why should you. I never talk about it. The memories are still too painful.'

Emma didn't know whether to be pleased he had opened up to her or disappointed that he so clearly still loved his dead wife. She could see that Dan had tears in his eyes. He brushed them away and suggested they return to the hotel and get some rest. It was still only nine p.m. here but back in the UK, it was getting on for two in the early hours of the morning. Emma had in effect missed a night's sleep so she was feeling very tired. It was clear Dan didn't want to talk any more. So they walked back to their hotel in almost silence and went to their separate rooms.

Emma slept really well. On waking, she looked at the clock on the bed side table. It showed the time was five a.m. She didn't normally sleep well in strange beds but this one was big and so comfortable she had slept solidly. She had a shower then rang down to reception to ask if she had any messages. The receptionist said she had two. One from a detective Lawson saying that he had arranged for them to meet a Miss Nina Simonenko at the offices of Condé Nast on Times Square at ten a.m. The second message was from a Dan

Brennan saying he would meet her for breakfast at seven at the deli across the street. She looked at her watch. It was now six o'clock which gave her about fifty minutes to finish getting ready. She put on the TV with the sound turned low so as not to disturb the occupants of the room on her left. The adverts were on. She remembered how annoying American TV was from her first visit. Any programme you tried to watch was constantly interrupted by inane adverts and it wasn't always clear where the programme ended and the advert began. ED seemed to be the advert of the moment. Emma didn't know what it was but by the end of the ad she knew more about Erectile Dysfunction than she could ever have wished. The side effects of the medication, which were listed in full at the end of the advertisement, seemed worse than the condition itself. She turned off the TV saying to herself, 'too much information.' She had brought her iPad with her. The hotel had free Wi-Fi. She decided to check her emails. After finding the hotel's network connection she was asked to enter her surname and room number. She did this but a message displayed telling her that the details entered were incorrect. She decided to use Dan's room number and surname. This time she was taken through to the Google homepage. She then remembered how Detective Lawson had misspelt her name so maybe the hotel had also registered her by the wrong surname. She had an email from her mother. Nothing important to report just the usual domestic stuff. The washing machine had broken and she was waiting for the man to come and fix it. Becky was behaving herself. She dashed off a quick reply telling her mother the flight had gone smoothly and the hotel was nice. She just had time to check the news back in the UK. A plane en route to China had gone missing. All countries were looking for it but it was a complete mystery as to where it had gone. Already conspiracy theories abounded. Some thought the Chinese had deliberately hi-jacked it to find out what information foreign countries could find out from their satellites. Others thought it must be terrorists. The Rosie kidnapping case was getting less and less coverage as time went on. The public was quick to forget. This was human nature. It was now five minutes before seven so she logged off, put the iPad in her bag, and headed over to the deli.

Even though it was still dark she could see that Dan was sat at the same table as the night before. He waved through the window to her as she approached. He had a cup of coffee in front of him but no food.

'Morning,' he said. 'I haven't ordered yet. I thought we could eat together.'

'That's nice,' Emma said picking up the menu as the same waitress who had taken their order the previous evening

229

arrived. She took a pencil and notepad from her pocket on the front of her apron and waited for their order.

'I'll have French Toast and a black coffee,' Emma said.

'I'll have two eggs – over easy, bacon, tomatoes, mushrooms, toast - better make that brown and some of those lovely pancakes with maple syrup,' Dan said.

'I don't know where you put all the food you eat,' said Emma after the waitress had taken their order and departed.

'I've always had a healthy appetite. I've got to keep my energy levels up. To survive growing up in my home town of Salford you had to be either a good fighter or a good runner.'

'Which were you?'

'I was definitely a runner. I was a scrawny kid.'

'What made you move from Salford to London?'

'The job. I was offered a promotion. At the time the Met. was struggling to fill the vacancies they had. All the talent was haemorrhaging to the city corporate firms.'

'And you don't fancy moving back?'

'To Salford, not really. I love the buzz of London. It would be a lot cheaper to live there though. People up north don't realise how lucky they are.'

'What do you mean? I thought people down south consider that they earn more money and look down on northerners.'

'Yes, they do earn more money but their living costs are much higher. If you look at disposable incomes, what people have left to spend after paying the bills, northerners are much better off. That's why they just smile when southerners scoff and look down on them. Who's the fool?'

'I've never thought about it like that. I must admit I couldn't afford to live in Oxford if I didn't share with my mother.'

'Exactly, for the price of a one-bedroomed flat in Oxford, you could buy a three or four bedroomed detached house with a large garden in the North.'

'How do you afford London prices?'

'I bought at the right time plus when Lucy died the insurance paid off the mortgage so I'm mortgage free now.'

'That's a big price to pay though?'

'The biggest. I would do anything to change what happened.'

'You must have loved her very much?'

'I did. She was the best.'

Emma was saved from the conversation by the arrival of their breakfast. Tucking in Emma told Dan that the meeting had been arranged for ten that morning with the reporter a Miss Nina Simonenko. They arranged to meet at nine in the hotel lobby for the short taxi ride to the Condé Nast offices. Emma went back to her room to work on some questions that she wanted to ask the reporter. Dan went to have a shower. He had been awake since two and had been walking around the city looking at the sights albeit in the dark. Emma thought this sounded a bit dangerous but didn't say anything.

They took a cab across the city. The cab got them to their destination in just the forty-five minutes they'd been told to allow but Emma had the feeling that they would have been able to walk it more quickly given the density of the early morning traffic in Manhattan. Emma decided she'd look at using the subway to get back. It must be quicker although she had heard that it was one of the world's most difficult underground systems to fathom. Surely it couldn't be more complicated than the Tube in London.

As expected the offices of Condé Nast were extremely plush. They had to take the elevator to the 35th floor. The magazine's office must have taken the whole floor because their reception was directly off the elevator and no other office was listed. They told one of the three receptionists that they had an appointment with Miss Nina Simonenko and they were invited to wait in the reception seating area. A low coffee table was in front of them with back issues of the magazine neatly laid out. Emma looked through them and soon found the one she was looking for. On the front cover, there was a picture of a handsome dark haired man in his forties. Above the picture the title 'America's Most Wanted' told readers to turn to page five for the full story. As instructed Emma turned to page five. She saw a block of ten photos of men of different ages and appearances. The man from the front cover was listed as number one. His name was Oliver Howard IV and he ran a highly successful law practice in the city. But Emma's eye was drawn to the picture of number two. This was a handsome man aged around fifty. He had white blond hair and piercing blue eyes. His name was Eric Bamber. He was an entrepreneur and founder of a hi-tech company based in California's Silicon Valley. Reading the article further Emma learned that he was educated at MIT, he was a self-made man and he was happily married with three teenage daughters. In his youth, he had represented the USA as a member of the Olympic rowing team. They had won a silver medal. Emma showed Dan the article.

'He certainly matches our criteria,' Dan said.

At this point, an elegantly dressed lady appeared in front of them holding out her hand.

'I'm Nina. You must be the English police officers who are interested in my article?' She said nodding to the magazine open in Emma's lap. 'You can keep that if you like. We have plenty more.'

Dan made their formal introductions then they followed Nina into her office.

She must have been very well thought of in the company as she had a large corner office with views out across the city.

'Nice view,' Dan remarked.

'Yes I love it but unfortunately I'm about to lose it. We are in the process of relocating our offices to the new One World Trade Center.'

Nina made a note of the pertinent information for both the UK officers including rank and full contact details before getting down to business. She had been duped by rival reporters posing as police officers in the past and wasn't going to fall for the same ruse again.

Satisfied she continued, 'John my boyfriend told me a little bit about what you are after but he was a bit sketchy with the details.'

Emma outlined what they were looking for. Successful, intelligent men around the age of fifty with blond hair and blue eyes. 'Someone like him,' she said pointing to the photo of Eric Bamber.

'That's rather specific,' Nina said. 'Can I ask why you are looking for this man? Has he broken the law?'

Emma didn't want to give the reporter too many details of their investigation. She just provided the high-level outline of their enquiry and told her that this was the kind of man who may be wanted in connection with a case they were working on in the UK. He wasn't a suspect though and they had no reason to believe he was willingly involved in anything criminal. He, or someone like him, could just have been an unwitting participant in a crime she explained.

'As you know I am a reporter. I respect that you can't give me the full details about this case but if I help you would you give me an exclusive when it breaks?'

Emma and Dan both nodded their agreement.

Nina opened her drawer and came out with a file. 'As you can see the magazine only printed details for the top ten men. Here I have a list of the top hundred. There was a one-page description of each man with a colour photo attached to the top right-hand corner. This is a copy I have prepared for you. You can keep it. I hope you are successful in your enquiries. Don't forget my exclusive and get back to me if you think there's anything more I can help with.'

With this, she rose from her chair and escorted Dan and Emma to the door. The short but beneficial meeting was over.

Emma put the magazine and folder containing the reports into her bag. 'I think we will take the subway back to the precinct,' Emma said. 'But can we stop off at the hotel first so that I can change these shoes? My feet are killing me. I wasn't expecting to do this much walking.'

"Fine by me' Dan replied. 'Which way is it?'

'I've no idea,' Emma said.

They asked at reception and the pretty girl offered them a map of the city and placed a red cross on the location of the nearest subway station at 42nd St - Bryant Park Station. They had to cross a couple of busy intersections but soon found the subway which was only a seven minute walk. Finding the right line and the right train was a different matter. In the end they had to ask at the information desk. The helpful man gave out a string of numbers and directions to which Emma and Dan both nodded. They both turned away from the desk.

'Did you get all that?' Dan asked

'No, I thought you did?' Emma said.

'Then why did you nod?' Dan asked.

'Why did you nod?' Emma asked.

'It's a man thing. We can't look dumb when it comes to directions,' Dan explained.

Emma started to giggle and Dan was caught up with her infectious laugh and joined in. Soon the two of them stood on the subway with tears streaming down their faces not knowing where to go. They looked at each other and for a moment Emma thought Dan was going to kiss her. The moment passed and he looked away sheepishly.

'I think he said to go to platform B and take the 145th Street bound train and get off at 81st street near the Natural History Museum, but I'm not a hundred percent certain,' Emma said.

An hour later they found themselves back at the police precinct with Emma now wearing a pair of comfortable trainers. Detective Lawson showed them to two desks facing each other. Both had a PC on them. I'll log you in then you can search the crime database to check if any of your men have been mugged. The database covers the whole country.

Emma split the names into two piles. Most could be dismissed as the men clearly weren't attractive enough. They ended up with sixteen names each to search.

'As we have so few I suggest we just enter their names and dates of birth. I know we are only looking for a potential match for Rosie but you never know we may find other donors,' Emma said.

'Agreed,' Dan replied.

Emma got a hit on her first attempt. 'I think I've got him,' she said.

'Who is it?' Dan asked.

'Eric Bamber, number two from the Most Wanted list. He was mugged in San José the previous year. Nothing was apparently taken. He received severe bruising to his lower body.

They continued through the list and managed to identify a further four similar cases that had occurred over the past ten years. Eric Bamber was the only one that seemed to be a match for Rosie so they decided to concentrate on him to start with.

'According to the magazine article and the police report he is still living in San José in the heart of Silicon Valley. I suggest we pay him a visit,' Dan said.

They printed out copies of the details for all five cases and asked Detective Lawson if he would arrange for them to meet up with the investigating officer from San José and arrange an interview with Eric Bamber. He was also kind enough to book their flights and hotel accommodation in Silicon Valley using the dodgy credit card.

64

Saturday 22nd March 2014 – California, USA

So next morning they found themselves on the first flight out of JFK international airport destined for San Francisco.

The journey through airport security was much quicker this time as they were on a regular scheduled internal flight. The wait for the bag on arrival, however, was just as long as ever. There just didn't seem to be a short cut to this process anywhere in the world. Emma wondered if it was a ploy by the airlines to discourage passengers from taking hold luggage.

They seemed to be the last of the passengers to exit into the arrivals hall. This time there was no police officer holding aloft a sign with their names showing. There was, however, a man of around thirty years of age sat in a wheelchair fast asleep. He had long dark brown curly hair and a matching beard. He had a piece of card face down in his lap. Dan thought he was either a beggar or given his dishevelled appearance an archetypal San Francisco police detective, though the wheelchair genuinely surprised him. He carefully took the card and turned it over. This time it said, "WELCOME TO SAN FRANCISCO - BRENNAN & BLACKIE ☺".

'I think this is us,' he said to Emma showing her the card.

She hit Dan playfully on the shoulder.

Dan gave the detective a prod. He quickly awoke with nothing but a cursory apology and without the slightest inkling of embarrassment.

'Sorry about that. I've been waiting for ages. I thought you must have missed the flight. I'm Detective Alex Green. You can either call me Al or as my colleagues call me Ironside. Though I prefer Al so I don't have as much to live up to.'

'Sorry. We had to wait ages for the bag,' Dan said looking towards Emma's suitcase.

'I thought you were only here for a few days?' Al remarked.

'We are!' Dan replied.

Both men gave a knowing shrug. As if to say - women, what are they like?

Emma set off towards the exit with both men in her wake.

It wasn't the heat that hit them as they exited the airport but the humidity. Emma felt her clothes beginning to stick to her during the short walk to the car park.

Al had an old large police cruiser just like you see on the TV cop shows. He pressed the trunk release to allow Emma to put her bag in.

'You'll both have to sit in the back. I've got to put my chair in the front.'

With a well-practised action, Al slid easily into the driver's seat and pulled his chair across himself and into the passenger seat. He must have had a lot of upper body strength to do that Emma thought. She wondered what had put him in a wheelchair. Probably a shooting incident.

'How far is it to Silicon Valley?' Dan asked.

'Silicon Valley isn't actually a place it's only a nickname given to the South Bay area of San Francisco. It is home to many of the world's largest technology corporations, as well as thousands of small start-up companies hence the link to the silicon chip. You will be staying in San Jose which is located in the centre of the area. At this time of day we should be there in about forty minutes it's only thirty-six miles.'

Al eased the cruiser to a stop outside the hotel. Emma was impressed. It was much more luxurious than the New York hotel. Once you get out of any major city your money obviously goes a lot further.

Al said he had set up a meeting for them with Eric Bamber in the hotel bar at seven o'clock that evening. Giving Dan a card with his details on he told them to get in touch as and when they needed him. As an aside he passed them a thin folder. 'This is a copy of the file relating to the Eric Bamber assault. I doubt there's much in here that will add to what you've already read in the online police report but I thought it might give you some additional ideas for what to ask him when you meet this evening.'

The hotel was a contemporary design. It had a large lobby with a shiny black marble floor and white leather chairs, settees and low coffee tables scattered generously about the place. A long reception desk was off to one side with three smartly dressed receptionists sitting behind it diligently working at their computers.

It was lunch time. The hotel receptionist they had chosen, the middle of the three, an efficient looking Asian man, told them their rooms wouldn't be ready for a couple of hours but they could leave their bags securely stored at the hotel. He gave them a map of the city and a list of local recommended restaurants. There weren't any visitor attractions mentioned which was to be expected in a mainly business area.

Since they had moved West the time difference with the UK had increased to eight hours. They both felt ready to drop not so much from the jet lag but rather the accumulative weariness that befalls long distance travellers. They walked out of the cool air-conditioned hotel into the hot midday sun. It wasn't the weather to be walking about, so they chose the nearest recommended restaurant which was literally just around the corner.

This turned out to be more of an upmarket diner. There was a long colourful menu on the table. Dan ordered a cheeseburger and fries. Emma ordered a chicken sandwich, cancelling the fries which seemed to automatically accompany everything on the menu. Both ordered a coffee to try to manage if not overcome their tiredness. Again the portions were huge and again Dan polished off his meal whilst Emma barely managed half of hers.

'How do you eat so much and stay so slim?' she asked.

'I have a lot of nervous energy. Everyone in my family is thin. I think we must have a high metabolic rate gene.'

'I wish I had that gene. I only have to look at a cheeseburger and I put on ten pounds.'

'Do you want to ask for a doggy bag?' he asked.

'No, I'll just leave it. I ended up throwing away the remainder of the pastrami and rye sandwich this morning. I don't know why people ask to take leftovers away; I can't believe that they ever eat them.'

'I wouldn't know. I've never had any leftovers,' Dan said reaching over to Emma's plate. 'You don't mind do you?' he asked taking the remainder of her sandwich from the plate.

'Go ahead. I hate waste. It's no wonder this country has an obesity problem. How does anybody cope with these huge portions?'

'I don't know,' said Dan talking through a mouthful of chicken sandwich.

'I'll just text McBride and let him know we have arrived,' Emma said to a distracted
Dan. 'Are you listening to me?'

Dan's eyes had moved to a television screen above Emma's head. 'It's just like being back in London.'

'What is?'

'Terrorists on the loose.'

Emma turned to see a picture of a man called Arif Tadeequi who the SFPD was hunting. He was believed to be in the area and planning a terrorist atrocity with a cell of up to six people. The CNN anchorwoman requested that any member of the public who knew the whereabouts of this man should ring the SFPD immediately. The man is armed and is regarded as highly dangerous she stressed with a pained smile. He shouldn't be approached.

'I expect all Western countries have the same problems,' she said as she sent the text hoping McBride hadn't already gone to bed as it would be late evening back home.

'True,' Dan said chewing the last bite of the sandwich. 'I just don't understand what it is these people are trying to achieve. They spend years trying to get to the west only to then start working to destroy it from within. Bizarre.'

'Only a few think like that. You will always get people who are unhappy with their lives and want to change it.'

'Well there are unhappy individuals but terrorists try to take matters to a whole new level. Their mission statement seems to be - *the greater the atrocity the better.*'

Emma didn't understand Dan's extensive rant about terrorists but decided not to pursue the subject further.

'What do you want to do now?' Dan asked. 'We still have an hour before our rooms are ready.'

'We could explore the city but I doubt there is much to see. Or we could look through the file Al gave us and formulate some questions to ask Eric Bamber later which is my preference?'

'Yes I agree we should prepare a questioning strategy for tonight.'

Dan attracted the attention of the waitress and ordered another two coffees.

As detective Al Green had suggested the file relating to the Eric Bamber assault was on the light side. It was clear that the police hadn't taken the crime seriously. Dan glanced through it and hadn't found anything useful that they didn't already know. Nobody had been apprehended for the crime. The police didn't even have a suspect.

'I don't think we will find out anything further until we speak with Eric Bamber. I suggest we get back to the hotel and see if our rooms are now available. I feel ready to drop,' Emma said with a yawn.

They asked for the check and left the waitress a large tip out of the money they had drawn on the credit card.

By the time they got back to the hotel it was two in the afternoon. There must have been a change of shift as the Asian man and the other two receptionists had been replaced by three new employees. They were greeted by a happy smiling Hispanic girl. Dan could have kissed her when she told them their rooms were now ready. She retrieved their bags and gave them their room keys.

This time to Emma's disappointment they didn't have adjoining rooms. They weren't even located on the same floor. Emma was on the seventh floor. Dan on the ninth. They agreed that they would have a much needed siesta. Emma stepped out of the elevator and as the doors closed told Dan she would meet him in the bar just before their meeting with Eric Bamber at seven.

Dan got to his room. He was impressed. It had the biggest bed he had ever seen. He decided to have a shower before his nap. The hot shower was wonderful. It had one of those rainforest shower heads that gives out loads of water. He wondered how a geographical area that freely admitted to having a water shortage could afford to waste so much of it but that was the USA for you, a country of excesses. He unpacked his small bag hanging his shirts in the ample wardrobe and putting his chinos into the trouser press. He then lay down on top of the large bed; before his head hit the pillow he was fast asleep. When he awoke he looked at the clock. He had expected it to be about five o'clock but it was five past seven. He couldn't believe it, he never overslept, he normally struggled to sleep for more than a few hours. He was late. He hated being late and chastised himself for not setting his alarm. He hoped Emma hadn't overslept. It would be so embarrassing if they missed their meeting with Eric Bamber. He hadn't done any of the extra preparation that he's planned to do. Why hadn't Emma phoned him? Had she also overslept?

Dan quickly dressed and made his way down to the hotel bar.

When he arrived he immediately saw Emma sitting with a very handsome man in a booth at the back of the bar. They were laughing together at something the man had just said. Dan suddenly felt something he had never felt in his life - jealousy. He strode purposefully across to their table.

'Why didn't you call me?'

'You are only a few minutes late Dan. It's not a problem I've been telling Eric here about our time in New York. Eric, this is my colleague DI Dan Brennan he works for the London Metropolitan Police.' Looking up at Dan, 'I've not asked him any questions yet we've just been making polite conversation.'

'Please to meet you Dan,' Eric said confidently holding out his hand for Dan to shake. 'What are you drinking?'

Dan felt a bit guilty about his brusque manner so quickly tried to recover the situation. 'I'm sorry for being late. I hate being late. It must be the jet lag. Mine's a beer please.'

Eric waved over a waiter. He was obviously well known in the bar given how attentive the waiter was dropping in his name at every opportunity.

'I hope you don't mind but I asked my wife to meet us here. We car share so I need to take her home.'

Dan and Emma looked at each other. They didn't like the idea of Mrs Bamber joining them. An individual tended to be more reticent with his partner present and some of their questions were on the delicate side.

Eric Bamber sensed their concern. 'Don't worry I've nothing to hide from my wife. We tell each other everything. You'll see what I mean when you meet her.'

Dan started the questioning. 'We want to know about the evening you got mugged?'

Just then an attractive woman gracefully walked across the bar towards them. The waiter intercepted her with an over exuberant greeting bowing before her, 'Mrs Bamber, so pleased to see you again. Will it be the usual?'

She nodded to him and came towards where they were sitting.

Eric stood up and pulled a chair out for her. 'This is my wife Rose,' he said.

She held out an elegantly manicured hand. Dan didn't know whether to shake it or kiss it. He took the option of just taking hold of it then letting go.

'Pleased to meet y'all,' she said in an exaggerated southern drawl.

'I was just about to tell the detectives about the time I was mugged,' Eric said.

'Well carry on,' she said as the waiter promptly arrived with a large cocktail that had a variety of fruit, an umbrella and a straw in it.

'I thought it was a case of mistaken identity,' Eric Bamber said.

'Why did you think that?' Dan asked.

'Well it clearly wasn't a robbery as nothing was taken and the guy kicked me in the nuts. I expect he thought I'd been messing with his misses then maybe noticed I wasn't the right guy and left it at that.'

'This is a delicate question but I have to ask it,' Emma said.

'You want to know if I've ever had an affair.' Eric said anticipating the question.

'Well yes. I have to ask.'

'The answer is no. I've never been unfaithful to my wife.' Eric replied looking at his wife. 'Rose is the only woman for me and always has been since the day I first set eyes on her.'

Taking up the questioning Dan asked, 'it says in the police report that you were tasered. So you were unconscious. So you didn't witness the man kicking you.'

'Well no but what else could have happened. I was black and blue down there. I was out of working order for weeks. Wasn't I Rose?'

'You sure were honey,' Rose replied in her southern drawl, not in the least bit awkward or embarrassed.

'Are you suggesting that this isn't what happened?' Eric asked perceptively.

Dan gave an outline of their case and how the UK police suspected that Eric's sperm had been stolen.

Eric was speechless for what seemed like ages as he took in the enormity of what had occurred.

'You mean there could be hundreds of little Eric's running about out there?'

'There may not be any yet. The girl who we think has been selected to be the mother of your children was only kidnapped a few weeks ago.'

'I'm willing to accept responsibility for any children I father. In fact, I've always wanted a son. Don't get me wrong I love my girls,' he said looking sadly towards his wife.

'I couldn't have any more after my last,' Rose said on a much more serious note. 'I feel bad that I can't give Eric a son.'

'Don't feel bad hon. We've been through this before you know that you and the girls mean the world to me.'

Dan could tell that they did. Eric had the same look on his face that he knew he must have had himself when he had talked about Lucy. He felt a little ashamed about the jealous thoughts he'd had earlier when he saw Emma and Eric laughing together.

'Could I meet him?' Eric asked.

'Who?' said Emma.

'My son of course,' replied Eric.

'One - we don't know if there is a child. Two - we don't know it's a boy. And three - if he exists we have no idea where he is,' Emma snapped.

She then felt bad about her reaction. He was obviously a good caring man who wanted to do right by any children he fathered. 'If we ever solve this case and we find a child we will certainly pass on your details if you want us to?' Emma said a little more diplomatically this time so keeping the Bambers on-side.

Eric and Rose both nodded their heads. 'We would like that,' they said together.

'Is there anything else you can tell us about the attack?' Dan asked.

'No, everything is in the police report. I was walking back to my vehicle in the car park. I'd just passed the back of a white van and bam I was out cold. I woke up thirty minutes later feeling like I'd done ten rounds with Mohammed Ali. Nothing had been taken.'

'Had your clothes been interfered with?' Emma asked.

'Now you mention it my belt was on a loser notch. I didn't think anything of it at the time.'

This hadn't been mentioned in the police report.

'What about the white van. Was it still there when you woke up?' Dan asked.

'No, it had gone.'

Another omission from the report.

'Thinking about it, it couldn't have reversed out of the parking space otherwise it would have run over me. I must have been moved then put back in the same place.'

Yet another omission from the police report.

'Thinking about the van. Do you remember any markings?' Emma asked.

'No as far as I can remember it was just plain white but then I only saw the back of it.'

'Do you always follow the same routine each day?'

'Pretty much. I normally leave the office around five. I call in at a couple of my manufacturing plants to check on things there. Then I pick up Rose from her work and we drive home.'

'So your attackers would have expected you to be in the parking garage around that time.'

'Yes, I expect they would if indeed this attack was planned as you suggest.'

They thanked the Bambers for their help and promised to get in touch if they needed anything further or found any news about any potential little Erics.'

When the Bambers had left Emma and Dan sat together with their drinks and discussed their next move.

'So we can assume that Eric's sperm was stolen. We know the date. Now we need to find out what happened after that and in particular who arranged and shipped it to the UK. There can't be many businesses that have the facility to store and ship sperm half way across the world. I suggest we speak to Detective Green in the morning and see if we can draw up a list of potential businesses offering this kind of service.

'What's with the Ironside nickname, I don't get it?' Emma asked.

'I think it relates to an old American TV detective who was confined to a wheelchair. Way before our time,' Dan replied.

'So what do you want to do this evening?'

'Let's park it all for tonight and see if we can't relax a little,' Dan said.

Emma had noticed the slight shift in the way Dan looked and spoke to her. She had thought when he first came into the bar that there was a hint of jealousy about him when he saw her in the presence of Eric Bamber. She wanted to exploit this as best she could and see where it would lead. Time was running out. If he didn't make a move here she thought there'd be no chance when they returned to the UK as they lived so far apart and both had such busy lives.

They decided to eat in the hotel restaurant. As is the norm with most hotel restaurants the quality was average, the portions were surprisingly small - especially for the USA and the prices on the high side. A bit of a disappointment overall. What it did have was a very good wine list. Dan ordered a bottle of Silver Ghost Cabernet Sauvignon 2013 Central Valley which was described as: A fruit-driven style of Cabernet that offers rounded, ripe red berry fruit with a plummy and easy-going feel. They laughed together about the description. How could a bottle of wine have an easy-going feel?

Emma now feeling blasé about using the credit card ordered a second bottle. After the meal, they took the remains of the wine back to the booth they had started off in earlier that evening. Emma was feeling decidedly tipsy by now. She couldn't think of a time of late when she had been so happy, though she was mildly aware that this was alcohol induced. She was just telling Dan about another funny story that only seemed funny because of the wine when he pulled her towards him and kissed her deeply.

'I've been wanting to do that since we first met.' Seeing her shocked expression he said, 'I'm sorry I shouldn't have taken advantage.'

'Yes, you should have. I've wanted you to kiss me since we first met. I thought you weren't interested.'

'I was interested. I'm just a bit out of practice. I've had women since my wife died but none of them mattered. Emotionally they just didn't register with me. I've never had feelings for a woman, like I have for you, not since I first met Lucy. I felt so jealous when I saw you with Eric Bamber.'

'Your room or mine?' Emma said not wanting the unexpected opportunity to get away.

'Yours is closer,' Dan replied taking her hand and leading her to the elevator. As the elevator doors were about to close a large group of Japanese business men entered. They pressed every button and the elevator stopped at every level. It seemed to take an interminable age before it arrived at Emma's floor but in reality it could have only been a couple of minutes.

They entered Emma's room and closed the door. Dan took her in his arms and gave her a long drawn out kiss. He knew she would be an excellent kisser and she didn't disappoint. They both wanted to savour the moment. Neither of them wanted to rush something that they had both been yearning for, for so long. Lust is one of the most powerful feelings a human being can feel and they were both overcome with their desire for each other. Emma started to unbutton his shirt whilst he undid the zip on her skirt and let it drop to the floor. She gracefully stepped out of it. She was wearing a pair of those sexy holdup stockings that show a white piece of thigh at the top. He slowly undid the buttons of her silk blouse whilst kissing the nape of her neck and the place where it gently curved into her shoulder. He slid the shirt down until it slipped to the floor. She was wearing matching black underwear. Her bra barely covered her heaving breasts. They weren't too big, they weren't too small, they were just perfect like the rest of her. He had never been a lover of women's perfume but the scent she was wearing was intoxicating. He kissed her across her cleavage as he undid her bra then as her breasts sprang free of their restraint he took her left nipple into his mouth running his tongue over it. He took the other nipple in his mouth teasing it until it became hard and swollen. He pushed her gently back onto the bed. He spent a moment gazing at her perfect form. He eased her panties over her hips then over her knees. She wriggled slightly kicking them off. All she wore now were the black stockings. Dan decided to leave them in place for now. He kicked off his shoes and removed his trousers, boxers and socks in one fluid movement. He then buried his face between her legs and ran his tongue over her wet sweet clitoris. She squirmed and made little animal noises pushing his head harder between her legs. She threw back her arms onto the bed as she gasped and came. Dan lifted her further onto the bed and lowered himself onto her. She guided his erect penis into the wet space between her legs. He took long slow strokes then harder and faster. Emma wrapped her legs around his back allowing him to go deeper inside her. They were both panting hard now. Both were uninhibited about the noise they were making. Faster, harder, faster, harder until together they both gasped in the climactic ecstasy that took them. Exhausted Dan fell back onto the bed and they both lay there naked with sweat glistening on their bodies.

The bathroom had one of those large Jacuzzi baths. Unconcerned now about the water usage they took a long leisurely soak together spending time getting to know each other's bodies. Then Dan carried her back to the bed and they made passionate love again taking longer this time to explore every contour, every sweet spot. Finally exhausted sleep took them over as they curled up together naked under the duvet their lust sated for now.

The morning after a first date is always a bit embarrassing. With his previous conquests, Dan had always been long gone by the morning choosing to creep away in the night rather than face a woman he had only been interested in having sex with. With Emma it was different. He lay beside her watching her sleep, looking at every detail of her beautiful face. The curve of her mouth, the way her long eyelashes curled, her pert little button nose. He felt love, a love he hadn't thought he would ever experience again. Suddenly he was overcome with fear. What if she didn't feel the same, what if she was taken away from him? He could feel the panic attack rising inside him. He couldn't breathe. Emma opened her eyes and saw the distress he was in.

She held him, 'breathe through it Dan, take deep breaths.'

He slowly let go of the panic and began to calm down taking long slow breaths. 'I couldn't go through it again.'

'Go through what?' She asked.

'Losing someone that I love.' He was now afraid that she would think he was some sort of obsessive madman. 'It's just that when you have lost someone you really love, it's really hard to open up again. I have to tell you now Emma I'm a mental car crash. I've been seeing a therapist for nine years. I struggle to sleep through the night without taking tablets. I think we may have a future together but you will have to be patient with me. I'll completely understand if you want to walk away.'

'Walk away. I think I fell in love with you the moment I first saw you. We can take things as slowly as you want to. I understand what you must be going through. When you have children you understand what loss can mean. The thought of ever losing Becky makes me panic.'

'Thank you. I don't think you can fully understand but thank you for caring.'

Emma pulled him towards her and kissed him on the lips holding his face in her hands. He kissed her back. Soon they were making love for the third time. Again they lay there spent. 'I think we had better start doing some work,' Emma said. 'We don't want to be late for our meeting with Ironside.'

'We can't go to work on an empty stomach. Breakfast first. I'll go to my room and change and meet you in the restaurant in twenty minutes.'

'Thinking of your stomach again?'

'No change there then. I need the energy. You're draining the life out of me.'

Emma threw a pillow at him as he sat on the edge of the bed pulling on his clothes.

65

It was nine on the dot when they arrived for their meeting with Detective Green at the local precinct. An officer named Simon Heal greeted them and introduced himself as Al Green's partner. He escorted them to the second floor where the pair of detectives shared an office and where Al was waiting for them. Dan and Emma ran through their interview with Eric Bamber.

'I have to admit that there hasn't been much effort put into this investigation,' Al began. 'It really didn't seem much of a priority given that nothing was taken and Mr Bamber wasn't seriously hurt. It seems to have been regarded as more of a prank than anything else .... !'

'I think his wife might disagree with you on that one,' Emma replied thinking of the two weeks her husband was out of action.

The two detectives looked worriedly at each other. 'She said that?' remarked Detective Heal.

'Not in so many words,' Emma said wondering why they were suddenly so concerned.

Dan interceded, 'I think you need to look at the mugging evidence in more detail and we need to look into how the sperm was stored and transported to the UK. There can't be many organisations that have the required facilities to store and ship sperm abroad.'

'We've already made a start on that for you,' Al replied passing a piece of paper to Dan.

On it was listed three company names along with an overview of their services. One of them was circled in red ink - Happy Families' Laboratories Inc. (HFLI).

'These three companies all carry out IVF treatment but only the one circled sends sperm donations out of the country. We thought it would be better if you went undercover just in case HFLI is implicated in this criminal activity. I've arranged an appointment for

246

you both with a Dr Charles Du Bois later this morning at eleven. I hope you don't mind but I've told him you are a couple from the UK looking for help with an infertility problem and you are looking for sperm from a top of the range donor.' Simon Heal said with a smirk on his face before adding, 'I hope you're up for it!'

66

As expected the medical facility housing HFLI was very plush. A stunning receptionist who sat behind a large highly polished desk greeted them. Stunning women was becoming the common factor of this case. Dan told her that they had an appointment to see Dr Du Bois. The girl pushed a form towards them and pointed with her long glossy red fingernail.

'You need to fill in your details here. There will be an initial five hundred dollar consultation fee. Further visits cost three hundred dollars. Dr Du Bois will see you shortly. Would you like a coffee whilst you wait,' she said indicating that they should sit on the leather sofa next to a water cooler across from her desk. A low coffee table with a spread of glossy magazines all neatly positioned offered an array of subjects.

'Not quite like the NHS, is it?' Emma said to Dan. 'Do you think we can put this on the expense account?'

'We don't have much choice but I don't want to be the one who has to explain it to McBride,' Dan said with a worried look.

They filled in the form as truthfully as they could but made out that Dan was infertile due to a bout of Chicken Pox in his early twenties.

Dan returned the form along with the credit card to the receptionist who promptly processed the payment and they waited holding hands together.

'At least we don't need to fake being a couple,' Emma said snuggling close to Dan. 'It should make things easier.'

Two cups of coffee were placed in front of them. Dan thumbed through a copy of Homes For The Discerning. 'Have you seen these houses?' he asked. 'They are just amazing. I've always wanted to live in America.'

'I doubt you could ever afford a house like that on a detective's income,' Emma snorted.

The receptionist stood before them. 'Dr Du Bois will see you now. Please come this way.'

They followed the long-legged receptionist through the frosted glassed double doors down a corridor until they reached another door with the name plate Dr Du Bois in shiny gold lettering. She knocked quietly and a deep voice boomed to come in. She opened the door and introduced Mr and Mrs Brennan and retreated back to her position on reception.

Dr Du Bois was older than Emma had expected but he had a kind looking face.

'Please come in and take a seat. Call me Charles. Is it OK if I call you Emma and Dan?' Not waiting for an answer he continued. 'It's not often that we have visitors from the UK. I expect you are here for gender selection?'

'No we are here looking for a sperm donor,' Dan replied.

'Oh, I see. Most patients from the UK are here for gender selection. Preimplantation genetic diagnosis, an expansion of IVF, can be used for sex selection,' he expanded. 'It is prohibited in the UK, except when it is used to screen for genetic diseases. The laws in the US are more relaxed on this subject. We mostly see Asian couples where bearing a son is seen as so important. I must admit I find the practice abhorrent. Think of all those frustrated males in twenty years who will be without a wife. I'd heard that the United Kingdom is suffering a shortage of sperm donors. No doubt down to the strict rules in place. In the USA there are no regulations governing who may engage in sperm donation. We just have recommendations and guidelines. The current guidelines limit a donor to twenty-five live births per population area of eight hundred and fifty thousand although even this is not enforced by law, there is no central tracking and lots of births go unreported. It is likely that some donors have over one hundred genetic children. Let me assure you that at my clinic we have much stricter controls in place. We have a limit of ten families per donor and we monitor all births.'

'Are the donors anonymous,' Dan asked.

'I'm assuming you are looking for the semen to be shipped home? For treatment at a clinic in the UK, the donor has to be Non-anonymous by law as the child has the right to know who their father is. We have very strict procedures at HFLI. We don't just take anyone. We have a very rigorous selection process,' Dr Du Bois said pulling a leaflet from a tier of trays at the end of his desk and passing it to Dan.

Dan scanned through the leaflet. He was surprised about the level of detail that the clinic went to thereby ensuring the quality of their donors.

'So do you ship to the UK?' Dan asked

Doctor Du Bois leaned over to his trays and produced two further leaflets. The first entitled International Deliveries and the second entitled UK Standard and passed them over to Dan.

Dan's eyes glazed over after the first paragraph which stated that HFLI delivered to forty countries worldwide via a designated carrier. He would read it in more detail later. Or maybe pass it over to Emma. He'd never been a great reader.

'We have quite a specific requirement for the biological father of our child,' Emma stated. 'He needs to be tall, blond, very intelligent and excel in sports and music. In other words, he needs to be exceptional. We also need the sperm shipped to the UK and we need a large supply so that we can produce siblings.'

'We only send enough sperm for one insemination. We do provide a vial buy and store option. This allows you to use the same donor for future insemination if unfortunately the procedure fails or you want the same father for a sibling. If you don't require the further sample we will even buy it back if it's still viable.'

The inevitable leaflet on the Vial Buy & Store/Vial Buy Back option slid across the desk.

'We require all our patients to be working with a licensed medical professional. The doctor or clinic needs to have an account with us. We can provide you with a list of clinics in the UK who specialise in reproductive medicine who we currently have registered or you can ask your own doctor to contact us and ask to be registered but I must warn you that we do carry out rigorous checks and it could take quite a while to process. To be honest with you both, and I shouldn't really say this, but it would be much cheaper and simpler for you to use one of the excellent facilities located in Denmark. With it being in the European Union you will have much less red tape.'

'So we can't have it shipped to our home in the UK?' Emma asked.

'We can do this in the USA but we can't send it to a home address abroad. Even in the USA, we need your health care provider to have an account and authorise the process. The sample has to be stored in a special freezer you can't just put it in your home freezer it wouldn't be cold enough. The chances of success would be very low so I can't recommend you follow this course of action.'

'How do you keep it cold enough during the shipping? Do you store it in dry ice?' Dan asked.

'All of our specimens are shipped in liquid nitrogen vapour tanks via FedEx or local courier. This has a temperature of –one hundred and ninety-six degrees centigrade. Dry ice has a temperature of minus seventy-eight point five degrees centigrade that is far below the temperature in which we store specimens and can result in a partial thaw process that is detrimental to the quality of the samples. The liquid nitrogen vapour tank is inside of a cardboard container. The inner canister known as the vapour tank is fastened using a cable tie to prevent tampering. Shipping papers attached to the outer case which contains a packing slip with the following information about your order: your health care provider's name and address, your name and address, your donor number and specimen preparation, number of vials, and post thaw count and motility for each unit. Also included is a summary of records detailing the donor testing and a statement of donor eligibility, specimen thawing instructions, return instructions and prepaid return label.'

'How long will the specimens remain frozen in the shipping tanks?' Emma asked.

Our standard shipping tanks have a guarantee to keep specimens frozen for seven days from the day of shipment; day one is considered the day of shipment. Upon request and for an additional fee we can send your specimens in a two-week tank in which the specimens are guaranteed to be kept frozen for fourteen days from the date of shipment.

'Everything seems very thorough and well controlled,' Emma said. 'Just one more question. Would it be feasible for a donor to bring another man's sperm into the clinic and pass it off as his own?'

That's a very strange question. No, it wouldn't be possible and I can't think of any reason why a donor would want to do this. All donors have to leave all their possessions in a locker and wear a gown before proceeding to the donation cubical.'

After receiving a raft of further leaflets they left the clinic with their heads buzzing. 'I don't think I could visit the other two clinics today,' Emma said holding her head.

'Me neither,' Dan replied. 'Let's go and get some lunch and we can talk through what we have learned.'

They found a small café in a nearby mall and slid into a booth well back from the other customers. Dan ordered his usual cheeseburger and fries and Emma ordered a prawn salad.

'The whole process is much more complicated than I could have imagined,' Dan said.

'And the regulations are far more stringent than I ever thought possible,' Emma added.

Dan continued with his take on things. 'We never thought that the perpetrator was keeping within the law. What we need to do is work out how someone could bypass all these procedures. It would need to be an inside job at either the clinic or the carrier. I'd bet on it being someone at the clinic. We need to get a list of all the employees and do some investigation into their finances.'

'Nobody is going to give us access to the employee records based on the evidence we have gathered so far. Which is zilch,' Emma stated.

'Legally no but what if we asked Laura Webb to take a look?' Dan suggested.

'You can't keep using Laura like this. You know it's not legal. It's not fair to her. What if she gets caught? What if we get caught? I can't afford to lose this job.'

'I don't like it but I can't see an alternative. I promise this will be the last time.

What time is it in the UK now?'

'Nine in the evening,' Dan calculated.

Dan rang Laura and spoke quietly into his mobile giving the details of the HFLI clinic.

'She'll get onto it straight away and report back as soon as she has something. I suggest we go back to the precinct and see if detectives Green and Heal have made any progress.'

67

Al Green and Simon Heal leaned forward towards the monitor intently watching the video from the camera which gave surveillance for the entrance to the parking garage where Eric Bamber had been assaulted. Luckily the tape had been retained as the case was still open. They had already found the time that Mr Bamber had arrived at the car park. They knew the time he had phoned 911 to report the assault. Now they painstakingly noted the registration of all vehicles arriving and leaving the parking garage paying particular attention to white vans. By the time the 911 call was made nine vehicles had arrived and forty-two had left including two white vans. One of the vans had a logo on the side with the name Ramano and Sons - Electricians At Your Service. The second van didn't have a visible logo. 'You take the electricians and I'll run a vehicle check on the other vans registration,' Al told Simon.

'Why do you always get the better lead?' Simon complained.

'Because I'm senior. Now get to it, else I'll give you the other forty-nine registrations to run,' Al remonstrated.

Simon returned to his work station cubicle and rang directory enquiries to obtain a phone number for Ramano's. He eventually got through to the office. He could feel the chill down the phone as soon as he announced he was phoning from the San Jose police department. Would the distrust between the Hispanic community and the police ever dissipate he thought? He eventually got put through to a Jesus Ramano who confirmed that he had been driving the works van that day. Yes, he had parked at the car park at the times Simon mentioned and yes he had been alone in the van. He had actually been working at the car park repairing some of the lights that were out. No, he hadn't witnessed the assault on Mr Bamber. Following the call, Simon rang the car park management company and confirmed that Mr Ramano's story was correct. They also confirmed that he had carried out work for them for the past five years and as far as they were concerned was beyond suspicion.

'I think we can cross my van off the list,' Simon said reporting back to Al with the information he had found.

'Mine also doesn't fit,' Al added. 'I traced the van to a rental company called Vans 4U,' he said looking at his notes. 'It was rented out to a school teacher who was taking his daughter to college in LA. I managed to speak with the daughter and she confirmed that they stopped off to get a bite to eat.'

'She could have been lying.'

'I thought the same so I rang the college and they confirmed her story. I also rang the school where the father teaches and the principal remembered him taking the day off as it caused a lot of inconvenience for the school having to find a replacement teacher.'

'So where can the van have gone that Eric Bamber saw?' Simon asked.

'It's a mystery, I don't know.' Al replied. 'All we can do now is follow-up the forty-nine cars we have identified.'

'That's going to take ages,' Simon moaned.

'The sooner you get started the sooner you will get finished,' Al said wheeling his way towards the elevator.

'What, you aren't going to help?' Simon groaned.

Al didn't reply and continued on his way.

They waited ages for a taxi to take them back to the precinct.

'I think we should hire a car,' Emma suggested. 'It's not as easy to find a taxi here as it was in New York.'

'Good idea.' Dan rang their hotel and asked them to arrange for a rental car to be delivered. 'It will be ready for us at the hotel this evening,' he reported.

It was three in the afternoon by the time they arrived back at the precinct.

Al was nowhere to be seen but Simon was talking rapidly on the phone in Spanish. He indicated that they should take a seat and held up a finger showing that he would be a minute. Five minutes later he came off the phone.

'Why can't people who come to live here learn to speak English? It's getting worse and worse. Some areas only speak Spanish now.'

'Sounds like you speak pretty good Spanish.' Dan said impressed.

'Needs must. You would never get anywhere in this area if you didn't speak Spanish. You would just get the response 'No hablo ingles, me no understandi.'

Simon brought them up to speed with the investigation. 'It will take me all evening to follow up all these car registrations. I suggest you come back tomorrow and we will discuss our next moves with Detective Green.'

When they got back to the hotel the receptionist told them that their rental car had arrived. She gave them the keys and pointed to a red Ford Sedan out in the parking lot.

'I've always wanted to visit Alcatraz,' Dan admitted. 'How about a drive along the coast to San Francisco?'

The receptionist provided them with a map and even booked them on one of the evening sailings to the island where Alcatraz was located, telling them how lucky they were to get a place as normally trips were booked up weeks in advance.

The evening was warm and balmy as they drove along the coast road. There was a fantastic sunset. They stopped off at one of the many roadside bars and sat sipping cocktails as the sun dropped down beyond the Pacific Ocean. The waves crashed down onto the rocks below and a light breeze ruffled their hair. Emma thought it was the most romantic occasion in her life and daydreamed about returning here with Dan on their honeymoon. San Francisco was smaller than she expected and seemed to comprise of the steepest roads she had ever come across. They arrived at the quayside and located the boat that would take them across to the old prison. As they waited in line Emma was amazed at the number of very large seals laid out on pontoons tethered in the harbour. By the time they arrived at the old prison on Alcatraz it was dark. For safety reasons, they weren't allowed to wander around the island. They queued up for the headsets which would give them a commentary as they toured the prison. Emma found it more interesting than she had expected as an ex-convict described life in the prison via the headset.

'I've always wanted to ride on one of those trolley buses,' Dan said pointing towards a queue of people as they docked back at pier 33. He dragged Emma towards the line of waiting people and they joined the queue. Ten minutes later they were aboard the old wooden trolley bus and ascending one of the steep San Franciscan streets. Getting off in the centre of the city they entered a trendy bar named The Brick and ordered some food and drinks.

San Francisco wasn't like other American cities. Emma and Dan both thought it seemed more European in its culture and in particular its food portion sizes. Following their meal at The Brick even Emma still felt hungry. It was only ten in the evening but all the other restaurants in the area had already closed for the night. 'Looks like everyone has gone to bed,' Dan commented.

'Then I suggest we do the same,' Emma said with a twinkle in her eye.

By seven that evening Detective Simon Heal had traced all the registration numbers but had found nothing significant. As he finished off his last coffee after a very long day he sat pondering the disappearance of the van Eric Bamber had seen. If it had been moved between Eric Bamber's assault and the police arriving but it hadn't left the multi-storey car park then there could only be one explanation, it was still in the car park but on another floor. The perpetrator must have known that the police would scrutinise the surveillance footage so he had remained there until later.

Simon switched on his computer and continued to watch the video again to see if a white van left the car park later. About an hour after the ambulance and police departed the building a white van could be seen leaving. Simon froze the image but to his dismay the registration plate was a blur. Something had been placed over the tag plate to distort the characters. He also couldn't make out the decals on the van as it drove directly at the camera before turning away out of view. He could just make out two figures inside the van but due to the tinted windows, it wasn't possible to even identify whether they were male or female.

As Simon rewound the tape to see if he could find the van arriving and hopefully have better luck identifying its origin he had another thought. It was a long shot but was worth a try. He phoned Romano and Sons. This time the office was closed but a recorded message gave a number to ring for electrical emergency call outs. Ringing the number the phone was answered by another member of the Romano clan. 'I'm after Jesus, this is Detective Heal, I spoke with him earlier and it's very important that you give me his number.' After some deliberation which involved a heated discussion with someone who Simon assumed was Mrs Romano the man came back on the phone and gave him a number before promptly cutting him off. Jesus didn't seem best pleased to hear from him and complained about Simon phoning at ten o'clock in the evening. An extremely loud TV was blaring away in the background and he shouted for it to be turned down.

'I've got one more question to ask you about the day at the parking garage. Do you remember a white van that was parked on the second floor moving to another floor around five in the afternoon?'

'Actually, I do. I noticed it on the second floor when I was fixing the lights there. It had such a silly name on the side. Then blow me it was there again on the fourth floor when I was fixing the lights up there.'

'Do you remember the name?'

'Yes, it was called Perfect Pooches and had a picture of a pink poodle on the side. Who would describe a pink dog as perfect, now an American Pit Bull that's what I call a dog.'

Interrupting his diatribe on what constituted the perfect dog Simon thanked Jesus and ended the call. In one movement he switched off the computer and pulled his jacket from the back of his chair. He knew exactly where he was going. He punched Al's speed dial number into his cell as he drove.

'Damn it Al, where the hell are you?' he said as voice mail picked up his call. 'I think I may have found a lead. As it's on my way home I'll just give it a quick recce now. I'll fill you in tomorrow if it looks promising.'

He knew where Perfect Pooches was located as it happened to be across the road from the insurance broker he used. He arrived outside in less than ten minutes. He had always assumed that Perfect Pooches was a dog grooming establishment but reading the blurb on the window it professed to prospective customers that they could keep their beloved pet dog alive forever. Cloning is now a reality it stated. Store your pets DNA and recreate him at any time in the future. Unbelievable Simon thought, is this even legal? The place was all closed up for the night. Simon decided to do some snooping around the back. Maybe the van was stored there and he could get a look inside. The yard was surrounded by a high fence with razor wire across the top. There was no way he would be able to scale it. He walked around the perimeter. At the rear of the building, a pair of solid looking gates allowed access to the yard. These were as high as the fence and topped by the same vicious razor wire. He was surprised by the level of security the building had. He peered through the narrow crack between the two gates. He could make out a row of identical vans but couldn't see the registration plates. He noticed several state-of-the-art security cameras high on the wall. Resigned to returning in the morning he was about to turn when a voice made him jump.

'Don't move I have a gun pointed directly at you. Who are you and what are you doing snooping around my premises?'

Deciding that the truth was the best way forward Simon replied in his most authoritative voice, 'I'm Detective Simon Heal from the San Jose police department. I suggest you lower the gun immediately.'

'And why are you here?' the voice continued not in the least concerned that Simon was a police officer.

'I'm investigating an assault that happened at the multi-storey Market & San Pedro Square Garage on N. Market St last year. I have reason to believe one of the vans from your establishment was there at the time and I would like to interview the driver.'

Simon's patience was wearing very thin. He was just repeating the fact that he was a police officer and in the process of turning round to confront the man when from the corner of his eye he saw the large fist of a huge black man flying towards his face, then blackness overwhelmed him.

Simon woke sometime later. He didn't know how long he had been out. His head was pounding and he was sure he had a couple of loose teeth as he gently probed around his mouth with his tongue. He attempted to raise his wrist to check his watch but found he couldn't move. He was securely bound to the chair he was sitting on with those plastic tie wraps that police forces across the world now used to restrain people. Light to carry and impossible to break even by the strongest suspects. This didn't stop Simon trying to get his hands and feet free even though he knew it was impossible. The ties just dug deeper into his skin and flesh until he could feel blood running from his wrists. Frustrated he gave up and took in his surroundings. It was dark, very dark. He couldn't see a thing in front of his eyes. He knew he was inside as there was no breeze and the air was musty. He thought he was in a basement. He was naked and cold. He shouted out but got no response. His voice became hoarse and he had no alternative but to wait for something to happen. After what seemed like hours a bright light suddenly shone into his eyes. He blinked and tried to turn away.

'I'm a police detective, release me immediately,' he shouted, not knowing if anyone could hear him.

A sinister high-pitched voice replied, 'We know exactly who you are Detective Heal. What we need to know is why you are snooping about our establishment. Now you can tell us the easy way or you can experience the most pain you have ever imagined and tell us anyway. The choice is yours.'

'Release me immediately,' Simon shouted. 'You are in enough trouble already. Don't make things even worse. I've already told your other goon why I'm here.'

As if not hearing him the man continued to speak. 'I've made a study of torture. It has always fascinated me the ingenuity of man to inflict pain to extract information. You have to get it just right. Too much and a prisoner will make up anything to make it stop. Too little and they will weave a web of lies.'

'Release me immediately,' Simon repeated angrily again.

'OK,' the voice replied as a blade arced downwards severing the plastic ties along with both Simon's hands. 'Your wish is my command.'

It took several seconds for the pain to reach Simon's brain. He immediately went into shock as his life blood pumped from the stumps where his hands had been. 'I learned that one from the African Congo. Over there they give prisoners a choice. Long sleeves or short sleeves. Nobody ever chooses short sleeves so I didn't bother asking you.'

Simon had fallen forward onto the cold dusty floor but was still tied to the chair by his ankles. The wetness of his blood pooled around his face. He screamed and screamed.

'We can't have you bleeding to death before you tell us everything you know,' the man said as he lit a blow torch. 'Now this is going to hurt a bit but I'm saving your life.'

The man walked towards Simon who was oblivious to anything other than the pain he was feeling. He licked the flame across the ragged stumps and the blood stemmed to a trickle. Simon howled even louder.

'I'm going to leave you for a little while now to contemplate your situation. When I return maybe you will be more co-operative.'

Simon hadn't heard any of this he had long since slipped into blissful unconsciousness.

When Simon awoke he thought he had experienced a nightmare until the reality that this wasn't a dream hit him. The pain from his wrists throbbed up his arms and into his neck. He had bitten through his tongue and it swelled painfully in his mouth. He groaned and tried to turn. The man must have been waiting for him to recover consciousness as he walked towards Simon and stood directly in front of him. He bent over and put his hands under Simon's armpits and gently lifted him with ease back onto the chair.

The man walked towards the wall and switched on a lamp. He picked up a syringe from the table there and turned to Simon and injected him in the arm. 'Morphine,' the man said; 'should take the edge off the pain so we can have a chat. I want to know what you and anyone else knows.'

Through his ruined mouth Simon told the man to go to hell.

'Oh I went there a long time ago,' the man replied. 'Detective Heal you disappoint me. We both know you will tell me everything I want to know eventually, so to save yourself a lot of pain I suggest you do it sooner rather than later.

The morphine had now kicked in and it was making Simon feel braver than he should have felt.

'I'll leave you a while for the morphine to wear off then I'll return and we can start again,' the man said with a sigh. 'I really don't have the time to waste on this Detective Heal; you are really trying my patience.'

It had been a long time since Simon had cried, maybe not since he had been a boy and had fallen off his bike and broken his arm. He remembered his mother comforting him and his Dad taking him to the local hospital to have it put in plaster.

He thought about how he would no longer be able to hold his wife's hand or stroke his daughters beautiful long brown hair. The tears of his loss flowed down his face.

After what seemed an eternity the man returned.

'I'll give you a choice. Do you want to lose your eyes or your manhood?' He said as he selected the appropriate tool from the table.

Simon couldn't answer the fear had paralysed him.

'If you don't have a preference I'll take your eyes. I always think sex is overrated.' Taking a poker and heating the tip with the blow torch until it glowed red he approached Simon again.

68

The following day Emma and Dan arrived at the precinct by nine. It was much easier to get around now they had their own transport. Al was sat at his desk looking worried. They couldn't see Simon anywhere.

'Any progress?' Dan asked.

'Yes and no,' Al replied. 'Simon found a lead last night and went to investigate. No-one has seen him since. He didn't make it home to his wife last night. I've tried ringing him several times since I got in but he's not picking up. I'm really worried. It's not like Simon to not report in.'

'Did he say what his lead was?' Emma asked.

'No. He left me a voicemail last night,' Al said turning on his phone and playing the message Simon had left. 'I'm so annoyed with myself. I went to my brother's birthday party last night and left Simon working here. I didn't think this case was that important and I'd missed his birthday for the last ten years because of work so I thought it was the right thing to do to attend. I didn't hear my phone because of the loud music. If only I'd picked up this wouldn't have happened.'

'There's no point beating yourself up mate. We just need to review everything that Simon was working on and find out what the lead was,' Dan suggested.

'That's what I'm doing now. I'm running through the surveillance footage from the parking garage again, maybe I missed something. Simon was looking at this when I left. Strangely he's wound it back to the beginning of the tape. I've also asked for a log of all the phone calls he made last night. I've asked for a trace on his cell but according to the tech team it's switched off.'

'Is there anything we can do to help?' Emma asked.

Al wheeled himself over to a large map posted on the wall. Taking a marker pen he reached up and circled a point on the map.

'This is where we are.' He circled a second point on the map about fifteen miles away. 'This is Simon's home. He said the lead he was following was located on his way home, therefore, I think it must be in this area,' he said drawing a wide circle around the two points. 'We know the exact time he left the precinct and we know the vehicle he was driving. We don't have many surveillance cameras but if we look at the footage from the few we do have then we should be able to narrow down the search area a bit.' Consulting a list Al marked the location of the cameras on the map. 'If you could map Simon's progress for me it would really help. I've set up this PC for you. Each camera has a serial number just punch it in with the date and time you require and it will show you the recording.' Al passed them the list of cameras along with a picture of the car Simon was driving.

The good thing was that at that time of night the roads were relatively quiet the bad thing was that because it was dark everything was in black and white so Simon's red car showed up as dark grey. They picked up the first sighting of the car quite quickly from the camera a block from where the precinct was located. Dan marked it on the map with the time of the sighting. He put an arrow pointing right to show the direction the car had turned.

'From this point he could have driven one of three directions. Two of the directions had cameras the other direction didn't have any. I estimate it would have taken about three minutes to drive between the first camera and this one or six minutes to this one,' Dan said pointing at the map.

They keyed in the data to retrieve the footage from the next camera and watched it for a good five minutes before and past the point Simon's car would have appeared had it taken that route. Dan put a red cross on the map then sat down again to look at the next camera. Again nothing showed up. Dan put a second red cross on the map.

'We have to assume that he went this direction,' Dan said putting an arrow onto the map.

'Or he could have stopped somewhere between the first and second cameras,' Emma added.

'True,' Dan conceded.

They had managed to reduce the search area considerably but it was still very large.

Emma pointed to the map, 'look what's within the search area. The Happy Families' Laboratories.'

As if on cue Dan's mobile rang. Looking at the display he said, 'it's Laura.'

Moving to a quieter area of the room Dan had a long conversation with Laura about Happy Families' and the staff employed there. He returned to Emma shaking his head.

'Laura's not found anything of interest. Apart from what we expected. Several of the staff lied on their CVs. One has three convictions for shop lifting. Another is an illegal working under a bogus name. Dr Du Bois seems genuine enough. There's nothing unusual about his finances. No sperm samples have been shipped to the UK in the last year. She said the security on their computer system was crap and advised us to tell them to get an overhaul. She also did a check on the other two fertility clinics. They don't even offer an export service and appear small outfits.'

'So where does that leave us?' Emma asked.

'All we can do is follow Simon's investigation and hope it leads us somewhere.'

Emma and Dan reported their progress to Al. He, in turn, updated them with what he had found.

'I think I know what Simon was thinking. If what Eric Bamber said is true and the white van moved but didn't leave the car park then it must have moved within the car park. I checked the surveillance tape for later in the day and sure enough, a white van left the parking garage an hour after the police and the ambulance carrying Eric Bamber left.'

'So we have a description and registration plate?' Dan asked.

'If only. The driver knew the camera was there and made efforts to avoid identification. Apart from knowing the colour and shape of the van we have zip. I also checked when it arrived and again it avoided detection.'

'Can't you check other street cameras like we have just done looking for Simon's car?' Emma asked.

'It was too long ago they will all have been overwritten long since. Remember until you came along this was considered a low-level crime. I'm afraid not much resource was put into it at the time and Mr Bamber didn't want to pursue the matter. We might have more luck with the phone records. They show that the two calls Simon made before calling me were to the electrician working on the lighting in the parking garage that day. I'm on my way over there now to speak with him if you want to tag along.'

When they arrived at Romano and Sons the closed sign was showing on the door. Nobody was around. Al wheeled himself to the launderette next door to ask if they knew where the family was. He returned to Emma and Dan with a grim look on his face.

'Seems there's been an accident. The family are all down at the O'Connor Hospital Emergency Department. We'll go there now and see what happened.'

When they arrived at the hospital Al showed his badge to the girl on the desk and was pointed to the direction of the lift down the corridor. 'They're in the burns unit on the third floor,' he told Emma and Dan. 'Apparently, Jesus Ramano had an argument with some live electrical wiring earlier today. It doesn't look good.'

Arriving at the burns unit they found a large Hispanic family crying and speaking loudly in Spanish.

'Are you the Ramano family?' Al asked holding up his badge.

A large man wearing a t-shirt bearing the name Romano and Sons stepped forward. 'You see I told you it wasn't an accident. Jesus was too good an electrician to touch a live wire.'

'Tell me what happened?' Al asked.

The man sat down heavily on a nearby chair holding his head in his hands. 'We got a call first thing this morning, as soon as we opened. The man said it was an emergency and promised to pay triple time if we would come out immediately. I told him I would take a look but he insisted that Jesus did the work. I thought it a strange request but who turns down triple time. Next thing I got a call from the hospital telling me Jesus had been admitted here with extensive electrical burns. That's as much as I know. No way would Jesus make a mistake like that. He might not be the brightest lad but he is a great electrician, I taught him myself.'

Al went over to the nurses' station and spoke to the nurse in charge. He then came over to report to Emma and Dan. 'It doesn't look good. He's still in theatre but they don't expect him to make it.'

'Has he said anything?' Dan asked.

'He hasn't regained consciousness so far,' Al replied.

Al went back to the family group. 'Is Mrs Ramano here?' he asked.

Two women stepped forward, one a heavy set woman of about sixty the other an attractive woman of about thirty. 'Are you Mrs Jesus Romano?' he asked the younger of the two.

'Yes, I am Marie Romano. Who has done this to my husband?' she asked.

'We don't know yet but I intend to find out. Did your husband receive a call last night from my colleague Detective Simon Heal?'

'Yes, it was just before ten. I remember as it interrupted my favourite TV program and Jesus asked me to turn it down.'

'Do you know what the call was about?'

'Not exactly. I think it might have been to do with the incident at the parking garage. I was busy trying to watch my program I wasn't taking much interest. He did say something about wanting to buy an American Pit Bull Terrier. A man's dog he said not like those Poncey poodles. That's the last thing he said. He went to bed and had already left for work when I got up this morning. Then this happened,' she said breaking down in tears again.

264

A grim faced doctor still wearing his operating theatre scrubs approached the family. 'Mrs Romano,' he said. The attractive woman turned to face him. Her eyes said it all as she waited for the death sentence to be delivered. 'I'm afraid there was nothing we could do. Your husband passed away five minutes ago. I'm very sorry for your loss.'

The whole family broke down in tears hugging each other for support.

Al knew he wouldn't get anything further from them. He asked the doctor. 'Was this an accident or do you suspect foul play?'

'That's impossible for me to say. You need to look at the place where the accident occurred to establish the cause.' With this he pulled the cap from his head and walked back in the direction he had come from looking defeated.

Al made several calls before leaving the hospital. 'I've arranged for us to meet an expert electrician at the warehouse where the incident occurred. I've asked that it be established as a crime scene until we get to the bottom of this.'

The warehouse looked disused. They were met at the door by a cheery short middle aged man who had a ludicrous comb over and wore a cheap brown suit. 'Definitely deliberate. The live and the neural wires had been swapped over and the mains switch had been tampered with. The electrician would have thought the power was off but it wasn't. If you notice there's a substation located directly behind this building. At the substation transformers reduce the voltage to a lower level for distribution to nearby commercial and residential users. The connection between the transformer and the power supply has also been tampered with meaning a high voltage current was allowed to flow directly into this building. As soon as he touched the wire six hundred volts would have gone through him. He had no chance. I'm surprised he didn't die instantly. This location was selected very carefully by someone who knew exactly what he or she was doing.'

Another uniformed officer approached them. 'Who raised the alarm?' Al asked. 'Looking at his note book the rookie replied, 'It was the auto repair shop across the road. The incident knocked out the power to the whole block. The mechanic came out to investigate and saw smoke coming from the warehouse. He found Mr Romano injured inside and called 911.'

Al went over to the garage and found an elderly guy in dirty overalls sitting smoking on the step. 'Are you the guy who phoned 911?'

'Yes sir,' he replied. 'I was just under the hood of a truck I was repairing when all the lights went out. I checked our power and couldn't get it to come back on. I was just going to speak with the people at the water cooler company next door when I noticed smoke coming from that abandoned warehouse across the road. When I looked through the door I saw a man smouldering on the floor. He didn't look good. I dialled 911 and waited with him until the ambulance arrived.'

'Did he say anything?' Al asked hopefully.

'No he just lay there lifeless.'

'Did you see any other people around the place this morning?'

'No I didn't see a thing apart from the electrician's van parked across the road. By the way, how is he?'

'I'm afraid he didn't make it.'

Al looked despondent when he returned to Emma and Dan. 'I don't know where we go from here. It seems like whoever is involved in this is one step ahead of us. I'm really worried about Simon. These people are ruthless.'

'If Jesus Ramano saw something then maybe one of the others parked there that day noticed something. I suggest we start ringing the list of people we identified and ask them if they noticed anything strange about a white van,' Dan said.

Emma gave him an exhausted look. She still hadn't got over the jet lag.

Dan felt sorry for her, 'I'll go back to the precinct with Al. You take the car back to the hotel and get some rest. I'll catch up with you later for dinner.'

Emma didn't like to let them down but knew she would be of little use, so she agreed to Dan's suggestion and set off back to the hotel. She would have a nice leisurely soak in that large spa bath and then a nap before meeting Dan later.

69

An hour later soaking in the bath Emma heard the hotel room door open followed by footsteps entering the room. She smiled to herself. Dan had managed to get away earlier than she had expected. 'I'm in here,' she called hoping that Dan would join her as the bath could easily hold the two of them. The bathroom door slowly opened. Instead of Dan Emma found herself staring down the barrel of a gun with a silencer on the end. A man's high pitch voice instructed Emma to get dressed. Keeping the gun train on her he threw a towel across the room. Emma's mind went into overdrive. If he wanted her dead he would have already shot her. He must want her alive for a reason. Her best option was to play for time. Dan would come back soon but then he too would be in danger. No, she had to get out of this predicament herself. Who was this man and why was he interested in her? Only a few people knew she was here in California. Maybe it's just a case of mistaken identity she thought.

'I think you have the wrong room?' Emma stammered.

'No Miss Blakely I have the right room. Detective Heal was very forthcoming with his information. In fact, in the end, he couldn't tell me enough. I know everything about your investigation and this is why you and DI Brennan have to be terminated. I don't like loose ends. I never leave anything to chance. Before I dispense with you I just want to carry out an extra little bit of interrogation. It's not very often I get to work with a woman. It should be fun, well at least for me. Now get dressed. You are going to walk out of this hotel quietly otherwise I start shooting and that will mean a lot more casualties than just you.'

Emma assessed her options. She could tackle the man, he wasn't that big and she was good at self-defence.

As if reading her mind he whispered in his girlie voice 'Don't try anything or I will shoot you.'

Emma dressed slowly in spite of her nakedness, life preservation overcoming any modesty she felt. Time was her greatest ally, the longer she could draw this out the greater the chance of making an escape. She tried to think of a way of leaving Dan a clue as to her plight. She undid the necklace from around her neck and placed it on the bedside table. She had told Dan the necklace had been a gift from her mother and she never took it off.

'Stop messing about,' the whiny voice told her. He strode towards her and grabbed a handful of her wet hair yanking her head painfully back so fast she thought a piece of her scalp would tear off. Tears sprang into her eyes and her heart slammed against her ribs. She kicked out towards his shins but he had anticipated her move and she met only air. He pressed the gun painfully into her ribs draping his coat over it to conceal its presence as he pulled her out of the door and into the corridor.

'I'm going to let go of your hair and you are going to walk quietly beside me to my van parked outside.' He pulled a baseball cap onto his head and pressed the elevator call button. Emma knew that there was a camera in the lift and silently mouthed *help* towards it as they descended towards the lobby. The man also seemed aware of the camera and kept his head lowered in an effort to avoid identification.

Emma thought her best chance of raising the alarm would be in the lobby. There would be several receptionists, the bell boy and a security guard who was armed. As the doors opened she could see a family including four children stood at the reception desk.

'Make any sudden move and I'll kill those children before the guard can even get his gun unholstered,' he whispered into her ear.

Emma felt deflated. She couldn't risk a gun fight here; there were too many innocent people around. The man took her through the front door and turned sharp right towards the staff car park. Emma looked around for an avenue of escape but there was nowhere to go. Even if she managed to get away from him she would be in the open with no cover. How could this be happening to her in broad daylight? He manoeuvred her towards a white van with a pink poodle logo on the side.

She saw her best chance of escape as being the time he opened the van door. She could use the van as cover whilst making a break for it. She braced herself to push him away and run. She planned it all out in her head. As he opened the door she would kick him hard where it hurts and run past the van towards the next row of parked cars. By the time he recovered she would have reached safety. She was so intent on her escape she didn't even notice the hypodermic needle he had taken from his pocket until she felt a sharp sting in her leg and everything around her went black as he bundled her into the back of the van.

70

'This is hopeless,' Dan said to Al as he got yet another blank response from yet another person who had been in the parking garage. Most people don't even remember being there that day never mind seeing anything.

'We knew it was a long shot but I can't think of any other avenue of enquiry to take. Maybe you should go and get some rest and you can start afresh tomorrow.'

Dan thought about Emma waiting for him back at the hotel but he didn't want to let Al down when he was helping them with their case. 'No I will keep going. We only have another dozen people to call.'

'Thanks, I'll get you a coffee to help keep you awake.'

Whilst Al was away Dan noticed Mrs Rose Bamber entering the room. She spoke urgently to an officer on the far side who pointed in Dan's direction. When she walked over Dan could see that she was visibly upset.

'I've got some bad news,' she said.

It didn't register with Dan. Why would Mrs Bamber be here and why would she be delivering bad news, was it something relating to her husband?

She registered his confusion. 'I'm the District Attorney,' she announced 'didn't anyone tell you?'

'No, nobody mentioned it but now I know why people were concerned about upsetting you.'

'Oh, the attack on Eric you mean. Yes, most of them thought it was a form of retaliation against me.'

'It was Detective Green I was after. Is he still here?'

'Yes, he's just gone to get coffee he'll be back in a minute.'

At that moment Al wheeled himself through the door.

'I'm sorry Al I've got bad news, it's Detective Heal, he's been murdered. The state troopers have just found his body out in the desert.

269

71

'You know I owe Detective Heal my life,' Al said as he drove Dan out of town towards the dump site. 'He was a good man. He was more than just a partner he was my best friend. When I woke up in the hospital and they told me I was paralysed from the waist down and would be in a wheelchair the rest of my life I hated him, really hated him. I wished he had let me die that day. He just continued to visit me every day no matter how much abuse I threw at him. He made me see that my life hadn't ended, it had just changed direction. I think being in a chair has made me a better detective. It certainly makes me look up to people he laughed as tears coursed down his face. How am I going to break it to Alysha and the kids? They will be devastated.'

Dan thought he had better phone Emma and tell her the news and let her know not to expect him back anytime soon. The phone rang and rang but she wasn't picking up. She must still be in the bath. I'll try again in another half hour he thought.

Dan could see blue and red flashing lights in the distance. Al slowed the car and they pulled up behind an ambulance. Two of the ambulance crew stood patiently at the roadside waiting for permission to remove the body. Several officers were fanned out several yards apart looking for clues in the undergrowth. A huddle of officers stood beside what Dan guessed was Simon's body. One young officer was wrenching his guts out over by one of the patrol cars. As they approached the officers one of them turned towards Al and put his hand out to stop him proceeding further.

'You don't want to see this Al; it's bad, really bad. I've never seen anything like it in the twenty years I've been on the force.'

'I need to see what they've done to him. I need to catch these bastards.'

Al pushed forward in his wheelchair and looked down at the remains of his friend. He lay there naked. Both his hands had been severed and an empty eye socket and one staring eye looked out from his ruined face.

'Have you found any clues as to who has done this?' he asked.

'Nothing so far.'

'Any sign of his clothes or his car?'

'No nothing.'

Al turned and wheeled himself back towards the car. Before he got in he fell forward to the floor racked with grief. Dan scooped him up and put him in the passenger side and loaded his chair in the back. They had brought this to the American's door. If they hadn't re-opened the investigation into Eric Bamber's assault none of this would have happened. Dan felt an overwhelming sense of guilt.

On the drive back Dan tried to get in contact with Emma again. Still no reply. He was getting worried now. He rang the hotel reception and they told him Miss Blakely had left an hour earlier with a man but hadn't left a message for him. Now he was really worried. He had intended to take Al home but decided to go straight to the hotel.

He raced up to Emma's room. Nothing looked disturbed but her bag was still there. She wouldn't have gone out voluntarily leaving her bag behind. He then noticed the necklace on the side table. Was this a message, a cry for help? She had told him only last night that she never took the necklace off. He went to question the security guard in the lobby. He had seen Emma and the man leave but hadn't thought anything suspicious about it.

Dan asked if he could see the surveillance tape. The one from the elevator showed Emma with the man. His heart sank as she mouthed the word *'help'* into the camera. At no point did the man look into the camera and his face was covered with a baseball cap. All he could tell was the man was white and slightly built.

'Are there any other cameras?' he asked the guard.

'We have one at the front of the hotel and also one in the customer parking lot,' he replied clicking on some buttons and bringing up the relevant footage. Dan could see the two of them leaving the hotel. It looked like the man had a gun pressed into Emma's side. No doubt this is how he had coerced her into leaving with him.

'It looks like the man was parked in the staff car park,' the guard said. 'Unfortunately, we don't have any cameras on that side of the hotel. Do you want me to ring the police?'

72

When Emma regained consciousness she found herself strapped to a chair in a dark dank cellar. Her body involuntarily shook in terror. The thick metallic smell of blood filled her nostrils but she knew it wasn't hers. A chill passed over her that could only be explained by a lack of clothing. She couldn't see anything. She strained her ears for any noise. She could just make out the sound of some yapping dogs in the distance. She called out then listened again but the sound hadn't changed. She pulled and tugged at her restraints but only managed to rub her wrists raw. The longer she sat there restrained with her senses deprived the stronger her fear grew. All her training told her this was what her captor wanted. Wear down the prisoner first then the interrogation is easier. It was working. After what seemed like hours she heard the click of a door opening. Next, a bright light shone into her face and the same high-pitched whiny voice of the man who had abducted her sounded in her ears. She felt her skin crawl. Sitting naked strapped to the chair she had never felt so scared and vulnerable. Her mouth and throat were so dry. When she spoke it was difficult to get any words out.

'What do you want with me?'

'Aarh, at last, you are awake. I'm hoping we can have a much more sociable chat than I had with that Detective Heal. I didn't like him. Not one bit. I've always liked the English. Such a nice accent and so well educated not like the mongrels we have in this country. I'm sure you must be thirsty,' he said putting a cup of water to her lips.

Emma drank thirstily not thinking about whether the liquid was safe or not. 'Do you know where Detective Heal is?' she asked.

'Oh yes, I know where every bit of him is.'

73

Back in England Laura Webb sat in front of her Apple Mac Pro Tower Desktop screen and thought about how she could aid the investigation. She knew the detectives were reticent about accepting her help but she couldn't just sit here doing nothing. Looking into the Happy Families' Laboratories computer system had given her an idea. She noticed that they always used the same carrier to transport the donor samples. Given the fragility of the contents and the fact they had to remain so cold throughout their transit, Laura thought that only a specialised company would offer to transport the packages. She was surprised to learn that FedEx offered this service.

Locating the FedEx office closest to San Jose Laura accessed their computer system. Much of the system was too secure for her to get into but one of their applications allowed customers to track their packages. This was an open system and was easy enough for Laura to hack into.

There were millions of packages registered on the database. Far too many for Laura to check through. She had to find a way of narrowing the search down. She needed something to identify the packages that required the special temperature controlled delivery. What she needed was an example of the type of package she was looking for. From her previous investigation into the Happy Families' Laboratories, she knew that they had sent a package to Europe the previous year. Entering the date of this delivery along with the Laboratories address she brought the record onto her screen. On a line at the bottom next to Special Transit Arrangements were the letters LNV. Laura assumed this stood for Liquid Nitrogen Vapour the cooling agent used to keep the sperm samples at the right temperature. Also on the screen there was another piece of useful information – Country of Destination. The example she was looking at showed Belgium.

Laura quickly wrote a search criterion to look through the FedEx database looking for LNV with the Country of Destination as the UK. Just in case they had used Great Britain, England or just Britain she added these in to be on the safe side.

The results brought up six companies in the San Jose area who had sent samples to the UK in the last five years. Five out of the six belonged to animal insemination companies. Only one belonged to a human research laboratory. Laura soon discovered that this laboratory wasn't even sending semen samples. It was working with another hospital in the UK to research a genetically rare disease and the two hospitals were sending blood samples from families in their area. This left the five laboratories dealing in animal semen. Laura expected that both human and animal semen had to be handled in exactly the same way. What better way to avoid the complex red tape of exporting human sperm than to disguise it as animal semen.

One company specialised in horse semen. Another dealt in farm animals. The other three dogs and cats. All five were minor concerns with only a small number of employees. As was the way with small enterprises the computer security wasn't up to much. This was until Laura looked into the last of the five companies. Trying all the hacking tools at her disposal she couldn't get into this computer system. This level of security wasn't cheap and would be way beyond the reach of a business the size of this one.

74

Dan returned to Al in the car. 'He's got Emma,' he said desperately.

'Who's got Emma?' Al asked.

'The monster who killed Simon he's taken Emma. We've got to find him before he hurts her.' Dan couldn't imagine how he would cope if Emma got hurt. He had to find her.

Dan thought about his promise not to use Laura again but this was an emergency. She picked up on the second ring.

'I was just about to phone you,' she said. 'I think I've found your sperm donor laboratory.'

Dan tried to be patient as Laura described her thought process.

'How confident are you of this result?'

'Ninety percent,' came the reply.

'We need to go to a place called Perfect Pooches run by a man named Raymond Hearns,' Dan informed Al. 'I'll explain everything on the way.'

75

Emma had always been good at reading people and her instincts told her that if she was going to get through this she needed to tell the man everything she knew. The outcome would still be the same, she was going to die at the hands of this madman but maybe if she was convincing enough she could save Dan and Al from the same fate. This man was obviously trying to eliminate anyone who knew anything significant about the case. She had one thing in her favour - they didn't know anything significant about the case, so she wouldn't need to lie.

76

'You haven't given me enough evidence for a warrant. In fact you haven't given me any hard evidence just conjecture. I want to get these bastards as much as you do but a judge wouldn't sign a search ,warrant based on what you've got.'

'Then we go in without a warrant,' Dan pleaded.

'What - a cripple and an unarmed man raid a highly organised criminal compound?'

'I think I have a plan,' Dan said 'It's risky but it might just work.'

77

'Aren't you going to plead for me to release you?'

'I doubt it would do me any good.'

'Wise decision Emma. I can call you Emma?'

'Call me anything you like.'

'Now we are going to have a little chat and you are going to tell me everything you know.'

'Ask away,' Emma said sounding far more confident than she felt.

'How did you find Eric Bamber?'

Emma explained about the Rosie Ware kidnapping and how the psychologist had believed that a network to produce designer babies was operating in England. This had led them to search for exceptional men used to father these babies. The assault on Eric Bamber had matched their criteria and led the investigation to San Francisco.

'And how did Detective Heal manage to trace the crime back here?'

'We didn't know he had. He didn't manage to tell anyone before he disappeared. We thought that he had gathered some evidence from Jesus Romano but the witness died before we could speak to him.'

'And this Jesus Romano didn't tell anyone other than Detective Heal what he had seen?'

'Apparently not. We interviewed the whole family and none of them was aware of the telephone call he had with Detective Heal.'

'Not even his wife.'

'No he went to bed immediately following the call from Detective Heal and he left for work the next morning before she woke.'

The man seemed pleased. 'This fits in with what Detective Heal told me and what Jesus Romano said; I think you are telling the truth.'

'So you were involved with Detective Heal's disappearance and the murder of Jesus Romano?'

'You've got me there Emma I have to confess that I might have had something to do with those events.'

'As you are going to kill me anyway you might as well tell me what you are up to here. Who are you, what's your name?'

'Still playing the detective, even though you are in such a hopeless predicament. I like your courage Emma. It's a pity you have to die. As you have been so cooperative I'll make it quick. That's the most I can offer.'

'Aren't you going to tell me what this is all about and who you are?'

'What's the point Emma, I think we both know the story. You are just hoping to buy more time so that your knight in shining armour can come charging through that door but we both know he hasn't a clue where you are. Nobody has a clue where you are.'

The man picked up a garrotte from the table at the side of the room and approached Emma testing the tautness of the wire as he advanced.

He stood behind Emma and placed the wire across her neck. At that moment an alarm sounded.

'Looks like we have visitors,' the man said. 'I'm afraid your termination will have to wait a moment.'

He went over to the table and switched on an old fashioned cream coloured monitor. Peering up into a camera aimed at visitors arriving at the front door Dan's face filled the screen.

'You are a very good liar Emma. I had believed you and was going to let Detective Brennan live. You have just forfeited your chance of an easy death. I can't abide being lied to. Now you will have the opportunity to see your partner die before I have a bit of fun with you.'

The man placed a second chair next to Emma then picked up a gun and left the room.

The monitor still showed Dan patiently waiting at the front of the building seemingly oblivious to the danger he was in. Emma shouted at the screen telling him to go but he couldn't hear her. She just had to sit there and watch events unfold unable to help in any way.

Dan banged on the door. He looked up into the lens of a camera with a blinking red light showing that it had been activated by his approach. The door clicked open but nobody appeared. He waited for a few moments then gently eased the door further open with his foot and peered into what looked like a reception area. All his instincts told him this was a trap but they also told him that he was in the right place and this was where he would find Emma. The thought of losing her gave him the courage to continue into the building. It was dark but Dan could make out a counter with another door beyond it. A large motif of a pink poodle nearly filled the wall to his left. It suddenly clicked into place. The comment Jesus Romano had made about buying an American Pit Bull and his remark about the poncey poodle. Whatever had been discussed had led Detective Heal here and to his untimely death.

'Detective Brennan, you are either very brave or very foolhardy,' a whiny voice said coming from an intercom sitting on the counter.

As his eyes adjusted to the dim surroundings Dan made his way towards the second door. As he did so the front door to the building swung closed and the lock clicked into place.

'I've got back-up coming. Give yourself up before you make things worse,' Dan said with more self-assurance than he felt.

'We both know there isn't any backup coming. It would be impossible to get a warrant to search this place on the evidence you have. That's the beauty of this country the authorities have to play by the rules but the criminals can play foul. Anyway, to get down to business I think I have something of value to you. I've been having an interesting conversation with Miss Blakely. I'm very impressed with your detective work. I would never have expected anyone to find out about our little operation here. You only just arrived in time. I was just about to terminate my friendship with the delightful Emma. Now I'm going to have to start all over and find out exactly what you both know.'

Dan edged his way slowly towards the door behind the counter. It comprised of tinted glass panels. There was nothing visible beyond. Dan's heart pounded in his chest. His thoughts went to Detective Heal's body and the torture Emma might have suffered but at least she was still alive so there was still hope. His instinct to come straight here had been correct. Al Green had insisted that he wait for back-up but Dan had jumped straight into the hire car and after finding the location of Perfect Pooches he had driven like a madman to get here.

All his senses were heightened as he pushed the inner door open whilst standing with his back against the wall to offer a modicum of protection, although the thin stud walls wouldn't stop a bullet. Creeping slowly forward into the gloom he stopped in the doorway straining his ears for any movement beyond. With a thumping heart, he waited, listening. No movement, no sound.

The room he was now standing in was clinically white; it was obviously some sort of laboratory. Several rows of work-tops comprising of the usual paraphernalia associated with the medical profession - test tubes, microscopes, expensive looking equipment. Laura had been right. They had been looking in the right area but to avoid the scrutiny that was associated with the human fertilization environment this criminal network had used the far less regulated world of animal reproduction. To transport human or animal semen the process was exactly the same. Laura had looked at the common link which was the mailing system. To store and transport samples half way across the world required specialised equipment and knowledge. You couldn't just put it in an ordinary mailbox. Laura had hacked into the computer system for one of the main parcel delivery companies in the USA. It didn't take her long to identify all their customers in the San Francisco area. Perfect Pooches wasn't the only client in this area but why it stood out to Laura was because of the security of its computer system. As she said The Pentagon would have been proud of this level of security. In Laura's opinion no-one including herself could hack into it. It was far beyond what a small dog breeding company would install. Her instincts had been right this company was just a front for something far more sinister.

Another red light blinked on in the far corner. His progress was being followed as he made his way through the building. There was still no sign of either the man or Emma in this part of the building. Dan could make out two further doors at the back of the laboratory.

His adversary was violent, merciless and worse of all smart. Dan knew he would have planned for this moment and would not surrender unless it was a last resort. He felt incredibly vulnerable but what choice did he have? He couldn't leave Emma in the hands of a man like this if there was the slightest chance he could save her.

Behind the first door, Dan could hear a scurrying noise along with the sound of metal bars being knocked against. Was Emma imprisoned in here he thought? He opened the door and a bright light immediately came on and he was greeted by a cacophony of barking dogs. Cages lined both sides of the room and each cage contained a dog of a different breed, big, small, long haired, and short haired. All of them looked at Dan, most wagging their tails expectantly, others growling and barking.

Dan quickly closed the door but the noise continued unabated. Dan's heart pounded even more against his ribs and sweat pricked across his forehead. He leaned against the closed door to get his breath back and still his racing heart.

'You've woken up my friends,' the voice came out of a speaker Dan hadn't noticed high up on the wall above where he stood. 'You are getting closer but do hurry up I haven't got all night.'

The second door opened up onto a corridor stretching ahead into the darkness. Office doors lined each side of the corridor. Silver nameplates indicated the people working in the building. Dan continued moving forward past the closed doors testing each one as he passed, all of them were locked, until he got to the far end. This door opened. Dan could see a staircase leading down into the bowels of the building. Keeping his back against the wall so that he could see both directions he gradually descended. Ahead he could see the flicker of a monitor. He turned the corner and there was Emma tied to a chair. Her eyes showed both fear and happiness.

Dan's immediate reaction was one of relief, relief that she was still in one piece and didn't appear to have been physically harmed. He raced forward to free her.

'He's still in the building and he's armed,' she stammered.

'Miss Blakely is correct and the gun is pointing at the middle of your back Detective Brennan. Turn round slowly and sit down I've prepared a place for you at the party.'

Dan turned to see a gun pointing directly at him.

'You must be on a suicide mission to come here alone unarmed. You must care about Miss Blakely very much and that gives me an instrument to extract information that's far better than torture. Now sit down. I won't ask a second time.'

Dan sat down heavily into the chair next to Emma. The man must have been in one of the locked offices. Dan had walked right past him. How could he have been so stupid? A novice police officer wouldn't have fallen for that old trick. Worrying about Emma had obviously dulled his thinking,

The man picked up a roll of electrical tape and threw it towards Dan. 'Fasten your ankles to the chair legs please.'

'Why should I do anything you say?'

'Because if you don't I'll put a bullet in Emma's knee. Do you know how painful that is?'

'I'll be long gone and you will both be long dead by the time the cavalry arrives to try and save you. Now I'm going to have to start my little operation all over again. It's a shame I liked the set up I had created here but I can't risk staying. I expect you have already told Detective Green your suspicions about this place.' He held up what looked like a remote control. 'The whole building is rigged with explosive. When I press this button I have ten minutes to get out of here then BOOM everything including you will be gone and the authorities will never find any trace of me.'

He stepped forward taking the tape from Dan and securing his arms to the chair then turned to go.

'I thought you wanted to interrogate us?' Dan said trying to stall his departure.

'I've changed my mind. I doubt you know anything of interest. It would have been interesting to find out how you found this place but I'm sure Detective Green is trying to organise a rescue party. Unfortunately by the time he manages that you will be buried under a pile of rubble.'

In a dramatic gesture, he pressed the button on the remote and a green light blinked on. Placing the remote on the table he disappeared up the stairs.

'I hope you have a plan to get us out of here?' Emma asked.

'Well I had a plan but I'm not quite sure of the timing. Ten minutes is a bit less than I was banking on.'

Dan managed to touch Emma's hand with his little finger. He knew without a doubt that dying here today with Emma was preferable to living without her.

Suddenly a loud noise made Dan look towards the monitor. He could see two men clad entirely in black wearing dark helmets swinging a battering ram to force the front door. The door swung open with great force but the two men didn't enter. They retreated back the way they had come.

'DON'T GO,' Dan shouted but there was no way they could hear him.

Next, he heard a distant voice over a megaphone - 'Come out with your hands up we have you completely surrounded there is no escape.' Gunfire from within the building answered the demand.

'Looks like he didn't get out in time,' Emma said.

'How much longer do we have before the explosives go off?' Dan asked.

'About seven minutes,' Emma replied.

'I don't think we have that long.'

Dan looked frantically around for a tool to use to release their bonds.

'If I can tip this chair over and knock that table over maybe there is something we can use to cut the tape.'

Dan began rocking backwards and forwards finally overbalancing and falling heavily onto the floor, unfortunately, he had fallen in the completely wrong direction and was further away from the table than ever. Dust rose around his face and a smell of dried blood hit his nostrils. He pushed back the repelling thought of lying in human blood and looked enviously towards the table. He was too far away. Pain racked through his body from the fall as he lay there in despair.

'Let me try,' Emma said.

'You'll hurt yourself.'

'What more than being blown up?'

Dan thought what a stupid comment he had made.

'OK give it a go but try and fall in the right direction.'

Emma swung back and forth and gave an extra heave forward towards the table at the tipping point. She crashed towards it and hit one of the front legs. At first, Dan thought nothing was going to happen but then seemingly in slow motion the table leg folded and the contents of the table started to slide towards where Emma lay dazed on the floor. The remote control for the bomb hit Emma on the head followed by a series of gruesome looking torture implements then to Dan's horror he saw the heavy computer monitor sliding towards her.

'Look out he called,' but still tied securely to the chair there was nothing she could do as the monitor slide mercilessly towards her falling off the table and giving her a glancing blow on the head. Emma fell unconscious onto the dirty floor. The monitor continued on its way towards where Dan lay breaking into pieces as it slowed to its final resting place. Still plugged into the socket on the wall sparks now fizzed from its remains and a smell of burning electrical circuitry filled the air. Dan shouted to Emma asking if she was OK but she was out for the count. At least she won't be aware of the end Dan thought. Dan felt pain in his hand. A pain that wasn't from his fall. Glancing to where his hand still lay bound to the arm of the chair he saw a sharp piece of metal protruding from the fleshy palm of his hand. It must have been part of the broken monitor. Blood oozed out of the wound mingling with the blood of the countless other victims who had spilt their lifeblood in this room. He managed to pull the piece of metal from his palm and was just about to discard it when he had a thought. Maybe he could use it to free his restraints. It seemed to take an age and he knew the time to the detonation must be getting close but he managed to cut through the tape. With one hand free it was easy for him to cut through the other bonds. Finding a very sharp sword which he guessed was one of the torture implements he sliced through Emma's restraints and picked her up then fled up the stairs. He could still hear gunfire at the front of the building.

'There must be a back way out of this place?' he thought out loud. Finding himself back in the corridor with the locked office doors he noticed the first door on his right stood wide open. This must have been where the man had hidden. Rushing through the open door with Emma still unconscious in his arms he looked frantically around for an exit. There was another door at the back of the room. Luckily it was unlocked. It led out onto a loading bay area. A row of identical white vans with pink poodle motifs on their sides stood stationary waiting for their owners to take them out. An expensive looking black BMW 4x4 sat beyond the vans. Obviously, this had been the man's means of escape but he was now pinned down at the front of the building. Past the vehicles, a high fence with razor wire around the top prevented their escape from the compound. The gates had a heavy chain securing them. Dan tried the nearest van door. It was locked. He expected all the others would also be locked. Maybe the BMW would be open if the man expected to use it. He ran towards it and with a great sense of relief the door opened and Dan noticed a bunch of keys resting in the centre console. He slid Emma across the front seat and pulled himself into the driver's seat. Pressing the start button the engine sprung to life with a gentle purr that only German manufacturing can guarantee. Revving the engine Dan put the car into drive and it lurched forward towards the gate. He had two worries. One - would it break through the gate and two - if they got through would they be gunned down by the Special Weapons And Tactics (SWAT) team surrounding the building? With no choice, he headed straight towards the centre of the gates. The car hit them head on and they flew outwards. Steam erupted from the broken radiator and Dan couldn't see anything in front of him. The airbags had deployed front and side and this cushioned the impact as he hadn't had time to fasten the seat belts. The car now immobilised rolled forward several yards beyond the compound before it came to a standstill. A voice told them to come out with their hands up. Dan opened the door and showing his hands shouted that he was a British police officer with an injured colleague and that the building was about to blow. Carrying Emma he ran towards the black clad SWAT officers ahead. The sense of urgency Dan expressed must have convinced the officer that danger was imminent. Speaking into a headset he told the other men to withdraw to a safe distance. He beckoned Dan still holding the unconscious Emma to take cover behind a Hummer that was parked a few yards away. They had only just reached it when there was an almighty explosion and the building went up in a huge fireball. The black BMW was thrown through the air and landed on its roof before it too went up in flames.

'We need to get Emma to a hospital immediately. She has suffered a severe head trauma.' Another officer took Emma from his arms and whisked her away. Dan was left standing in the dark surrounded by a group of heavily armed police.

'On the floor now,' a voice ordered him.

Dan lay down with his arms and legs spread out. One of the men patted him down and told his leader that Dan wasn't armed. A pair of handcuffs was roughly fastened to his already sore wrists and he was dragged back to his feet.

'How many other terrorists were in that building?'

'None that I know of,' Dan replied.

'Does the name Arif Tadeequi mean anything to you?'

Remembering the news article he had watched in the diner on the day they arrived he responded, 'Yes, he's the terrorist that is on the loose I saw it on the TV.'

The plan he had formulated with Al Green had worked. Legislation put in place following 9/11 when the twin towers in New York had been destroyed allowed for a swift response to a terrorist threat. There was no need to wait for a court order if national security was being threatened. The Patriot Act had even trumped the world famous American Constitution. In Dan's eyes, the USA was a strong country that protected its people. Its people were allowed to love their country and to respect their flag – they were encouraged to be patriotic. So different to England where to display the English flag was seen as xenophobic. Where to question the values of Islam was seen as racist. Dan hated the direction his once great nation had taken; it had become so politically correct it just tied itself in knots. In his opinion, the only salvation would be to free the country from the shackles of the over-bureaucratic European Union and follow the example of its American cousins. If it didn't change and change soon then it was doomed.

'Nice call phoning in an anonymous tip off of a sighting of a suspected terrorist. You must have known that it would get our arses into gear,' the SWAT team leader said with a hint of admiration in his voice if not a little disappointment that they hadn't caught their terrorist.

78

Detective Al Green drove back to what remained of Perfect Pooches the next morning. The scene of the explosion and fire wasn't hard to find as tendrils of black smoke rose into the bright blue Californian sky. Fire crews still had their hoses trained on the remains trying to damp down any burning embers. The surrounding businesses had closed for the day as the approach road was still officially sealed off. Dirty black water gathered in puddles and ran into the gutters. The roof had caved in and twisted metal beams stood erect like a grotesque piece of modern art. The neighbouring units were peppered with shrapnel. An office chair sat twisted and charred on the path leading to where the front door had once been.

Al sat in his car taking in the devastation. Anything that could burn had gone or melted. Without even speaking to the fire chief he knew that they wouldn't get anything useful from the site. As he pulled himself out of the car the stench of barbequed meat wafted over him.

Al had already managed to obtain some basic details about the company. The director was an American named Raymond Hearns. It employed a staff of twenty people including a security guard, an African American named Otis Jackson, who was at present unaccounted for.

The fire chief walked over to where Al waited.

'What can you tell me?'

'Well, the building was definitely rigged with explosive. I expect this was C4 looking at the damage but the lab will have to confirm that. So far we have identified one human fatality plus a couple of dozen roast dogs.'

'Have you managed to ID the body?'

'No it's burned beyond recognition and as expected not in one piece. You will need DNA or dental records in order to make a positive ID.

'Black or Caucasian?'

'Impossible to tell. All the skin had gone. You will have to wait for the autopsy results. There was one interesting thing. There's an escape tunnel. It led from the building and came out beyond that hillock over there,' the fire chief said pointing to a scrubby hill a few hundred yards away.

'So someone could have got out of the building before it blew?'

'It's possible.'

Al wondered if Raymond Hearns had escaped and maybe the cadaver belonged to the security guard. He hoped not as he knew he wouldn't rest until he had caught Simon's killer.

79

The questioning seemed endless. It always came back to how Dan had known that Emma was being held at the dog cloning laboratory. Dan didn't have an answer. Well, he didn't have an answer he could tell his interrogators. No way was he going to drop Laura in it. He kept to the lie that he had received a tip-off. How had he received a tip off? When had he received a tip off? Detective Al Green was nowhere to be seen. He asked repeatedly how Emma was and when could he see her. The only response he got was that she was out of danger and he could see her when he started telling the truth.

'Why don't you ask the man who kidnapped Emma?' he asked the detective.

'There isn't a piece of him left that's bigger than a quarter.'

'Have you identified him?'

'I'm asking the questions not you.'

Dan just had to keep to his story. They didn't have enough to charge him with. He hadn't broken any laws. Finally, in frustration, they let him go.

When Dan entered the hospital room Emma was sitting up in bed chatting with Al.

'How are you?'

'Apart from a bad headache and ten stitches, I'm fine. They say I'm out of danger. They want to keep me under observation just in case I have a brain bleed. I told them that us Blakely's are renowned for our thick skulls but they wouldn't listen. Al's been filling me in on what happened. I'm really sorry about Simon.'

'Did you get a grilling?' Dan asked Al.

'Sort of but I think they were secretly pleased we caught Simon's killer. Homeland Securities weren't best pleased that they didn't catch their terrorist.'

'Have you got any information on Perfect Pooches?'

'Nothing so far. On the face of it, it was a legitimate business. We can't find any trace of the killer. He went by the name of Raymond Hearns, an American citizen, but prior to 1995 there is no record of him. He must have assumed a false identity. We have been interviewing the other staff from the business but they all seem above board. They know next to nothing about their boss. All of them say he kept to himself but that he travelled abroad a lot. They didn't even know where he lived. The security guard Otis Jackson has disappeared he went by his real name but gave a false address.'

'Surely Hearns had to pay his taxes. He must have given the IRS a home address?'

'He just used the business address.'

'So there's no trace of him? We just have another dead end,' Dan groaned.

'The USA investigation may be a dead-end but Laura has given us the address in the UK where the sperm sample was delivered to,' Emma reminded him. 'At last we have a lead to where Rosie and the other women are being held.'

'How long will they keep you in?'

'I have to stay another night then hopefully I can be discharged.'

The door to the room opened and the District Attorney Rose Bamber entered with another woman Dan and Emma didn't recognise. The woman looked as if she had been crying. She had red-rimmed eyes. She wore no makeup and her hair was pulled back in an untidy ponytail.

'This is Alysha Heal, Simon's wife. She wanted to thank you both for finding the man who murdered her husband.'

'You don't need to thank us. If anything you should hate us for re-opening this investigation and getting Simon killed. I'm very sorry for your loss. Simon was a fine man.'

'You were doing your job. Just like Simon was doing his. I don't hate you. It's the criminals that did this to Simon, not you.'

'When is the funeral? We would like to attend,' Dan said turning to Emma who nodded her agreement.

'It's next Friday but I'd rather you didn't come. Not everyone in the Department thinks like me, many will blame you. It's better that you get back to England and continue the investigation whilst you have a lead. There's nothing that you can do for Simon here.'

Rose spoke up, 'we aren't going to charge you with anything. I've already arranged your flights back to the UK the day after tomorrow. We will continue the investigation at this end. If we turn anything up we will let you know.'

Dan felt relieved that they could leave. They had brought nothing but trouble to their kind American hosts.

Two days later they boarded their flight. McBride had arranged for them to be upgraded to first class due to Emma's injury. She was still very groggy and slept for nearly the entire journey. Dan stayed awake enjoying the excellent food and service that was to be expected for the exorbitant cost of the tickets.

80

Friday 28th March 2014 - OXFORD

On their return to the UK Dan and Emma had reported their progress to the Operation Silver Team. Emma suggested to McBride that her and Dan pose as prospective customers and make a visit to the Top Dog Kennels the name of the business where the sample had been posted.

When Emma picked Dan up she looked anything but a serving police officer. She looked more like Sandy Olsson out of the film Grease. She was wearing tight black shiny leggings and a pink fluffy angora sweater. She had tied her hair up into a high swinging pony tail covering up the stitches that still held together the gash in her scalp with a wide hair band. Large hooped earrings dangled from each lobe. Her makeup was exaggerated. Dan thought the look trashy but very sexy. He wanted to pull her into his flat but she was double parked outside. To look more the part she had borrowed a red two-seater sports car from a friend. The day was cold but sunny. This allowed them to have the car's soft top roof down. Emma turned the heater on full which streamed hot air across their bodies keeping the cold wind at bay.

They knew they were in the right place by the noise of a multitude of yapping dogs that assailed their ears as they drove along the drive leading towards the kennels.

'It's no wonder they put these places deep in the countryside,' Dan said.

They had phoned the Top Dog Kennels the previous day to enquire about finding a mate for their pedigree Pomeranian. An appointment with the owner a Mrs Benyon had been arranged for eleven o'clock that day.

They parked in the large yard. The place comprised of a bungalow on one side that seemed to be used for the owners living accommodation and the kennels office. On the other side, there were two parallel rows of dog kennels. Each cage housed a different breed of dog. Some dogs were large some were small but they all seemed to be pedigrees. There was no sign of any mongrels. Three kennel maids were hurriedly moving between the cages carrying bowls of food and water.

Dan and Emma got out of the car and walked to the nearest girl. She was slightly on the chubby side but had a pleasant friendly smile. She asked if she could help them. They told her they had an appointment with Mrs Benyon and she directed them to the office attached to the bungalow.

'Mr and Mrs Griffiths,' Emma said introducing themselves using their false name. 'We have an appointment with a Mrs Benyon for eleven.'

'Of course,' the young receptionist said, 'please take a seat Mrs Benyon will be with you in a moment.'

Dan and Emma seated themselves on a leather three-seater settee. In front of them were several magazines on dog related subjects. A water cooler sat in one corner. Posters of a variety of different dog breeds adorned the walls. There were lots of winning rosettes pinned to a cork board which Emma assumed had been won by the many dogs that Mrs Benyon boasted about in her literature? Emma had spent some time on the internet yesterday looking at the Top Dog website. It told prospective clients that the kennel only used champion dogs and they could expect to produce prize winning litters if they used their services. An inner door opened and a petite smartly dressed lady approached them holding out her hand.

'Mrs and Mr Griffiths, it's a pleasure to meet you. Would you like to come into my office?'

Emma and Dan followed her through. It looked a bit like a doctors consulting room with medical posters showing the internal workings of what Emma assumed were dogs rather than humans. It reminded her of their recent visit to see Dr Du Bois in San Jose.

Dan took up the conversation with Mrs Benyon explaining that he had bought his wife a pedigree Pomeranian two years ago and how she now had the desire to breed her.

Emma putting on an exaggerated Essex accent which she could tell immediately grated on Mrs Benyon said, 'yer, my baby Trixie wants to be a mummy. We are hoping you can find her a suitable boyfriend. It certainly looks like you have some handsome studs outside for her to choose from.'

'We don't keep any dogs here,' Mrs Benyon replied in disdain. 'All the canines here are bitches. We only use frozen semen for the insemination. You bring your pet here at the right time then we inseminate her with the semen of the dog that has been selected. You take her away and hopefully sixty-one days later your puppies arrive. If you wish to sell them via us we have an excellent after service sales scheme.'

'I told you darling. I told you that's how it would be done nowadays,' Dan said. Looking towards Mrs Benyon Dan asked, 'what sort of price are we looking at for the whole package?'

'It varies a lot depending on how successful the stud dog has been at the shows. For a Cruft's champion, you would be looking at a total cost of fifteen hundred pounds. This would include the insemination and the boarding fees for up to two weeks stay here. You would make a tidy profit from the arrangement, Puppies fetch upwards of five hundred pounds each and the average litter is six.'

'I'm not sure I could leave my little Trixie here,' Emma said. 'She would get awfully homesick.'

'Maybe if we could have a look round then my wife could satisfy herself that Trixie would be happy to stay?'

'Certainly, Mr Griffiths. I'll get one of my girls to give you the guided tour.' With this, she lifted the telephone and spoke to the receptionist and asked if Tara could give the Griffiths's a tour of the kennels. 'She won't be a minute. Would you like a tea or coffee whilst you wait?' Dan ordered a coffee and Emma ordered a tea.

The receptionist must have already had the kettle on as two minutes later she came through with a tray holding a mug of coffee for Dan and a pot of tea with two cups for Emma and Mrs Benyon.

As they drank Dan said, 'It's a nice operation you have going here. You seem full up at the moment.'

'Yes, we are very busy.'

'Where do you get your studs from and how do you manage to get the frozen sperm delivered. I expect it can't be sent through the Royal Mail.'

'It comes from all over the world Mr Griffiths. We have a network of franchises located in twenty-five different countries. Each kennel collects the donations from their area then ships them to where the order has been placed.'

'A bit like Interflora,' Dan said.

'A similar concept but we use a specialist shipping service to send the product. A temperature of -196°c has to be maintained at all times otherwise it is ruined.'

At this point, Tara knocked on the door. Mrs Benyon asked her to give Dan and Emma a tour round the kennels and explain the procedure.

Rising and shaking their hands Mrs Benyon said, 'hopefully it will put your mind at rest and you will let us help Trixie fulfil her potential.'

With this, she sat back down behind her desk and continued with her paperwork dismissing the three people before her.

Tara took them first to the kennel area. All the cages looked warm and clean. Each kennel has its own heating to keep the girls warm Tara explained. It certainly looked to Emma to be a first rate establishment. They continued to the back of the kennel building. There were four further rooms here.

'This one is our staff room,' she said opening the door to reveal a room containing a table surrounded by four chairs, a settee covered with a bright orange throw. A work surface at the end had a kettle, a microwave and a selection of cups, plates and cutlery. The next room she explained was the insemination room. There wasn't much visible in here it looked like a vets treatment room. It had a large table in the centre and cupboards and a sink down one side. The room opposite she explained was the storage room. This contained a number of fridges.

'These aren't like the fridges you would find at home. The temperature is much colder. We also have a backup generator that kicks in if the power ever goes down.'

'So how often do you get deliveries of dog semen?' Dan asked.

'Not very often. It's an expensive process so we tend to buy in bulk. I'd guess we have about four deliveries a year. It depends on what orders we get in. They come from all over the world you know? This is better for the breed. It stops the interbreeding that happened so often in the past.'

'What's Mrs Benyon like to work for. She seemed a bit brusque to me,' Dan said.

'Oh she isn't, she's a great employer, really kind. She can be so spontaneous. She thinks nothing of suddenly giving us the afternoon off.'

Dan wondered if this was to allow privacy for the delivery and collection of the human sperm samples.

'You can see that we have a list of all the breeds currently available but we can obtain any breed you require,' Tara said pointing to a list on the wall. Next to each breed there was a corresponding number plus a date. The number indicates which container the sample is held in. It wouldn't do to get them mixed up.'

'What does the date mean?' Emma asked.

'That's the date the sample arrived,' Tara explained.

'These numbers where there are question marks shown next to them what do they mean?' Dan asked.

'They are just empty containers, waiting for the next delivery.'

After the tour, Tara returned them to Mrs Benyon.

'I hope you have enjoyed your tour and have come to a decision,' Mrs Benyon asked.

'Very much so and we are very impressed,' Dan replied. 'Can we look at some price options?'

'Certainly,' Mrs Benyon said typing some details into her computer. 'I'll print out a list of donors and the price for each. You will find a synopsis for each dog showing his pedigree, achievements and breeding prowess.'

'A bit like a dog CV,' Dan laughed.

'Exactly. The dog world is a highly organised professional establishment.

Mrs Benyon passed Emma five sheets of paper each one contained the details of Pomeranian studs. The price for each varied from four hundred to fifteen hundred pounds.

'I'm sure you will want to study these print outs before making a decision.'

Emma had a quick scan down the sheet. The dogs were sorted according to their cost. Stopping at the first American dog on the list Emma asked, 'this one here looks a possible match - Benjamin one thousand eight hundred dollars - he's won the USA National Dog show and also the Eukanuba National Championship. He also won best of breed at the Westminster Dog show.'

'A very good choice if I may say so,' Mrs Benyon replied.

'How do you get the goods sent all the way from the USA?' Dan asked. 'Won't it be very expensive?'

'It does increase the price of course but it has already been included in the amount you see on the list. We have several collection sites in the US and a contract with FedEx. They ship it over here in a special container. If you go on our site and enter the registration number for Benjamin you can see a video of him.'

'Hey darling, we will be able to show it to Trixie see if she likes him.'

'I'm sure Trixie will love him,' Mrs Benyon said sarcastically.

Dan looked at the prices and whistled, 'it's not cheap is it?'

'It's an expensive process especially if the semen is coming from abroad. The semen coming from overseas is shipped in a special container called a vapour shipper because it is primed with liquid nitrogen it is classified as a dangerous good. We try to keep the costs of freight and handling down by importing multiple breeding units at one time this is why we only have a few deliveries each year and store the sample in our own cryogenic unit on site. We offer a full end to end service here at Top Dog Kennels. We ensure the donor dog is free from any infectious diseases, obtain a copy of the Collection Certificate, deal with the import permit then when the sample arrives store them until they are required. Your Trixie will stay here at the kennels and we will check when there is a rise in her progesterone levels. At the most optimum time, we will carry out the insemination procedure.

If the cost is a concern for you I can tell you that it is cheaper if you choose a mate from here in the UK as we can use chilled rather than frozen semen. However this only remains viable for around four to five days but it is better to carry out the insemination within twenty-four to forty-eight hours. Ovulation timing using blood assessment of progesterone concentrations is essential. The initial rise in progesterone values allows the inseminating veterinarian to predict when ovulation will occur. Ovulation generally occurs two days after the initial rise, and maturation, which must occur before the eggs can be fertilised, this can take two to three days. From then the eggs remain viable for about twenty-four to forty-eight hours.

Insemination is the same regardless of how the semen has been stored and takes about twenty minutes. The semen is warmed and evaluated prior to using transcervical insemination.'

'What's transcervical insemination?' Emma asked.

'Transcervical insemination. It just means that the semen is placed directly into the uterus, we find this method gives a far greater chance of fertilization. Here we use an endoscope and camera so we can view the bitch's cervix and insert a fine catheter to ensure the semen is injected into the right place.'

'Will my Trixie be anaesthetised?'

'No, Trixie will remain standing and since she thinks she is ready to mate she should accept the procedure without sedation.'

'That's the end of the process?' Dan asked.

'It can be but we also offer an excellent after insemination service. At four to five weeks an ultrasound can be carried out. This will tell you if your bitch is pregnant, however, if you want to know the numbers of pups, this is best assessed by an x-ray at around eight week's gestation.'

'And what's the chance of success?'

'Unfortunately the UK is quite far behind our American and European counterparts when it comes to breeding dogs via artificial insemination which is why we prefer to get our semen samples from overseas. It also has the added benefits of reduced interbreeding and gives you a greater choice of mates. The industry standard is a fifty-six percent success rate but here at Top Dog we pride ourselves in achieving over seventy percent.

'So it might not work the first time?'

'Nothing can be guaranteed so you need to prepare yourself for several rounds of treatment.'

Dan and Emma thanked Mrs Benyon for her time and said they would get back to her when they had decided on the right mate for Trixie.

Back in the car Emma said, 'did you notice the samples delivered last summer? These tie up with those sent by Perfect Pooches in America however we know three were delivered but only two are shown on the chart. I think the third one belonged to Eric Bamber.'

'Yes, I agree but proving it is going to be another matter. We can't use any of the information Laura has given us and so far we don't have a concrete link to Perfect Pooches in California. Remember that business was being run as a legitimate concern. There's no way we can get a search warrant based on what we have at the moment.'

I expect the Top Dog is also being run as a legitimate business. Julie Benyon certainly knows her subject and it's quite possible she is totally unaware that her business is being abused in this way. It could quite easily be one of the kennel maids.'

'I don't think so. The fact that Julie Benyon knows her business so well would make it very difficult to pull the wool over her eyes.'

81

The answering machine was flashing as Dan and Emma opened the front door to his flat. Emma went to put the kettle on whilst Dan walked over to the machine to listen to the waiting message. Al Green's tinny American voice came out over the speaker.

'Dan it's Al Green. We have just got the DNA results back from the human remains we found in the ruins of the Perfect Pooches building. They don't belong to Raymond Hearns, I repeat they don't belong to Raymond Hearns, he's still on the loose. We have a match and it seems the body belongs to an Otis Jackson. He was employed as a guard at the facility. He was a nasty piece of work and had a rap sheet as long as your arm. We've put out an APB for the arrest of Hearns but I think he will be long gone. I doubt he will be coming your way but I thought I'd better warn you.'

The answering machine clicked and a mechanical voice announced 'that was your last message.'

Emma now standing behind Dan gave a shiver, 'I thought he was dead.'

Dan wrapped his arms around her, 'it's OK he can't harm you anymore. I'll keep you safe.'

82

Monday 31st March 2014 - OXFORD

'The time is 9:30 am, Monday, the 31st March. This is our daily briefing for Operation Silver,' McBride announced to the team assembled in the Major Incident Room. I'll pass you over to DS Emma Blakely who has a report from the visit she and DI Dan Brennan made to the Top Dog Kennels on Friday.'

As the investigation was now being cut back weekend overtime had been suspended. Chief Superintendent Mike Harding had tried in vain to keep the case in the public eye but interest was fast waning and leads were fast running out.

Emma explained to the team their findings.

'So what more do we really know?' Rod Hartley asked.

'Well, we know that three samples were dispatched from the USA but that only two samples have been recorded as being received at Top Dog Kennels. Our assumption is that the third sample belonged to Eric Bamber and was forwarded onto or collected by the person holding Rosie.'

'But that's all you have assumptions. No judge in the land would give us a search warrant based on what you have.'

Emma felt annoyed with DS Hartley. They had put their lives on the line getting this lead. What had he contributed to the investigation? Nothing of any significance that was for sure. He just spent all his time travelling around Scotland looking a disused building where the women might be held.

'I'm going to apply for a warrant with what we've got. Maybe we will get lucky and get an understanding judge,' McBride announced.

83

Tuesday 1ˢᵗ April 2014 - OXFORD

Arriving in the office McBride had a message to see Chief Superintendent Mike Harding immediately. It would have to be quick as he was due to travel down to London to interview Jacqui Bates. When he arrived at Harding's office he was busily packing his belongings into several large cardboard boxes.

'I'm being sent on secondment to Hong Kong,' he announced. 'This offer has come completely out of the blue but I've been asked to head up a joint operation between the Hong Kong and British authorities looking into a Triad gang who have been involved in people smuggling to the UK and importing drugs.'

'How long will you be gone?'

'One maybe two years. Gill is coming with me and the girls are finishing their exams at boarding school here in England and coming over in the holidays.'

McBride wondered for a moment if he was going to be asked to step into Mike Harding's shoes whilst he was away but this idea was soon dispelled.

'My replacement is acting Chief Superintendent Geoffrey Vicars.'

McBride thought maybe it was an April Fool's Day joke but quickly realised it wasn't.

Mike Harding must have seen the look of horror on his face.

'No, it wouldn't have been my choice but the powers that be have insisted. I'm sure you will be able to manage for the short time I'm away.'

McBride knew from experience that secondments always lasted far longer than anticipated and that when the person returned they invariably went into a new position. He also knew that he couldn't do anything to influence Mike's replacement so he would have to make the best of it. Geoffrey Vicars had a reputation as being officious, overbearing and pompous. Totally the opposite to Mike Harding.

'When do you go? And more importantly, when does Geoffrey arrive?'

'I'm leaving today. We fly out next week. I'm renting out the house here. Geoffrey will start in the morning'

'I'm pleased for you. I'm sure you will enjoy the experience,' McBride said truthfully but barely unable to contain his disappointment.

'I'm sorry to leave you in the lurch especially during such a high profile case but I really didn't have a say in the matter. It was all a done deal before it even got mentioned to me. Believe me, it is as much a shock to me as it is to you.'

It flashed across McBride's mind that maybe Harding was being moved out because they were getting too close to the truth about Rosie Ware's abduction. Vicars was renowned for closing cases down. He dismissed the thought. How could the person involved in Rosie's kidnap be able to influence such things?

McBride hated London. There was too much traffic and too many people for his liking. The meeting had been arranged for one o'clock at the Methodist Central Hall building. It had a large café area in the basement that was open to the public and was just down the road from Jacqui Bates's office in Westminster. Too late to go anywhere else but too early for the meeting McBride wandered around the magnificent old building. An elderly bespectacled steward with grey receding hair approached him.

'Would you like a tour?'

McBride hesitated for a moment.

'It's free,' the steward added, 'and it would give me something to do.'

'Sure,' McBride replied not wanting to disappoint the old man.

Following him further into the building the stooped old man began his spiel.

'Designed by Edwin Alfred Rickards and built in the Baroque and Edwardian architecture style the building was completed in 1911 to mark the centenary of John Wesley's death. John Wesley along with his brother Charles had formed the Methodist church back in the 18th century.'

McBride was surprised to learn that the building wasn't as old as he had first thought. He was led into a splendid circular room with a domed ceiling.

'This is the main auditorium called The Great Hall where we hold meetings and conferences. It has a capacity of two thousand three hundred people. The domed ceiling is reputed to be the second largest of its type in the world. Many famous figures have stood up and spoken in this room including Mohandas Gandhi, Martin Luther King, Jr. and Winston Churchill. But the room isn't only used for speeches - in 1968, Central Hall hosted the first public performance of Andrew Lloyd Webber's Joseph and the Amazing Technicolor Dreamcoat. It has also had its moments of controversy. Back in 1966 whilst the FIFA World Cup trophy was on display here it was stolen only to be found seven days later by a dog named Pickles.'

Taking a lift and going down a long corridor the steward took a set of heavy keys from his pocket.

'I don't normally show visitors this part.'

The door opened out onto a balcony and McBride followed the steward as he stepped outside. It gave a splendid view towards the front of Westminster Abbey.

'This is where the television cameras are located for filming the royal weddings. It gives the church some extra income.'

Next, they travelled down to the basement. The steward showed him one of the dozens of ledgers stacked on the shelf.

'This is one of the account books showing the donations made by our parishioners in order for this great building to be constructed. The building work was funded between 1898 and 1908 by the "Wesleyan Methodist Twentieth Century Fund" or the "Million Guinea Fund", as it became more commonly known. The aim was to raise one million guineas from one million Methodists. The fund closed in 1904 having raised 1,024,501 guineas or £1,075,727 in today's currency.'

McBride imagined all those poor souls from around the world giving money they could ill afford to build this sumptuous place. Few if any would ever see it. Why did religion feel the need to spend money on lavish buildings? A donation box stood off to one side. Making an appropriate contribution McBride thanked him for the tour and made his way into the café area.

He noticed Dr Darleen Clutterbuck seated alone at the far side of the room with a large piece of cake and cup of coffee in front of her. She wasn't difficult to spot dressed in her usual bright clothing this time comprising of an orange and purple shirt and a long flowing skirt in the loudest shade of yellow he had ever seen. McBride waved and indicated that he would buy a drink and join her. As he reached the head of the queue Jacqui Bates arrived looking somewhat flustered. She was wearing a smart navy blue skirt that ended just above her knee and a matching jacket. All eyes in the café looked towards her as she made her way across the room towards the counter. She strode with the confidence of a catwalk model.

'DCI Ian McBride from Thames Valley Police,' he said introducing himself. 'Tea, coffee, something else?' he asked.

'Just a still spring water for me,' she replied.

They joined Darleen and McBride introduced everyone.

'Did you do as I asked?' Darleen said to Jacqui.

For the benefit of a puzzled looking McBride, she added. 'I asked Jacqui to write down everything she remembered about this man. People remember so much more when they have the time to think about it. I'm sure when she spoke to Dan Brennan she didn't mention most of what she knew about him.

'I did as you asked but as I told DI Brennan most of what he told me was a lie.'

'Clever liars always use an element of truth. It makes things easier to remember and less likely for them to slip up and be found out. Now it's our job to try and pick out the truth from the lies.'

Jacqui handed Darleen a piece of paper with a surprisingly long list written on it.

Everyone sat quietly sipping their drinks as Darleen read through the list. McBride glanced towards Jacqui Bates as she took a mobile phone from the small wristlet bag she carried and began texting someone. The reports about her beauty were not in the least bit understated. She looked more beautiful in the flesh than she did in the photograph he had seen attached to her missing person's report. Now she was thirteen years older than when that photo had been taken but her maturity had only enhanced her beauty. Her sleek dark hair was pulled back and fastened at the nape of her elegant neck by a mother-of-pearl clasp. She gazed down at her phone with soft brown eyes. A slight Mona Lisa smile spread across her face and lit it up with a radiance of happiness. She closed her phone and looked towards McBride.

'My fiancée,' she explained.

'Where and when did you first meet the man we are interested in?' Darleen asked her.

'It was whilst I was a university doing my PhD. I was in one of those old small dusty bookshops, you know the ones that now only survive in historic towns. I was looking for a first edition copy of Brave New World, by Aldous Huxley as a present for my father's birthday. Mr Gove the bookshop owner had phoned me to tell me he had managed to locate a copy. Whilst he was in the back of the shop getting me the book I noticed a man browsing through the travel section. He looked towards me and our eyes met. I'd never really believed in love at first sight but this was as close as it gets. He had the most intelligent face with eyes that held you spellbound as if you were the only woman in the world. He introduced himself as Niklas Hoffman and told me he was a WWII historian visiting England for a few weeks. He asked me if I would go for coffee with him and maybe show him around the area. That's how it all started.'

'Had you ever seen him before that day?'

'That's the strange thing; I could have sworn that I had seen him before. I mentioned it to him but he laughed and dismissed the idea. He swore that this was his first visit to England.'

'Did he tell you which country he came from?'

'He told me his family originally came from Germany but found themselves backing the wrong side during the war so had fled to Switzerland in 1938. He was born there in 1958. He definitely had a European accent.'

'Do you think he might have been Jewish?'

'I don't think so. He certainly didn't look Jewish, if you know what I mean.' Her cheeks blushed with embarrassment at the memory, 'and he loved English bacon sandwiches.'

'You have made a note on your list that he liked boats.'

'Yes, it wasn't something he told me but during our time at the cottage I noticed him reading a German magazine about boats.'

'Why did your parents report you as missing? You were only gone a couple of weeks.'

'I hadn't mentioned my relationship with Niklas to them. They wouldn't have approved. He was quite a bit older than I was. Whilst we were away at the cottage my apartment was broken into. The police couldn't find me and they contacted my parents. I hadn't told anyone I was going away so they were worried that I had been abducted. A missing person's report was filed. When I turned up safe and sound I expect it never got withdrawn. I didn't think about it again until your lot contacted me.'

Opening her purse Jacqui removed a crumpled old photograph. 'This is the only picture I ever had of him. I remember when one of my friends took it he was furious saying that he didn't want anyone photographing him. I thought it strange at the time.'

She smoothed out the photo on the table. It showed a couple sitting together in a crowded terrace bar overlooking a river. The girl was clearly Jacqui. The man was less clearly defined. He had his head turned to the side and he was wearing a pair of dark sunglasses.

'Even after all these years the sight of him still makes my heart flutter. We only spent six weeks together but I've never really got over him.'

She pushed the photo towards McBride, 'Take it. It's time I moved on. I've got a loving fiancée and a bright career in front of me. You never did tell me why you are looking for him?'

Before McBride could answer.

'On second thoughts I don't want to know. Niklas Hoffman, or whatever his real name is, is in my past and that's where I want to keep him.'

Looking between McBride and Darleen, 'I hope you find whatever it is you are looking for.' With this Jacqui rose from the table and swept out of the room.

84

Wednesday 2nd April 2014 - OXFORD

The office was furnished but devoid of any personal possessions. Geoff Vicars, the replacement for Chief Superintendent Mike Harding, sat in the comfortable leather swivel chair and turned slowly looking up at the white painted ceiling thinking. He had sold his soul but he had got a good price for it. The phone call had arrived the week before totally out of the blue. An opportunity of a lifetime and all he had to do was slow down an investigation that was going nowhere anyway. He'd thought about the offer and for a moment contemplated turning it down but then his ambition got the better of him. He knew he wouldn't get promoted again on merit as the competition for the next rank was too strong. The police force no longer operated on a dead man's shoes basis where if you just served your time you would move up to the next rank. Nowadays you either had to know the right people, which was the same in most professions, or you had to be good at the job. He satisfied neither criterion. For some reason, which escaped him, he had never been welcomed into that inner circle of senior officers who looked out for each other. It had been the same all his life through school and college and then after he joined the force. He had people he hung around with but never anyone close that he could call a true friend. Well, now he had made good. He picked up a discarded broken elastic band from the top of the desk and flicked it across the room. There was a knock at the door and his underling opened it and peered in.

'I didn't tell you to come in,' he boomed.

'Sorry, sir. I just wanted to let you know that your things have arrived and the men are bringing them up straight away,' the embarrassed junior officer said reversing quickly out of the door.

He had been assigned DC Barry Attwell as his minion. He had expected his current assistant to move with him but for some reason, he couldn't fathom, the man had chosen to remain behind. Hopefully, this new man would be easily bullied and would jump whenever Geoff demanded it and would never question an order. Always have the right grunt in place was his ethos.

Another knock on the door and this time it didn't open. Geoff waited ten seconds and then said in a loud voice, 'come in.'

The same young man opened the door wide and a procession of removal men walked in each carrying a large square cardboard box containing Geoff's personal effects.

'Where do you want these?' a gruff man wearing a brown boiler suit with Archer's Removals stencilled across the back asked. He was clearly annoyed at having to stand outside for so long holding the heavy box.

'Just put them on the floor over there.'

Each man placed his box on the floor and marched out of the room without another word.

'Not you,' Geoff said to DC Attwell. 'I want you to arrange for me to meet the Operation Silver Team this afternoon. I also want a breakdown of all the officers assigned to the case plus a synopsis of the evidence that has been gathered so far.'

'Yes sir,' the harried officer said backing out of the door before he got yet another order.'And bring me some tea whilst you're doing nothing. It must be in a teapot I don't like tea brewed in the cup.'

A distant 'whatever whatever' could be heard. Geoff smiled to himself. He liked being in charge and he liked giving orders.

He only intended emptying one of the boxes, the one with his most prized possessions inside. The others containing mostly manuals from the dozens of training courses he had attended during his career he would leave for DC Attwell to unpack. Why do a job yourself if you can get someone else to do it, another ethos.

85

'I've called you all together so that you can meet our new acting Chief Superintendent Geoff Vicars. As you might have already heard Chief Superintendent Mike Harding has been seconded to the Hong Kong police to assist on a case they are working on. I expect Geoff to arrive any minute but in the mean time we can catch up on the progress we have made in the last few days.' McBride didn't want to colour the team's opinion of their new chief so didn't pass on any of his own sentiments about the man. 'Darleen, have you got any further insights for us?'

'I've taken a look into the how Rosie's kidnapper might have subdued her. In the initial police report, it stated that some form of Chloroform may have been used. However, I've found out that it is nearly impossible to incapacitate someone using chloroform. It takes at least five minutes of inhaling an item soaked in chloroform to render a person unconscious. After a person has lost consciousness due to chloroform inhalation, a continuous volume must be administered and the chin must be supported in order to keep the tongue from obstructing the airway, a difficult procedure even for an anaesthetist. It has never been demonstrated that "instantaneous insensibility" has been achieved using chloroform alone. I have come to the conclusion that another form of sedative was used.'

'Any idea what could have been used?' McBride enquired.

'Take your pick Fentanyl, propofol, pentothal, methohexital, etomidate or ketamine. We know he used Gamma-Hydroxybutyric to subdue and kill Jennifer Shepherd. Many of these drugs wear off after a few minutes or kill if the dosage is too high. I expect he would have later administered something longer lasting like methadone which would keep her unconscious for at least eight to twelve hours. The initial tranquilliser would certainly have been administered by injection rather than inhalation. More importantly than what he used is the fact that your man had both the access to these type of drugs and more notably the skill to administer them in the correct dosage which adds to my belief that he has medical knowledge and training.'

At this point, acting Chief Superintendent Geoff Vicars strode purposefully into the room and made his way straight to the front. With not so much as an introduction, he launched into a tirade of abuse against McBride's team. 'The only member of this team who seems to have achieved anything is PC Gary Hope. He puts the rest of you detectives to shame. From what I've read it was his suggestion that these criminals might be using a canine breeding operation that put you on the scent of these villains. In fact, I'm so impressed with Gary that I've decided to promote him to the job of being my personal assistant. How's your tea making skills, boy? They've got to be better than my current aide. I've decided to take a much more hands-on approach to this case than my predecessor did. To my mind, it seems to have lost its direction. Sloppy is the word I'd use.'

McBride stepped in, the last thing he wanted now they had a good lead was to have his team demoralised. 'We are just waiting for the warrant to come through to enable us to search the Top Dog premises. Is there anything you can do to speed it up, sir?'

'I've already cancelled the request,' Vicars announced to the stunned group. 'In my opinion, it would be a complete waste of time and effort. I agree this was probably the route the criminals used to get the semen sample into the country but I doubt the kennels would have any idea about their involvement in this crime. Mrs Benyon is a personal friend of the Home Secretary. It would be an embarrassment for us all to implicate her in this sordid business. No, we need to look at other avenues of enquiry.'

Scanning the notes DC Attwell had written up for him. 'I like this lead you investigated on the Isle of Sky. I know you dismissed it but to me it smells of a cover up.' Looking directly at McBride, 'I want you to take a team back there and dig deeper, find the location where these women are being held. Also, the hotline has produced a number of interesting ideas as to the identity of the kidnapper plus there have been several sightings of Rosie Ware. I want you to concentrate on following these up.'

In McBride's opinion, the hotline with the excessive reward on offer had only slowed the investigation down. Members of the public rang in giving names of people they thought suspicious or they just plain didn't like. There had been alleged sightings of Rosie in Europe, Asia, Africa, North and South America, and even one in North Korea. They had checked out any promising leads but as McBride had expected they all turned out to be dead ends. He had concluded early on that the time and effort involved following up these spurious leads just wasn't worth it. Although they had continued to man the hotline he had instructed the call centre staff to only pass on highly credible tip offs. He had never liked Vicars but now he was making McBride's blood boil. What did he think he was doing hijacking their investigation and at a point where they had their best lead yet. McBride decided to play along for now but he vowed to get to the bottom of this obvious derailment of his case.

Next Geoff Vicars turned on Dr Darleen Clutterbuck. 'And we can certainly dispense with your services. I've never understood psychologists' mumbo jumbo. To my mind you are just a complete waste of money. Too much American television giving credence to your profession if you ask me.'

McBride wanted to step in to defend Darleen but he needn't have worried she was quite capable of fighting her own corner.

Raising herself to her full height she reminded McBride of an Amazon warrior, 'What's the saying - "Dead wood floats"?' Implying that one way to get rid of a useless member of staff is to promote them above their abilities. 'And you acting Chief Superintendent Geoffrey Vicars are just that – rotten and useless.' With that, she picked up her briefcase and left the room.

McBride thought the berating was over but he was wrong. Vicars turned back to him. 'These reports you have submitted they are shoddy with scant detail in them. Take that surveillance operation you carried out on Mary Shepherd's home in Lytham St Annes. It must have cost us a fortune and you didn't even get the name and address of this supposed granddaughter. Why is that? Smells of a cover up to me. I want her found and I want her charged.

McBride's instincts to keep Laura Webb's name out of the reports had been proved right. Something was wrong with Geoff Vicars' approach. He was doing everything in his power to derail the investigation. Maybe Mike Harding's secondment to Hong Kong had just been a ruse to get this man into the heart of the investigation and steer it away from finding out what had really happened to Rosie Ware. If this was the case then the perpetrators of this crime had clout at the very highest level. McBride would have to tread carefully, very carefully from now on. He would have a quiet word with those of his team at the centre of the investigation. Geoff Vicars had to be sidelined. They would need to appear to follow his directions which would waste time but behind his back they would continue to investigate their own leads. McBride knew he was putting his own career and maybe the future careers of his team on the line but he was incensed by what appeared to be a gross misuse of power on the part of his supervisor.

Geoff Vicars turned to leave the room taking Gary Hope with him.

86

Late April 2014 - OXFORD

The trail, if there had ever really been one, had gone cold. The newspapers had moved on, the public had tuned out of Rosie's plight and turned their attention to the next big story – the spread of the Ebola virus, the war on terror, immigration and the rise of UKIP. Rosie Ware's disappearance had become yesterday's news. People soon forget. Only Tom Ware religiously rang McBride every week for an update only to end the call in disappointment.

The arrival of Geoff Vicars had definitely obstructed the investigation. He became known to the Operation Silver Team as the mobile chicane. At every turn he put obstacles in their way slowing them down and stopping them from following promising leads. He had cut down the size of the team to only McBride and Emma Blakely. Dan Brennan and Cathy Grainger had been sent back to their respective units. He had terminated Dr Darleen Clutterbuck's consultancy arrangement almost immediately citing the cost as gross mismanagement of tax payers' money.

McBride walked along the canal; the same canal where Rosie had disappeared. He reached the spot where they believed the abduction had taken place. The blue and white police tape had long disappeared. The nearby bushes were festooned with yellow ribbons indicating the popularity of Rosie Ware. An Oxford university scarf tied to a branch fluttered in the breeze. Many burned out candles and bunches of long dead flowers sat alongside the canal where her friends had held a vigil in the days following her disappearance. The scene was a shrine to Rosie. A place where people could leave their mark of respect. Without a body, Rosie wouldn't have a permanent resting place. The place looked so different from the icy cold January morning when he had first seen it. Now bright green leaves covered the trees and bushes. Spring flowers grew alongside the canal. A weak but warm sun brightened the scene. McBride knew from his long career as a police detective that the longer an investigation took, the colder the trail became, and the harder it would be to conclude. He still hung on to the hope that Rosie was alive. All their investigation pointed to the fact that she had been taken for a purpose and was not just some random act of violent gratification.

McBride never let go of a case. Other officers might box up the evidence and send it away to some cold case storage unit and move on to their more current work load but for McBride, he never let go, never stopped looking. Like the loved ones of the missing he took them into his heart and never gave up the search. He still had unsolved cases going back to the start of his career that he regularly went over. Constantly applying new forensic breakthroughs hoping that a new lead would open up. All these cases weighed heavily on his heart. He always felt a sense of failure if he couldn't solve a case. He ran through different scenarios questioning his actions, his decisions, things he could, maybe should, have done differently.

87

Sixty miles away Dan Brennan sat in Dr Darleen Clutterbuck's office for what they had agreed would be their last session.

'What's stopping you taking the next step in your relationship with Emma?'

'Fear.'

'Fear of what?'

'Fear of commitment. Fear of loss. Fear of forgetting,' Dan said sighing and leaning forward in his chair resting his head in his open hands covering his eyes.

'What does Emma think?'

'We don't talk about it.'

'Don't you think that's strange?'

'Maybe. I sometimes think she thinks the same way.'

'Why is that?'

'Well she has her life in Oxford and I have my life here. Neither of us wants to change that so we don't raise the subject.'

'Dan I think you know how difficult it would be for Emma to move to London. She has a daughter to care for.'

'Yes I know I should be the one to move but I just can't do it, not yet.'

'Then maybe you don't love her enough?'

'But I do. I think about her day and night. I count down the minutes until I can see her again.'

'Let's wind the clock forward. You and Emma are in your sixties. Becky her daughter has long since left home. You have both retired. Can you leave London now?'

'I don't know, I'd be betraying Lucy's memory. I'd be leaving baby Tommy behind.'

Darleen took her glasses off and looked directly at him. 'Dan you don't need to be in London to remember Lucy and Tommy. They will always be a part of your life but you have to move forward. If your relationship with Emma is to grow you have to learn to let go of your past otherwise it will poison the future. Think of a place that was special to you and Lucy. A place the two of you would go on a special occasion.'

'We used to like to walk in woods in spring when the bluebells came out.'

'Use this as the place where you visit Lucy when you need her. Compartmentalise her in your mind in the woods with the bluebells. Now you can take her with you wherever you decide to live.'

'Now let's look at your fear of commitment and loss which are two of the same thing. If you had known at the start that Lucy was going to be taken from you would you have rather the two of you had never met, never shared the time you had together?'

'Definitely not.'

'So why are you holding back in your relationship with Emma. Very few of us know what the future holds. Maybe the two of you will only be together for a short time or maybe it will last into your old age. All you can do is seize the moment. Live for today. Follow the course fate has given you. Don't live your life for maybe's that might and probably never will happen.'

'I love Emma more than anything else in the world. I want nothing more than for us to have a happy life together. I'm going to do it. Take the plunge. I'll apply for a transfer to Oxford. That's if Emma wants me.'

'You've come to me because you need someone to tell you what you already know. You want someone else's permission to let go of the past and take responsibility for another person's life. Now go and get on with that life. You don't need me anymore. Well not as a therapist but hopefully we can remain friends.'

Dan got up to leave. He turned and gave Darleen a hug. 'I don't know how I would have got through these last few years without you.'

Darleen watched him go hoping that the story would have a happy ending. She also suppressed a feeling of loneliness in her own life as she picked up the case notes for her next patient's appointment.

88

Three months Earlier – Rosie's Story

For Rosie, it had been the worse two days of her life. The water and chocolate had long run out. Rosie had expected the gentle swell to turn into a maelstrom throwing her from one side of the crate to the other but this didn't happen. She had never been good with boats and expected to succumb to seasickness but the water continued to be calm. Maybe she wasn't at sea; perhaps she was on a river or canal. She knew she must look a complete mess. At least no man would be interested in a woman in this state. The boat began to slow. At last the end of her journey she thought and perhaps her best chance to escape. This is when she heard a slow hiss and a noxious chemical smell assaulted her nostrils. She started to cough and feel drowsy and although she fought it fell unconscious.

89

January 2014 – The Facility

The man flipped the light switch and the fluorescent lights raced down the long corridor lighting the way to the end. He stood at the first window and marvelled at his new prize. The view took him back twenty-eight years to another scene and he got the same elated feeling as he had back then. The girl lay like Sleeping Beauty waiting to be kissed by her Prince. She had been bathed and her hair washed and brushed flowing across the pillow showing off its magnificence. The glass was one way only. On the other side the girls would just see a large mirror. Sometimes the man would stand for hours watching his collection.

He rubbed his left hand. That damned dog had bitten him as he threw it into the hedgerow after it had completed his intended task of stopping Rosie on the tow path. He had the medical knowledge to clean the wound and put some stitches in but it hurt like hell. He hoped it wouldn't get infected as he couldn't risk going to a hospital A&E.

90

When Rosie awoke the rough crate had been replaced with a soft bed with crisp expensive Egyptian cotton sheets. She had an IV drip in her arm. At first, she thought that she had been rescued and admitted to hospital but when she viewed her surrounding it was more like a windowless luxury hotel room. Rosie pulled the needle from her arm and slowly swung her legs out of the bed. She was dressed in her own pyjamas. How on earth had the kidnappers got hold of these she thought then remembered they had been in her rucksack. Her legs felt like jelly as she made her way to the door, she tried the handle but found it locked. Banging on the door and shouting for help brought no results so defeated she sank down onto the settee and waited. There was no clock and her watch had been taken so she had no idea what time it was, hell she had no idea of what day it even was or what country she was even in. It was strange that after the claustrophobic constraints of the coffin-like box on the boat that the mind welcomed the relative luxury of this replacement prison and made the abduction less abhorrent. Maybe this was the psychological intention of her abductor. The knowledge that things could be worse, much worse.

Sometime later the door opened and a stunningly tall mixed race woman entered the room. Rosie eyed her warily not sure whether she was friend or foe.

'My name is Ruth and I'm here to explain your situation and the rules that apply here.'

'What is this place? Where am I?' Rosie asked.

'I don't know where it is. All I know is that it's underground and there is only one door into the facility.'

'I won't have sex with men I don't know, I'll never play your game, never ever,' Rosie cried.

Ruth smiled, 'don't worry that's the least of your problems, you won't see any men around here. I've forgotten what a man even looks like.'

'Then why am I here, have you kidnapped me for ransom?' Rosie asked hopefully.

'Unfortunately not. I'm a prisoner here just like yourself. This is now your home. There is no future for you beyond these walls,' Ruth explained trying to console a distraught Rosie.

'But, but I had such a great future, I was going to be a scientist and help the world,' Rosie cried.

'Oh, you can still be a great scientist and help the world just not in exactly the way you expected,' Ruth explained.

'I don't understand,' Rosie sobbed.

'There's no easy way to tell you this so I'll be direct. This is a human stud farm. You have been selected because you are considered to be a supreme human specimen. You will be expected to breed until your reproductive system fails.'

'Then what? They will let me go?'

'I don't know, some women continue to work here others just disappear, I've only been here eight years, some women have been here nearly thirty years. I don't have all the answers.'

'I won't do it, I'll just refuse, they can't force me.'

'Don't fight; it's just not worth it. Every one of us had the same thought as you when we arrived. If you comply you will be treated well, you can continue your education and have an interesting job here. If you become a troublemaker, well, let me just show you what happened to the last woman who tried to start a mutiny.'

Ruth led her out of her room and down a long white corridor with fluorescent lighting. Rosie took everything in as they walked. If she was going to escape then she had to learn everything she could. The place looked like a medical facility. Everything was white, glass and chrome. It smelled like a hospital.

In a room similar to her own, a woman of around forty-five years of age lay on a bed covered with a white sheet. Only her head was visible. The woman had the most gorgeous red hair that Rosie had ever seen; she turned her gaze towards Rosie and the saddest most beautiful emerald green eyes fixed their gaze on her. A tear formed and ran down her face. Ruth pulled back the covers and Rosie let out a terrifying scream. The woman had no arms below the elbows and no legs below the knees. She was obviously pregnant as her abdomen swelled out of proportion to the size of her. The woman let out a pitiful animal noise. Not only did she have no limbs but her tongue had also been removed.

'This is what happens to women who cause trouble,' Ruth explained. 'They only need your womb and genes, everything else is redundant. Kelly O'Connor here serves as an example of what happens to those who don't comply. She's expecting triplets in June.'

Rosie felt physically sick, 'what sort of monster can do this to another human being?'

'I don't know,' Ruth replied, 'I just hope I never find out. All I know is that he refers to himself as The Perfectionist.'

Rosie remembered the note she had received that was signed "P", this must be what it had stood for. 'What happens to the babies, are we allowed to raise them here?'

'No, after the birth they are taken away from us and adopted out in the real world. We aren't even allowed to breast feed them for the first few days or weeks they are here. They want you back to being reproductive as soon as possible and breast feeding suppresses this.'

Ruth took Rosie further down the corridor into a room with a large glass window. Behind the glass were several rows of baby cots. Currently, five of the cots were occupied by new-borns none of which was more than a few weeks old. Besides the cots were several arm chairs where two women perhaps in their mid-thirties sat chatting amiably. Both had very large ponderous breasts and attached to each a baby suckled hungrily. This is Hannah and Sophie two of our wet-nurses. They have had birth complications so can no longer breed. They have been retained to feed the newborns; they won't be used for future breeding but still have a use here. One of the women gently removed one of the babies from her breast and laid it carefully back in its cot. Milk oozed from her vacant breast and ran down her front. She picked up another baby and its mouth searched out the nipple and attached itself. The woman sat and resumed her conversation.

'How can two women feed so many babies?'

'We have two more wet-nurses. Only the good milk producers are kept on.'

'I thought a woman only produced milk for a few months after giving birth,' Rosie enquired. Her inquisitive mind getting the better of her frightening predicament.

'That's not true, a woman can produce milk for years as long as she keeps breast feeding. In years gone by wealthy women all had a wet-nurse to feed their babies.'

Rosie's mind raced with more questions, 'who provides all the medical services, the doctors, nurses, scientists, who cooks the meals and does the cleaning?'

'That's easy, we do. We have the finest female minds in the country. We have the best laboratories, libraries and teaching aids. You will be asked what field you want to go into and the full resources of the institute will be at your disposal. I can't say that any of the women here would have chosen this life but some actually seem to enjoy it. The worst part is being separated from the babies. None of the women ever get used to that. It's heartbreaking.'

'How many women are here?' Rosie asked.

'You make the number back up to twenty. It would have been twenty-one but Jennifer disappeared last week. You look a lot like her actually. I'm going to miss Jennifer she was my closest friend and was the matriarch here as apart from Dr Williams she had been here the longest.'

'Why would they get rid of her?' Rosie asked.

'She had complications after giving birth to triplets a couple of weeks ago. Dr Williams said that her breeding days were over. A week later she was gone.

'And the babies?' Rosie asked.

'They are the three tiny ones on the left. They are a bit underweight but doing OK,' Ruth explained.

Rosie looked at the three babies. Two with blue blankets one with pink. She assumed the babies under the blue blankets were boys and the one under the pink one was a girl. She thought how sad it was that they wouldn't be with their mother, never even know their mother. Looking at the babies Rosie swore to herself that she would find a way to escape. No matter how long it took she wouldn't be kept a prisoner here like a caged animal.

It was as if Ruth knew what she was thinking. 'There is no way out of here. Don't you think we haven't all tried? The only way out of here is in a body bag.'

Rosie vowed to herself that she would find a way.

'There must be interaction with the outside world. How do supplies get in? How do the babies get out?'

'The airlock at the end of the corridor. We put any waste out and they put fresh supplies in.'

They can't remove the oxygen from the babies when they are moved out.

'No, but you can hardly hide a grown adult in with a baby.

'How did they get Jennifer out? Did they kill her here first?'

'Every night we have lock-down. All the girls have to be in their rooms. Unless there is a birth taking place. Have you noticed the large mirror in your room? Well, this is a two-way mirror. They can observe you from the other side. Each room has a ventilation system. We assume that they can pump knockout gas into the room. Jennifer went to her room one night. The next day she had gone.'

'You must have a way of communicating with the outside world? To ask for supplies?'

'We have access to an intranet system. Do you know what this is?'

'Yes, it's a closed computer system. Only computers on the network are connected. No external communication is allowed in or out.'

'We can request goods, books, research papers, medicines etc.'

'Has anyone tried to bypass it?'

'Of course, we have but we just have dumb terminals at this end. We don't have access to the server. It's good that you are thinking of how to escape but as time goes on you will accept life here.'

'I'll never accept being kept a prisoner,' Rosie said bitterly.

'We all went through the same process. Some girls even take their own lives. Depression is the biggest problem here. It's the hardest thing to have your babies taken.'

'What about the fathers of the babies? Where do they come from?'

'Sperm samples are delivered for insemination. We have no idea where they come from. We do know that they have been carefully selected as the babies tend to have the same traits as the mother. Take Jennifer, for example, she had twenty-five babies and every one of them had blue eyes with blonde hair. Kelly's babies nearly always have red hair with green eyes. My babies are always dark skinned with black hair.'

'Don't you feel like mixing them up to get these people annoyed?'

'What's the point? If you don't produce good babies then you don't survive. We once had a girl who had a downs syndrome baby. Next day they had both gone.'

Ruth seemed to sense Rosie's anger and returning her to her room suggested she have a lie down before lunch. Agreeing Rosie lay down on her bed trying to assimilate all the information she had been given. There must be a way out of here and she was going to find it.

After a couple of hours sleep Rosie awoke feeling refreshed. For the first time, she really looked around her prison cell as she had decided to call it. Opening the doors of the small wardrobe she found four track suits in various colours with three sets of plimsolls all in her size. She had a chest of six drawers containing underwear and socks all in plain white and in utilitarian no-frills cotton. There was a desk with two drawers and a Personal Computer on the top. The top drawer contained a selection of stationery, pens, pencils and erasers. The second drawer held paper, some lined and some blank. Some of the contents from her rucksack had been placed next to the PC. Rosie's diary which she had kept since the age of fourteen; a photograph of her parents, that she always carried with her; a Mount Blanc fountain pen her father had bought her last Christmas. Anything that could have been used to communicate with the outside world had been removed. Her laptop and phone were both missing. She read through the two entries she had made in this year's diary which she had started at the beginning of January. Both related to

Ben and both seemed so frivolous and unimportant now. She lifted the paper from the second desk drawer and hid the diary there. She decided she would keep a record of her time here. This is when she noticed a letter deep in the drawer. Taking it out she opened it and looked at the bottom. It was signed Jennifer Shepherd. Wasn't that the woman Ruth had just mentioned? The one who disappeared a few days ago? The mother of the triplets? Rosie didn't want to intrude but her inquisitive mind got the better of her. As she read the letter her eyes misted over and tears ran down her face.

My name is Jennifer Shepherd. I know I only have a few days left in this world. I can see it in the eyes of the other women here. They look at me not just with pity but with the sure knowledge that one day their turn will come, like a clock ticking down to their execution date but without the hope of a reprieve. I know this because I have looked at other women here in the same way. This is why I'm writing this letter. Not in the hope that I will be rescued, there is no hope, but to set the record straight; to tell my parents that I didn't run away as the police would have them believe.

I went missing on the day the 'A' Level results were issued back in August 1986. This day turned out to be the best and worst day of my life. The day couldn't have started better. It was one of those rare English summer days when the sun shone, the sky was clear blue and the breeze was light and warm. It was one of those "good to be alive" days.

I remember being so excited as I cycled down the seafront from my home towards the school. Lots of other pupils were milling around the entrance hall waiting to receive their results envelope. As each envelope was opened there were either whoops of glee or despondent groans. You see those white envelopes determined the course of the next stage in our lives, they were important. I opened mine and relief flooded through me. I thought I had done well but until you get the confirmation doubt always clouds your mind. I had got straight As and with this an assured place at Cambridge University to study architecture. I'd always wanted to be an architect. As a child, I would pester my parents to take me to London to see the many grand old buildings alongside new super modern structures. My only thought was to return home to tell my parents. You need to remember that back in 1986, we didn't own mobile phones so I couldn't ring them.

Maybe if I hadn't been so excited I would have noticed the black van following close behind me. It all happened so quickly. As we came to a quiet stretch of road with sand hills either side it came up alongside me and cut me up. I had no alternative other than to stop. Next thing I knew a man of about thirty came up to me and stuck a needle in my leg. My head swam and I sank to the floor looking up at that clear blue sky and bright yellow sun. That was the last time I felt the warmth of the sun on my face. That was the last time I breathed fresh air. The next thing I knew I woke up in bed in this facility. I have been here ever since.

I don't need to explain to you what goes on here. You will already have been told.

Back in 1986 this facility had only been opened a couple of years. Most of the rooms were empty. Only four other girls were held captive. Of those original girls, only Elizabeth Williams remains. She has made herself indispensable. A wise move if you want to stay alive. Cheryl committed suicide back in 1990. Depression is

323

one of the biggest problems here. This is why we are allowed to study and have televisions and radios. A caged animal with nothing to do will go mad. Kimberly went through an early menopause in 2008. She disappeared several months later. Donna was removed last year. I really miss Donna we had become great friends. She was from Zimbabwe and had won a Rhodes scholarship to study At Oxford University in the UK. She was taken on her way from the airport.

My first child, a girl, was born in 1987. I named her Sophia. Of course, she will have been renamed by her adoptive parents and won't remember me or her original name. I was allowed to hold her and breast feed her for the first week of her life before she was taken from me. Having bonded the loss was so much greater. This is why Dr Williams now takes the babies immediately and gives them to a nursemaid to suckle. We didn't have the luxury of nursemaids back in the early days.

My second child was a boy named Christopher. That was a difficult birth as he was breech and Dr Williams was still studying obstetrics so didn't have the knowledge to perform the delivery well. Luckily we both came through it.

Test tube babies had only just been introduced back in those early days and the women here didn't have the expertise to carry out the procedure so we continued the conceptions using the old method. I don't mean using a man but using the self-insemination method of that time. As more women arrived the pool of experts grew until we had one of the most efficient clinics in the country.

By the early '90s women weren't just having single births but twins, triplets and we even had a set of quads. I had my first set of twins in 1991. A boy and a girl. I named them Luke and Melony. I was good at having babies. In total, I have had twenty-five children. None of which will ever know me. I just hope for my parent's sake that one of my children will one day find them. Being an only child I hate to think that my parents will die without knowing that they have so many grandchildren. I also want to put their minds at rest. It must be terrible - the not knowing.

I don't know if this letter will ever get out. I can only hope it will. Whoever you are reading this please don't despair. Life isn't too bad here. I know you will feel like your life has ended. I used to worry about my babies but of course they will be oblivious to their beginnings. I just hope they are having happy successful lives and are being allowed to pursue their goals. I have been assured that they have all been placed in loving homes with parents who really want them. I have to believe for my own sanity that this is true.

As my end draws near I meet it with a sense resignation and relief. I wish I could believe in a God but I don't. I think that being dead is like the time before you are born just nothingness but I do go in the knowledge that I am leaving many beautiful intelligent children behind. My life hasn't been in vain. So don't cry for me but also don't give up. One day this facility will be found and the women

inside released. Then hopefully my story will
also get out.

Jennifer Shepherd x (20ᵗʰ January 2014)

Attached to the letter was a list of the names that Jennifer had given to her babies plus the date each was born. Rosie wondered where all these children were now. One child, a girl named Grace, had been born only two days before Rosie herself. Carefully re-folding the letter and list she placed them in the back of her diary for safe keeping. When she escaped she would ensure they got delivered to Jennifer's parents.

91

For the first couple of months very little happened. Blood samples were taken. Injections given. At first Rosie just sat in her room looking at the four walls but the interminable boredom soon drove her to the library and social areas. It was true what Ruth had said; the library was one of the best she had ever seen. Soon she was taking books every few days and avidly reading them from cover to cover. If she wanted a research paper or article from a particular publication she only had to put a request in on the intranet and the publication would arrive shortly after. The other girls were fun too. Rosie made a point to learn all their names and details of where they came from. Once she escaped she wanted to be able to contact their families to let them know that their daughters were still alive.

They were allowed to watch television and had access to a large selection of DVDs. At first Rosie had followed the police investigation into her disappearance avidly. A DCI McBride was in charge of the investigation. He reminded her of her father. Not in looks but in his personality. He had kind eyes and spoke with determination assuring her parents and the public that all efforts were being made to trace Rosie's whereabouts. She had shouted at the TV when she saw how far away from the truth they were. She had cried when she watched her parents and Ben speak at the news conference. After a few weeks news about her disappearance appeared less and less until it stopped altogether.

After being in the facility two months one morning Dr Williams knocked on her door.

'Rosie, We need to harvest your eggs today,' she said.

Rosie was overwhelmed with panic. 'I'm not ready to be a mother. Can't we wait a bit longer?'

'Now is the optimum time. If we don't do it today then we will miss the window for this month. If we don't get you pregnant in the next few months then you will be disposed of. If you can't breed then you are no use to the programme.'

Rosie nodded her acceptance and followed Dr Williams down the corridor to one of the medical rooms.

Dr Williams explained the procedure. 'We will do an egg extraction today. The viable eggs will then be fertilised in vitro.'

'You mean a test tube baby?' Rosie asked.

'Yes,' Dr Williams replied.

At least she wouldn't have some strange man's sperm inside her. The thought of this made her feel sick.

Dr Williams carried on her talk. 'We will only be putting one viable egg back inside you. The others will be frozen for use later.'

'So I won't be expected to have triplets?' Rosie asked.

'No. We like to have just a single birth the first time. As you get more experienced we will increase the number of fertilised eggs but we never put more than three back,' Dr Williams explained. 'In the early days, the procedure wasn't as good and one woman had quads. We struggled to keep them alive and lost two of them.'

So Rosie didn't put up the fight she had expected to. Like a lamb to the slaughter she allowed them to carry out the procedure. Four days later one fertilised egg was put back into her body. Now she had to wait two weeks to see if it had taken. When the result came back positive she cried for the rest of the day. She thought that she would be different. She thought she would be the one to change things. She was just like all the rest. Powerless to do anything.

92

June 2014 – The Facility

Rosie felt a bit sick in the mornings but overall she felt strong and well. The facility had a small gym and Rosie regularly took exercise. It was now June. She had been here nearly five months. She was twelve weeks pregnant. Already she felt a sense of love for the baby growing in her womb. She had a deep feeling of desolation about having to give it up. This is what sent Rosie on the reckless course of action that she decided to embark on.

When it happened her chance to escape came out of the blue.

One morning in early June there was a loud keening noise, which sounded like a wounded animal, coming from down the corridor. Several pairs of feet ran past Rosie's door. Rosie put her head out and asked what the commotion was about.

'It's Kelly. She's gone into labour but something's not right. There's blood everywhere.' One of the girls said.

Rosie crept down to the operating theatre and listened at the door. Dr Williams was talking to several of the women who assisted her.

'It's not good, I'm afraid it's either Kelly or the babies.'

'You've got to save Kelly,' one of the assistants replied.

'She will need a hysterectomy. When he finds out Kelly will be history anyway. She would want us to save her babies,' Dr Williams said.

Behind their surgical face masks, several pairs of wet eyes nodded their agreement.

'Let's get on with it. The sooner we get those babies out the better chance they have,' Dr Williams said.

A couple of hours later the news went round the facility that Kelly had died on the operating table. The three babies had survived but it was touch and go. They were in incubators in the ICU their little faces covered with oxygen masks.

Rosie went to the ICU and peered through the window at the three babies. They were tiny and pink with a shock of red hair the same colour as their mothers. Next she went to the operating theatre where Kelly still lay on the table. She seemed so small and pale in death. She had finally escaped from the torturous existence that she had suffered for so many years. As she stood next to the body Dr Williams came up beside her.

'What will happen to her now?' Rosie asked.

'We need to prepare her for transport,' Dr Williams said.

'Will they send her back to her family in Ireland,' Rosie asked.

'I doubt it. I don't know what happens to them. When we have a death we just have to put the cadaver in a body bag. There will be a lock down tonight and the body will be removed. I don't know what happens to them after that. Will you help me prepare the body?'

Dr Williams went to a cupboard, removed a thick black body bag and spread it out next to Kelly's mutilated corpse.

'Why is the bag so heavy?' Rosie asked.

'For some reason it has lead weights sewn into the bottom. I've never understood this. Maybe it's to weigh the body down when it's disposed of. Perhaps they are thrown into water.'

Between the two of them, it was easy to put Kelly into the bag and zip it up. They placed the body on a gurney like those used in ambulances where they could be collapsed down to go into the back of a vehicle.

Rosie thought back to something Ruth had said to her when she first arrived. "The only way out of here is in a body bag". This is what gave her the idea. The curfew was in two hours. Not much time to prepare but enough. It was now or never.

First Rosie went to the supply cupboard. She took out two pillows, a small oxygen cylinder and mask normally used for the premature babies, a scalpel, a five hundred millilitre bottle of water and a packet of biscuits.

Next, she went to find Ruth and explain her plan. She would need some inside help if this was going to work. When she told her Ruth was horrified.

'But you can't be sure that they dispose of the body in water. What if you get buried alive or thrown into an incinerator. Even if they do throw the body in water you will drown trapped inside the body bag.'

Rosie explained that she had weighed up all the facts. She had been brought here by boat so the facility must be near to water. The body bag was weighted down so that it would sink. What other possible explanation could there be? Also, she was an excellent swimmer so would have a good chance of swimming to safety. Rosie knew that she sounded more confident than she felt but she also knew that this was her one and only chance of escape.

'What if you get caught? You know he will be looking for another girl to make an example of to replace Kelly. How can you risk winding up with no limbs?' Ruth said.

'I've got to get out of here and this is my only chance,' Rosie said.

'OK. What do you want me to do?'

Rosie explained that she needed time to get away. If her escape was discovered whilst she was still on the boat then she would get caught. She asked Ruth to remove the pillows the next morning and to make excuses to anyone who asked where she was. All the women were in the same position and it was unlikely any of them would inform on her but she didn't want to take the risk.

'Do you want help getting into the bag?' Ruth asked.

'I think I'll be OK. I can work the zip from the inside. I don't want anyone to know you were involved in this.'

'OK. If you do get out you will come back for us won't you?' Ruth pleaded.

'Of course I'll come back for you.' Rosie said hugging her friend.

Time seemed to tick ever so slowly as she sat in her small room. Rosie wanted to avoid the areas where the other women would be. Although she would have loved to say her goodbyes she didn't think she would be able to keep her emotions under control. These women had become like family and close friends. The thought of never seeing them again and abandoning them to an early death was more than she could cope with. The facility was already in a subdued state having lost one of their longest members. It wasn't far from anyone's mind that a replacement for Kelly might be sought.

Rosie took her diary out of her desk drawer. She had made entries since the day she had arrived determined to leave a legacy of her time here. She had contemplated taking it with her but as she wanted to keep weight to a minimum and it would get ruined in the water she had decided to leave it behind. If she failed to make it then maybe one day in the future it might be found and her family would find out what had become of her.

She started to read from the beginning. Was it only five months? It was the longest five months of her life but Rosie felt as if she had developed from a girl into a woman in this time. Her boyfriend Ben, who had been the centre of her life back in January, hardly entered her thoughts anymore. She still missed her parents though. It worried her the strain her disappearance would have had on them.

<u>*Rosie's Diary*</u>

Monday, January 27th, 2014

At least I think this is the right date. It may be a day either side as I don't know how long I was knocked out for. There is no natural light down here so it's impossible to know if it is day or night but the women seem to follow a strict regime. Breakfast is at nine, lunch at one and dinner at six. When I awoke this morning I thought at first I had been rescued and was in a private hospital. This soon turned out to be a delusion. Although I was in a luxury prison it was a prison none the less. My hopes were further dashed when I found out that I hadn't been kidnapped for ransom but had been selected for some mad man's human breeding programme. This place has been running for around thirty years and no-one outside these walls apart from its orchestrator, or orchestrators, knows of its existence. How could all these women have been abducted and no-one in the outside world be aware of it? This morning I was shown round the facility by Ruth. She has been nominated to be my mentor until I settle into life here. I vow on day one that I will never settle into life here. I will make it my mission to find a way to escape. Although Ruth is my guard I can't help liking her. Lunch time is my first meeting with the rest of the women. When I walked into the dining area it was like walking backstage on a Miss World contest. I have never seen so many beautiful women in one place. I had always considered myself to be good looking but I paled into insignificance next to these beauties. The big difference between these women and the Miss World contestants was that most of them seemed to be in various stages of pregnancy. Ruth introduced me to them. It will take me a while to remember all their names. They fussed around me like I was a new addition to their tribe which I suppose I was. Apparently, there isn't much new of interest around here so a fresh face is always welcome. I learn only one new girl a year joins the group but this depends on how many he has culled from his collection. He always likes to keep the total number of woman around twenty I don't know if this is to fill the number of bedrooms or if it is to meet the demand for the babies. I have been chosen to replace the recently departed Jennifer. Ruth tells me that I have a meeting with Dr Williams tomorrow. She wasn't in the dining room today as she was attending the latest birth. Tomorrow I will learn what is expected of me. I am now back in my room writing this diary. You can't see it but tears stream down my face. I long for Ben to hold me in his arms. I long to talk to my parents. I long for this nightmare to end.

Tuesday, January 28th, 2014

Today I met Dr Williams for the very first time. She doesn't have a single medical qualification but she knows more about obstetrics than almost any other doctor in the country, probably the world. She has been here since the age of eighteen and has learned her profession via books and videos. The other women bestowed on her the title of doctor. Her first name is Elizabeth but no-one ever uses it. She is one of the few women who has remained in his collection even though she has now gone through the menopause. In fact he hasn't used her for breeding since she took control of the medical facility aged twenty-seven. I asked her why she does his bidding. Her reply was that doing nothing wasn't an option. She said that if I had been here in the early days when they had little in the way of medical knowledge and equipment I would have also chosen to help. I know I'm not in a position to judge but I get the impression that Dr Williams loves her job. An assistant named Heather takes my blood pressure then weighs and measures me. She then sticks a needle in my arm and draws what seems an excessive amount of blood. I'm given a bottle to fill with urine and left in private to complete the task. I think about messing up the sample but then think 'what's the point'. Making life difficult for the other women here isn't going to help my predicament. Heather returns and takes the sample from me. She gives me a six page form to fill out. The form contains only medical questions about me. I'm surprised that there are no questions relating to my parents. When I've had medicals previously the doctor seems more interested in the genetics of my parents than me, as if trying to predict problems I might encounter in the future. It doesn't take long to fill in the form. I'm a very healthy person. In fact I can't remember the last time I was ill. Heather gives me another appointment card for two days hence. This makes me laugh it's not as if I'm going anywhere or have a busy social life.

Wednesday, January 29th, 2014

Today I had a meeting with the education advisor a lady named Rachel. She shows me around the library and gives me instructions on how to use the intranet and how to request books or papers I want for my research. It is left up to me what I choose to study. I can carry on with the course I am taking at the University of Oxford or I can switch to something completely different. I tell her I will think about it. Resuming my studies is the furthest thing from my mind at the moment.

I return to my room wanting to catch the twelve o'clock news. Yes, surprisingly enough we are allowed access to the outside world but it is only one way. I'm still making the headlines. I shout and scream at the TV telling them I'm here but of course no-one can hear me. There is a re-run of Sunday's television appeal which I had missed. My parents and boyfriend Ben are pleading for my safe return. At this stage they still think I've been kidnapped for money. My parents look strained as if they haven't slept for days which I expect they haven't. Ben looks as handsome as ever. How I long to be with them. The policeman in charge of my case is a DCI Ian McBride. He looks intelligent and competent which gives me some hope.

Thursday, January 30th, 2014

Today was my second consultation with Dr Williams. My test results are all back in. It's not as if this facility has the usual NHS backlog, is it? Anyway, everything is hunky dory and I can proceed to the next stage. Dr Williams talks as if it's my life ambition to get pregnant. Yes, I want children one day but not now and not like this. The baby will be conceived by IVF. Even in couples with infertility problems the success rate is now forty percent. For someone as fit as me, using the sperm of the male who has been selected to father the baby, she tells me I have an excellent chance of success. The word 'success' isn't what I would use. Dr Williams explains that I have to start taking a drug called Lupron as soon as I have my next ovulation. I'm given an ovulation predictor kit together with my next appointment card for a date in two weeks. As soon as I get back to my room I look for somewhere to bin the drugs. I push them one by one into a hole I have made in my mattress. There's no way I'm going to make this easy for them.

Friday, January 31ˢᵗ, 2014

I've decided to carry on with marine biology the same subject I was studying at Oxford. Ruth tried to persuade me to switch to human biology but the thought of being press-ganged onto Dr Williams's medical team or even becoming her successor appals me. I might never see the ocean again and the only fish might be dead on my dinner plate but at least I'll be able to dream of a world beyond this prison. Rachel was correct when she said the learning facilities are excellent. We have access to thousands of online books and DVDs. I've been given a Kindle so that I can download books and documents from the intranet.

Saturday, February 1ˢᵗ, 2014

Today in the library I met Wendy for the first time. She is the lady who was giving birth on the day I arrived. It was her first child, a boy. Wendy is only one year older than me, she was the newest girl before my arrival. I went over to introduce myself but she seemed subdued and intent on her studies. Suddenly she looked up and said 'I didn't even get to hold him. He was so tiny with black hair and dark blue eyes. He cried when they took him away as if he knew. Dr Williams said that it's better for the mothers if they don't bond with the babies.' I told her she would be able to see him through the nursery window but she said it would only make her pain worse. It was better to forget about him. I changed the subject and asked what she was studying. She told me she was writing a paper on human characteristics and their star sign. It seemed a strange subject to study but she explained animals gave birth at a particular time of year to give their offspring the best chance in life whereas humans gave birth all year round. Her study looked at whether children born at certain times of year had a social advantage. It also looked at the diet of the mothers and how this influenced the growing foetus. Was it better for a baby to be born in winter when the mother had eaten well during the early stages of pregnancy or was it better for the baby to be born in the summer when the mother would be able to produce ample milk and nutrition to the child? I left her to her work.

Saturday, February 8th, 2014

It's been a week since my last entry. Two reasons for this – one, nothing much has happened and two, I've been engrossed in my studies. Ruth wasn't in the dining room for lunch today. I found her in her room crying. She is pregnant again. This will be her tenth pregnancy and she's only thirty-two. She doesn't think she can go through it all again. She tells me she never even wanted children. Her last delivery was twins, a boy and a girl. Dr Williams is trying for triplets this time. I tried to comfort her but I didn't know what to say.

Thursday, February 13th, 2014

Back to see Dr Williams again today. I don't mention having disposed of the tablets. She confirms with me that my period started the day before which it had, I'm always as regular as clockwork. More bloodwork and this time an ultrasound is done. Dr Williams refers to this as the baseline. She wants to check my oestrogen levels, specifically my E2 or estradiol. This is to make sure my ovaries are "sleeping," the intended effect of the Lupron. The ultrasound is to check the size of my ovaries and look for ovarian cysts. I don't have any cysts everything looks OK so my treatment moves on to the next step. The next step is ovarian stimulation with fertility drugs. Dr Williams tells me I'm lucky as I'll only need one injection a day. Some women need as many as four. In the outside world, women self-administer but here Dr Williams likes to ensure all the women have their correct shots so I am told to report each day at ten o'clock. I've no opportunity to avoid this one! Do they know I'm hiding the drugs?

Friday, February 14th, 2014

Valentine's Day. No flowers, chocolates or cards just a great big needle. I've always hated needles. I pity the poor women who have to have four of these a day. I've been put on cooking duty from today. Obviously no-one has checked up on my cooking abilities. I don't expect to be in the job long. I'm taking over from Ruth who has chronic morning sickness. She doesn't appear for lunch so I take her some soup. Normally her skin is a beautiful honey colour but today it's deathly ashen. Just one look at the soup sends her running to the toilet.

Tuesday, February 18th, 2014

In addition to the daily visits to have the ovarian stimulation, injections I have to attend the clinic every fourth day so Dr Williams can monitor the growth and development of the follicles. More blood is taken to check my estradiol levels, and an ultrasound is done to access the oocyte growth. I know how a pin cushion feels!

Dr Williams says that monitoring the cycle is important as it helps her decide whether or not to increase or decrease the dosage of the medication. Apparently I need to be checked until my largest follicle is sixteen to eighteen millimetres in size.

Wednesday, February 26th, 2014

The next step in my IVF treatment is to trigger the oocytes to go through their last stage of maturation, before being retrieved. This last growth spurt is triggered with human chorionic gonadotropin (hCG). Dr Williams is using a drug called Ovidrel.

Timing this shot is vital. If it's given too early, the eggs will not have matured enough. If given too late, the eggs may be "too old" and won't fertilize properly. The daily ultrasounds at the end of the last step are meant to time this trigger shot just right. Usually, the hCG injection is given when four or more follicles have grown to be eighteen to twenty millimetres in size and your estradiol levels are greater than 2,000pg/ML.

Thankfully this shot is a one-time injection (yeah!).

Dr Williams is pleased with my results. She complains about the difficulty of working with the older mothers. Nature isn't kind to women as they age. The timing of my egg retrieval is very important and I'm told to report back in exactly thirty-four hours.

Thursday, February 27th, 2014

This is egg retrieval day. I'm gowned and prostrate on an operating table. Natasha the anaesthetist has given me a light sedative to relax me and make me sleep through the procedure. Dr Williams has explained everything to me. She will use a transvaginal ultrasound to guide a needle through the back wall of my vagina, up to my ovaries.

She will then use the needle to aspirate the follicle, gently sucking the fluid and oocyte from the follicle into the needle. There is one oocyte per follicle. These oocytes will be transferred to the embryology lab for fertilization.

I feel really woozy after the procedure. Dr Williams is very pleased she has managed to retrieve a dozen oocytes.

I feel like I'm getting my period but Dr Williams tells me this is very common. At least I've got out of dinner making duties. While I recover from the retrieval, my follicles are aspirated and searched for oocytes or eggs. Apparently not every follicle will contain an egg.

Dr Williams gives me some progesterone supplements and tells me to take them each day. These go straight into the mattress with the other drugs.

Friday, February 28th, 2014

I wasn't going to involve myself in the technical side of the IVF process but curiosity got the better of me. It was for this reason that I found myself in the laboratory early this morning asking Sue the embryologist numerous questions.

She went through the process with me. Firstly she evaluated the eggs. Any overly matured were discarded as fertilization is unlikely to be successful. Any not mature enough were stimulated to maturity in the lab. Fertilization of the eggs must happen within twelve to twenty-four hours she explained.

I watched as Sue puts each of the selected eggs onto a petri dish. Next she took a vial containing the semen. This is the first time I'd met the father of my child. She puts this through a special washing process, which separated the sperm from the other stuff that is found in semen (yuck). Then she chooses the best looking sperm, placing about ten thousand in each culture dish with each egg. The culture dishes are kept in an incubator then after twelve to twenty-four hours checked for signs of fertilization.

She told me that out of the ten eggs she had selected about seven would fertilize but I'd have to call back tomorrow to check.

Monday, March 3rd, 2014

Implantation day. Today I returned to the clinic to have one of the eggs put back inside me. Eight eggs had fertilized but the other seven would be cryopreserved for future use. The procedure was surprisingly simple. No anaesthesia was required and no injections!!!

I ask Dr Williams what happens if the IVF fails.

If the pregnancy test is still negative twelve to fourteen days post-transfer, then I am to stop taking the progesterone (not that I've been taking it in the first place), and we wait for my period to start. Then we start the procedure all over again but this time one of the remaining fertilized eggs would be used.

I asked her what would happen to my spare eggs. It upset me when she said some of them would likely be implanted into some of the other women. Apparently blue eyed blondes are highly desirable and if there wasn't a request for some of the other ethnicities then they would be used as surrogate mothers. This was the first time it struck me that this is only a business and the women here are just commodities like cattle at a market.

Wednesday, March 12th, 2014

Today my period was due but there is no sign of it. I don't feel pregnant though. I went to discuss this with Ruth. She said that all the drugs could be messing with my cycle so not to worry.

Monday, March 17th, 2014

Still no sign of my period and today I have to visit Dr Williams for my pregnancy test. I have mixed feelings. Part of me wants to succeed. Maybe this is my competitive nature. Part of me is dreading the test being positive.

Monday, March 24th, 2014

Well, it was positive. It's taken me a week to be able to write about it. I'm still in shock. I still don't feel any different but I'm sure my boobs are getting bigger. The only other news is that I've been taken off cooking duties. Luckily Ruth is feeling better and has returned. I'm now in the laundry.

Rosie closed the diary at this point as it was time to go. Leaving the diary was like leaving a best friend. Writing had kept her sane over these last five months. She hadn't made an entry today and didn't intend to. She didn't want to mention her escape plan just in case her absence was noticed and her room was searched. She hid her diary behind one of the drawers in her desk carefully securing it in place with some of the surgical tape she had acquired earlier.

Thirty minutes before the curfew started she returned to where Kelly's dead body lay. Unzipping the bag she used the scalpel to cut through the stitching that held the lead weights in place. She extracted all four of them and hid them inside one of the cupboards behind some other supplies. In their place she put the oxygen cylinder, mask, water and biscuits. Next she went back to her room.

They didn't have a lot of clothing and Rosie's small wardrobe only held three track suits. Turning out the light, in the hope that anyone watching through the two-way mirror wouldn't see what she was doing, she quickly put on the three suits one on top of the other. Next she put the two pillows on her bed under her blankets and positioned them so it looked like there was someone sleeping there. She carefully wrapped the scalpel, to protect herself from the sharp blade, and put this in her pocket. The facility was quieting down now as the girls returned to their rooms. Rosie crept along the deserted corridor and returned to the operating theatre. She didn't meet anybody on her way. This was her last chance to back out she thought.

Unzipping the body bag she climbed in next to Kelly. It wasn't like snuggling up to a warm soft human being. By this time Kelly was cold and stiff. She had thought to remove the body and hide it somewhere but she couldn't risk it being found whilst she was still escaping. Because Kelly was limbless and had lost most of her blood there was plenty of room for Rosie to fit comfortably alongside her in the bag. She calculated that with the lead weights removed the total weight of the bag would only seem like that of a normal body.

As Rosie lay in the bag her thoughts started to run away with her. She felt so frightened and she thought back to the day that she had been kidnapped and brought here. Now though it wasn't just her, she had other responsibilities. She had the baby growing inside her plus all the girls imprisoned here whose only hope of salvation was down to her. As a mantra she went through the names of all the women trapped inside these walls. This calmed her down.

Curfew had long since passed when she heard the first sounds of movement from the end of the corridor where the air lock was. She had the oxygen cylinder ready just in case they decided to expel the air but she didn't think they would do this. There's not much point starving a corpse of oxygen. She was correct and she felt the gurney being wheeled out through the door. She felt a sudden elation about being free but then realised that she was a long way from the end of her journey. There was no talking around her so she suspected that only one man was doing the extraction. After ten minutes the air changed and Rosie realised that they were outside. Fresh air had never smelled so good. Rosie resisted the urge to breathe in deeply knowing that she couldn't make even the slightest noise.

This was the point where things started to go badly wrong. The bag together with its contents was tipped unceremoniously into a hole. Rosie had to bite her lip to avoid crying out. Fear gripped her. Was she being buried alive? She heard the sound of a lid being closed above her and a lock clicking into place. It had been dark inside the bag but now it was pitch black. Rosie hardly dared breathe. Everything was still then after several minutes the deep throaty sound of a motor sounded and the smell of a boat's engine fumes assailed Rosie's nostrils. It dawned on her that she was back in the same box that had been used to bring her here, however this time she didn't have the luxury of a torch to provide some light. If it was a similar journey to the one that brought her here then she could be stuck on the boat for a couple of days. Rosie had envisioned getting out of the body bag and slipping off the boat whilst nobody was looking. She now realised that she was trapped in the box until someone opened it to dispose of Kelly's body. She thought about the scalpel inside her pocket but soon dismissed the idea of using it to cut her way out of the box. Scalpels are designed for cutting flesh, not wood. She had no other option than to wait it out.

After a few hours, Kelly's body started to smell. Firstly that cloying smell of drying blood then other bodily odours. The zip was cumbersome to undo from the inside but eventually Rosie managed to unzip the bag and stick her head out to get some fresher air.

Rosie estimated that it had been about thirty hours when the boat suddenly stopped. In the last half hour, the swell had become noticeably heavier and Rosie suspected that they were somewhere out at sea. This was not good news. Depending on how far they were from land and the temperature of the water this would determine Rosie's chance of survival. She knew that in June the sea would still be extremely cold around the British Isles. Without a survival suit, she maybe had about an hour tops. She zipped the body bag shut and held onto the scalpel in one hand and the oxygen in the other. She placed the mask over her mouth and turned the knob on the cylinder to on. The remaining water and biscuits she abandoned.

It was a bit like waiting for the big drop on the log flume at a theme park but in this case death was a real possibility. She heard the lock being removed from the box and the lid scraping from the top. She was then hauled out. She could hear at least two men talking but couldn't make out the words. Grunts of exertion accompanied Rosie's progress from the bowels of the boat to the deck. She held her breath hoping that they wouldn't notice the bag contained more than one body. Next she felt herself falling. Hitting water even from a small height knocks the wind out of a person. The mask was pulled away from Rosie's mouth and she felt like she had been dropped onto concrete. This thought was soon dispelled as icy cold water started to flood into the bag. She thought it was going to be cold but nothing prepared her for the numbing shock of the freezing water filling the bag. Rosie could feel herself sinking and more and more salty seawater flooding in. She was now sinking rapidly tumbling over and over. She had to get out of the body bag fast before she was dragged into the ocean depths. She had no time to fumble with the zip, she doubted her cold numbed fingers could have worked it open anyway, so with a sweep of her hand she brought the scalpel in an upwards arc slicing through the plastic material. Letting go of the scalpel she pushed the sides of the gap apart and forced herself upwards. Kelly's dead body still inside the bag sank slowly below her. Something caught around Rosie's arm. It was the tube leading from the mask to the oxygen cylinder. At first her instinct was to shake the tangle free but then she realised this may be the difference between life and death. She didn't know how far she had sunk but she knew that a human could only hold their breath for one maybe two minutes. She could feel the bubbles escaping from the mask against her face. Quickly she placed the mask over her mouth and her lungs automatically sucked in the clean fresh air. She felt like a student in one of those helicopter crash simulation exercises where they are plunged into a dark swimming pool and taught how to escape. Rosie hadn't had any survival training. She just knew that a frogman wasn't at her side to assist if she got into difficulty. Her first problem was orientation. She didn't know which was up or down. She just knew it was pitch black. Don't panic she told herself. Taking a deep breath from the oxygen cylinder she removed the mask and felt the direction the bubbles went. Air rises so this was the way up. She didn't know how deep she had gone and whether she needed to think about the bends but she did know that time was ticking away and she had to get out of the cold water as quickly as possible.

Rosie swam strongly upwards. She broke the surface and paused to try and get her bearings. She looked around wildly. The night was pitch black. There wasn't even a moon. Rosie could make out the retreating lights of a boat, presumably the one that had carried her here. She watched it as it sailed into the distance. It couldn't help with her rescue but at least it showed her the direction in which to swim.

The oxygen tank was of no further use to her and would only hamper her swimming so she let it sink from her grasp. Rosie set out in a crawl towards the direction the boat had taken. She had no idea how far from shore she was. She had never realised how cold sea water could be. Her swimming had always been done in either the pool at the family home or the Olympic sized pool that she had practised in when she swam for the Newcastle Aquajets team.

After thirty minutes she felt like she was making no progress at all but she had no other choice than to continue. After another ten minutes, she noticed a dim light off to the right on the horizon. At first her hopes rose thinking it might be a boat. Didn't people say that the English Channel, where she assumed she was, was the busiest shipping lane in the world? Then she realised that it was the sun rising in the eastern sky. Dawn was approaching. She continued her swim but with every stroke she felt weaker. She recalled a book that her parents had given her on her twelfth birthday. It was entitled A History of Female Heroines. One of the chapters was about an American woman named Gertrude Caroline Ederle who was the first female to swim the English Channel in 1926. This gave Rosie inspiration. If the Queen of The Waves as she was known could swim the full twenty-one miles across, from France to England, surely it was possible for Rosie to swim this short distance. At least she had her liberty and dying a free woman was better than dying a prisoner in a human breeding farm. The cold was really getting to her now and she felt more and more exhausted. Her teeth chattered so much she thought they would shatter. This is the end she thought. In her head she started to say her mantra of the names of the other women who were depending on her. This gave her the will to continue. She stopped and trod water for a moment to see if anything was visible on the brightening horizon. Was it in her mind or was there something ahead of her breaking the line between the sea and sky? She continued to tread water. There was definitely a boat up ahead coming straight towards her. She had a sickening thought that it might be the same boat that had transported her here. Maybe her escape had been noticed and the boat had been instructed to turn round and search for her. This was a gamble she had to take. She knew she couldn't survive much longer in the cold water.

As the boat drew nearer she could see several fishermen preparing pot and nets on the deck. They were engrossed in their chores and no-one looked up to see Rosie. As the boat loomed nearer Rosie shouted as loud as she could but her voice was drowned out by the sound of the engine. The boat sailed past her only yards away. Rosie looked forlornly after it with a sinking heart. She was just about to turn round and continue her swim when the boat suddenly started to turn back towards her. She frantically waved both her hands to try and attract their attention. This time three men stood along the side of the boat pointing towards her and shouting instructions for the skipper to cut the engines. Rosie swam to the side and two sets of strong arms pulled her from the water.

Rosie's teeth were chattering so much she couldn't even speak. Someone found a thick woollen blanket and put it around her shoulders.

'Well we have a fine catch this morning,' the skipper said. 'A bit nippy for an early morning swim isn't it lass?'

Rosie smiled as a hot steaming mug of tea was thrust into her shaking hands.

'You need to get out of those wet clothes. There are some dry garments down in the cabin. They will be a bit on the large size but I doubt you care much about appearances. I'll ring the coastguard and arrange for an ambulance to meet us back at the dock. You will need to be medically checked out. What's your name lass?' The skipper asked.

'Rosie Ware,' she replied.

The men looked around at each other. 'Isn't that the name of that girl that got kidnapped six months ago?' one of them asked.

'That's me,' Rosie said.

Down in the cabin, Rosie stripped off her cold sodden clothing and dressed in a t-shirt, a thick woollen jumper that went down to her knees and a pair of scruffy trousers that smelled strongly of fish. She had never been so happy with an outfit in her life before.

There was a knock at the door and a smiling face appeared. 'Are you decent?'

'Yes, come in,' Rosie replied.

'I've radioed ahead. We should be back in about twenty minutes. You lie down and get some rest. I'll come and wake you when we arrive,' the skipper said indicating a bunk that ran down one side of the small cabin.

Rosie climbed onto the bunk and wrapped herself in the warm duvet and fell fast asleep.

93

Dan was out on another job when the call came in.

'DI Brennan,' he said into his mobile phone.

A confident female voice he didn't recognise said, 'I understand you are one of the detectives working on the Rosie Ware kidnapping case. I just thought you might want to know that she has been found out in the English Channel.'

Dan's heart sank. 'Where are they taking the body to?' he asked thinking that maybe the post-mortem might reveal a clue as to where she had been held captive. It was too late for Rosie but maybe it wasn't too late for the other missing women.

'Oh, she's not dead, she's very much alive. A fishing boat picked her up early this morning. She was originally taken to the A&E at Southend Hospital but when they found out who she was it was decided to transfer her to the University College Hospital on Euston Rd, London. They thought a larger hospital would be able to handle the publicity better when the story breaks. The ambulance is on its way there now. It should be arriving any minute.'

Dan was only about ten minutes away from the hospital. 'I'll be there as soon as I can,' he said into the phone. 'Tell everyone involved to keep this news quiet for now.'

During the trip he placed a call to DCI McBride. The manpower on Operation Silver had been reduced to only McBride and Emma Blakely. As their leads had failed to shed any further light on the kidnappings and where the women were being held, the original size of the team couldn't be sustained. Dan had been sent back to the Met. He did spend some of his own time continuing the investigation often visiting St Katharine Docks to watch the boats there, particularly one boat. He had been told to keep away but the whole case smelled of a cover-up.

McBride was as surprised and pleased as he was.

'How did she end up in the English Channel?' He asked.

'I don't know any of the details yet. I'm just on my way to the hospital to talk to her,' Dan replied.

'I'll find Emma and we will come straight down,' McBride said.

'Don't say anything to the parents yet. I want to confirm it's her before we get their hopes up,' McBride continued.

When Dan saw Rosie in the hospital bed he knew at once that this was indeed Rosie Ware. Although she was white as a sheet and her hair was straggly and matted she looked just like the photo he had so often gazed at.

'Are you up to making a statement yet?' Dan asked.

'The doctors want to give me another check over first. They are worried about the baby. After that I'm all yours,' Rosie smiled.

Whilst the doctors did their examination Dan let McBride know that he had confirmed the girl was Rosie and he could go ahead and let the parents and the press know that she was safe and well. He then took the opportunity to contact Darleen Clutterbuck.

'You will never believe it. Rosie Ware has managed to escape. I'm with her now in the hospital,' Dan told her.

Dee was really pleased but had a worrying edge to her voice. 'Listen if Rosie is fit to travel you need to get her out of there as soon as possible. If the kidnapper behaves as I expect he will, he will come after Rosie again either to kill her or take her back. He's not the sort of person who will have his prize taken from him like this. Take her away to somewhere he won't know to look. Don't use any of the police safe houses or anyone connected to her family or the investigation team. As you know this man has powerful friends.'

Dan thought about it, 'I know the perfect place,' he said. He was just about to tell Dee the details when she interrupted.

'Don't tell me, don't tell anyone. The fewer people who know her whereabouts the safer she will be.'

'Aren't we swapping one prison for another,' Dan said.

'Yes, but it's only until we catch him. Rosie escaping will make him mad, very mad. He has lost his prized possession. He has been successful in the past because he is so calm and calculating. Hopefully this will get him to make a mistake. Remember you still have lots of other women somewhere out there to rescue.'

'Leave it with me,' Dan said. Speaking quietly he asked her to phone DCI McBride and tell him the plan and that he would be in touch as soon as he had Rosie safely accommodated.

Before returning to Rosie he searched around for a pay phone. Luckily hospitals still had lots of pay phones due to the ban on mobile phones. Not that anyone observed the *no phones* rule any longer. He made the call and explained what he wanted and returned to the ward where Rosie was waiting for him.

'Is everything OK?' he asked.

'Mother and baby are doing fine,' she replied.

'You don't look pregnant,' Dan said.

'I'm only twelve weeks gone. I've got a long way to go yet. The doctors want to keep me in for a few days just for observation, and then I can return to my parent's home in Newcastle. By the way has anyone spoken to them yet?'

Dan told her about his discussion with the psychologist Darleen Clutterbuck.

Rosie wasn't happy. 'I'm not exchanging prisons. I can't live like that. I want to see my parents and my friends.'

'There are some things you need to know. If at the end of it, you still want to go home then I'll drive you myself,' Dan said.

'I don't know how you will take this but your parents aren't your biological parents,' Dan began.

Rosie didn't look too shocked. 'I've always thought that I was adopted but I could never have wished for better parents. I've never felt the need to ask the question. If my real parents didn't want me then I don't want to meet them.'

'Your real parents did want you. At least your mother wanted you,' Dan said.

Dan explained about finding the body the day after Rosie was kidnapped and how it turned out that it belonged to Rosie's biological mother.

'Jennifer Shepherd,' Rosie said lifting her hand to her mouth to hide her shock.

'How did you know,' Dan asked.

'I didn't but I know she disappeared just before I arrived at the facility.'

Rosie remembered back to the three small babies she had seen on her first day there. She hadn't known it at the time but these were her brothers and sister. She had no idea where they were now. As with all the babies they had been moved out within a few days or weeks of their birth.

'My mother. Was she next to me on that boat when I was abducted?'

'Maybe, I don't know.'

'I'll do whatever you think is best. My main concern is finding where I was held and releasing the others.' Looking down, 'I can't leave looking like this. I don't suppose you could get me some clothes?' she said indicating the hospital gown she was wearing.

Remembering the shops located near the front of the hospital, 'I'll be right back,' he told her.

94

The man couldn't believe his ears when he heard the news about Rosie's escape. Surely it wasn't possible. He'd moored the boat back in St Katharine Docks early that morning after disposing of the Irish troublemaker's body and was on his way back to the facility by car. He had his eye on a new acquisition for his collection and was already getting excited about acquiring it.

He made a 'U' turn on the A road he was travelling along. Horns blared out and brakes squealed but undeterred he jammed his foot hard on the accelerator. The powerful engine of the BMW 4x4 kicked in and the car surged away from the angry drivers leaving them in his wake. The news broadcast had reported that Rosie had been taken to the University College hospital. Keying the location into the satnav on the car's dashboard the polite English voice told him he would reach his destination in approximately forty minutes.

She must have escaped inside the body bag containing Kelly's body. It was the only way she could have got out. He admonished himself for not checking the bag. What a stupid mistake to make. He had thought it seemed heavier than expected but just thought it was his age catching up with him.

Luckily traffic around London wasn't too bad and he made good progress to the hospital. As he approached he saw a gaggle of reporters and film crews milling around the steps up to the hospital main doors. They were just setting up their equipment. Some of them even had step ladders to afford them a better view. Good, he thought; she is still here. Parking was his next problem. He drove towards the back of the hospital and found a driveway marked *Hospital Personnel Only*, ignoring the sign he drove straight through and reversed into a parking bay with *Consultants Parking* painted in white on the floor. A side door led directly into the hospital bypassing the media throng out front.

Having studied certain aspects of the medical profession in his youth he had a good working knowledge of hospitals. He knew that a large hospital like this one would be full of doctors and nurses who by and large would be strangers to each other. Confidently walking down a long straight corridor he followed signs to the laundry located in the basement. Steam rose through the doorway and he could hear voices speaking in a foreign tongue he was unable to recognise. Stacks of freshly laundered uniforms lay on several trolleys outside the room ready to be delivered around the hospital. He selected a set of blue operating scrubs and retreated down the corridor until he found an empty store room. He quickly put the scrubs on covering his lower face loosely with the surgical mask as if he had just come out of surgery and placing the cap on his head.

Next he had to find the ward where Rosie was located. Making his way up two flights of stairs he found himself outside the geriatric unit. Sitting in a wheelchair an elderly woman in a dressing gown and slippers grabbed his arm. 'Are you here to take me to X-Ray? I've been waiting hours.'

Looking down at the plastic wrist band showing her name as Florence Robotham, he said, 'Yes, Mrs Robotham sorry to have kept you waiting.'

'Miss Robotham. I'm not married,' she replied curtly.

'How can a lovely creature like you not have been snapped up,' he said turning on the charm.

'Oh, I've had plenty of men. I've just not found The One,' she said giving him a cheeky wink.

Taking charge of the wheelchair he turned and made his way along another long corridor following signs towards X-Ray. If anyone wondered why a surgeon was doing the job of a porter no-one questioned it.

He stopped beside the reception to the Cardiology Unit where a flustered young nurse was sorting through a pile of medical charts. Out of earshot of Mrs Robotham, he asked the nurse if she would check the location of his patient nodding towards the old lady.

Nurses are always in awe of surgeons and she immediately stopped her work and turned towards the computer on the desk. 'Certainly what's the name?'

'Miss R Ware,' he said not wanting to alert her to Rosie's full name just in case she recognised it from all the news reports. He knew he was taking a risk but he had to get Rosie back and his desperation was evident in his uncharacteristic reckless behaviour.

Tapping in the name, 'she belongs on Ward 7 but I would have expected her to be in geriatric,' the young girl responded puzzled. 'Maybe they are full,' she added more as an afterthought to herself.

Thanking her for the information he continued to push Miss Robotham towards X-Ray. He didn't want to leave her here and cause suspicion.

95

Luckily for Dan hospitals in recent years had become much more commercialised and in addition to the usual florist shop they now contain food and clothing outlets. This one even had a Gregg's bakery. He wasn't sure how this had come about.

He wasn't used to buying women's clothes. The young shop assistant seemed to know this. She probably had lots of men coming into her shop in the same predicament where their wife or girlfriend had unexpectedly ended up in hospital without the correct attire.

Ten minutes later Dan was armed with two bags containing underwear, sandals and a smock dress, a track suit and a pair of Nike trainers. He even had some cosmetics, a hair brush and a toothbrush. He was sure Rosie would be impressed with his efforts.

96

After parking Miss Robotham at X-Ray, the man made his way up to Ward 7. Now he just needed to get hold of a sedative to enable him to overcome Rosie and get her out of the hospital and back where she belonged. He knew that all medicine was held under lock and key and obtaining a sedative wouldn't be easy. What he needed was a distraction. Off to the side of the corridor to Ward 7 a number of private rooms were located. Private rooms either held rich patients who could afford to pay the extra charge or the critically ill patients who needed peace and quiet. He looked through the glass window of the first room. This contained a teenager with his leg in plaster raised in the air in traction. Two people who could have been his parents sat either side of the bed. This wasn't what he wanted. He strode to the next room. Through the window he saw a middle-aged man lying unconscious in bed attached by wires to several machines that beeped and flashed. He gently pushed open the door and stood at the end of the bed and unclipped the patient's chart and quickly glanced at it. A heart attack patient – ideal. Stepping over to the heart monitor he loosened the wire until the horizontal green line flat lined at zero. He heard panic erupt at the nurses' station as he stepped into the en-suite bathroom. Seconds later the door was flung open and two nurses with a third pushing a crash cart rushed into the room. A doctor in a flapping white coat followed in their wake. As the four of them examined the unconscious man he deftly took a syringe and a bottle of sedative from the cart and exited the room.

He made his way onto the main ward. The nurses' station was deserted. After filling the syringe with the correct dosage he disposed of the bottle and glanced around. About ten beds lined each side of the room. Most of them were occupied. Some patients were sat upright reading or watching TV others were lying down snoozing. He saw a girl sat up in one of the beds and made his way towards her holding the syringe out of sight.

97

When Dan returned to the ward Rosie wasn't there and his heart missed a beat but then Rosie stepped out of the bathroom at the end of the ward wrapped in a towel with another around her hair.

'I couldn't smell of fish for my first outing with a man,' she laughed.

Dan pulled the hair brush from one of the bags. 'I think you will need this,' he said.

Rosie pulled the curtain around the bed leaving Dan on the outside. Five minutes later she was dressed in the sundress and sandals ready for inspection. 'How do I look?' she said giving a twirl.

'Beautiful,' Dan replied honestly.

They stopped at the nurses' station and Rosie signed the necessary forms to discharge herself.

'Where are we going?' she asked.

'Wait and see, it's a surprise,' Dan told her.

98

The man couldn't see his Rosie anywhere. Selecting a young girl near the centre of the room he asked where he could find a patient, a girl of around eighteen with long blonde hair who had been admitted that morning.

'Oh, you mean Rosie. She was moved to Ward 8 across the corridor about an hour ago.'

The man turned and raced out of the ward colliding with two of the nurses who were just exiting the heart attack victim's room rebuking some poor colleague who they blamed for not correctly attaching the wire to the heart monitor and causing the code red. Offering his apologies he made his way back to the main corridor and into Ward 8.

This time he went straight to the nurses' station but was careful to have the surgical mask loosely across his lower face and asked where he could find Rosie Ware.

'You just missed her she discharged herself about five minutes ago and left with a young man.'

Racing back to the main corridor and looking out of the window he was just in time to see his Rosie getting into a car at one of the hospital side entrances.

There was no way he could catch them. He was enraged.

99

After driving for thirty minutes Dan parked the car outside a pretty town house in one of London's quieter suburbs. He opened the car door and escorted Rosie together with her meagre possessions to the red front door. He rapped on the door using a large brass knocker. He was obviously expected as ten seconds later the door opened and a beautiful woman stood in front of them. She was the spitting image of Rosie just slightly older. Instantly Rosie knew who she was even though she had never seen her before.

'I'm Laura. I'm your sister. Come in I've had the kettle on.'

Dan and Rosie followed Laura through the house and out onto a sunny patio area at the back. The day was a lovely hot summer's day, rare in Britain.

'I thought you might like to sit outdoors,' Laura said. 'I expect you have spent enough time indoors to last you a lifetime.'

Rosie instantly liked this sister she never knew existed before today. She had always hated being an only child. She had always envied her friend who had siblings.

'I expect you two have a lot to discuss. I'll go and finish the tea,' Laura said.

It took several hours for Dan and Rosie to swap stories. At the end of it, Rosie was crying.

Laura appeared in front of them, 'Dan you had better come and see this.'

Dan followed her into the small comfortable lounge. A mid-sized flat screen television was on in the corner. An excited female newscaster was in full flow, 'and now over to our outdoor correspondent Andrea Orr who is currently outside the University College hospital.'

The camera switched from the quiet indoor studio to a live location outside the main door of the hospital. A handsome middle aged presenter looked earnestly into the camera trying to stand her ground amongst the jostling crowd.

'This is Andrea Orr for Capital News live from the University College hospital; where we have unconfirmed reports that missing heiress Rosie Ware has been admitted for treatment after being discovered early this morning somewhere in the English Channel. According to a source, she was picked up alive by a fishing boat at four-thirty this morning. Where she had come from and how long she had been in the water is still a mystery. A hospital spokesperson has confirmed that DI Dan Brennan, one of the lead investigators, from the Operation Silver team was at the hospital this morning to interview the missing girl.'

The journalist beckoned to someone off screen and a pretty young woman appeared by her side.

'This is Tammy Holroyd who worked in the Occasions Fashion Boutique located in the hospital.'

The presenter turned slightly towards the girl thrusting the microphone in front of her face.

'I understand that you spoke to DI Brennan this morning and he bought several items of ladies clothing from your store?'

The nervous girl bravely looked into the camera and started to reel off a list of the items Dan had purchased. The presenter quickly cut her short not wanting to bore the audience. She fired off a series of questions at the girl who clearly knew no more information than she had already revealed. The presenter having no further information, or people to interview, returned the viewers to the news studio.

'We can now go over to Rosie's parents' home in Newcastle,' the studio newscaster said.

A young male reporter took up the story. 'All is quiet at the home of lottery winners Tom and Sara Ware. A neighbour has told us that a visitor did arrive shortly before we got the news of Rosie's release. At this time we don't know if a ransom has been paid and if so for how much.'

There was a commotion behind the reporter who turned towards the gathering crowd.

'It seems that we have some movement from within the grounds.'

The camera panned towards the large iron gates which had started to swing open. A car slowly emerged from the driveway. Dan could clearly see the face of DCI McBride through the window. People knocked on the window but McBride continued to look straight ahead. When he was clear of the crowd the car sped off down the road. The camera panned back towards the reporter.

'I believe that was DCI Ian McBride who is head of the Operation Silver Team that has been investigating Rosie's disappearance for the last six months. This is Tim Bradford for Capital News. I will now hand you back to the studio.'

The newscaster picked up the story again and told the viewers that they were to be taken to the see the fishing boat and crew that had saved Rosie from the clutches of the cruel sea. Dan had heard enough and pressed the standby button on the remote control. The TV went off and the house returned to its quiet state of existence.

'Quite a circus out there isn't it?' Laura said.

'I'm just glad we managed to get Rosie away before they took up siege around the hospital,' Dan replied. 'They seem to think she is still a patient there. She should be safe here. Only myself, Emma and McBride know that you exist.'

'And my grandmother,' Laura added. 'But she knows not to say anything about the case.'

The police had kept the connection between Jennifer and Rosie out of the press.

'What do we do next?' Laura asked.

'We need to try and identify the location where Rosie was held prisoner. Can you join the discussion? You may be able to give us some assistance.'

Laura joined Dan and Rosie in the garden. The three of them sat in silence for a few minutes just soaking up the late afternoon sun and contemplating their next moves.

'We have to try and locate the facility,' Dan said turning to Rosie.

'That's the problem. I don't have a clue where it is? I thought I could rescue the other women but I'm no help at all.'

'I'm sure there are little things you know that will help us narrow down the location,' Laura said.

'Do you have a map of the South of England?' Dan asked Laura.

Laura gave him one of her looks and brought out her laptop. She entered a few key strokes and brought up a Google Maps view of the South of England.

'Right we know that you were found eight miles off the South coast. How long do you think the boat journey took and how fast do you estimate the speed was.'

'The journey took about thirty hours and I'd say the speed was about five knots at the slowest and eight knots at the fastest.'

Laura entered this information into the laptop and turned the screen towards them. 'Allowing for some errors in the estimated time and speed I think the facility is somewhere in this area.'

The circle took in a large area of the South of England and Northern France.

'Did you drive to the boat?'

'No, the facility was next to the water,'

'So we are looking for somewhere on the coast,' Dan said.

'We weren't at sea very long. I think we came down a river.'

'Good. That rules out the majority of the search area.

'I think we can also rule out France,' Rosie said. 'I felt the boat turn around and it headed back towards England.

'It looks like the location is somewhere next to the river Thames. That's the nearest estuary to where you got picked up by the fishing boat.'

Dan cursed all the time the police had wasted looking at remote islands around Britain but this was the nature of police work. Endless dead ends hoping for that one key piece of evidence that would give them a break.

'You're doing well,' Laura said to encourage Rosie. She could see that her sister was beginning to tire after her exhausting day.

Laura entered the new data into the laptop and the search area reduced once more.

'Right now let's talk about the facility,' Dan said. 'What could you see from the window?'

'There weren't any windows. We were underground. It was some sort of hospital or laboratory.'

'What about the doors?'

'There was only one entrance. It was some kind of air lock. A bit like those you see in films where they keep samples of the plague secure.'

'That should narrow it down. There can't be many places matching that description.

'How big would you estimate the area to be?'

'I'd say about three thousand square meters.'

'And what age would you estimate the building to be.'

'I'd say the 1980s or maybe the 90s.'

Dan thought the building was likely to have been built in the 70s or 80s prior to the date Jennifer was abducted. They wouldn't have risked moving the girls.

Laura zoomed into the area they were interested in. Lots of buildings crowded the banks of the Thames and the tributaries running into it. 'I'll be able to narrow it down when I get the information on the bio hazard facilities.' After some more frantic typing, Laura looked up. 'This is going to be more difficult than I first thought. Because of terrorism, this type of information is highly classified. I may be able to hack into some of the Police databases but hacking into the MoD and MI5 is beyond my abilities.'

'Don't worry,' Dan said. 'With the information Rosie has given us we should be able to get search warrants for the facilities that match the criteria.' He didn't realise how difficult this would turn out to be.

'You get some rest now Rosie. You've done great. If you think of anything else that might help pass it on via Laura.'

Out of earshot of Rosie Dan asked Laura if she could send the list of names for the other missing women to Cathy Grainger. He expected that there would be other bodies at the point where Rosie had been dumped in the English Channel. When they managed to retrieve them they would need the dental records Cathy had in her files in order to identify them.

Dan was tired but elated as he drove back to his flat. He never imagined he would see Rosie Ware alive. He managed to park his car on the street parallel to where he lived. As he walked around the corner, a gaggle of reporters rushed towards him, thrusting microphones in his face. A barrage of mixed up questions assailed his ears. He didn't need to understand what they were he just said 'no comment' as he pushed his way to the front door of his apartment block. Closing the door on the melee he was now in the cool quiet hallway that formed the space at the foot of the stairs that lead up to his 2nd floor flat. He turned and placed his forehead against the heavy door to gather his strength before starting up the two flights of stairs. As he put his key into the front door lock of his flat it opened before he could turn it. Emma stood before him holding a glass of red wine. 'I thought you might be in need of this,' she said passing the wine to him.

'You wouldn't believe what a day I've had,' he said. 'I thought McBride was coming down with you?'

'Change of plan. We thought someone should speak with the Wares and put them in the picture and you know how McBride hates coming to the city.'

'Yes, and I know how much you love coming to the city,' he said kissing her deeply on the mouth.

Since their time in America, they had taken every opportunity to visit each other. Early in their relationship, neither of them raised the subject of moving in together both knowing that the other wouldn't want to relocate but then out of the blue Dan had recently informed Emma that he had put in a transfer to the CID office in Oxford. It would probably take months but it gave them a happy future to look forward to.

Emma served up a once frozen pizza whilst Dan relayed the events of the day. Men always seem to think that all women are great cooks. Unfortunately cooking had never been her strong point. Her mother did most of the cooking at home. If cooking was a way to a man's heart then Emma would have to find another route.

Looking down at the sad offering on his plate Dan put down his knife and fork and picked up the list of the women who had been imprisoned with Rosie and passed it over to Emma. 'She memorised everyone's name and where they came from. She also had a list of the other women who she had never met who had passed through the facility before her time there.

Emma noticed Jennifer Shepherd's name amongst them. 'Rosie must have one hell of a memory,' Emma said.

'She has. You will get to meet her when all this dies down.'

'I hope so. I just get the feeling it's all far from over yet.'

'Me too,' Dan said.

'So let's make the most of this calm before the storm,' she said pushing her own plate away and leading Dan towards the bedroom.

100

The next morning was an equally hot sunny day. Emma looked out of the window.

'They are still camped out there,' she said indicating to the reporters milling around the entrance.

'Well we can't make much progress from in here so I suggest we run the gauntlet,' Dan said.

'Breakfast first,' Emma said popping two pieces of bread into the toaster and spooning coffee into the percolator.

'I suspect there are other bodies dumped out at sea so my first job today will be to get a police diving team out to the location near where Rosie was found,' Dan said. 'Can you go back to Oxford and speak with Cathy Grainger. Ask her to draw up a list of possible sites for the facility. Once this is ready get McBride to obtain the warrants.'

'Yes sir,' Emma said saluting Dan.

He gave her a slap on her behind and she laughed as she consumed the toast and marmalade.

Neither noticed the man standing across the road. He was dressed in a smart suit with a man bag on his shoulder.

They left the flat separately. None of the reporters hassled Emma as she left. She hadn't been mentioned in the news report so they were unaware of her involvement in the case.

When Dan left it was a different matter. They thronged after him asking questions all the way to where he had parked his car the previous night. He just continued to give his 'no comment' statement.

The man in the charcoal-grey suit across the road didn't move until they had disappeared around the corner. A master of disguise he could blend into any situation. Today he looked every inch the respectable businessman in his off the rack wool suit, white starched shirt and navy silk tie. To complete the picture he wore wire rimmed spectacles even though he had twenty-twenty vision.

Making his way to the front entrance of Dan's block of flats, he carefully inserted a lock pick into the key hole and was through the door in the time an ordinary person could have used a key. He strode up the staircase to Dan's flat and did the same thing there.

Opening his black leather briefcase he removed several listening devices and began placing them at various points around the flat. Withdrawing a small screw driver he dismantled the telephone and inserted a device inside. He was outside the flat again within five minutes. He had already planted a tracking device on Dan's car together with a listening device inside. Unlike older devices that could only track a short distance this one was state of the art and linked to a satellite. It could track Dan's car anywhere in the world. Not that he thought Dan would be leaving the country. Sooner or later it would lead him to his beloved Rosie. Then he would take her back where she belonged.

Now he just had to get a listening device into Dan's mobile phone. He had already formulated a plan for achieving this. He took out a wig, false moustache and a different pair of glasses from the briefcase. He didn't want Dan to be able to identify him when he put his plan into action.

Dan drove to where the police underwater team was stationed. He had met with the team before and always found them a strange group. But you would have to be a bit strange to volunteer for a job working in the cold murky waters around London. As part of his police training, he had once spent a day with the team. He had never been as frightened as when he had been asked to search for a gun in one of the local canals. He hadn't been able to see more than three inches in front of his face and had to feel his way across the bottom of the canal. He couldn't believe the rubbish that was there. Old Bicycles, abandoned shopping trollies, even a false leg which at first Dan had thought was the genuine article. The gun was never found. Dan decided that this police speciality wasn't for him and resumed his career on solid ground.

He had already phoned his superior Chief Superintendent Danny Hughes and got permission to start the search. The team was waiting for him as he arrived.

'We've just got a few more pieces of equipment to load on the boat and then we will be ready to set off.'

'Great,' said Dan. 'Do you want me to come with you?' he asked.

'No, we should be OK,' came the reply. 'We know where to look and we know what we are looking for.'

Dan was relieved. Although he liked boats he had other avenues of the investigation he wanted to follow. Finding the living was his priority. He set off to speak with the Port of London Authority based in Pinnacle House a few miles upriver.

101

The man followed Dan at a discreet distance. He could tell from the red dot on the satellite navigation screen exactly where Dan was going. So far he hadn't attempted contact with whoever was harbouring his Rosie.

Dan parked about five hundred yards away from his destination. Parking was always a nightmare in London. Most roads were now *resident only parking* which was great for the residents when they wanted to park in their own neighbourhood but caused everyone a problem when they wanted to travel elsewhere.

To get to the Port of London Authority building he had to cross a busy junction. An elderly lady appeared at his left-hand side. She was pulling one of those wheelie bags that old people so often have. A menace to other pedestrians Dan thought.

'Nice day again,' the old lady cheerily said.

'Very nice,' Dan replied.

As they waited for the traffic lights to turn to red, so that they could cross, neither of them noticed the man sidle up behind them. The red number 15 double-decker bus was travelling quickly towards them from the right hoping to get through the lights as they changed to amber. The woman leaned forward so that she could see beyond Dan in readiness for making the dash across the road.

The man stood close behind her. As the bus approached he shouted loudly 'NOoo...' as he pushed the woman into the path of the bus. Dan turned to see the woman falling into the road with the man's arms outstretched trying to save her.

The bus driver had no chance of stopping. The woman disappeared under the bus and her wheelie bag exploded as the front wheel ran it over, spreading the contents before Dan's feet.

'Oh my God, Oh my God,' the man shouted. 'Ring for an ambulance.'

Dan instinctively took his phone out of his pocket.

'I'll ring. You check if she's OK. I can't bear to look,' said the man taking the phone from Dan's hand.

Dan let the phone go and knelt down to look under the bus. He couldn't see anything and went round the side of the bus to look further back. By this time shocked passengers started to disembark. The dazed driver grabbed Dan by the arm. 'She just stepped out in front of me. There was nothing I could do.'

'I know. I saw everything,' Dan said. 'Don't worry I'm a police officer.'

As the commotion unfolded the man removed the back of Dan's phone and placed a listening device behind the battery where it wouldn't be easily noticed. He put the phone back together then calmly rang 999 giving the details and location of the accident.

Dan returned from the bus shaking his head. 'She's a goner I'm afraid.'

The man gave the phone back to Dan. 'How sad. I've rung for the police and an ambulance. I saw her falling. I reached out to try and save her but I was just too late.'

'I know you did. Can you wait for the police to arrive and give them a statement?'

'I'm really late for an appointment. I'm on my way to an interview for a job. I've been unemployed for four months and this is the first interview I've had. The recession has really hit the city hard. Can I give you the statement and be on my way?'

Dan hadn't remembered telling the man he was a police officer. He must have overheard the conversation he'd had with the bus driver. He felt sorry for the man and took out his notebook and began writing down the man's version of events.

Satisfied he let the man continue on his way. He didn't fancy his chance of getting the job after witnessing such a traumatic accident.

The man continued back to his car. He removed his disguise then set up the listening system that would trigger each time Dan made or received a call. The first call Dan made was to the Thames River Authority telling some man named Brooks that he would be late for their appointment.

It took two hours to finally get away from the scene of the accident. Dan continued to his meeting with Neil Brooks. 'What I need are details of boat access between here and this area,' he said indicating the search zone marked on the map he had printed off at Laura's house. 'I also want to know the time it would take to navigate to these locations.'

Brooks explained the complex routes that would need to be taken to navigate to some of the places on the map. 'The Victorians were very clever. They used waterways as we now use motorways. The rivers and canals in Britain are all linked where possible. Even if it meant building elaborate locks to lift the boats. As you must understand the time it takes a boat to cover a distance depends on the tide and the number of locks it has to navigate.'

'What does the tide have to do with it? I thought that only applied at sea.'

'The river Thames is tidal. Right up to this point,' Brooks said pointing to an area on the map. 'It makes a huge difference to a boat's progress and the distance it can travel.'

Dan remembered that Mike Robson had mentioned this when he gave his talk about St Katharine Docks. This made Dan think that their search area may be more complicated than he first thought. Places much nearer as the crow flies, which was the way they had measured it, would take longer to reach. He would need to adjust the calculations.

'We do have route planners,' Neil said. 'People on boating holidays use them to calculate how long it will take them to reach their destination.'

'That would be a great help,' Dan said

Brooks returned armed with a handful of pamphlets covering the South East of England. 'There's probably an iPhone app that you can purchase that does the same thing. I expect that will be much more accurate.'

Dan thought he would mention this to Laura. She was into all these new-fangled devices. He didn't have time to learn how to use these. He didn't even own an iPhone.

Dan looked at his watch. Should he go around to Laura's house to pass on the information and perhaps quiz Rosie again or should he head back to his office and report back to his boss. Normally his boss left all aspects of an investigation to him but for some reason, he was taking a keen interest in the Rosie Ware case. Dan expected this was the potential for some high-level publicity. His boss liked nothing more than appearing on national television. He had already asked Dan to give him a briefing so he could make a statement on tonight's Capital news program. From his previous dealings with his superior on this case, he was very wary about the information he gave him. He didn't know why but some instinct told him to keep any information about the case close to his chest. He already knew that the kidnapper had friends in high places and although he had no evidence to back this up he couldn't help but think that Chief Superintendent Danny Hughes may be connected in some way.

Before he had made up his mind about what to do next his phone rang. It was the police underwater unit. Linda Smith the head of the unit was phoning with an update.

'We have found three adult bodies so far. Plus one of them had the skeleton of a baby with it. Luckily there is a sand bank beneath the dump site so they aren't too deep plus being in body bags has preserved the skeletons intact. My divers have been able to make a number of dives. They have now reached their dive time limit so we are packing up for today. We will resume at first light. I'll arrange for the bodies to be taken for examination by a forensic anthropologist - a bone expert to you and me. As you already have a list of names we should be able to match them up with the bodies within a couple of days when we get the dental records.'

Dan thanked her for the update. This was big news and made his mind up that he should give his boss the promised update prior to the evening news being broadcast rather than re-interview Rosie.

102

The man was getting more and more annoyed. Dan hadn't visited Rosie's hiding place or made any phone calls connected to her location. He needed to get Rosie back and quickly. More drastic action was needed.

He picked up his mobile and punched in a number.

Dan made his way through the rush hour traffic back to the office.

He knocked on the Chief Superintendent's office door.

The chief wasn't happy. 'You can't keep Rosie Ware hidden away. She needs to be out there in front of the cameras. The public wants to know what's happening. I've arranged a press conference for tomorrow at six thirty in the evening. I want both you and Rosie there.'

Dan tried to argue that it was in the interest of Rosie's safety that he was keeping her hidden but the chief would have none of it.

'Have her there or consider yourself suspended,' he said.

After Dan left the room the chief made a phone call. 'It's all arranged she will be at the press conference tomorrow at six thirty,' satisfied he replaced the receiver.

103

Dan debated whether to go against his boss's order and face disciplinary proceedings or produce Rosie at the press conference. He decided to let Rosie make the decision. He took out his phone and rang Laura.

'Laura, it's Dan. Can I speak to Rosie?'

Dan told her his predicament. Rosie wouldn't listen to his argument for going against his bosses wishes. She insisted that he take her to the press conference. After all, they couldn't be sure that her kidnapper would target her again. She couldn't hide out forever. She promised that she would return to Laura's as soon as the press conference ended. No one would be any the wiser as to where she was staying.

The man picked up his mobile and redialled the previous number. It was answered at the other end after three rings.

'She's staying with someone called Laura.' I want you to check all the associates of Rosie, her parents plus the Operation Silver Team and find out if anyone is associated with a woman by this name.'

Danny Hughes replaced the receiver with a heavy sigh. He didn't like the fact that he was being drawn deeper into this conspiracy. He knew very little about the organisation he had become involved in. It seemed a win-win situation in the early days and the organisation had propelled him through the police ranks as promised. In return, all he had to do was provide them with a certain amount of information and steer cases in the direction they wanted them to take. Never before had he been asked to manipulate a high profile case such as this.

104

Next afternoon, taking a circuitous route, to ensure that nobody was tailing him, Dan drove to Laura's house.

He managed to park at the end of Laura's street. He walked back to Laura's house. Rosie looked much better today. She was wearing a new outfit which Dan guessed had been loaned to her by Laura. She looked even more beautiful than her picture. They set off towards the hotel where the conference was taking place.

The man watched them walking back towards the car. He saw a beautiful woman standing in a doorway watching them go then close the door. So this is where she had been hiding he thought. He made a note to check who lived at the address. He craned his neck round to read the number off the door.

Now he knew where Rosie was staying he could make plans to abduct her again. He could now get rid of the meddlesome DI Dan Brennan and also that bitch police woman Emma Blakely. He had listened to the taped conversation from the night they had stayed together. It had disturbed him how much information Rosie had been able to glean about the facility. Luckily the location they were looking in was miles off-course.

105

Dan explained to Rosie how the press conference would be conducted.

'I don't want you to give any details about the investigation. The less the press know the better. The last thing we want is to panic this man into shutting down his little scheme and disposing of the remaining women.'

Dan prepped Rosie as to the questions she might be asked and the answers she should give. Any awkward questions Dan would step in and state that due to the ongoing police investigation they couldn't give an answer at this time.

Arrangements had been made for Tom and Sara Ware to travel to London to attend the press conference.

Dan had pulled in as many favours as he could to have a large police presence around the hotel where the press conference was being held. Being out in the open like this left Rosie vulnerable. Dan was still fuming about being forced to take this unnecessary risk.

Rosie was reunited with her parents before the interview took place. The three of them were so happy both Sara and Rosie had tears of joy streaming down their faces.

McBride had driven down from Oxford to be there and being in charge of Operation Silver took the lead at the conference. He reiterated Dan's earlier advice and stressed the importance of keeping the direction of the investigation quiet.

Surprisingly the press conference went off without a hitch. When the reporters asked about where Rosie had been held and how she had escaped McBride skilfully steered the questioning away from the subject. He implied that Rosie had been kidnapped for ransom as originally thought and after months of skilful negotiations this had led to her release. The only awkward question was around why she had been dumped in the English Channel. He quickly recovered the situation stating that the kidnappers had been spooked and they believed that they had fled to France by boat where Interpol was currently searching for their whereabouts.

Maybe Dee had been wrong and the kidnapper wouldn't try and take Rosie again. Dan certainly felt more relaxed and at ease than he had done earlier that day.

He dropped Rosie back off at Laura's home and returned to his flat.

106

It was dark. A new moon, barely visible, in the night sky. The man looked round to make sure nobody noticed him as he bent down and put the bomb under Dan's car. It was magnetic and jumped out of his hand greedily attracted towards the metal of the engine sump. He carefully flicked a switch on the side of the device. He knew a red light would now be glowing but this would only be visible to someone on their hands and knees looking under the car. It would be activated as soon as the car went round a corner. The mercury in the see-saw detonator would roll to the opposite side; complete the electric circuit, and then boom.

When news of DI Dan Brennan's death was confirmed he would set off to Oxford to sort out the other thorn in his side DS Emma Blakely.

107

The sunny spell had broken as suddenly as it had arrived, typical of English weather. Today was grey and overcast as Dan looked out of the window. He wondered how long the reporters would be camped outside his place. He thought maybe he should ask Laura if she would put him up. He would feel better if he was nearer to Rosie. He felt really uneasy again, his euphoria after yesterday's interview had disappeared. Something in his gut told him this situation was far from over. He phoned Emma to ask her opinion but his phone was acting up. He would try her again later. Picking up his car keys and jacket he made his way to the door. On his way to his car he slipped into a mobile phone shop around the corner hoping to lose the reporters following behind. Five minutes later he checked the coast was clear and made his way to his car. He pressed the remote to open the door and put the key in the ignition. He smiled to himself as he thought about seeing Emma again.

108

The man sat in his car round the corner from the house where Rosie was hiding. He removed the new Glock 17 from the secret compartment in the glove box and screwed the suppressor onto the end. The gun he had used to shoot the old man to obtain the yellow Labrador dog back in January was long gone. Stripped to its component parts each piece had been disposed of separately in waterways and dustbins around Oxfordshire. The man never took unnecessary chances so never used the same gun twice. Unlike other criminals, he didn't have a problem getting firearms into the country. Next, he removed the plastic bag containing the fentanyl loaded syringe that he would use to subdue Rosie. He placed the gun and the syringe into a small cardboard box. Today he was dressed as a postman.

His plan was to ring the bell. If the woman looked through the peep hole she would see the postman with a package. No-one could resist opening their door to receive a parcel. He would immediately shoot the older blonde woman. It was a shame to eliminate such a wonderful specimen. He would have liked to have her for his collection but she was a bit older than he liked and he didn't want to risk handling two feisty women. He would inject Rosie with the Fentanyl then drive her to St Katharine Docks where he would lock the unconscious Rosie inside the box on the boat before travelling to Oxford to sort out that other detective.

He was happy. He liked it when he had a good plan. He whistled a tune as he walked up the steps to the house and rang the bell.

Inside Laura and Rosie were just eating breakfast when the doorbell rang. Toast in hand Laura went to answer. Maybe it was Dan she thought? She looked through the peep hole and saw a postman, package in hand, standing on the doorstep. She took the chain off the door and reached for the doorknob.

109

Emma tapped quietly on McBride's office door.

'You wanted to speak to me sir,' she said poking her head in.

'Come in Emma. Sit down.'

'I'm OK standing sir. I'm in a bit of a rush.'

'I'm afraid I have some bad news for you,' McBride said.

It's amazing how time seems to stand still between two sentences. All possible scenarios flooded into Emma's mind. She immediately thought it must be about her mother and daughter. Becky had finished her exams last week and her mother had taken her for a week's holiday to an apartment she owned on the Costa Blanca in Spain. They had flown out of Luton early that morning. Had the plane crashed?

'It's DI Dan Brennan. I'm afraid he's dead.'

First relief that it wasn't Becky and then dismay flooded over Emma. She felt her legs give way and now knew why they got the recently bereaved to sit down before telling them bad news. She slumped into the chair opposite McBride's desk.

'I don't understand what's happened. He was fine the other night,' Emma said.

'He's been murdered. His car was blown up by a bomb early this morning.'

'Are you sure it's him?'

'Pretty sure. Who else would be driving his car? The body was burned beyond recognition. We can't be a hundred percent sure until we check the dental records.'

'But you can't be sure,' Emma reiterated.

'Look Emma, I know you don't want to accept it. You and Dan were close. Hell, I don't want to accept it but there is so little hope that it's not him,' McBride said with a sadness in his eyes that Emma hadn't seen before.

'But there is some hope,' Emma said still not wanting or willing to believe the facts before her.

'I'm worried about you,' McBride continued. 'If Dan has been targeted then you might be next. I want you to pack up your things and take the week off. Is there somewhere you can go?'

'Emma thought about joining her mother and daughter in Spain but then thought better of it. She couldn't put them in danger.

'I've got an old school friend I can stay with for a few days but I want to work the case sir. I want to find whoever has done this to Dan.'

'That's not going to happen,' McBride said. 'You are now officially off the case. I want you to pass all your evidence on to Anthea Bowker. I don't want to see you back in the office until all this dies down. That's an order.'

Emma knew there was no point arguing. McBride was stubborn. When he made up his mind he rarely changed it. Surely he himself was at equal risk of being targeted. With a heavy heart she returned to her desk and packed up her belongings. She was about to close down her computer when she noticed an email flashing in her inbox. It was from the anonymous source who she now knew to be Rosie's sister Laura Webb. She opened the mail and began to read the contents:

All is not as it seems. You are in danger. Leave everything behind. Your bag, mobile and car. Take only some cash. Don't tell anyone where you are going. Take the bus to Oxford railway station. Catch the next train to London Paddington. I will contact you there. Delete this mail.

Emma would trust Laura with her life. She followed the instructions deleting the email and closing down the computer. Putting all the cash she had into her pocket she locked her bag, car keys and mobile in her desk drawer then quickly left the office.

She walked past her car on the way to the bus stop. She hoped it would be safe parked on the quiet side road where she had left it that morning. What a stupid thought why was she worried about a car when her whole world had fallen apart. She had never caught the bus into town before but many of her colleagues commuted to the police station each day so she knew how to get there. She waited the ten minutes it took for the bus to arrive, nervously scanning the streets around her. At the railway station she fed the machine with the right change for a one-way ticket to London Paddington. After another anxious twenty minutes wait the train arrived. It was only when she was safely sat on the train that the enormity of the situation hit her and she started to shake with shock. She had heard of delayed shock but had never experienced it before. A young woman with a baby who was sat opposite asked if she was OK.

'I've just had a shock. Someone close to me has been killed,' Emma said now crying into a hanky.

'I'm so sorry,' the woman replied not really knowing what help she could be and secretly wishing she hadn't asked.

The woman got off at the next stop. 'I hope things go alright for you,' she said to Emma not knowing what else to say but thinking whatever she said would sound crass and unsympathetic.

'Thank you,' Emma replied, glad to be left alone in her grief.

A young girl took the seat that the woman had recently vacated. Emma didn't have to worry about her striking up a conversation. This girl was immersed in her own world, her head bobbing away to a tune coming through her headphones. Emma could just about hear the tinny sound but couldn't make out the song. She gazed out of the window at the still, cold, sleeping English countryside waiting patiently for the morning summer sun to bring it alive and thought she would never feel alive again. It had taken all her life to find the love of a good man and now it had been cruelly snatched away from her.

As with most daytime trains, which seemed to stop at every station, many that Emma had never heard of, the journey seemed to take forever. In fact, it was only fifty-six minutes. Emma got off the train. She didn't know where to go. She looked around for Laura but couldn't see her anywhere. She sat on one of the many benches and waited. After five minutes a young black pimply-faced teenager came and sat next to Emma.

'A lady said that you would give me five pounds if I gave you this message,' he said holding up a piece of paper just out of Emma's reach.

Emma searched in her pocket but the smallest note she had was ten pounds. She doubted the lad would have change, so she thrust the money in his hand and took the note from him.

'Cheers lady,' he said and quickly disappeared from view.

Emma opened the note.

Meet me in the ladies toilets. Furthest cubicle. L

Trying not to look too eager Emma walked casually towards the Ladies. The door on the cubicle at the end was locked. Emma gave it a quiet tap with her knuckle. It immediately changed from red to green and a hand came out pulling Emma inside.

Laura instantly put a finger to her lips indicating that Emma should stay quiet. She then began feeling round the collar of Emma's coat and even got her to take off her shoes so that she could check they hadn't been tampered with.

'OK, you seem clean. We can talk now.'

'What's going on?' a frustrated Emma said. 'I've had the morning from hell. Did you know Dan has been killed?'

'Yes. No.' Laura replied.

'What do you mean?' Emma asked.

'Yes I know everyone thinks he's been killed but he hasn't,' Laura explained.

Emma slumped down onto the toilet seat putting her head in her hands, the relief flooding over her. 'What happened?' She asked.

'I'll let him explain it himself. He's outside in the car,' Laura said.

Emma stood and opened the door to leave but Laura pulled her back. 'First, put this on,' she said holding out a burqa.

'Isn't this a bit James Bond like?' Emma said.

'You don't understand the organisation we are dealing with here. They think Dan is dead but they will still be after you.'

Emma quickly donned the outfit which covered her own clothes from head to toe.

'I can't see where I'm going,' Emma said peering through the small black mesh window.

'Wait two minutes then go to the car park. Look for a dark grey Ford Focus parked in the ten minute waiting bay.'

Laura left the cubicle and Emma looked at her watch. She had a big smile on her face; not that anyone could have seen it behind the mask she was wearing.

After the two minutes, she made her way out to the car park. She instantly spotted the car even through the veil. Desperate to see Dan she stepped out into the path of a car that blew its horn sharply at her. She quickly retreated back onto the pavement wondering how women wearing these garments lasted a day on the busy London streets.

When she opened the car door a laughing Dan greeted her. He had tears rolling down his face.

'I've never seen anything so funny in my life,' he chuckled.

Emma gave him a friendly slap then threw her arms round him. She had never been so glad to see anyone in her life and she realised how strong her feeling for Dan had become.

'I thought you were dead. What happened?'

'Hey, you aren't supposed to throw yourself at men dressed like this. You are supposed to be respectful and walk ten feet behind me,' Dan admonished.

Emma gave him another slap.

Dan explained how he had got up that morning and tried to ring her but his phone was acting up. 'I decided to take the battery out to check it was seated properly. I found a listening device behind it. I checked round my flat and found another six bugs. I worried that if someone had managed to plant these bugs in my flat and mobile they had probably done the same thing with my car. I went out and bought a pay-as-you-go phone from that mobile shop around the corner from my flat. I rang Laura and told her what had happened and asked her to move Rosie straight away. I wasn't sure if I had been followed to her house yesterday.'

Laura picked up the story. 'I was just about to open the door to the postman when my phone rang. I don't know what made me stop and answer it. Some inner intuition perhaps. When Dan told me what had happened. I became suspicious. I wasn't expecting a package. I grabbed my bag and Rosie and we left out the back,' Laura explained.

Dan took up the story again. 'It was Laura who told me to go to my car, unlock it and leave the keys in the ignition. We thought that if a car thief took it then any tracking device would lead the villain away from us. I didn't know he had planted a bomb in the car. Obviously, someone took the bait and got really unlucky.'

'I feel really bad about that. I saw someone do this in a film and thought it was a good idea,' Laura said.

'You weren't to know and it did save Dan's life,' Emma said. 'What do you suggest we do next?' Emma asked. 'I've been taken off the case and in spectacular fashion so has Dan.'

'We go off the grid and undercover,' Laura said enjoying playing the spy.

'We don't have any money or contacts though,' Emma said. 'There's not much we can do.'

'But, you've got me.' Laura said. 'And I'm a mastermind at going undetected. The first thing we have to do is find a safe-house. Any suggestions? We can't go back to mine as we don't know if I've been rumbled.'

'I've got an idea of somewhere we can hide out.' Dan said.

'Where?' the girls both said together.

'Darleen Clutterbuck, my therapist. She has a large house in Islington. Nobody will think to look for us there. I suggest we split up and meet at her house. And Emma...'

'Yes,' Emma said.

'Lose the burqa. It might look commonplace in this area but it will stick out like a sore thumb in Islington.'

'Gladly. I can't wait to get it off. How do women wear these things? They're so claustrophobic.'

'I suppose they get used to them,' Laura said passing a plastic bag over to Emma.

'What's this?' Emma asked.

'Your next disguise,' Laura said.

Emma opened the bag and took out a pair of sunglasses and a head scarf. Laura passed a similar bag to Dan. His contained a pair of sunglasses and a baseball cap.

Before they separated she warned them to only use cash. No credit or Oyster cards.

'We don't know how sophisticated this man is but looking at the bugs he planted at Dan's flat he's got access to some very hi-tech surveillance equipment. I'll dump this car in a rough area and leave the keys in it. It should get stolen within a few minutes. If he does manage to trace it hopefully he will be taken on a wild goose chase. I'll pick Rosie up on the way. I've left her at the Westgate shopping centre with a fistful of cash.'

Emma hated splitting up with Dan. They decided that Emma would get the bus whilst Dan took the tube. For a reason Emma didn't understand Dan had an aversion to buses. It took Emma ten minutes to work out the buses she needed to take. The journey consisted of three separate buses. The first bus stopped outside a McDonalds. She took the opportunity to nip inside and dump the burqa emerging minutes later in her new disguise together with a burger and coke. Earlier she had thought she would never want to eat again, now she was ravenous.

Dan was the first to arrive at Darleen's house. Luckily she was in. She opened the door and Dan could see immediately that she had been crying. When she saw who it was she looked like she had seen a ghost. She flung her arms round him.

'It said on the news that you were dead,' Dee said.

"I can confirm that rumours of my death have been greatly exaggerated," Dan said quoting the author Mark Twain with a grin.

Dan got hit again for the third time that day.

'Can I come in?' he said.

Dee opened the door for him. 'What's with the disguise? You look like an America tourist.'

Over a fresh cup of coffee, Dan explained what had happened and asked if it would be OK if the four of them spent some time hiding out at her house.

'I'll be glad of the company. I just rattle around this big old house.'

'I've got another favour to ask?' Dan said.

'Shoot,' said Dee.

'You're friends with the Home Office pathologist Ken Atkinson aren't you? I wonder if you could have a word with him.'

Dan went on to outline his plan to Dee.

An hour later Emma arrived. 'I can see now why you didn't want to take the bus,' she said.

Dee and Dan gave each other a knowing look and for the second time that day Emma thought she was missing something regarding Dan and his aversion to buses.

It took another forty-five minutes before a sweaty Rosie arrived. They nearly didn't recognise her. She was wearing a track suit and had on a long dark wig.

'I ran the last five miles,' she said bending forward holding her knees trying to get her breath back. Being held hostage has made me really unfit.

Darleen didn't think she had ever been able to run five miles. Even walking five miles was a stretch nowadays.

'Laura's dumping the car. She should be here in about an hour.'

'I'll show you all to your rooms. You can freshen up whilst I put some dinner on,' Dee said.

Dee loved to cook. She also loved to eat and had put on more than a few pounds in the last few years. She was just stirring the pasta sauce when an exhausted Laura arrived.

They all hungrily tucked into the pasta carbonara and shared an excellent bottle of Spanish Rioja called Cianza, apart from the pregnant Rosie who had to make do with a sparkling mineral water.

After the meal Dan suggested they have a brainstorming session. Dee brought in an old fashioned white board that she used for some of the teaching sessions that she sometimes gave.

'Right if everyone throws out the clues and evidence we have gathered so far we can see if it leads us anywhere.

The Kidnapper

Male
Age Mid 50s
Foreign ?
Tall
Slim ?
Dark hair ?
Brown Eyes

Facility Location

By a river or canal
Abandoned Medical facility (with bio hazard containment area)
Three thousand square feet footprint
Built pre-1980s
Possible search area criteria – map with area circled?

Boat

Medium size
Sea worthy
St Katharine Docks?

Persons Of Interest

Frances Prescott the Director of undergraduate admissions at Oxford
University?
Julie Benyon - Director of Top Dog Kennels

Dan put a question mark next to the facts they were unsure of.
'We don't have much to go on do we,' Emma said.
'Let's talk through the facts with the question marks.
Firstly we think he's foreign because the two women involved with
Rosie's birth both confirmed the man had an accent and Lawrence
the down and out saw the man with a European style man bag. So I
think we have enough evidence to confirm this is true.
Dan rubbed the question mark out. As he did so a thought came
to him. 'The man who was the witness at the number 15 bus
accident the other day. He had an accent.'
Dan took out his note book and looked at the name and address
the witness had given him. 'Laura, can you check out this address?'
Laura typed the address into her iPad and shook her head. 'It
doesn't exist.'
'The bastard. He deliberately pushed that old woman in front of
the bus just to gain access to my phone to plant the listening device.'
'So you got a good look at him?' Emma said.
'Yes, but thinking about it I suspect he was wearing a disguise. I
can confirm he was still tall and slim,' Dan said.
Emma rubbed the question mark out from next to the TALL and
SLIM clues.
Next, they looked at the facility location clues.
Rosie said, 'You've put abandoned next to the Medical Facility.'
'That's right. It must be abandoned to keep so many women
secretly hidden for nearly thirty years,' Dan said.
'I can't be sure but I don't think it was an empty building. I could
hear sounds from above. It had soundproofing but I definitely had the
feeling other people were nearby,' Rosie said.
Darleen joined in, 'think about it. If you had a facility that
contained bio hazard material then access to that area would be
strictly controlled. Staff could work in the building for years and not
expect to go there.'
'So the whole floor might be out of bounds,' Emma said.

'That's right. Nobody would suspect a thing because it's the norm. Only a few members of staff would have the clearance to go down there. In fact, the staff may not even know there's a basement there,' Dee said.

'That makes perfect sense. It would be much easier bringing supplies into a working building than an abandoned one,' Dan said rubbing out the word *abandoned* from the list.

Next, they went on to discuss the search area. Dan told them about the discussion he'd had with Neil Brooks at the Thames River Authority.

'So we might have got the search area completely wrong,' Laura said. 'How stupid of me. Of course we would need to allow for locks and possible routes where a boat could navigate.'

'Don't beat yourself up,' Dan said. 'None of us thought this through properly. We were rushing. Remember investigations take time. We can't expect to solve this in a few hours.'

Dan brought out the pamphlets that explained the waterways of the South East of England. 'Neil Brooks said that there might be some sort of App that we can use to calculate time and distance.'

'Leave it with me,' Laura said. 'I'll do a better job on it this time and see if I can narrow down the search area.'

Next, they moved onto the boat.

'Have you had any more thoughts about the boat Rosie?' Dan asked.

'Remember I didn't actually see it. Well, I did see it sailing into the distance after I was thrown overboard,' Rosie said.

Darleen said, 'I could put Rosie under hypnosis. It's amazing what patients remember.'

'Wouldn't that be bad for Rosie reliving the trauma,' Laura said looking worried.

'Not if it's done properly,' Dee said.

'I'm up for it,' Rosie said. 'Anything to help rescue my friends.'

Darleen explained the rules. 'I'm the only one who can talk to Rosie whilst she's under. If any of you have a question then write it down and I'll ask her. At no time must you interrupt. Is that clear?'

They all nodded their agreement.

They moved into Dee's consulting room. Rosie sat in a comfortable reclining armchair. Dee sat on a stool by her side. The room brought back memories to Dan of the times he had laid on the couch in this room pouring his heart out.

Darleen put Rosie under. 'Rosie, can you hear me?' Dee started.

'Yes,' Rosie replied.

'I'm going to take you back to the time when you were alone in the water looking towards the boat. What can you see?'

'It's so cold and I'm so scared,' Rosie said visibly shivering.

'You can no longer feel the cold Rosie and you have a guardian angel on your shoulder who is going to look after you. You feel warm and safe. Now, look towards the boat. What can you see?'

'I can see lights.'

'What colour? How many?'

'Red lights. Four of them.'

'What else can you see?'

'A flag.'

'Where is it? Is it on top of the boat or on the back of the boat?'

'It's on the back of the boat.'

'Can you see what's on the flag? Can you see what colour it is?

'It's so hard to see. It's still dark. Wait a door has opened at the back of the boat. I'm frightened someone will spot me in the water. I'm so frightened.'

Rosie curled up into a ball to try and make herself smaller.

'Nobody can see you Rosie. Remember it's dark and you don't have a light. Your guardian angel won't let anyone see you.'

Rosie noticeably relaxed.

'The light from the doorway is shining on the flag. Can you describe it to me?' Dee continued.

'I think It's red and white. Yes, I can see it clearer now it's definitely red and white.

'Good girl. You're doing great,' Dee encouraged. 'Can you see what's on the flag?'

'Yes, it's got a red stripe then a white stripe then another red stripe. There's some sort of black emblem in the centre but I can't make it out. Maybe it's a bird I'm not sure.'

Before she had even finished Dan knew what the flag was and where he had seen it previously. Everything fell into place.

Dan wrote a note out and passed it to Dee.

'Rosie, can you see the name on the back of the boat?' Dee said

'I can see a name but I can't make out the letters. It's too dark and the boat's too far away now.'

'Can you see how many words there are or how many letters?'

'It's only one word. It's a long name. Nine possibly ten letters.'

'Could it be *PERFECTION*?' Dee asked reading from the note Dan had passed her.

'It could be but I can't see it clearly. I can't be certain.'

'You've done really well Rosie. You are going to rest now. You are no longer in the water. You are safely here back with your friends,' Dee said.

Dee clicked her fingers and Rosie instantly came awake.

'Was it any help?' She asked totally unaware of the interaction she had just had with Dee.

'It was a great help,' Dan said.

Dan thought back to his search of St Katharine Docks. He thought of the constant obstructions he had met and how the diplomatic immunity card had been played and stopped his investigation into one particular boat.

They all moved back to the white board.

Dan added the name *PERFECTION* under the list of boat clues and removed the question mark from next to St Katharine Docks. He also added the name of the man from the Austrian embassy who he had interviewed about the boat - Count Maximilian Schütte-Rainer III to their list of suspects.

Doing a search on the laptop he brought up a picture of the Austrian flag with a description underneath:

> The Austrian civil flag consists of two red stripes
> edging a white one and dates back to 1230. It is the
> oldest flag in the world after the Danish one. The
> Austrian State flag carries a coat of arms in its middle,
> which was introduced in 1919. This consists of a black
> eagle with a gold crown on its head. It holds a hammer
> in one talon and a sickle in the other. These represent
> the sun and moon. A chain would connect the two
> symbolizing the binding between Heaven and Earth but
> this lays shattered as imposed shackles have to be
> broken.

Rosie stared at the picture of the flag, 'Broken shackles,' she muttered. 'That's just what I feel I've done in escaping from the prison where I was held.'

Dan told the group what he already knew about the boat. 'It belongs to the Austrian embassy. They use it for entertainment. When I was investigating the disposal of Jennifer Shepherd's body I thought that she may have been moved there by boat. Only three boats had entered the dock that evening. I managed to rule out two of them but the third, *Perfection*, was cloaked in secrecy. My boss at the Met warned me off investigating it big style.'

'Do you think your boss might be involved?' Rosie asked.

'I don't know. I hope not. I thought we were just dealing with one or maybe two men but maybe this is bigger. Much bigger,' Dan said.

'We know that the Austrian embassy owns the boat could the man you interviewed Maximilian Schütte-Rainer be our perpetrator?' Emma asked.

'He definitely didn't look or sound like the guy I met where the old lady was killed by the bus even taking the disguise into account. He also doesn't look like the sketches provided by Irma Barras, Stella Hodson or Jacqui Bates.'

'It's looking more and more like this is a bigger group of people but why would an organisation be involved with such a mad scheme? What is there to gain?' Laura asked.

No-one could answer her.

'I suggest we sleep on it,' Dee said. 'You must all be tired. We will go through it again in the morning and work out our next step.'

They agreed and went their separate ways to their bedrooms.

110

Laura had been up and working for a couple of hours when the others still drowsy with sleep arrived in the kitchen for breakfast.

'I've managed to narrow down the search area.' Laura had found a projector in Darleen's study which she had connected to a laptop. She tapped on a few keys and a map of the South of England projected onto the whiteboard. Laura pointed to a large area in pink. 'This is the area where I think the facility is located. I've also got a list of companies that match our criteria. There are twenty-four companies connected with medical services located in the area.'

'It's still a massive area and a lot of companies to look into,' Emma said looking at the map glumly.

'Maybe not,' Dan said, all eyes turning towards him. 'Laura can you enlarge this area of Oxfordshire.'

As the map expanded the names of more of the smaller towns and villages displayed on the map.

'There,' he said pointing to a small village. 'It's something Dee said early in the investigation. Do you remember Jacqui Bates the girl who ran away with the man? The one he released because she couldn't have children. Well that's the name of the village where he hired the holiday cottage.'

'That's right. I said I suspected it would be near where the girls were being held so he could be close enough to visit them.'

Laura tapped again on the laptop and twelve red dots showed on the screen. 'Unfortunately Oxfordshire has the highest number of biomedical facilities in the country but at least it's reduced the number. These are the ones located next to water that can be reached by boat.'

Rosie asked, 'Is it possible to identify companies that have ordered the drugs used for IVF treatment?' Rosie reeled off the list of drugs that had been given to her whilst in captivity.

'That's a good idea,' Darleen said. 'The production and movement of drugs is tightly controlled. We should be able to trace which if any of the twelve companies procured these or have had them delivered.'

'I'll get on to it.' Laura said.

'And I'll start cooking breakfast,' Darleen said. 'We can't have you working on an empty stomach.'

'What should the rest of us do?' Emma asked. 'I feel that Laura is doing all the work here.'

Darleen laid out a breakfast buffet fit for a 5* hotel. As they all tucked in she turned on the TV to catch the nine o'clock news. The outside broadcast was being beamed from the scene of a burned out car. Police tape hung loosely from what remained of the car. A tow truck was positioned behind it; obviously ready to take it away for further forensic examination.

'This is Andrea Orr from Capital News reporting from the scene of yesterday's car bomb attack. I can now tell you that the body from the car has been confirmed as belonging to DI Daniel Brennan who was an officer working for the London Metropolitan Police. Dental records had to be used to make the identification as the body was so badly burned. I can also tell you that DI Brennan was one of the lead investigators on our other main story, the kidnapping of the heiress Rosie Ware. At this stage we don't know whether the two incidents are connected. Terrorism hasn't been ruled out and the City has been put on high alert. An Anti-Terrorist Branch task force team has been set up to investigate the incident. I will keep you informed as the story develops. This is Andrea Orr for Capital News passing you back to the studio.'

A shocked Emma said 'How did they identify that body as yours?'

'The pathologist Ken Atkinson is a close friend of mine.' Dee explained. 'I asked him to do me a favour and keep the body's ID a secret for as long as possible. It is better for all of us if Dan remains deceased for now. Ken went a step further and confirmed the body belonged to Dan. He must have had his reasons.'

'Won't he get into trouble?' Rosie asked.

'Mistakes happen all the time. Everyone will be so pleased when Dan reappears they won't make much of a hoo-hah,' Dee said. 'Anyway kids I'll have to leave you to it. I've got some hospital patients I need to visit today. I'll be back about four. If you need to go out take the Jeep. Here are the keys. I'll take the Jag as it only fits two people comfortably.' With that she was gone.

After two hours Laura reported back with her finding. 'I managed to hack into eleven of the twelve laboratories that we are interested in. None of them seem to be involved in In Vitro Fertilisation. The twelfth place named Fischer Bio International (FBI) is the one that really sparks by attention. The IT security it has in place is the best.

Like Perfect Pooches in America and the Top Dog Kennels it's way above the level of security one would expect for this type of company.

'So it's a dead end,' Emma asked.

'I didn't say that. I can't get the information from their end but what I can do is search for pharmaceutical companies that are delivering medical supplies to them. I've written a search programme that will go through all the inventories looking for deliveries to our mystery firm. Also I've looked at their corporate website and can confirm that the laboratory isn't involved in any form of In Vitro Fertilisation so if we find a delivery of the drugs in question then I think we will have found our location,' Laura said drawing a circle on the map indicating the whereabouts of their prime suspect. Emma maybe you could use Dee's computer and see what you can find out about Fischer Bio International (FBI). Have a look at Companies House to see who the registered owner and directors are.'

Emma was happy to be useful and set about doing the investigation. She came back with the information thirty minutes later. 'It's a family owned firm. The families name is Fischer and get this, they are Austrian. I've printed out the Wikipedia entry for the Managing Director a man named Hans Rudolf Fischer':

Hans Rudolf Fischer

Born in Vienna, Austria in 1958, to a German father and Czechoslovakian mother (both of which were distinguished bacteriological researchers) Fischer attended grammar school in Gstaad, Switzerland, and then the University of Zurich, from which he graduated in 1979. He went on to study medicine at University College London but dropped out during his third year following the untimely death of his parents in a tragic car accident in the French Alps in 1982. As the only heir to the Fischer fortune, he took over the reins of the family biomedical company Fischer Bio International (FBI) which has operations in Austria, Germany, Switzerland and the UK. Since this time he has been perceived as rather a reclusive figure choosing to spend most of his time around his English home in the Oxfordshire countryside. He has never married and has no known children. He has ranked as high as thirty-first on the World Ranking Most Eligible Bachelor table. He is estimated to be worth in the region of one hundred and twenty million US dollars. He is credited with taking over a failing company and turning it into a modern day success.

'He certainly seems to fit the profile. He has the money and the medical knowledge to set up this type of operation. He also fits the age and has a European background.'

'Is there a photograph of him?' Laura asked.

'I couldn't find one but I'll keep searching.'

'The search program has come back with the results and Fischer Bio International has been receiving substantial amounts of the drugs used for infertility treatment,' Laura said.

'So what do we do next? Do we have enough to get a search warrant?' Emma asked Dan.

'We need more than this. How about if I go to the place and do a bit of reconnaissance? I'm the only one of the four of us that nobody is looking for.'

'I don't like it. It's too dangerous,' Emma said not wanting to risk losing Dan a second time.

'I won't go inside I'll just scout round the surrounding area.'

'I still don't like it. We don't know how many people we are dealing with here.'

'Well what's the alternative? We can't just sit here and do nothing. I can at least see if they have a boat dock and if The Perfection is there. I promise I won't make contact with anyone.'

Emma couldn't think of any other solution so she finally agreed.

Dan took the pre-paid phone and Dee's car keys and set off. He promised to ring them with any news as soon as he could.

He punched the post code into the GPS system on the Jeep's dash. A one and a half hour drive if the traffic was good. At least it would still be light when he got there. Dan had borrowed a pair of binoculars from Dee. Like everything Dee owned they were top quality. Laura had pulled him off a Google maps image showing the location of the laboratory. It was quite isolated surrounded by a wooded area. It had one access road. They could make out the waterway beyond the building but any boat dock was obscured by the structure.

111

Laura stood looking at the whiteboard with the updated information.

The Kidnapper

Male
Age Mid 50s
Foreign possibly Austrian?
Tall
Slim
Dark hair?
Brown Eyes

Facility Location

By a river or canal
Medical facility (with bio hazard containment area)
Three thousand square feet footprint
Built pre-1980s
Printed map showing search area?
Near Oxfordshire village

Boat

Medium size
Sea worthy
St Katharine Docks
Austrian Flag
Named Perfection?

Frances Prescott the Director of undergraduate admissions at Oxford University
Julie Benyon - Director of (TDK) Top Dog Kennels
Maximilian Schütte-Rainer III – Austrian Embassy Liaison Officer?
Hans Rudolf Fischer - Fischer Bio International (FBI)

'Can you see any more clues?' Emma asked coming to stand beside her.

'I was thinking we could ring the Austrian Embassy and make some enquiries about the boat. Also, I thought I would take another look at Ms Prescott and Mrs Benyon. If they are connected to this organisation they must have a way of contacting each other.'

'OK. I'll take the embassy. You delve further into these two,' Emma said indicating the persons of interest.

Emma looked up the number for the Austrian embassy. The phone was answered by a helpful lady with a soft European accent. Firstly Emma asked about hiring the boat. She told the woman that she worked for an advertising agency and her bosses wanted to hire a boat to take some clients out on the Thames to see the sights. The woman told her politely that it was embassy policy not to hire out the boat. She hoped Emma understood that it would be a security risk hiring the boat to strangers. Emma agreed and thanked her for her assistance. As a parting comment, she said that a Mr Schütte-Rainer from the embassy had hinted that it could be chartered. The woman said she didn't know where Mr Schütte-Rainer had got that idea from he should know better being the Security Chief.

Emma looked at the information from Companies House and there it was in print the name Maximilian Schütte-Rainer was listed as a director of the company Fischer Bio International. So they had a link between the Austrian Embassy and the biotech firm. Could the Austrian Government be involved in something this sleazy? Emma found it hard to contemplate that this could be the case. She thought it much more likely that Rainer had taken the job at the embassy to give the operation the cloak of diplomatic immunity.

Reporting the new evidence to the others Laura told them how she had also found a link between Frances Prescott at Oxford University and The Top Dog Kennels in Kent.

Laura explained to them how she hadn't been able to break into the Top Dog Kennels computer system but she had gained access to Julie Benyon's home system. 'I trawled through all the phone records and all the email transactions and couldn't find any links between the two. I then had an idea. I searched for email addresses that they had both accessed. Both of them had logged onto the account takecontrol69@hotmail.com. I checked all the transactions but no emails had ever been sent or received from this account.'

'So how could they have communicated if they never sent an email?' Emma asked.

'That's what puzzled me at first. Let me show you. It's very simple but very clever.'

Laura walked to where Emma was sitting at the computer on Dee's desk. 'Right log on to one of my email accounts,' she said telling Emma an email address and password. 'Now type out a simple email but don't send it. Just save it in the Draft Folder.'

Emma did as she was told then logged out. Laura typed into her iPad. Accessed the same email account's draft folder and read out the email Emma had just typed. Then she deleted it.

Emma said, 'so there's no record of an email ever been sent?'

'That's right. The transaction would only be recorded if it left the server. In this case, the message has never left the email account. And get this my search also reveals that this email account has been accessed from dozens of sources which I assume equates to people but without more details, I can't even start to find out their identities.'

'So messages could be accessed by multiple people. Whoever had the email address and password just left a message in the draft folder then whoever picked it up deleted it once they had read it. As you say so simple but so brilliant. It works like the old fashioned *dead-letter drop* system that spies used to use in the cold war,' Emma said. 'So we now know that Hans Fischer isn't working alone here in the UK. We need to warn Dan. He's walking into something much bigger than we originally thought. This isn't the work of a lone person or a couple of people, this is an organisation and by the looks of it a big one.'

Emma took one of the pay-as-you-go phones that Rosie had purchased from the Westgate Shopping Centre the previous day and sent Dan a message explaining what they had found out.

112

Dan slowly drove past the driveway that led to the facility. He could see a barrier with a security hut with at least two guards. The facility was surrounded by a high fence with razor wire across the top. It also had plaques every few metres showing the universal symbol to tell any potential intruder that it was electrified. This put paid to any thoughts of getting into the grounds of the laboratory. Dan stopped in a layby a hundred and fifty yards further down the road and looked at the map again.

If he continued down the road a short distance it started to climb up a steep hill. He calculated that he could park the car and walk parallel across the hilly terrain and would then be at a point where he could look down onto the facility and be in a position to check if it had a boat dock.

Another hundred yards up the road a 1:4 sign indicated that he was approaching a steep hill. The 4x4 Jeep took this in its stride and didn't even slow down. About half way up the hill Dan noticed a track leading off to the right that hadn't been shown on the map. He turned onto its rough surface that had obviously seen little use over the years. After about two hundred yards the track started to peter out. Dan thought it was probably an old logging road used to manage the thick forest that surrounded the area. Leaving the car he took the binoculars and phone and set out in the direction of the fence.

It was tough going, as the trees and undergrowth were dense. Dan checked the phone. No signal but what could he expect in this remote place. Eventually, he came out onto another track that ran parallel to the electrified fence. Dan stepped quickly back into the trees and surveyed his surroundings. This track was wide enough for a vehicle and had signs of much more recent use than the logging trail he had come in on. He could make out the facility below him and the river beyond. Using the binoculars he zoomed in on the building. He didn't know what he expected to see but nothing jumped out as being suspicious. It must have been home time for the employees as a steady stream of cars wound their way down the driveway. He could make out the car park which was already nearly empty. From this position, he couldn't see if there was a boat dock.

Hugging the tree line he made his way along the route of the fence until it abruptly came to an end at a cliff edge. There was no way to go any further. It was a sheer two hundred foot drop down to the river below. He couldn't go further but he was now in a position to see the river side of the facility. Again he raised the binoculars and could clearly see a boat dock at the rear of the building. It was empty. Dan guessed that Perfection was currently moored at St Katharine Docks. It would only be brought here on the rare occasion when a body needed to be moved. Either a new girl coming in or one for disposal going out. Looking out across the river Dan checked the phone again but still didn't have a signal. His report to the others would have to wait. He was just about to turn round to make his way back to the car when he heard the distinctive sound of a round being chambered in a gun. A voice he immediately recognised as that of the man from the bus accident spoke.

'DI Dan Brennan, I thought I had disposed of you already? Turn round slowly and put your hands up.'

As Dan turned he let the cell phone slip from his hand. It tumbled silently over the cliff edge. Dan couldn't risk the man being able to contact the women. Dan looked straight into the barrel of a Glock 17 with a suppressor on the end. He suspected this was the same gun that had been used to kill George Banks - the old man with the Labrador dog.

'Don't you think that we have top of the range security here? I'm disappointed that you just blundered in like this. You were spotted as soon as you walked towards the perimeter fence.' The man threw a pair of handcuffs towards Dan. 'Put these on, please. Then raise your arms so I can search you.'

Dan wondered if he could push the man over the cliff but he kept the gun trained on him at all times. With the other hand, he frisked Dan. The man pocketed Dan's wallet and car keys. Dan frantically thought about what was in his wallet but couldn't think of anything that would link him to Darleen Clutterbuck and give away the whereabouts of Rosie and the others. Then he worried about Dee's car. If he found it on the logging track he would be able to trace it back to Dee. It was too late to worry about any of this now; he just needed to find an opportunity to escape.

'Why don't you just shoot me?' Dan said looking down the barrel of the suppressor.

'Too messy. I like to dispose of my bodies more thoroughly. Plus I want to have some fun with you first. I need you to tell me where Rosie is.'

'I'll never tell you,' Dan said more bravely than he felt remembering what this organisation had done to Detective Simon Heal in America.

'Oh, you will tell me. You will be begging to tell me in a few hours. You will be pleading for me to end your miserable pathetic life. First I'm sure you would like a tour of the little menagerie I have created here. It's not often I get to show off my collection.'

With Dan two feet in front and the gun pointed at the centre of his back they made their way along the edge of the fence. After walking ten minutes beyond the point where Dan had joined the track they came across a gate built into the fence. The man entered a code into the security pad and the gate swung open. They descended down a path towards the facility. Dan noticed with dismay that the car park was now empty.

'Don't expect anyone to rescue you. The security guards are both at the entrance they won't be doing their rounds for another couple of hours yet.'

They approached the side entrance of the three-storey building. Again the man entered a code into the keypad and roughly pushed Dan inside the building.

'Walk along the corridor. You will find an elevator at the end. Press the down button,' the man said.

Dan walked to the end and pressed the button. They waited in silence as the elevator arrived and the doors opened. The control panel showed 1, 2 & 3 for the ground and upper floors. It showed -1 and -2 for two basement levels. There was another button with no markings on it. Next to this button was a keyhole. The man took a key from his pocket and inserted it into the hole and turned it. A panel that hadn't been visible before opened up next to the control panel. This was a keypad with nine numbers plus a biometric finger print reader. The man entered a four digit number that Dan couldn't see. A green light illuminated. He then placed his thumb on the plate and pressed the blank button. The elevator started to descend past the -1 and -2 levels to a third basement floor. The doors opened into a long dark corridor. The man flipped a switch and fluorescent lights flickered on, lighting the length of the corridor. Dan could see lots of windows down the left-hand side. Each one gave a view into what looked like a hotel bedroom. The first room was empty. It contained a neatly made double bed, a desk with a PC on it, a TV, a wardrobe and a settee. There were two doors one of which was obviously the exit the other Dan assumed was an en-suite bathroom.

'This is Rosie's room,' the man said. 'It's waiting for her return. You see I give them all the home comforts they could wish for. Now let's take a look at my collection. I think you will be impressed.'

Waving the gun at him he got Dan to walk down the corridor. At each window he could see that each room was occupied by a woman. The woman ranged in age and appearance. Most were white some were darker skinned. They all had one thing in common they were all exceptionally beautiful. Another thing many of them had in common was that they were pregnant.

'Quite a collection I've put together. What do you think?' The man asked.

'Think? I think you are mad,' Dan said.

'That's because you don't understand what we are trying to achieve. How could you understand you are of inferior intelligence?'

'Well explain it to me then because what I see here is the work of a madman,' Dan said trying to buy more time hoping to find a chance to escape. 'How can it be an achievement to keep these girls locked up down here like caged animals? How can you justify torturing them when they try and escape?'

'I assume you are referring to Kelly O'Connor my red-headed Irish beauty. Oh, Kelly was one of my favourites. She was a feisty one. I never did manage to tame her. From the minute she arrived, she tried to escape. She refused to co-operate with any of the treatments. She incited rebellion amongst my other girls.'

'So you cut her limbs off?'

'Well, she started to self-harm. She tried to harm her unborn babies. I couldn't have that. Could I?'

'Why cut out her tongue?' Dan asked.

'I had no choice. She just screamed and screamed. This level is very well sound-proofed but I couldn't risk my employees upstairs hearing her. She also served as an excellent deterrent to stop any others from misbehaving. There's nothing like the threat of ending up like her to keep the new girls in line.'

Dan's anger bubbled up inside him. 'These women have done nothing wrong yet you keep them caged down here like battery hens and then when their breeding days are over you snuff them out as if they are just a piece of worthless junk. What does it feel like to take another human beings life? What does it feel like to deprive a beautiful intelligent woman of her future just to satisfy some egotistical arrogant belief that you are making a better world – playing God?'

'Oh don't get me wrong I take no pleasure from killing my girls. I love them all. But what am I to do? I have limited space here. My work must go on. I always put them down in a humane way. They don't suffer.'

'So you don't think that Jennifer Shepherd suffered when you left her to freeze to death in a London alleyway?'

'I sedated her first. She would have felt no pain.'

'What about the pain you have caused her family? The pain you have caused all these girls families? The years they have spent searching for their children not knowing if they are dead or alive.'

'I'm afraid that is just a necessary evil.'

'What about Mr Banks?'

'Who is Mr Banks?'

'The old man you shot in order to steal his dog. You see you don't even know his name. You don't have any respect for people.'

'His death served the greater good. He was old; he would have died soon anyway.'

'I suppose you think the same about the old woman you pushed under the bus just to get hold of my phone?'

They had now reached the end of the corridor and Dan could see an airlock that led into the unit where the girls were being held.

'We will have to go to my office so I can show you why my work here is so essential,' the man said.

Together they retraced their steps but instead of getting out on the ground floor they continued up to the third floor. The man showed Dan into a large plush office. He approached the desk and switched on the computer. After some typing he turned the screen towards Dan. Dan could see a graph. Along the bottom it clearly showed dates going from 1600 to 2060. At the side going upwards were numbers. A red line ran across the graph. For the first few hundred years there was little change then when it reached 1960 it started to rise at a rapid rate. By 2060 it had gone off the top of the graph.

'I think you need to recalibrate your graph,' Dan said.

'No need,' the man said. 'When it reaches that level mankind is doomed. This graph shows the growth in the human population if nothing is done to manage it. Projections show that when it reaches 2060 the world can no longer sustain the number of inhabitants forecast.'

He typed in another set of commands. The first graph disappeared. In its place a picture of the world appeared. Along the top, on the left, it showed the date followed by the total human population followed by the total number of life forms on the planet. Red dots on the various countries seemed to indicate their population.

'This is a simulation showing the future of the planet if nothing is done to slow the relentless growth of the human population,' the man said.

The date on the left climbed ten, twenty, thirty years as did the human population figure in the middle whilst the figure at the end representing other life forms reduced at an alarming speed. The red dots spread across the different countries, some faster than others. When the date reached 2060 the human total started to drop alarmingly.

'This is the tipping point. The toxic by-products and effluent produced by this huge population will have caused irreversible damage to the food chain from contamination. Do you know that the majority of the world's inhabitants rely on fish for their existence? What do you think will happen when most of the life forms in the sea are dead? The land will have suffered from so much industrial pollution and habitat destruction that it cannot support these people. When most food and water resources have been consumed the human population will start to starve to death. Is this a future you want your descendants to experience?'

He typed in another set of commands. The same screen appeared but this time when the date reached 2030 the total human population started to level off and the reduction of life forms also stabilised.

'This is the projection if the actions we have already put in place are allowed to continue to fruition.'

'Surely if you show this to the world governments and leaders they will take the necessary action,' Dan said.

He laughed, 'they have been corrupted by greed, wanting nothing more than to exploit the world for money and power. Do you really think a politician would be re-elected if he proposed couples only had one child and consumed less of the world's resources? Look at how China is rebuked for following this policy and condemned for their human rights. Do you think any government with a policy to control human breeding could hold office for the time needed for it to be effective? They just bury their heads and leave it for someone else to try and fix. You need to look past your social programming and see the bigger picture. If nothing is done soon we will be passed the point of no return.'

'So if we do nothing the world will be destroyed?' Dan asked.

'No, the world will continue just not as it is now. There have been many such mass extinctions in the past. Many biologists believe we may be at the beginning of a sixth mass extinction of species. Eventually, nature will impose the necessary correction via food and water shortages causing mass starvation and resource wars. The population will drop to sustainable levels and the world will continue and recover but why go through all the pain when we can easily avoid it?'

'I still don't get it,' Dan said. 'If you want to reduce the world's population why are you breeding more people?'

'The salvation of this planet will be down to the scientists.'

It suddenly all made sense to Dan. 'So you are trying to breed a super race. Then you can annihilate the rest of us?'

'No point having all queen bees with no worker bees. We are just looking to address the imbalance of overpopulation. We don't intend to kill people only reduce the world population back to a sustainable level. Think of us as farmers managing their livestock.'

'But humans aren't livestock.'

'No but if they continue along their current unmanaged path both humans and the majority of life forms on this planet will be wiped out. When a species is left to go out of control it becomes vermin. Statistics show that the most intelligent humans are having less and less offspring. Unfortunately, the lower the IQ a person has the more children they produce and they expect the hard working intelligent people to pay for them. The pool of high achievers is getting smaller and smaller. What we aim to do here is breed humans with the greatest potential. We put the babies into loving families so that they can be nurtured. We then place them into our organisation so that they can work on projects to protect the planet.'

'Why do they need to be beautiful?' Dan asked. 'Beauty doesn't equal intelligence.'

'If you can have both brains and beauty why not? Beautiful people are always more successful. Also, it makes them easier to place if we can guarantee the adopting couples a beautiful intelligent child.'

'All this, trying to save the world' Dan said pointing to the computer, 'it's not why you are doing all this. You aren't concerned with your fellow man or in saving the planet. Breeding perfect children is your obsession and I expect it's quite a lucrative pastime.'

'You've got me there detective. You are right our efforts are futile. In fact, we have only made things worse. To succeed in getting the world population back to stable levels means mothers only having 2.1 children. This has been achieved in many of the advanced countries of the world. The problem we now have is with the third world countries where religions promote a multiply-and-conquer philosophy. All the main religions strive to increase their own group size so they can outnumber the others in their quest for survival and domination. They will never be persuaded to adopt policies to curb population growth, no matter what incentives are given. We even tried mixing these people into Western society "The Multicultural Experiment" but that has failed miserably. For some reason these people cling to an idea of faith and become even more radical. I came to the conclusion many years ago that meddling in population control was a recipe for disaster.'

'So you decided to branch out on your own and set up this little enterprise?'

'I persuaded a group of philanthropic people who had more money than sense that my project here would provide a rich source of future scientists to help them combat the effects of population growth but I'll admit to you that I got a lot of satisfaction from improving the species and the income from it has been quite substantial. My family always had money, a lot of money, but the Second World War changed all that. Prior to the war we owned many businesses and had several estates. Unfortunately for us, the majority of them were located in the East of Europe. First, the Nazis took them, then the communists. We were left with barely enough income to sustain our lifestyle. I'd always been interested in breeding livestock. I used to get great satisfaction in selecting a mare and a stallion and producing a prize foal. For some reason humans seem to think genes don't play a part in creating intelligent children. It's laughable that your Government produces statistics showing that the children of the rich do better at school and university and try and address the balance by foisting children from poor backgrounds into our elite education system. It's like taking a pony and expecting it to win The Derby. At the end of the day, humans are just the same as animals; those with the best genes rise to the top and those at the top produce the best children. If a childless couple has money they want to buy the best and that's what I provide. If I had time I'd show you the success my little project has achieved.'

'So it's all a lie that the planet is doomed.'

'Oh no, the facts speak for themselves. All intelligent people who look at the figures agree with the outcome I have shown you. It's just that I won't be alive to see it happen, I'll be long dead by 2060 and as I don't have any children to worry about my only concern is living well in the present.'

'Tell me what happened that night. The night you took Rosie and killed her mother.'

'Ever the detective. What does it matter?'

'It matters to me. You can't have had time to abduct Rosie, bring her back here then take Jennifer to London.'

'I didn't. The boat with Jennifer aboard was already moored at Chiswick Quay Marina in London. It's only a one and a half hour drive from Oxford to Chiswick then a couple of hours boat ride to dump Jennifer's body in the English Channel during darkness. What I didn't foresee was that the Thames Barrier would be closed by the time I got there. This gave me a major headache. I couldn't wait for the barrier to reopen the next morning as I couldn't take the chance of disposing of Jennifer's body during daylight hours. I decided to moor the boat at St Katharine Docks and risk leaving her in the alleyway behind the dumpster. I expected her death to be classed as natural causes.'

'So Jennifer was lying right beside her daughter on the boat?'

'And Jennifer seemed to know it. When I took her for her last walk she kept asking for Grace the name she had given to Rosie as if she knew she was close by. You see humans aren't that different from animals. Maybe we don't have as acute a sense of smell but Jennifer knew her daughter was close by and she even knew which baby it was. It's nice don't you think that they had that little reunion before, well you know what.'

'You're a sick bastard.'

'I never expected you to link the two cases together. By the way, how did you do that?'

'Well, that's one of the down sides of producing genetically superior humans. They make very good detectives. We didn't link the cases until we got outside help from one of your protégés.'

'Laura Webb? I should have guessed. She was always one of my masterpieces. I guess she was the beautiful woman harbouring Rosie?'

Ignoring the question - 'And how does Maximilian Schütte-Rainer III fit into the picture.'

'Oh, Max's grandfather and mine were colleagues during the war. I won't bore you with their wartime exploits but suffice it to say they weren't fighting on the side of the British. You could say that it was the two of them that had the vision to put together our little organisation. Max is a fixer and his position at the embassy allows me to bring certain items into the country. The diplomatic pouch can be very useful at times. He also provides the boat when I need it and helps me out when I have a two man job.'

'What about Frances Prescott? Where does she fit in?'

'I think you have already worked that out. She selects suitable candidates for me but I always have the final choice.'

'I think we should adjourn now to the roof top,' he said as if suggesting they partake in after dinner brandy and cigars. 'You are beginning to bore me.'

Waving the gun at Dan he marched him out of the office and back down the corridor. Half way along he directed Dan to turn right and ascend a rough concrete set of stairs. At the top of the stairs, a door led out onto a flat roof top.

Breathing deeply, 'I love it up here in the summer. It has glorious views out over the countryside, don't you think?'

'I'm not really in the mood to look at the view,' Dan said.

'I suppose not. Let's begin shall we?'

The two men stood on the roof top facing each other.

'Our work here is bigger than any of us. It's about mankind's salvation.'

'What kidnapping girls and treating them like animals; forcing them to have children; killing them when they are no longer any use to you?'

'Sit down,' he said throwing a second pair of handcuffs in Dan's direction. 'Chain yourself to that metal rail,' he said indicating a stanchion that held a water cistern above them.

Dan had little choice than to obey. He needed to buy time.

'Right tell me where Rosie is? Or tell me which knee do you want me to shoot first?'

Dan didn't reply.

'There's no point making it hard on yourself. You can tell me now where she is and I'll kill you quickly or I can keep shooting you until you tell me. Your choice.'

He raised the gun and pointed it at Dan's right knee. His phone then started to ring. He answered it. He listened intently then told the caller he was on the roof.

'You really shouldn't have borrowed someone else's car to drive here. My men found it on the logging trail. I've had the registration traced back to a Dr Darleen Clutterbuck. A friend of yours I believe?'

Dan couldn't help the surprised and shocked look that registered on his face. He felt so annoyed with himself that he had so easily led this man back to Rosie, Emma and Dee.

'I have no further need of you. I so hate unnecessary violence so I can just shoot you now I have the information. Then I can set off to retrieve Rosie and eliminate your troublesome friends.'

A second man's voice sounded from the direction of the stair well. Obviously the person the man had just been speaking with. Dan didn't recognise it but he detected a slight European accent in his almost perfect English.

'Hello Hans.'

Dan tried to turn to see who it was but the water tank blocked his view.

'I'm glad you are here,' said Fischer. 'You can help me dispose of the body I can't get hold of Max.'

This wasn't good news for Dan. Obviously, the two men knew each other. Dan had hoped that Fischer was working alone in the UK or at least with only a couple of people who might not even be aware of his operation here. He had come to believe that he was the sole madman behind this insane scheme. It occurred to Dan that this operation was bigger than he had first believed. This was an organisation rather than a lone wolf. The thought frightened him even more than the predicament he was in.

'I've explained to DI Brennan that our plan is bigger than one man and he has to make the ultimate sacrifice. Do you want to shoot him or shall I?' Fischer asked.

'I'll do it. I think you have done quite enough,' the man said.

Hans Fischer lowered his gun. 'I think this is goodbye, DI Brennan. I can't say it's been nice knowing you,' he said.

Dan closed his eyes waiting for the moment when the bullet would end his life.

He heard the pop of the suppressor equipped gun firing. Nothing happened. He opened his eyes to see a shocked expression on Fischer's face. He had a hole between his eyes. He fell forward dead; face down onto the rough concrete roof top.

The other man spoke. 'We are not the ruthless organisation that you might think. What we do is only to try and save the planet. Hans here lost his way. He became a danger to our organisation. As he said this plan is bigger than one man. I'm sorry I can't release you. I can't risk you following me. I'm sure someone will find you in a few hours. Before I go I will give you a piece of advice. Don't pursue this investigation further. It would be, what do you English say "like pissing into the wind" but you have my assurance that no more women will be kidnapped and forced into having children against their will.'

With that the man turned and disappeared down the steps. Dan heard the door close. He was alone, left to his own thoughts with nothing to gaze at apart from the body of the man he had spent so many hours pursuing.

113

It was seven o'clock the next morning when a surprised caretaker came up to the rooftop to do a maintenance check. He was even more surprised to find Hans Fischer's dead body. Dan identified himself as a police officer and asked the man to call the station.

'Tell them to bring some handcuff keys,' he added.

The maintenance man lent Dan his mobile phone. Whilst he waited for the police to come and release him he made a call to Emma to let her know he was safe. She said they had all been frantic with worry. She told him about the links to the other suspects.

'I got in touch with McBride and he's been trying all night to get search warrants for Top Dog Kennels, Oxford University Admission Services and Fischer Bio International. He's been going in circles trying to find a judge to sign them but he keeps getting blocked.'

'I think we need to get this business into the open for our own sakes. This organisation is much more powerful than we could ever have believed. It will be better for them if we all just disappear.'

'That man could have just shot you but he didn't,' Emma said.

'True. He seemed an honourable sort but we don't know about the rest of them. Give that woman from Capital News a call, what was her name, and ask her to get a film crew down here? If we get this into the public domain we will be much safer.'

'Andrea Orr. That was her name,' Emma replied.

The maintenance man returned with a large pair of bolt cutters.

'These should cut you free,' he said.

Dan explained to the maintenance man that there were many women locked in the basement.

The man looked at him as if he was quite mad. 'I can assure you sir; there is nobody other than workers on the basement floors.'

'How many floors do you think there are in this building?' Dan asked.

'There are five floors, sir. Three above ground and two below,' he replied confidently.

'Well you are a floor short,' Dan explained. 'You will find that there are three floors below ground and on the lowest floor there are many women held captive.'

Dan took the man to the elevator and pointed out the blank button with the keyhole next to it.

'I asked what that was for when I first started work here and I was told that it was just redundant as the lift had been designed for a six-storey building.' The man thought for a moment then said, 'You know workers here have always thought that this building was haunted. Several members of staff have said they heard strange noises and the sound of babies crying. We just dismissed it as their imagination.'

'The problem we have now is how do we get these women out? To access the lowest floor we need the key, the code and his thumbprint,' Dan said pointing towards the roof where Hans Fischer's dead body still lay on the floor. By the way, what's your name?'

'Graham sir. Graham Rigby. We can get the key. It should be in his pocket. And we can also get the thumb,' he said holding up the bolt cutters. 'I can't help you with the code though.'

'We should be able to work out the code,' Dan said. 'Do you have any old printer toner cartridges?'

'Yes, we have stacks of them. We collect them then send them off for recycling. We are a very green company.'

'Also we will need a brush of some sort. A small paint brush will do.'

'I have one in my tool box,' Graham said.

'Meet me back here with the toner cartridge and the brush. I'll bring the key and the thumb.'

Graham left to gather the things Dan had requested. Dan returned to the body with the bolt cutters. He found the key in Hans Fischer's jacket pocket. Next, he picked up the bolt cutters. Dan had never done any form of body mutilation before. He picked up Fischer's hand and placed the cutters around his thumb. He closed his eyes and brought the two handles together. A first he thought nothing had happened as he felt no resistance. He opens his eyes and saw the thumb on the ground surrounded by a small puddle of blood. He took an evidence bag out of his pocket. As with most policemen, he always carried a couple with him, on or off duty. He picked up the thumb and placed it in the bag.

When he got back to the elevator Graham was already there. He had wedged a broom to keep the lift doors open.

'We don't want any early arrivals to call the lift, do we?' he said.

'You're in the wrong job. You should consider joining CID,' Dan laughed.

Dan inserted the key and as previously happened the panel slid down to expose the key pad. He opened the print cartridge and dipped the brush into the residue of black powder that remained. Next, he carefully brushed the powder over the numeric keys. Immediately the powder stuck to the fingerprints highlighting the four digits that formed the code. What it didn't show was the order they had been pressed in. Dan thought back to when Fischer had entered the code. He definitely pressed four separate numbers. The first was at the top. The only number covered with black print from the top three numbers was number two. Dan pressed it. The other three numbers were four, six and nine. He tried them in that order but nothing happened. He must have the order the wrong way. He tried again this time two, six, nine then four. Again nothing happened. Dan was starting to get worried. He thought there may be some security mechanism that would set off a timer to blow the building up if the wrong code was entered more than so many times. He remembered how the building in San Jose had been rigged to explode. Computer passwords normally gave you three attempts so he went ahead with another combination. He entered two, four, nine then six. This time the green light came on. He took the severed thumb out of the evidence bag and placed it on the fingerprint reader.

'You stay here, Graham. We can't risk both of us being trapped down there. If I'm not out in twenty minutes, get help.'

Graham looked visibly relieved that he wasn't expected to go down and rescue these women. If they had been imprisoned for years there's was no telling what their reaction would be. They might mob him in their rush to escape.

Dan removed the broom and pressed the blank button. The elevator doors closed and the lift started to descend. First floor 2 then 1, -1, -2 then it continued downwards. As before the doors opened to reveal the long passageway that ran alongside the glass windows. Dan flicked the switch and the lights came on. This time many of the rooms were empty. Curfew must have finished Dan thought thinking back to Rosie telling them how they had to be in their rooms by a certain time. The door at the end opened into a containment area. He had to use the thumbprint and code on each door; luckily it was the same code. Dan passed through the airlock and deeper into the underground facility. The final door was made of solid steel. There was a logo etched into the metal. It looked like a small Noah's Ark. He pushed the severed thumb against the biometric reader beside it. The heavy door slid open. Worry passed through Dan's mind. These women had been trapped down here for many years. What would their reaction be? Dan was thinking along the same lines as Graham that these women would be enraged and attack him for a chance to escape.

He stood with his back to the door and shouted, 'This is the police. Rosie Ware has sent me to rescue you all.' He repeated the same statement several times until a small group of shocked women stood in front of him.

A beautiful caramel skinned woman pushed her way through the crowd. 'See I told you Rosie would make it and send out a rescue party,' Ruth announced triumphantly.

'Well I'd hardly call it a rescue party,' Dan said. 'There's only me.'

'But you can get us out of here?' Ruth asked.

'I can certainly do that,' Dan said. 'I can only fit six people in the lift at a time so you will have to form into groups. Ruth, can you come in the first group? I will need to leave you above ground to care for the women whilst I come down for the rest.'

It surprised Dan how orderly the women were. He had expected them to all make a rush for the door. Some even hung back as if they were reluctant to leave. He escorted the first six women out of the building. By this time a large police presence was gathered outside the building.

DCI Ian McBride stepped forward. 'You look rather well for a dead bloke,' he said. 'You seem to have solved our case and several other missing person cases,' he added looking at the six beautiful women blinking at the strong sunlight and holding their arms up to the sky.

'There's plenty more of them still in the basement, sir. I need to get back and bring them out,' Dan said.

At this point McBride's radio crackled. He listened and said, 'let them through.' Turning back to Dan he said, 'It seems some of your friends are here to see you.'

Dan looked down the drive to see a Jaguar sports car with Dee at the wheel. Sitting next to her was Emma with Rosie and Laura uncomfortably crushed into the tiny back seats. Dee and Emma gracefully got out of the car and the two girls literally fell from the back seats trying to unfold their cramped long limbs.

'I think that box I was locked in was more comfortable than that car,' Rosie wailed.

Rosie saw the six recently released women she had spent so much time with milling about on the grass. One of them saw her and the group rushed to embrace the girl with hugs and kisses.

Dan took Dee aside, 'I'm glad you are here. I think we might have some trouble getting some of the women to leave their captivity. They look very frightened.'

'It's to be expected,' Dee said. 'It's like when animals are freed from captivity it takes some of them a long time to leave the safety of their cage. It will help if Rosie and I go down there to speak with them. Remember some of these women have been here for decades.'

For the next trip, Dan took Rosie and Dee along. Dan could see from Rosie's face the effort she had to make to force herself to return to the scene of so much pain.

After speaking with the remaining women for twenty minutes Dee returned to Dan.

'Some of these women need serious psychological help. It's going to take a long time before they can return to a normal life. Two of them have recently given birth and they are refusing to leave their babies.'

Dan had totally forgotten that there would still be babies down here.

'What do you propose,' he asked seeking Dee's advice.

'We need to get all the women to a secluded location where they can receive the treatment they require. I can get some of my colleagues to help with the treatment but I don't know of anywhere that has the capacity to admit this number of patients. I'd prefer if possible to keep them all together.'

'I think I might be able to help with that,' Rosie said. 'Give me a few minutes.'

She turned from them and rang a number from her mobile. After an intense conversation, she turned back to Dee and Dan.

'I've just been speaking to my father. He has a country house about thirty miles from here. He uses it for corporate events. It has been closed for the last few months undergoing renovation. The contractors are just in the process of finishing off the final work. They have finished ahead of schedule so he doesn't have any bookings for the next four weeks. He has agreed to make it available for us to house the women until we can assess their individual requirements.'

'That's brilliant,' Dee said.

Rosie gave them the details and Dan arranged for a bus to take them to their new temporary home. Dee arranged for some of her fellow professionals to meet them at the house to help the women begin their long road to recovery. Darleen knew the trauma that lay ahead for these women. The media attention they would face. The reunion with their families. The search for their missing children. All of them would deal with the situation differently but Darleen knew that it would be a long road ahead with many ups and downs. Those that had been in captivity the longest would probably suffer the worst. The families of these women would also have an ordeal ahead of them. They had lost a teenager whose memory had been frozen in time and who wouldn't be the same person that they remembered. So often a person whether dead or just missing is placed on a pedestal with all their faults and foibles forgotten. Now they would be faced with a new version of their loved one that they may struggle to bond with. It was important that these women and their families receive one to one counselling immediately. Tom Ware's offer of a secluded country estate was ideal for this healing process to begin. Cathy Grainger had agreed to help with the logistics of informing the families and making the arrangements for them to be reunited with their missing daughters.

'We do really need to get the remaining women above ground. I don't know how long this severed thumb is going to keep working,' Dan said.

Two hours later all the women and babies were aboard the bus and on their way. Dan took a last look around the basement facility as he waited for Rosie. So much pain and heartache had been suffered by these women. Was it worth it to save the planet? Dan couldn't believe it was. Surely there was a better way. He thought about what he had learned. He was in no doubt that the facts regarding overpopulation were true. He thought about what Fischer had said about the world's politicians only being concerned with their own careers. This was also probably true. What would he do if he knew about the impending extinction of the most of the world's life forms? About the pain and suffering his descendants were imminently going to face. Could he continue in his quest to bring this group to justice? He thought about what Fischer had said about this being bigger than any of them and how futile it would be for the investigation to continue. He wondered now if some of his superiors in the Met had been involved or at least warned off the case like he had been. It made sense. He thought back to how his boss had behaved trying to close down the Jennifer Shepherd murder investigation. It was so out of character for him.

He was still deep in thought when Rosie returned clutching a book under her arm. 'My diary and the letter my mother left,' she explained. 'Now let's get out of here I never want to see this place again.'

They returned to where Emma and McBride were orchestrating things above ground.

'I've finally got the arrest warrants for Frances Prescott and Julie Benyon,' McBride told Dan. 'I want you and Emma to go and serve them and search their homes and work addresses. I'll stay here. We have a major incident to investigate plus a dead body still on the rooftop to deal with. Dan, I'll need a statement from you as soon as you have apprehended the rest of the group. As you are a serving police office the Police Complaints Commissioner will need to be involved.'

An officer gave Dan and Emma a lift back to where Dee's Jeep was still parked on the logging trail. Dan had managed to retrieve the car keys from Fischer's office.

'Who do you want to visit first?' Emma asked.

'I don't mind,' a distracted Dan replied.

'You seem very low,' Emma said reaching across to him and cupping his face gently in her hands.

Dan broke down and held Emma tight. The events of the past couple of days weighed heavy on his already fragile mental state. He literally felt the weight of the world on his shoulders. He told Emma about the future that an unsuspecting world would face if no action was taken. Could he really help bring down an organisation that might be the only chance to save it? Did the ends justify the means?

Emma told him that if the organisation was as powerful and widespread as he suggested then minions like them wouldn't be able to bring it down.

'David brought Goliath down,' Dan said.

'All we can do is our job. Let's go and speak with Frances Prescott and Julie Benyon and see what they have to say.'

Emma decided to go to Oxford first and serve the arrest warrant on Frances Prescott. When they arrived at her office they knocked on the door.

'Come in,' a deep male voice said from within.

They entered to find a strange man sitting behind Frances's large desk.

'We are looking for Frances Prescott,' Emma said.

'She's gone. She phoned me last night and handed her notice in. When I say notice she said she was leaving with immediate effect. Her desk has been completely cleared out. She must have done it after she phoned me. I thought she was happy here. I couldn't get her to give me a reason for resigning. She just said it was a personal family matter.'

Next Dan and Emma went to the flat Frances Prescott rented in the centre of Oxford. They knocked on the door but there was no reply. They went to find the superintendent. At first, he was reluctant to open the door of Frances Prescott's flat but when they showed him the official looking warrant he passed them a spare key.

Dan opened the door as soon as he entered he knew the flat was empty. It had that echo that empty spaces have. There was nothing there. Not a stick of furniture. Nothing.

'She must have done a moonlight flit,' Dan said.

They spoke to one of the neighbours a Mrs Smithson. She told them she had spoken to Frances yesterday and she hadn't said anything about leaving. She had heard furniture being moved in the middle of the night but hadn't been interested enough to investigate.

410

Another neighbour said that he had seen a removal van outside. He couldn't remember if it had any logos on it.

They decided to visit Top Dog Kennels to serve the arrest warrant on Julie Benyon. Dan knew it would also be a dead end; that she would also be long gone but he had to show that they had at least tried.

They drove up the gravel drive to the kennels. It looked like a normal working day. Several kennel maids were wheeling barrows about containing goodness knows what. Emma spotted the girl that she had spoken with previously.

Producing her police ID badge and holding it in front of her, 'Tara, we are police officers and we are looking for Julie Benyon. Is she around?'

Tara looked surprised. 'Aren't you the couple who were enquiring about mating your Pomeranian?' Not waiting for a reply she continued. 'She's gone on holiday. She rang me last night to say that a relative abroad had died and she had to go there urgently. She's left me in charge,' she said looking very pleased with her sudden promotion. 'Are you here about the break-in? She said that the police would be coming round sometime today. They've taken all the computers and paperwork. I can understand the computers but why would anyone take the paperwork? I'm not sure how I'm supposed to run this place without the information they contained. I hope you have brought some good news? Have you found the culprits?'

They had been hoping to seize all the computers and paperwork. It looked like this was another dead end.

Emma phoned McBride and told him that both the women had done a runner. He cursed, 'If those warrants had been signed earlier we would have had them.'

'Have you managed to get any information from Fischer's office?'

'No, it had also been cleaned out. The suspect must have done it after he shot Fischer. So all we have are dead ends.'

'What do you want us to do now?' Emma asked.

'There's not much you can do. I get the feeling we won't get much support for continuing the investigation. All the women have been freed. We know where the bodies are buried. As far as the Police Commissioner is concerned the case is sewed up. I suggest you come back here and help with the interviews with the women. We need to identify them and get in touch with their families. Cathy Grainger is currently with them but we need to get this done before the TV and newspapers tell the public. I still don't know who informed that Capital News woman. She has been at the gate all morning trying to get an interview.'

'What about the babies?' Emma asked.

'A doctor has checked them over and they are all in perfect health,' McBride replied.

'I didn't mean the ones we have rescued. I mean the hundreds that have been taken away from their mother's in the past.'

McBride was thoughtful for a moment. 'I don't know, that's a bit of a dilemma. These kids are blissfully unaware of all this. If we did have a way of tracing them would it be in their best interest to know the truth?'

'I'd want to know,' Emma said.

'Yes, I expect you would. All I can say is that we will keep the case open. I expect it will pass to Cathy Grainger's team. You know how tenacious she is. If there's a way of linking these children with their real mothers then she will find it but I expect it will take many years.'

So that was it effectively the case was closed. The top brass took the credit for bringing a lone madman to justice. No doubt the organisation was already making plans to re-establish their breeding program in the UK.

Dan couldn't condone their methods but a small part of him secretly hoped they would find a more humane solution to fixing the problems facing the Earth. The thought that there were people out there dedicating their lives to saving this wonderful planet made him feel somehow more secure.

There was one more obligation Dan still had to fulfil. He looked up the international phone number for the Condé Nast magazine offices in New York. An efficient sounding operator answered his call and he asked to be put through to Nina Simonenko.

'Hello, Nina Simonenko speaking.'

'Hi, it's DI Dan Brennan from the London Metropolitan Police. Do you remember when I paid you a visit a few months ago to discuss your article on America's Most Wanted?'

'Yes, I remember Dan.'

'And do you recall my promise to give you an exclusive once the case was over?'

'Yes.'

'Well do I have a story for you ......'

114

A week later back at the station Emma finally got McBride alone. 'The funding for our trip to America; there never was a corporate entertainment budget for big-wigs was there?'

'No. I went to the Commissioner and he wouldn't hear of me sending officers to America to look for the sperm donors. Then I remembered Tom Ware saying that if there was anything he could do to help, to let him know. He gave me the funding with no questions asked.'

'You put your job on the line?'

'Yes and I'd do it again. Sometimes you have to bend the law a bit to do what's right.'

Emma had never felt as proud of this man that she had come to respect over the years. She reached up and kissed him on the cheek.

'You're a good man McBride.'

'Well if it gets me kisses from a beautiful young woman then it's worth it,' he said giving her a fatherly look. 'By the way, how's your relationship with Dan Brennan going?'

'How do you know about that?'

'I'm a detective, aren't I? It wasn't by chance that I sent the two of you off to America together. I could see from the way you both looked at each other that there was a mutual attraction there. You need a good man in your life Emma.'

'Thank you sir,' she said turning to leave. 'And the answer is yes, it's going well, very well.'

The phone on McBride's desk rang. It was Tom Ware. 'I wanted to thank you for all you and your team have done to solve this case. You are all a credit to the police service. Is there anyone in particular who deserves all or part of the one million pound reward I offered? I'd like it to go to someone deserving or at least a good cause.'

McBride thought for a minute. 'There is an organisation that could benefit from a donation like that.' he explained about the Missing People charity and gave Tom Ware the name of the Chief Executive Peter Tetley.

115

Laura took Rosie to Lytham St Annes to meet the grandmother she had never known. Mary Shepherd clung to her two granddaughters. The previous few months had been full of highs and lows. 'I thought I would go to my grave never knowing what had happened to Jennifer.'

Rosie removed the letter Jennifer had written to her mother from her bag. 'Jennifer wrote this letter to you before she died.'

Mary Shepherd picked up her reading glasses and placed them precariously on her nose. She slowly unfolded the letter like it was a precious manuscript. She read it through three times before raising her head and clasping Rosie's hands in hers, 'You've made an old woman very happy my dear. At last, I now know what happened to my Jennifer.'

She ran her finger down the list of names on the separate piece of paper, 'all these children are my grandchildren?' she asked.

'Yes, and I intend to look for them all,' Laura added.

'They're releasing Jennifer's body tomorrow. I've made arrangements for her to be buried next to her father.'

116

It rained at Jennifer Shepherd's funeral. It was a sad valediction on such a promising life that the number of police mourners exceeded those of friends and family. Three people stood huddled together under a large black umbrella. Two beautiful young women supporting an old lady wizened by arthritis but with eyes that held a belief and understanding that her only daughter's life had not been in vain. Each threw a single stemmed rose on top of the white coffin then the three of them turned and walked slowly towards the black funeral car. These women, strangers not long ago, now had the solidarity that only family and the tie of blood can forge. They were now bound together for the rest of their lives. Dan caught up with them. Rosie and Laura turned to acknowledge him as he approached but their grandmother just focused on the car as if she could only manage one task at a time. They gently guided her into the roomy interior and Dan noticed tears falling from the old lady's gentle blue eyes.

'What are your plans now?' Dan asked.

'For the wake or for life,' Rosie asked.

'For the future,' Dan clarified.

Rosie answered first, 'well I'm set for motherhood,' she said cupping her protruding belly, 'then I'm going to finish my education and try and improve the world.'

'And what about you Laura?'

'I'm going to continue searching for the rest of my family. There are at least another dozen or so siblings out there blissfully unaware of their beginnings, plus I have a father to find and get acquainted with. I've got the list that my mother left showing when each of her babies was born.'

'Don't you think they should be left in their blissful world?' he asked.

'I would want to know and I'm sure they will too,' she replied with a zealots gleam in her eye.

With that they climbed into the car next to their grandmother and closed the door. The big car slowly splashed down the cemetery road and out of sight into the rain filled mist in the distance.

Emma now stood beside Dan, 'fancy a drink to celebrate the closing of the case?' she asked.

He cleared his throat, 'Why not, I think we deserve it.'

117

Epilogue - Somewhere in Austria, Europe

Paul Vettle gazed around the room as he waited for the others to arrive. He always arrived early as he loved to soak up the history of the place. The 13th-century house had originally belonged to a member of the Knights Templars. A group not unlike his own; in the fact that they were rich, powerful and secretive. This hadn't saved them as the Catholic Church had virtually wiped them out as they were seen as heretics, or perhaps more accurately, he thought competitors. The occupants of this very house had met a particularly grizzly end. On the night of Friday 13th of March in 1307, following orders from Pope Clement V and King Philip IV of France, a group of soldiers broke into the house and murdered the entire family. This had been a carefully coordinated and extremely successful attack against all the Templar strongholds across Europe. The contents of the house had been ransacked and all documentation burned. This very room had however escaped the carnage as it had been extremely well hidden, one of the reasons the group used it today. Many of the most treasured Knights Templar books had remained intact until their discovery in 1942 when a Nazi general had made the house his base and one of his soldiers had discovered the room whilst searching for hidden Jews, which many of the ancient houses hid within their walls. The General immediately swore the soldier to secrecy, as a history scholar he knew the immense value of the find. Several days later the soldier had a most unfortunate accident when he fell from the high parapet of the building and broke his neck. The General kept the room a secret and after the war ended purchased the house. This had been Paul's grandfather Josef Vettle. The house had been passed down to his father and then to him. Both had been invited to share the secret room when they were initiated into the Ark Club.

The Ark Club had been formed in 1972 when it became clear that the biggest potential threat to the planet was overpopulation. A small group of philanthropic individuals saw it as their duty to reverse the trend and do away with the thinking that it was a human right to have as many children as a person wished to have.

The Group had worked tirelessly over the last forty-two years to put in place plans to reduce the fertility of the masses. Their top scientists had produced chemicals that were added to food and water supplies that reduced fertility by as much as 40% and although it had the side effect of producing more gays and lesbians it had ultimately succeeded in its aim to reduce the birth rate. Inoculations against many childhood diseases had been laced with fertility impairing drugs of which the recipient would be unaware for many years until they tried to reproduce. Of course, many couples in Western countries sought infertility treatment but this was a small number in the greater scheme. In the third world countries where the problem was most acute, the population explosion was beginning to be reversed.

The Group's plan was to take things slowly and keep well under the radar. This is why the men and women who sat on the board today were the only ones who knew the ultimate plan. They didn't want to be compared with the likes of Hitler or China. Countries like China had been severely criticised for adopting a one child, one family policy but having suffered a famine in the 1960s that wiped out forty-three million of their people wasn't it a humane policy rather than inhumane? Hitler's plan had gone so disastrously wrong because he tried to force his vision on a world that had different views and values. He would have been dismayed that his idea for a superior white race had actually set in motion its demise. The reduction in the workforce in the nations involved in the two world wars had created a vacuum which had been filled by Africans and Asians. Over the next few hundred years, the white race would be obliterated by the interbreeding of these groups whereas the home nations of the Asians and Africans would remain pure. The white man's very success would cause their downfall as economic migrants clambered to gain access to their shores and their politically correct Governments failed to stem the tide. Centuries from now intellectuals would look back at history with great puzzlement as to how a once great race had been invaded and annihilated without a shot being fired. The Group just saw this as a weakness and following the natural selection process and survival of the fittest and strongest saw no need to intercede although a few of the group thought it unfortunate that the diversity and beauty of the white race might be lost. Others thought that with the advancement of gene manipulation the race wouldn't be lost as when designer babies became the norm in the future the preference would always be to have a blonde blue eyed baby as who would choose brown skin and dark hair like the masses possessed.

Paul thought back to the meeting where Hans Rudolf Fischer had first proposed his idea to produce children with the potential to become great scientists and leaders. These children would grow into intelligent, wealthy adults armed with the qualities needed to save the planet. Fischer put forward a strong argument. He explained that as with any animal the best traits could be bred into a species and the human race was no different. He would carefully select the breeding females and males. Their offspring would then be placed into carefully chosen families in order to nurture them to their full potential. The children's progress would be followed into adulthood and the best placed in the many companies that the group controlled. He had acknowledged that the potential of the breeding females would be cut short but this was a small price to pay for the dozen or so progeny that they would issue into the world to make it a better place. He had convinced the group that they would be improving the human race where natural selection had been suppressed by the liberal lefties of the many countries that saw it as the right of the masses to reproduce at will.

The proposal had been met with a mixed response from the group as at that time the memories of Hitler's vision of a superior Aryan race was still fresh in their minds. Paul remembered his Grandfather's tales about Hitler's dream of creating a blue eyed blonde Aryan race and how flawed his thinking had been. Eugenics had become a dirty word. The sole aim of The Ark Club was to protect the planet for the enjoyment of future generations. Their group had no ambition to create a race based on skin, hair and eye colour but the prospect of a pool of highly intelligent scientists did appeal to a majority of the group. The additional fact that the project would be self-funded from the sale of the babies swung the decision and the motion to implement the scheme had been approved by a slim majority.

Paul had only been a junior member at the time. Even at this young age, he had deep reservations about the plan. In his mind it went against everything that he had believed the group stood for. He had been in a quandary about it and had discussed it at length with his father who had explained that sometimes bad things had to be done to achieve the greater goal.

He didn't doubt that the objectives of the programme had been met. Some of the groups finest scientists had been obtained from Fischer's experiment and the benefits would continue far into the future but had it been worth the price the women involved had paid?

Paul was roused from his thoughts as the board members filed into the room. One chair remained empty. There were eleven people including himself, five men and six women. The group saw no evidence in the suggestion that males were superior. To them this was just a myth perpetrated by religions over millennia to dominate and suppress women. Hadn't many of the great leaders in history been women?

As the others took their seats around the table Paul Vettle rose and addressed the meeting. 'We have had a problem with the UK child breeding operation,' he stated. 'Unfortunately, it has been compromised and I am proposing to the group that we now close it down completely. It has served its purpose. The benefits from the children already born from the process will last us well into the future.'

'What went wrong,' a Swedish board member asked.

'I've prepared a detailed report into the root cause of the problem, I'll summarise my findings for you today and you can read the full report before you leave.' He continued to address the meeting. 'There are two main reasons for the problems,' he started, 'firstly the weather stopped the disposal of the body of one of the breeding females. Normally they are wrapped, weighted down and transfer by boat down the Thames then dropped into the English Channel. On this occasion the Thames Barrier had been raised due to high water levels so the boat was trapped on the River Thames. The corpse was placed in an alleyway hoping it would be dismissed as a down and out who had succumbed to the cold. This would have worked had it not been for the fact that the girl selected to replace her in the breeding programme happened to be her daughter.'

Gasps and mutterings erupted around the table as one of the golden rules of the group was that breeding females weren't to be directly related. Paul Vettle coughed and the meeting quietened so he could continue.

'The Police managed to link the DNA from the unidentified body to the DNA from the missing girl Fischer had kidnapped.'

'Why was the daughter selected to replace her, you know our policy is to never use our own offspring to breed from,' one of the members asked in a high pitch American voice.

This was rich Paul Vettle thought the question having come from that American nutter who had tortured and killed a police officer only a few months ago. The group had needed to get him out of the USA quickly and set him up with a new identity. Paul didn't show his contempt for the man. 'Fischer was infatuated with this breeder. He thought she produced the best human specimens he'd ever seen. When she stopped being productive he was obsessed with continuing the line. We have rules for a reason. We can't allow one man's obsession to jeopardise our work here. I'm afraid he had to be eliminated,' he said nodding towards the empty chair.

'Do you think the group is in danger of being exposed?' a smart Asian woman asked.

'No, the episode has been contained but I've had to call in a lot of favours to smooth things over. Many of the world's governments suspect that we exist. They understand the importance of our work they just don't want to be seen as culpable if the truth ever comes out. They prefer to remain blissfully ignorantly hoping that we will sort out Man's future survival. This incident though has put at risk everything we have worked for which is why I'm proposing we end it now.'

All the heads around the table bar one nodded their agreement.

The whiny voiced American Raymond Hearns rose from his chair. 'I think we should re-establish the breeding farm in America. It is the ideal location for us to carry on this invaluable work. I already have a facility in mind and can get things up and running in no time. I still have all the male sperm samples stored away. I can assure the group that nothing will go wrong whilst I'm in charge.'

Paul Vettle had known that any dissent would have emanated from this man. He had worked closely with Hans Fischer who had nominated him to join their group in the first place. Paul had never liked him. Members of The Ark Group were much more closely scrutinised nowadays. Only rich altruistic people were put forward as potential members. 'We no longer need the money that is generated from this venture and the risks from it are far too great. By the time any babies born now reach maturity the world's future course will already be set. There is no benefit to us in re-establishing this scheme. All those in favour of terminating this operation please raise your hand.'

Ten hands were raised only one remained lowered.

Seeing the vote had gone against him Raymond Hearns stormed out of the room.

The group continued through the rest of the agenda. Under Any Other Business Paul Vettle only had two points one of which he had only just added. 'Firstly, we need to find a new member to replace Hans Fischer and secondly, we need to ensure that Raymond Hearns doesn't put the group in jeopardy.'

The group discussed the options and put forward their choice of a successor for Fischer's position within the group. Paul was nominated to sort out their other problem. The meeting was closed and the members left the room and headed back to their respective countries.

Paul Vettle closed the door and pulled the lever taking the room back into concealment until the group's next meeting where he expected a vote for another new member would be enacted.

The following week Paul Vettle sat reading the morning paper whilst he sipped his cappuccino coffee. He smiled to himself as he read the heading of a small article on page two - *American police killer found dead in Paris Hotel Bedroom – Suicide suspected.*

118

The rest of Rosie's pregnancy went perfectly and in early December that year, she gave birth to a healthy baby boy. Laura had travelled to Oxford to act as Rosie's birthing partner. She was so proud of her sister.

'What are you going to call him?' Laura asked looking down at her beautiful nephew.

'Eric – after his father. The whole Bamber clan have already booked flights to come and visit their newest relation. Eric and Rose have been so supportive.'

'How's the family reunification programme going?'

'Fantastic. Thanks to the publicity and the donations we have received from so many generous people we have so far managed to reunite six offspring with their biological mothers and siblings.'

Laura had set up the charity to help locate the missing children for the women who had been released from captivity.

'And how's the search going for our own family?'

'Not so well but it's early days yet. You have to understand that until a child gets to the age of eighteen they can't legally approach us for assistance. Most of our siblings will still be under age but I'm hopeful that as time goes on there will be more coming forward to be genetically tested. Unfortunately, under UK law, it is illegal to try and make contact with an adopted child, at least until they turn eighteen years of age.'

'How come so many children believe that they have been adopted by their parents?'

'I expect it's similar to Ali and Yasmine Pahlavi. They just have a feeling that their parents aren't who they say they are. We have also had a few cases where the adoptive parents have come forward. Up until the story breaking, they had no idea that their baby had been forcibly taken from the birth mother. All of them had been told the same story that the mother had been a student who didn't want the child. It has been heartbreaking for so many families but with the help of many dedicated professionals we are making positive progress.'

Ali and Yasmine Pahlavi had been Laura's first success in identifying a biological mother and child relationship. One of the women rescued from the facility had been a match for the childrens' DNA. Getting this acknowledged by the courts had however been a major obstacle. English law had not kept pace with scientific discovery and the names entered on an official birth certificate still held sway over that of a DNA test. Lots of cases involving biological fathers had been heard in the courts but never one involving a biological mother. Without the adoptive parents consent and without a court directed DNA test the evidence they had was useless. The charities lawyer said that the only way to gain custody without the parents' permission would be to bring criminal charges against them for kidnapping the children. Ali and Yasmine wouldn't even consider this option. Although they always felt the Pahlavis weren't their real parents they did care about them and didn't want them to be hurt in any way. Sitting down with a family mediation officer, the children, adoptive parents and the biological mother had come to an agreement about access rights and custody. A Parental Responsibility Agreement was signed and filed with the court. This gave their biological mother access rights. Laura received regular emails from the children updating her on their progress. Everything seemed to be working out fine with this joint custody arrangement. They were fantastic children and so mature for their age.

'So what are your plans now?'

'Finish off my degree – well that's the plan. Mum and Dad have bought a house nearby and they have agreed to look after Eric whilst I'm studying.'

'How are things with you and your boyfriend Ben?'

'They aren't. It's funny really I thought he was so perfect, so mature but when we met up again everything had changed. We are still friends but he just seems so immature now. We have both moved on. I've only got room for one boy in my life at the moment and that's Eric,' she said gazing lovingly at her new baby.

119

5 Years Later

Rosie Ware, despite being a single mother, managed to gain a 1st class honours degree in marine biology and went on to get her doctorate.

Her professor phoned her one night, 'Rosie, there's someone I want you to speak with, can we meet up for lunch tomorrow, say 12 o'clock' at Fandango's?'

'Sure, as long as I am away by three to pick up Eric from school.'

Not knowing who she was meeting she didn't know what to wear and plumped for a simple black trouser suit and a blue silk blouse. Fandango's was one of her favourite Spanish restaurants and she regularly went there. As she entered she was met by the seemingly ever present Maître d', Ronaldo, who kissed her lightly on both cheeks as part of his standard over the top welcome, simultaneously effusing;

'Buenos dias seniorita, que tal hoy?'

She smiled at his exaggerated Spanish accent. He had once told her that he was actually called Ronnie Sinclair and was from the West Coast of Scotland. He had never even been to Spain.

She immediately spotted Claire her university lecturer sitting at a table with a handsome, middle-aged tall blond man. Claire waved and beckoned her over and the two of them rose to meet Rosie.

'This is Paul Vettle an old friend of mine. I've been telling him what a brilliant scientist you have become.'

Rosie coloured slightly at the compliment and offered her hand to Paul. The man spoke with a slight German accent. 'I've been looking forward to meeting you for so long Rosie, I've heard so much about you from Claire. I won't beat about the bush as you English like to say, I'm here to offer you a job of a lifetime. I work for the Ark Charitable Foundation, you may have heard of it?'

Rosie smiled, 'Oh yes, I've heard of it, you are doing pioneering work to save coral reefs around the world.'

The time flew by as they talked about global warming and how ocean acidification was damaging the marine life, how fish stocks around the world were now decimated and unable to support the half a billion people who relied on fish for their staple diet. Paul explained how the Ark Foundation had been set up to safeguard the dying species of the coral reefs, how a breeding pair of each specimen was being carefully collected and housed in giant aquariums.

'This is the project I want you to work on Rosie. Of course, it will mean relocating to Australia.'

Rosie couldn't believe her luck, this was her dream job.

120

Two months later with visas in hand and little Eric in tow Rosie sat on the huge jumbo jet more excited than she could ever remember. She had kissed her parents and sister goodbye at Heathrow airport with the promise that they would be out for a visit as soon as she was settled. The flight was really long with changes in Singapore and Darwin. On the final leg of the journey, the plane approached Cairns just as the sun rose bringing the dawn of a new day. It was the most beautiful sight Rosie had ever seen with crystal clear blue water lapping gently onto palm lined white sandy beaches.

She was met at the airport by one of the team. 'Hi I'm Rob I'll take you to your accommodation and get you settled in, you will need a few days to get over the jet lag.'

Rosie had hoped that Professor Paul Thomas would have taken the time to meet her as he was the person who she would be working alongside. When she asked Rob where he was he told her that Paul was a very fiery character and only had time for the job. Rosie felt a bit disappointed but nothing was going to detract from the euphoria she currently felt. Eric rubbed at his eyes and yawned as they made their way towards Rob's car. She liked Rob instantly, he was a typical Aussie guy with a great sense of humour and easy to chat with. He drove quickly along the coast pointing out places of interest as they went. The housing was so different to what she was used to in the UK, mainly low rise with corrugated iron roofs. The colours all around her were so vivid. They finally arrived at a private complex. Rob waved to the guard on the gate and the barrier was raised to allow them to drive through. The complex was neatly set out with three rows of six bungalows, all painted in different pastel shades, with a larger building at the far end.

'The cottages are where the staff live and the main building houses the labs and work rooms. This is your cottage here,' Rob said.

He pulled up outside a lovely little yellow cottage that had direct access onto a pristine white sandy beach. Rosie could see a jetty at the end of the beach with a slick white boat docked at the end.

'Paul will be on the boat getting it ready for the expedition that he's taking out next week. He's a bit of a workaholic but his heart is in the right place I'm sure you two will get on.'

Rosie's priority was to get Eric settled and also to get some much needed rest after the long flight. She dumped their bags in the hallway and after tucking Eric into his new bed she fell fast asleep without even managing to take off her clothes. She had arranged for a nanny to care for Eric during the day but she had insisted that the job would not entail late nights as she didn't want to miss out on Eric growing up.

Next day she was up at five in the morning as her body clock hadn't yet adjusted to the new time zone. She unpacked their clothes and settled down on the porch to read an article on how krill was dying out in the Polar Regions. She was so engrossed in the article she didn't notice a man approaching her new home. When she looked up a distant memory stirred. The man looking down at her had the most gorgeous red hair and the most beautiful emerald green eyes.

'Hi I'm Paul Thomas, welcome to Cairns.'

Printed in Great Britain
by Amazon

32399354R00245